WANTED

WIFE ~~FOR~~ 4 NAVY SEAL**S**

DEE PALMER

ISBN-978-0-9957038-3-4

Warning: ADULT CONTENT 18+ This story is on the filthy side of smut and isn't suitable for those who don't enjoy graphic descriptions that are erotic in nature, but for those that do, enjoy ;)

For free stories sign up to my Newsletter on the contact page at deepalmerwriter.com (Promise No Spam)
or go here http://eepurl.com/biZ6g1

OTHER BOOKS BY DEE

The Choices Trilogy

Never a Choice
Always a Choice
The Only Choice

Never a Choice 1.5
A Choices Novella

Ethan's Fall

The Disgrace Trilogy

Disgrace
Disgraceful
Grace

DEDICATION

The Chosen Ones & Divas
You're my favourite distraction <3

"Find your Tribe and Love them Hard"

I Love my Tribe

Authors Note:

This story was inspired by an advert on Craig's list….I have no idea if the ad was genuine but it sparked my imagination…the story is all mine ;)

This is edited in American-English BUT Finn is British so her speech and thoughts will have English-English spellings…which essentially means Finn keeps the 'r' in arse. Hope you enjoy :)

CHAPTER ONE

"JESUS, FINN, YOU SURE YOU'RE NOT EMIGRATING?" HOPE laughs out a dirty throaty sound, as she struggles with the last of my suitcases. Stacking the final piece on the back seat on top of the mobile mountain, which pretty much contains my life or what was my *pathetic* life. I flash a tight smile, which sticks to my teeth, and a punch of guilt hits me in the gut, which I clearly fail to hide in my expression. "Finn?" I can hear the wobble in my best friend's voice, her tone pitched with genuine concern.

"No, I'm not emigrating." I make a show of rolling my eyes at her dramatics, even as I mumble 'probably' under my breath so as not to be accused of lying outright, if all *does* go well. "One month is a long time. I need a lot of shit."

"There's a lot and then there's *all* your shit. I should know, since you've been camped on my sofa for the last three months. My flat looks like it's been burgled, it's so bare. I think the only thing you haven't packed is Dolly here." She pats the soft-top roof of my ancient Citrëon 2CV.

"I would take her if I could." I tilt my head and cast an affectionate glance at the car that has rescued me from many a disaster, the most recent, moving everything I own from my home with Dave to the aforementioned sofa in Hope's flat. Luckily Dolly is like the frickin' Tardis, and I only needed to make one trip. Come to think of it, that isn't lucky at all, it's just sad. I'm twenty-six years old, and I spent ten of those with the love of my life, yet all my worldly possessions fit inside a 4-door, antique car, which has wildlife growing in the footwells.

"It's only a month; I'll take good care of her." Hope's face fails to achieve the smile she's desperately trying for, and I take that as my cue to jump in the car and avoid eye contact. *I'm such a coward.*

We chat for a while, and the car falls silent. Hope reaches over and her bony hand grips mine, which is clutching the steering wheel. Her eyes are glazing again, and I try, with enormous effort, to swallow the lump in my throat, but it won't budge.

"I'm going to miss you so much," she tells me for the umpteenth time. "Do you really have to go? He could be a psycho." I twist my hand in hers so our fingers are now threaded.

"He could be, but he isn't," I reassure her.

"I still think you're crazy." She states this with certainty but no judgment.

There are many reasons she has been my best friend since primary school. For a start, she's the keeper of all my secrets. The morning after every sleepover since my early teens, she would take delight in embarrassing me, regurgitating every word I spilt throughout the night when I talked in my sleep. The worst of all habits, in my opinion, because there was nothing I could do to stop myself, and I was, by all accounts, shamelessly honest and open. I bought a dreamcatcher, which seemed to help. Nevertheless, in the end, I begged her not to keep me talking. I asked her to wake me or even add a gag as a preferable alternative to sneaking a peek inside my subconscious. She told me I was a spoilsport but agreed, because above everything else, she always has my back. Even if she doesn't agree with my choices, she's undoubtedly my one-woman cheerleader, crossing everything she has and wishing me all the luck in the world without so much as a twitch of a judgmental brow.

"No. Crazy would be giving Dave another chance to humiliate me and waste another God knows how many more years of my life." My laugh is rightly humorless and filled with contempt.

"Yeah, that would be crazy. But the States? Do you really have to go all that way to find *one* decent guy?" I choke back a cough and feel my cheeks burn with the truth and lie I'm about to serve.

"Orange County, California, and yes, it would seem so." Not technically a black lie, it's vague enough. And if my damn cheeks aren't flashing like a fucking beacon, I might get away with it.

"What *aren't* you telling me, Finn?" Hope shifts in her seat, and her tone is deadly serious. *Dammit.*

Now I could lie, but she would know. If we lived in the Dark Ages, she would've been burnt at the stake years ago; it's kind of spooky, her witchy ways. But the truth? If I tell her the actual truth, she's likely to grab the wheel from my hands and flip a one-eighty in the middle of the motorway, rush hour traffic be damned, and probably end poor Dolly in the process. So, I have to give her something meaty, the truth, but not quite the *whole truth* and maybe a little bit of, *nothing but the truth.*

"He's asked me to marry him." I think that counts as meaty, and I try for a casual delivery with my level tone, though I don't think it matters.

"What the fuck, Finn?" she hollers, causing my shoulders

to shoot up to protect my ears because my hands are occupied. "Are you out of your fucking mind? You've 'known' "—she exaggerates her air quotes and lays the sarcasm on thick with her condescending tone—"him for what, three months? And now, you're going to marry the dude?"

"I didn't say I *was* going to marry him. That's what this month is about. It's a trial." My words are stark in the silence of the car. They sound ridiculous when spoken out loud. Who does this? What sane, normal woman would? She's right; it's nuts. I'm out of my fucking mind. Which is why none of that matters.

I'm a crazy woman, and three months ago, I said, "Fuck it." *I* made this decision, and I'm not backing out.

"Oh, well, that's all right, then." The sarcasm is like treacle now, and her tone is tinged with bitter disbelief and disappointment.

This is not how I wanted today to go. I fix my mouth tight shut for fear of saying something I can't take back. The tension is palpable, and I cringe when Billy Idol's "White Wedding" crackles through the retro radio hanging from a makeshift hammock under the dashboard. *Perfect.*

We reach the airport and Hope helps me load my cases onto the trolley. She still hasn't said a word. I hand her the keys to Dolly and go to walk away. She's double parked, so I know she has to get going. She grabs the sleeve of my denim jacket and pulls me into her tiny, surprisingly strong hold.

"Wow, the gym's been paying off for you, too. You hug like a heavyweight." I groan under her hold.

"Or like I might never see my best friend again." Her soft words hit me hard.

"Hope…" I sigh and return her embrace with a gentle heartfelt squeeze around her shoulders, her head resting against my neck. I feel her body shudder with the first gasp of a sob. It's enough to make my nose tingle, and a slew of big fat tears fall onto my cheek.

"But it's true. That might be the case." She sniffs, sloppy wet sounds she doesn't try to hide.

"No, it's not true." I pull back and hold her gaze with mine, her dark green eyes fill with tears, matching my own. I blink to try and keep focus.

"Stay, Finn...please," she mutters, her fat lip wobbling.

She's killing me. "I can't, Hope." I shake my head, and the heaviness in my heart, the sadness I feel is a fraction of the sorrow I have endured, and she knows this. "I wasted ten years of my life with a man who had no intention of marrying me, H, and he even took delight in humiliating me about the fact in front of all my friends. He made me feel utterly worthless, and now..." I stutter and draw in a fortifying breath. "I have these men, and one of them promised to marry me. I get to choose... me, I—" I clamp my mouth shut at my apocalyptic fuck-up.

"Men?" she snaps.

"Man, I meant man." I wave my hand to dismiss my seemingly silly mistake,

"You said *men*," Hope corrects and then gasps. "Finn you didn't answer *that* advert?" Her hands fly to her mouth, eyes like saucers, and we both suck in a shocked breath.

"I...I..." I can't construct a sentence. She steps up to me and interrupts so I don't have to. *I wish she didn't.*

"That's who you've been talking to so secretively these last three months every spare minute. That's what all this gym shit you've been dragging me to morning, noon, and night for the last three months has been all about. It's because you need to be fit enough to take on four guys?" She stares at me, and her mouth is open so wide it's comical, but I'm not laughing. I'm waiting for the scream, the howl of judgment to rain down on my slutty arse. I draw in a breath and brace.

"Yes." I tip my chin, and time comes to a halt...and remains still as I frown at my friend, the statue. Her wide emerald eyes are fixed and focused, though I'm not sure on what. I wave my hand in front of her face, but she doesn't flinch. *Is it possible to be catatonic standing up?*

"Hope? Are you okay? You're kind of freaking me out." I look around to see if anyone else is observing my friend's weird behavior, but no one is paying us any attention. Well, other than the parking officer who is scowling between Dolly and the No Waiting sign. "Hope!" I hiss a little loud, and she blinks and gives a full body shudder, regaining her senses.

"Four guys?" she asks with a degree of awe in her tone.

I hesitate before answering.

"Yes."

"At one time?" She arches a brow, and her lips begin to curl into a wicked smirk.

"Not necessarily. We haven't actually gone over the logistics," I reply, a little straight-laced given the topic, after all, we're hardly in a secret-sharing environment.

"But they wanted a twenty-year-old?"

Her incredulous face pisses me off, and I place my hands on my hips and tip my chin, my tone a little on the defensive side. "Well, they got a *mid-to-late* twenty-year-old, who has worked her arse off to knock the last several years off her clock…literally." I straighten my back and subtly tighten my tummy in lieu of drawing in an obvious slimming breath.

"Oh babe, you do. You look smoking hot; don't worry about that." She pats my arms and flashes her best friend a reassuring smile. "No. You need to worry more about the fact you don't have enough holes, because, babe, that's something you can't fix at the gym." She bites her lip to hold in her trademark filthy laugh, but I crack first and she's quick to follow. She throws her head back, full-on belly aching, dirty laughter falling from her lips, eyes streaming, shaking her head. "Oh my God, you're going to be kept busy around the cock." She doubles over at her own joke and waves me down because I think she has another gem. "They're in the Forces right? They're going to want everything to run like clockwork."

"Okaaaay, then, are we finished?" I pat her back as she attempts to regain her composure.

"Sorry. So sorry…too tempting. You're right, you have a flight to catch. The cock is ticking. No time to be *dicking* around now." She snorts with another laugh.

"Hope." I sigh.

"Look, Finn. I still think you're batshit insane, but if you have to go crazy, at least you'll have lots of nuts to keep you company." She pulls me in for a final hug, and I can see she's genuinely smiling. Her face is a little wet from her tears, but her expression doesn't hold any anxiousness or tension. There's a little worry, which is understandable. *Maybe I should've told her sooner.* "I want you to promise to do one thing for me." She clears her throat; her tone is soft but serious.

"What's that?" I wait with bated breath for her to tell me what she'll need from me to ease her mind, and will it be anything within my power. She hesitates a moment before her shoulders start to shake.

"Pictures…I want *lots* of pictures." She snickers some more.

"I'm gone. I'll call you when I land." I turn on my heel and start to push the half-ton trolley away from my best—annoying—friend.

"With pictures!" she calls after me.

"Sure, with pictures." I turn my back to the trolley so I'm facing her while pushing the beast up the ramp.

"You go, girl. Take one for the team! Oh wait, no. Take *four* with the team!" She shouts with the volume of a crowd control foghorn over the entire departures drop-off area. I cringe, but raise my hand to wave her off. Her own hands are flapping at me like a crazy person before she sinks into the car. The parking officer has finally lost his patience and points for her to leave or get towed. *Dolly wouldn't survive a tow with all that manhandling.* I watch the cream and raspberry car filter into the traffic and disappear. *Shit, I hope I'm in better shape than Dolly when it comes to being manhandled.*

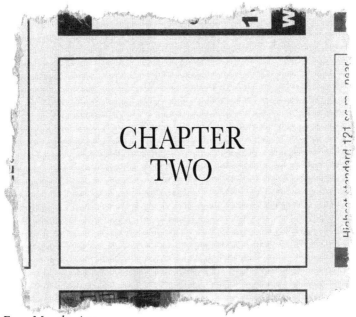

CHAPTER TWO

Four Months Ago

"YOU CAN'T BE HERE WHEN HE GETS HOME, HOPE. IT will kind of ruin the surprise." I slam the oven door shut, having checked the chicken is doing whatever it's supposed to do in the oven, when I'm not allowed to drench it in a decadent cream sauce or rich wine gravy. The best I can manage within my boyfriend's tight 'health freak' guidelines is a light pan fry to give it some color, and then steam the little fella in the oven to try and keep it tender and juicy. Dave owns an elite gym in the West End of London with a superstar clientele, and appearance has become a bit of a focus for him. I guess it always has been, but I'm more conscious of it now, perhaps, since it's become less important to me.

"Oh, don't worry about that," she says, with enough horror in her tone to convince me she isn't joking. "I don't want to be here when you start dry humping your man as soon as he gets in the door."

"That wasn't the surprise I was going for." I narrow my eyes and stick my tongue out at her disturbed expression.

"But sex is...I mean it's why, under that coat you look like you're auditioning for the *Rocky Horror Picture Show*." She leans over and pulls the lapels of my Mac wide open. I squeal and re-tighten the loose material, cinching it firmly at the waist. I take a quick peek myself, because now I'm filled with panic.

"What? You're kidding right?" I laugh nervously, searching her implacable face for any signs she's joking. "I was hoping for agent provocateur seductress, not transvestite."

She rolls her eyes, tutting and shaking her head with a light admonishing smile.

"I'm kidding, Finn. Jeez, you're easy to tease when you're strung out or frustrated." She snickers, a deep, filthy, wicked laugh, and reaches for my hand to offer some genuine comfort. I'm all over the place with uncertainty and zero confidence. "You look fucking hot under the Mac. Is that part of the get up? He's into the whole flashing-in-public thing?" She takes another sip of my wine despite having declined her own glass, and has proceeded to drink nearly all of mine.

"Hardly. No, I was hoping we could go for a quick drink, and this might turn him on. I mean I'm practically naked under here." I hate sounding tentative about this, but I'm more than a little out of my comfort zone.

"Shit, Finn. You could wear a used bin liner, and you'd turn most men on. What makes Dave so special you're worried it won't? Does he have a golden dick or something?"

"No. I just..." I hesitate as I struggle to articulate feelings I don't really understand myself. "He's my best friend, Hope, apart from you, obviously."

"That's a given. Continue." She beams a smile which crinkles her bright green eyes and widens her even brighter painted red lips. Her wild, glorious red hair is slicked back in a severe bun, practical for work but a little harsh for her soft pixie features.

"Sometimes I feel that's *all* I am. I don't know when it happened but I worry we've slipped from lovers to mates, and I miss feeling…wanted…desired, you know?"

"Um… Only ever one-night stands over here, so not really." She gives an unapologetic shrug. I didn't really expect her to understand. Her longest relationship is with me. She was with me when, underage and out looking for fun, we snuck into club. We ran straight into Dave and his mates. In borrowed heels and the tightest dress this side of indecent, I literally fell on my arse at his feet. He owned me from that night on. I never stood a chance. I fell for him and didn't look back. I do have my doubts about Hope, on the other hand. I don't think she'd fall if she was hit with a fucking freight train.

"We've been together for a long time, Hope, and I think he's a little bored. So I thought I'd spice things up a bit."

"And is he making the same effort?" She purses her lips in an effort to temper her underlying objections. She does this a lot when we talk about Dave, however, this time, she's very wrong.

"I think he's going to do more than that." I rush out the words with a surprised blurt of excitement, which seems to pique her interest.

"Oh really? What?" She leans in closer to me, her face mirroring my smile.

"I think he's going to propose to me on Saturday." I drop my mouth in mock shock. Well, not mock since I am shocked.

"Why Saturday?" Her face is unchanged. No more excitement, no less either; however, she looks a little skeptical.

"It's his birthday, and he's been really secretive. It's not like him. I normally organize everything we do socially, but this time, he's called all our friends, booked a private room at the new club on the high street. He's even sorted the caterers. Every time I offer to help he says he's got it covered, and all he wants from me is to say, '*Yes*'." I clap my hands together in a rapid-fire mini applause.

"Fuck!" Now that tone *is* utter shock.

"I know." I giggle and bounce on my toes. "Honestly, Hope, all this time I thought he was going off me. I know he loves me, but he really hasn't shown much interest *sexually* for ages."

Hope wrinkles her nose with distaste. "Eww…Do we have to? I can't help having a visual when you talk details." She sticks two fingers down her throat as if her tone isn't enough for me to get the level of her abhorrence.

"I'm serious." I flick the end of the tea towel and catch her with an impressive snap on her arm. She yelps and scowls, and I ignore the fiery stare. "I've been really busy at work, and I haven't been to the gym in like forever. This"—I grab my squidgy midriff and then shift my hands to my size D-cups—"is not the body he signed up for."

"What? The body from when you were sixteen, you mean? Well, no fucking shit, Sherlock. Whose body is? Listen very carefully. You are fucking hot, any size you choose to be, so don't give me that shit. Has he actually said that, because I will cut him—"

"No! No, he hasn't." I wave her down as she brandishes a spoon as if it was a mighty blade of body-shaming retribution. "He wouldn't say anything like that. But, I know image is important to him, so I'm sure it's in the back of his mind, and I can't help thinking—"

"The proof of the pudding is in the eating, and if he isn't eating…" She wiggles her finger in the general direction of my crotch.

"Exactly." I sigh. "I honestly don't remember the last time he did *that*." I mouth the last word silently.

"Too many carbs?" She lets loose an unladylike snort, and I

blurt out a laugh. I love that about her; she always makes me feel better. "So the big seduction thing is a preemptive thank you…a timely reminder of how fucking lucky he is?"

"I hope so."

"You know I fucking hate this about you? No, not *you*. I hate how he makes you doubt yourself. I don't get the whole marriage thing, but I know it's important to you and he does too. So the fact he's kept you waiting all these years chips away at your self-esteem and you're all, 'Maybe I'm not attractive to him anymore. Or maybe he sees me as just a friend'. It's billy bollocks. You fucking rock, and he's damn lucky to have you. There are hundreds of guys who would think the same as me. You happen to have fallen in love with a bit of a dick." She holds her hands up to signal the end of her little speech and draws in one more breath. "I'm not judging, just stating fact."

"It's complicated." I shrug off her tirade, because I have heard it before, and it stings because it's true.

"No, it's simple, although I'm jumping down from my soapbox because, he may be a dick, but he's *your* dick, and you are the only one who matters in the equation. Your happiness and you've wanted that white dress since we used to play dress-up when we were kids." She steps around the kitchen island to my side and wraps her arm around my waist.

"I still love to dress-up." I snicker, looking down at my kinky ensemble.

"The outfits have become a little dirtier—a little more leather than lace."

Hope wiggles her brow.

"And at least I fit into the heels." I lift up my leg to showcase my most spectacular shoes.

"Killer heels, and if they don't seal the deal, I don't know what will. I can guarantee it won't be that meal you're cooking."

"It's his favorite." I try to sound offended and defend my

efforts, but she's right. *Again.*

"Bollocks. That's no one's favorite: steamed chicken, brown rice, and broccoli. Oh God, I'm going to gag." She starts retching, and I push her away then walk over to the hob to make sure as bland as this meal is, it's at the very least perfectly cooked. "Okay, I'm going to be off. Do you want me to meet you for lunch tomorrow? I'm working at the spa round the corner. I could pop in." She slips her bag over her shoulder, then grabs her keys and phone from the counter.

"Depends on whether you're coming to see me for lunch or coming to fuck my boss." I point an accusatory wooden spoon her way, and she boldly returns my stare with no shame, a fiery spark in her eyes.

"Well, he is *very* fuckable."

"Hope..." I warn.

"Fine! Lunch." She holds her palms flat in an act of supplication. "I promise no fucking. Maybe a quick handjob, but definitely no fucking."

So much for supplication.

She grabs her coat from the kitchen stool and makes to run from the room. Not that I could catch her with my skyscraper slingback stilettos.

"See you tomorrow. I can tell you all about it," I call after her.

"Please don't. I've only just stopped gagging from the food." She pops her head round the door, her shoulders jerking and her cheeks puffed out holding in pretend vomit.

"Out!" I point my finger and give my dismissal in a firm and final tone.

"Love ya', Finn." Her reply is delivered sing-song, which always leaves me with a smile.

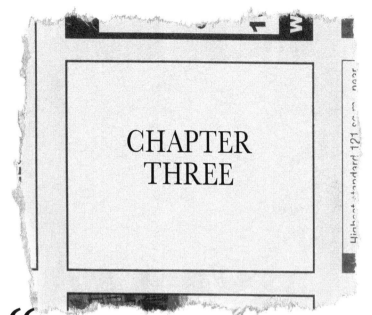

CHAPTER THREE

"Hmm...something smells good, RP, what's the occasion?" Dave walks into the kitchen dropping his gym bag and briefcase. His near-black hair is still damp from the shower he would've taken before he left the gym. He is religious with his workouts, and I have to admit he looks damn good because of it. He's not overly tall, five foot eleven. I'm five foot five, so he's tall enough. He has wide shoulders, trim, narrow waist. His thighs are kind of weird now though, bulging and distorted with muscle mass, it makes finding jeans that fit a challenge. Every muscle from his tanned nose to his pedicured toes is toned to perfection, if a little bulky for my taste. I felt he reached perfection a few years ago, but apparently, that wasn't perfect enough. His face is bright with a wide smile, and his jacket strains at the seams when he draws in a deep breath through his nose, capturing the aroma of the meal I have tried so desperately hard to make interesting. He strides straight past me to the fridge, grabs a bottle of water, and peers over my shoulder at the pans simmering. He ruffles my hair that I had artfully fashioned into a messy bun. I thought at the time, *It is amazing how much effort is required to look effortless.* "Why have you got your coat on, if we're eating in?"

"I thought we could go out for a quick drink before dinner?" I give him a genuine, shy smile as I feel a surge of nervousness start to grip my tummy.

"Have I missed an anniversary or something?" He frowns, taking in the fact my face has little make-up and my coat isn't all I'm wearing.

"No, I thought we could try something a little *different*." I twist around so I'm now facing him, and with a boldness that surprises both me and him, I drag my leg up his thigh. The gap in the front of my coat widens and falls back, exposing my long leg, stocking, and suspender. I press the spike of my heel against his butt, impressed I can, one, get my leg up that high and, two, maintain my balance.

"You want to go out like that?" His derisive tone is as harsh as a slap in the face, but his mocking laugh is worse.

"Well, For a start, I'd quite like you to maybe not laugh at the suggestion." I slip my leg back down. I don't want to sound hurt or angry, or this evening will be a non-starter.

On the other hand, right now, I can't ignore the real pain from the slice of rejection that cut deep with his response.

"I'm not laughing. I'm a little surprised, is all. This isn't like you, RP—"

"Could you maybe not call me RP tonight?" I watch as more bemusement twists his features.

"Why? You know I don't mean anything by it. It's a nick-name." I can see he's struggling to understand, but I don't want to go into details. I want a bit of fun and *a lot* of intimacy.

"I know. Just maybe not tonight." I try and keep my plea lighthearted but earnest, because it really is a shitty nickname.

"Fine. You're acting really weird, Finn. Are you on your period?"

"Oh, my God!" I hold my breath and count silently to ten, thanking all that's holy I don't have a knife at hand.

"Sorry. Clearly not, although…" His accusation hangs in the air like a noose swinging silently in the gallows, along with the remainder of my surprise evening.

"Jesus, Dave." My voice catches with an equal mix of fury and emotion.

"What? What have I done?" His tone has switched from confused to inflammatory with a tinge of aggression. "I walk in and, bam, you're acting all weird, wanting to have sex and go outside with me, while looking like a stripper."

"I'm weird for wanting sex?" I take a step back and cross my arms tight around my waist, covering as much of myself as I can. I still feel more than naked, utterly vulnerable.

"That's not what I said." He lets out a heavy sigh, his hands deep in his pockets, and he shifts uncomfortably from one foot to the other. "Look, can we start this again, and maybe you can talk to me and tell me what the hell's going on?" His tone softens, and I think that's worse. I get an intense prickle at the bridge of my nose, and I have to blink to stop the tears from welling. *I won't fucking cry.* I shake myself and straighten, pulling myself together.

"Fine, but I'm going to need a drink." I grab my empty glass and the bottle of white wine from the cooler.

"Really, RP? You know that's like a meal in itself. Do you have any idea of how many cal—" He wisely snaps his big, fat mouth shut as I spin to face him with thunder, and possibly murder in my eyes.

"If you say calories, I swear to God, Dave, this bottle is going where the sun don't shine, and it's not going in narrow end first." I wave my weapon of choice at his startled face. The only words playing in my head are Hope telling me I fell in love with a bit of a dick. I pour a large glass of wine, making a childish point to fill it to the top, slurping from the lip of the glass before I can lift it. I watch Dave intently as he nervously draws small sips from his bottled water.

"Do you love me, Dave?" I hold his gaze as his eyes widen with worry.

"Is this a trick question?"

"It really isn't." I let out a sigh, feeling the warmth of the alcohol hit my bloodstream, calming me some. This conversation feels a little weightier than I was anticipating. *I wasn't expecting much conversation at all.*

"Then yes, of course I love you. You're my best friend, my little RP. Well, not so little."

"Really, Dave? Is that seriously the problem here? That I've gained some weight?" I take another gulp.

"I was joking, and I never said that." He has a look of mock hurt blazing across his face that I could make such an accusation.

"We hardly ever have sex, so there has to be some reason."

"I love you, Finn. I'm not going to lie and say you are at your most beautiful now, because I personally think you'll look more gorgeous when you lose a little weight." He tips his head like that will soften the shallow, passive-aggressive insult.

"Just like I think you are most handsome when you're not so bumpy with all those gross muscles." I counter in all seriousness.

"No, but joking aside, Finn…" He barely gives my insult any recognition, and he certainly thinks it was a joke. "…you're a very beautiful woman, and I'm a lucky guy." He steps forward and sweeps his arms around me, pulling me close and holding me tight. *This is all I wanted, to be held…well, held and some cock. I'll take being embraced over indifference.*

"And the sex?" I push, because, actually, I would *really* like some cock. I think I've healed over.

"I guess I've just had a lot on at work, and I know this might come as a shock, but guys don't think about sex every five minutes." He laughs out loud and playfully taps me on the nose. I'm not entirely convinced, but he holds my gaze, and I do see the love in his dark hazel eyes. It's always been him, even if he can be a bit of a dick.

"So, we're good?" I ask and grind a little against his erection, which is most definitely just as keen as I am.

"We're more than good, Finn. You are my perfect woman, and on Saturday, I'm going to prove it."

"Saturday?" I ask, hoping for more, then not. I'm all tingly with the anticipation, and I kind of like the feeling.

"Nuh-uh. I'm not saying another thing." He kisses the tip of my nose, then my cheek. His lips brush mine, and as soon as I open my mouth to take a little more, he withdraws everything. His heat and his body. I sag from the loss, but he takes my hand. "Come here." He pulls me over to the kitchen island and slides his hands over my shoulders, squeezing the tense muscles and massaging with just the right amount of pressure to make me moan. What am I saying? I'm so horny a gust of wind would make me moan.

"I'm starving," he declares, and all ministrations cease. I tip my head up to meet his gaze. He has a relaxed smile, and I sigh, a little defeated but only a slight amount. I still have Saturday.

"So, do you want your dinner now?" My hope that he wants to give me more flatlines with his answer.

"Yes! Then you can give me a blowjob, how about that?" *Talk about throwing the dog a bone.*

CHAPTER FOUR

"AND I TAKE IT YOU BIT HIS DICK OFF, AND WE'RE off to visit him in hospital so your best friend can laugh her arse off." Hope has her arm threaded through mine as we head back to the salon where I work as an artistic director, second to the owner, Carlos. I'm a hairdresser. I can polish it up however I like, but I'm a stylist, a fucking good one at the best damn Salon in Chelsea, London—most probably the whole of the UK if you believe Carlos's hype.

"I shouldn't have told you. It always sounds worse when I say it out loud. I like giving blowjobs. I mean I got off so, it was a win for me too." I sound feeble even to my own ears. *When did I become so pathetic?*

"But that's not what you were hoping for, right? For the evening, I mean. So, it wasn't a win, by any stretch. Where the fuck is your backbone?" She's keeping her tone remarkably soft, considering the furious glare sparkling in her green eyes.

"It will be a win on Saturday," I mumble.

"You'd say yes? After that? I mean, after everything you've told me, you'd still say yes?" She stops in her tracks and faces me, utter astonishment shining from her pale complexion.

"I love him, Hope, and he loves me. No relationship is smooth sailing. Everyone's shit stinks. At the end of the day, though, he picked me." I can't hide the catch in my voice. "I've never been picked for anything. Parents, foster care, even my grandmother didn't really pick me. I was dumped there. I know marriage isn't the be-all end-all, but it means someone wants to commit their life to me forever. Dave wants me."

"'Even if one in two marriages end in divorce." She throws out a random statistic which happens to suit her argument.

"Yeah, even then, because for now and for each day in our one-day-at-a-time relationship, he has chosen me." I nod in affirmation with a little 'so-there' thrown in.

"You get the partner you deserve, Finn, and right now, he's being a dick, and you're being a doormat."

"Hope!" My eyes water instantly, because she's never voiced her view with such a mean spirit before, and she looks mortified right away.

"I'm sorry, Finn! God, I'm so sorry. I didn't mean—"

"Yes, you did," I bite back, and my voice cracks.

"Yes, I did. But you know I only want you happy." She cups my face, her hands like silk from all the massages, and her eyes are as wet as mine. She holds my gaze as silent tears trickle down my face. She gives a tight nod. "All right, angel. But just so you know, if I swung your way, you would've been well and truly chosen a long fucking time ago." She pushes out a light laugh, which is just enough to ease the tension.

"And I would've chosen you, but even though you have the most amazing green eyes I've ever seen, I'm still more of a penis girl." I push the front door to the salon as she laughs with me. She's just as much my world as I am hers, and I know she has my best interests at heart. It doesn't mean she's right, but it does mean she'll always have my back.

"Preaching to the choir, sister. Speaking of penises, or is it penii? Carlos!" Hope calls out to my boss. The salon is packed, but Carlos is lounging in the luxurious waiting area, spread-out like a glorious God on the cloud-like, puffy, white sofas. His dark skin glows and thick, jet-black hair, hangs strategically for maximum impact across his handsome face. His sultry eyes, the shade of midnight, are just as bewitching. "Damn, sometimes I hate my one-night-stand rule." Hope flashes me a wickedly carnal smile, and I suddenly fear for the safety of my boss. This is a match made in hell.

"Hope, you look quite edible." Carlos sits up, and Hope leans down to kiss his cheek in greeting.

"Don't I, though."

I pull her back and step between them. It's like rutting season; they're both as bad as the other, and I know I'm grumpy about it because I'm hopelessly horny.

"Hope, when are you going to persuade Finn here to let me loose on those platinum locks? You know it's a crime to work in London's most prestigious salon and have glorious but utterly *boring* hair. She's never had so much as a tint washed through it." He drags his long fingers along my scalp and loosens the tie holding the mass of curls at bay. His fingers shake and pull the strands free. I think I might whimper. Hope certainly snickers.

"You're on a fat chance there, Carlos," Hope replies, and I seem to have entered a dream-state. "Dave likes the natural look: no color, no cuts, no tatts. Completely natural. You'd have more luck trimming her bush than cutting any length off her hair." She snickers at her comment.

"Hope!" I choke out a cough and feel my cheeks burn with embarrassment. She may have bumped uglies with Carlos and now obviously thinks she has no need to engage her brain-to-mouth filter, but he's still my boss.

"What? I'm just saying…" She waves off my concern with a shrug. "You haven't changed your appearance since you were sixteen, and he nearly threw a shitfit when we both got our noses and navels pierced. He said I was a bad influence." She drops her tone to mimic Dave's reprimand, but ends up laughing.

"You *are* a bad influence." I join in, because she's too infectious not to.

"I like her essence." Carlos's rough grumble and thick accent make Hope sigh loudly.

"Influence," I correct.

"Oh I heard what you said." His gaze cuts to Hope like she's the only person on the planet; it makes the hairs on my neck stand at attention. *I miss that.* I'm seriously suffering from sensory deprivation if I can get this turned on by my boss's husky voice and a few choice words in the middle of my work shift.

"At least let Carlos do something special for Saturday?" Hope goads after some seriously heated seconds of eye fucking, then winks conspiratorially at my boss.

"Oh, yes, the big day. Please, angel, I will make you utterly irresistible. Not that you aren't already, but I will make the icing. Yes?" He turns his attention to me, and I notice Hope fans herself while his gaze is diverted.

"Fine! But you're not cutting the length, because Dave likes it long." I hold up my index finger to indicate that is my number one rule.

"Who doesn't?" Hope gushes under her breath, and I cringe because, for the love of God, she's now blatantly staring at my boss's pants. *Ground, swallow me now.*

"So Saturday, you're coming, Carlos?" I ask quickly to keep his eyes on me and not on my wayward friend.

"Of course." His smile is bright, wide with perfectly straight, dazzling teeth. *Killer smile.*

"Good. Dave's friends and family always makes me conscious of the fact my side of the room looks like someone forgot to mail the invites." I half joke.

"It won't look like that this time. He has invited the whole salon, and what we may lack in number we make up for with style and glamour." Carlos wiggles his thick, dark brows wickedly.

"And interest. Dave's mates are narcissistic boring fuckwits. Again, I'm not judging, I'm stating a fact." Hope holds up her hands and tightens her lips as if she has finally finished with the unsavory comments. *Unlikely.*

"Oh God!" I slap my hand against my head with a sense of doom and exasperation.

"Ah, don't be like that, Finn." She jumps onto my part of the sofa and throws both her arms around me, squeezing until I can't breathe. "It's going to be fun with a big fat capital F."

CHAPTER FIVE

Present day

"NAME?" THE LADY AT THE CHECK-IN DESK FAILS to hide her irritation, but judging by the exaggerated roll of her tarantula-lashed eyes, she really isn't trying very hard. I may be holding up the queue, but this trolley is possessed by Satan, won't go where I push it, and does in fact weigh about the same as my car. *Oh, if she huffs one more time, I swear.* I abandon the trolley, jutting across the path between the desks and the roped-off hordes of impatient travellers.

"Sanderson." I pinch out a tight smile, and even then, I'm being generous.

"Have you checked in already?"

"That's why I'm here at the check-in desk." I smile for real this time because I get to use my own dramatic eye roll. "No, I haven't, but I'm all good to go now."

"Would you wait a moment? There seems to be a problem." Her eyes dart from me to her screen and then back to me. Her brows furrow with confusion and now her nervous smile, although genuine, makes my anxiety reach new heights. I know I have the right day. I double-checked the booking and there's no fucking way I'm hauling all my stuff back to Hope's. If it isn't the right day, I'll just stay here. After all it's not like I don't have my *whole* life in those cases.

"I'm sorry, Ms. Sanderson, you are in the wrong queue." Her smile now dazzles it's so wide and white.

"Um—"

"Please follow me." She is all bright-eyed and bushy-tailed, and I take a step back at this miraculous transformation. "The porter will bring your bags."

"Porter?" I numbly follow her at the gentle tug on my sleeve, watching with my mouth agape as a burly porter pushes my trolley and follows us to the first class check-in desk.

I snort out an unladylike sound, cupping my mouth to contain the sound, and laugh. I look around for the prankster; this has Hope written all over it. Not that she has the money, but she'd think nothing of causing a little chaos.

The lady who brought me over, hands me to an elegant, immaculately groomed man with a deep tan and bright blue eyes.

"I'm so sorry for the confusion. Marc will take very good care of you." She smiles again, and I'm sure her cheeks must be aching with the stretch of her lips.

"Not a problem." My brain hasn't engaged, and I'm still waiting for the big reveal.

"Is that all of your luggage, Ms. Sanderson?" Marc drags my attention away from nervously scouring the area for where Hope might be hiding.

"Um, yes, but we can stop this now. I get the joke. Really very clever, but—"

"I'm sorry? What joke?" Marc asks with genuine confusion.

"The flying first class joke." I drop my hip and tilt my head in lieu of another eye roll.

"You don't want to fly first class?"

"No."

"No?"

"Well, obviously I do; however, I booked economy." There's a hushed inhale like I have thrown out the C-word at a nuns convention.

"You were upgraded, Ms. Sanderson. I can assure you this isn't a joke. I'm also pretty confident you will want to fly first class." His warm grin matches the friendly gleam in his eyes.

"Really? I mean really, I was upgraded? By whom?" I try to peer around his screen, but it has some sort of privacy cover blurring out any details.

"I don't believe I'm allowed to give out that information," he warns.

"Well, I don't believe I will be getting on the plane and maybe you will have to haul those cases back down to economy," I sass and fight the urge to click and wave my fingers in his face.

"Give me a moment." He smirks at my attitude, and I give a light shrug. Yes, I'm the idiot kicking up a fuss about being upgraded. He returns with a triumphant smile. "Elemental paid for the upgrade."

"Oh." The instant recognition makes my lips spread into a wide, warm smile. "In that case…" I thrust my passport forward and lay it on the counter.

"So you're happy to travel now, Ms. Sanderson?"

"Very happy, yes." I nod enthusiastically. Elemental is the name of the house where the men live …and my future husband. *Oh God.*

I downed the first glass of champagne. It really didn't touch the sides of my throat and I notice first class has a bar—a real bar. So I'm pretty sure my nerves won't be a problem for much longer. The seats are massive and recline into a full bed. Not that I'll be able to sleep, but I might fall into an alcohol-induced coma at some point on this ten-hour flight, so a horizontal option is good. I pull the crumpled piece of paper from my back pocket, or the *catalyst* as I like to call it. Smoothing it out on my knee that won't stop shaking, I read it for the millionth time.

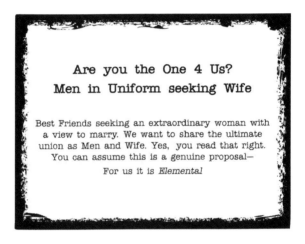

Are you the One 4 Us?
Men in Uniform seeking Wife

Best Friends seeking an extraordinary woman with a view to marry. We want to share the ultimate union as Men and Wife. Yes, you read that right. You can assume this is a genuine proposal—

For us it is *Elemental*

Hope showed me the advert three months ago. By then, I'd already spent one month on her couch, and she thought I could do with a giggle. The ad had been making the rounds on social media, and she laughed about it—we both did. Joked about 'if only'. But I had a twinge in my tummy that pushed me to take the next step from 'if only'. My heart was broken, my head was all over the fucking place after *that* Saturday, but my instinct was right on the money. My instinct said, "Fuck it, Finn. Why the hell not?"

You can question my sanity, and fine, you can question my

motives too, but once I was satisfied this was, indeed, a genuine offer, I doubt I would have chosen any differently at the end of the day, or more specifically at the end of *that* Saturday four months ago.

CHAPTER SIX

Four months ago

"**Y**OU LOOK STUNNING, FINN. I WOULD SO DO YOU."
Hope stands back with her hands crossed over her chest and a sappy smile on her flawless face. I have straightened her hair so it hangs around her face, and I put some fiery gold streaks in it to match her lipstick. She looks a little breathtaking herself. I give a mock curtsey at her compliment and turn to look in the full-length mirror on the back of my bedroom door. Dave left much earlier to get 'things' sorted, and Hope and I have been getting ready ever since that morning. Well, getting slowly tipsy and getting ready.

I chose a red halter neck backless dress, loose-fitted, shimmery with fringing. I know it's sexy as fuck, but it also doesn't hug my love-handles, so it's flattering too. I wear some gold, strappy Jimmy Choo sandals and will carry a matching small clutch. My hair hangs in long, loose, luscious curls, courtesy of

Carlos, and I'm a bundle of excited, nervous anticipation.

"Ah, thanks, babe. Right back at ya." I bump my hip against hers and draw in a deep breath. I'm ready.

We are ushered upstairs into the private room, which is heaving with familiar faces and some not so familiar; Dave does know a lot of people. He sees me walk in, and I get a small thrill as his eyes widen with approval. He strides forward and sweeps his arm around my waist.

"Hmm…RP, you scrub up well." He kisses my cheek, and I ignore the hiss from Hope, standing just behind me. "Hope, you look stunning." Dave leans over to kiss Hope on the cheek, and I can see from the tick in her jaw she still hasn't let my nickname comment go.

"He doesn't mean anything by it," I whisper into her ear. She raises her brow. "Not tonight, Hope. Let's just enjoy tonight, okay?"

"Fine. I will need another drink though. It's like a fucking convention for Dave wannabes in here." She points at the crowd of men at the bar, and I snicker. They do seem to have a uniform stroke clone look going on.

"Come on, let's dance first." I tip my head to the relatively empty dance floor. I prefer it like that because I get to throw some serious shapes without the fear of taking someone's eye out. The men are too busy checking their own reflections to bother us, and besides, I'm with Dave and they all know that. I wonder if they know what he's planning.

We have danced nonstop for hours, refueling when Carlos arrived and joined us on the dance floor, but my feet are starting to ache. I motion to Hope that I'm going to take a breather when I see Dave start to move my way. My stomach flips, and I get a flash of tingles that ignite my skin. This is it.

The music fades, and I hear Dave's voice through the speakers. He is all mic'd up to the sound system.

"RP…" He exhales, and I wince. "Finn, my beautiful girl-friend…" He holds out his hands, and I place mine in his. My chest feels tight, and the residual beat of the music is still thumping in my ears, or maybe that's my heart. I can't breathe. "You are my best friend, and I love you." He drops to one knee and the whole crowd collectively inhales a breath and holds it, just like I do. "For my birthday it would make me the happiest man alive if you would…" He pauses and pulls out a large square velvet box. He pops the lid and his face crumples with a smirk.

I don't understand.

I look to his eyes for clarification, which he is more than happy to oblige. "If you would let me go to Amsterdam for the week with my mates." There's a howl of deep laughter from the bar, and I stare, transfixed, at the golden condom nestled in the velvet ring box in his outstretched hand.

"I don't understand, Dave." I manage to whisper, my skin flaming from my toes to my hairline.

"I don't want to cheat on you, Finn, but I want to go for a break. You know?" He wiggles his thick brows. "What goes on in Amsterdam, stays in Amsterdam." He twists over his shoulder and winks at his friends, who are all still doubled up at this 'joke'.

"I thought you were going to ask me to marry you." I bite my lip to stop it from fucking wobbling, but I can't hide the tears in my voice.

"Fuck, no!" He barks out a laugh and stops when his gaze meets my eyes. I blink to try and focus, but the tears are too fat to hold. The dam bursts, and they fall onto my bright, red cheeks. "Finn…" He cups his hand over the mic, and his face darkens. "Babe, don't be like that. I thought you'd be cool. I could've gone and cheated. I'm being honest, at least. I'm not an arsehole." His voice is clipped, indignant at my response.

"You did this in front of everyone, Dave?" I grit out, anger starting to bubble up and replace the debilitating humiliation.

"It was a laugh, Finn. Jesus, you used to be able to take a joke. Besides, I thought you were more likely to say yes like this." He is still scowling, like I have done something wrong.

"You want to go and fuck some hookers for your birthday?" I snap.

"Christ, Finn. Do you have to put it like that?" He glances nervously over at his friends. I'm sure every eye in the place is glued to us; however, I don't care.

"You won't have sex with me, but you want to go and pay some stranger? I just want to make sure I'm getting the whole picture." My voice is loud enough now that I don't need the microphone he is still clutching. His eyes flash with anger, and he straightens his shoulders and meets my deathly glare head on. He's mad. I'm embarrassing him, and I'm fucking heartbroken this is the only thing he's thinking about in this fucked up, twisted situation.

"Yes," he states with a snide and spiteful tone.

"Then go." The pain in my chest is crushing me from the inside, yet somehow I hold myself together and turn with grace. I don't quite manage a smile, but when Dave shouts into the mic, "She said yes!" and the crowd erupts with a joyous cheer, my knees give out, and I start to fall. I don't remember much more. I didn't hit the ground, but I did hit rock bottom.

The Morning After the Night Before

"What a complete fucking arsehole, shitbag, motherfucking, cunt!" I'm still swaying with the dangerously high levels of alcohol swimming in my veins. I believe I'm pointing at my best friend as I test out the full extent of my Anglo-Saxon vocabulary, but there seems to be three of her. I hedge my bets and aim at the middle one. My face is still wet from the tears that fell like

Niagara fucking Falls the instant I left the club, but I have moved on to vitriolic rage. *I can't believe I didn't kick him in the balls.*

"Yes. Yes, he is. What are you going to do about it?" she goads me. I take the glass handed to me, hoping it's more vodka, because that's what a best friend should be offering, some much needed hair of the dog before the inevitable hangover comes and bites my arse and finishes me off. I take a sip and screw my face up at the ice cold water and hand it back to her. *Traitor.*

"Am I all packed?" My eyes widen with a dizzying head rush when I whip my head around too fast to survey the room and the neatly stacked tower of suitcases Hope has been stuffing all night on my behalf. I have been just as busy and even with my coordination shot to shit, I have managed to cut the crotch out of every single pair of jeans, trousers, and underpants that Dave owns. *He's so keen to share his dick, might as well make it easy for him.* Hope cleared the debris and made sure the clothing was folded away, so he won't suspect I have gone a little *Fatal Attraction.* It's the very least he deserves.

"You are." She pushes the glass in front of my face once more. I reluctantly take it and drink the water down this time.

"And you're sure I can stay with you?" I let out a deep breath and hand the empty glass back. Her kind eyes soften with the sympathetic tilt of her head.

"You know you can, babe. *Mi casa es su casa.*"

"Only, I don't have any—" Fuck, more fucking tears. She's by my side, perched on the bed as I am, her arms holding me tightly, offering me solace. My body shudders and shakes as I fight the rolling waves of sob after sob that wrack my body. I can't believe I have any fluid left. I'm utterly battered and bruised, and my tummy muscles scream in agony from all the sorrow. Her hold comforts me while she rocks me and makes soothing sounds to try and ease my pain. I'm falling so deep, I can no longer see any light. "I was so humiliated, Hope. How could he do that? How could he think it was funny? After everything I've been—"

"Because he's a cunt." She drags me closer with a tighter, chest-crushing squeeze, and I let out a hollow laugh as she pulls me back once more from the abyss.

"He really is."

"And we're not going to give him any more time, okay?" She holds my gaze, and I blink the tears away. She nods slowly, and I find myself mirroring her movements, like a small child might do.

"Okay." I reply on autopilot, because with the numbness, the unbearable hurt, and copious quantities of alcohol, I'm not sure much is going in. Nevertheless, I trust my best friend; she's all I've got now.

"You are coming to stay with me, and if that piece of shit so much as enters my post code, I will cut his precious cock off with a rusty spoon and feed it to the pigeons in Trafalgar." She pinches her thumb and forefinger together with the smallest of gaps, and her other hand is holding an imaginary and equally tiny spoon with which she motions a rough chopping action. I lean my tipsy head onto her shoulder, feeling it's too heavy to hold up. I let out a slow breath and a hiccup.

"There aren't any pigeons in Trafalgar anymore," I muse out loud, because that is how my drunk brain works, focusing on the *pertinent* parts of a conversation. Not that my heart isn't broken, bleeding out from this relationship wreckage, or that I'm a tangled, mangled mess of unstable emotion. No, I'm thinking about where all the fucking pigeons are. I must be suffering from alcohol poisoning, or I might have actually lost my mind.

"There are still pigeons, babe, and if there weren't any, I'll happily stick it down his self-serving throat." She narrows her eyes with a fierce scowl, looking her meanest and most sincere.

"Just make sure he swallows!" I blurt out, and she joins me in our first real laugh of the night—well, morning now.

"It ain't love unless you swallow, babe, and that man, he fucking loves himself." She wiggles her perfect brows, but the glint in her eye is so serious it makes me shiver. *I love her so much, because she means every damn word.* "Come on, babe, let's get you out of..." She pulls me to standing.

"My home?" I blurt my interruption. My voice catches on my question, and my tone is a mix of resignation and desolation.

"*His* home." Hope emphasizes this with a wince of sadness, but the truth of it can't hurt me anymore than it already does.

"Yeah. Let's get out of *his* home and life. I've wasted enough time." I sniff out a bitter laugh. I may have nothing of value in those five cases, but I'm worth more than a fucking gold condom in a velvet gift box. It wasn't me who kissed ten years together good-bye, but it is me who has finally seen that I deserve to come first for a change.

$$\triangle \triangledown \triangle \triangledown$$

"I hate this, Hope. I don't want to date. I just want someone to make that decision for me. Choose *me*." I thump my chest and grunt my best impression of a Neanderthal man. "Very caveman, you know? You my woman. You my wife."

"You do not." She rolls her eyes at me and pushes another online dating form my way. It has been a month, but when I realized there was little love lost, at least on his part, it was pretty easy to pick myself up. Maybe, if I could've pinpointed the moment in time when we moved firmly into the friend zone, my relationship with Dave would've ended years ago. For whatever reason, though, I didn't see it, and now I am, for the very first time, 'putting myself out there'. I'm being proactive and upbeat, which does make me think the decision to leave Dave was the right one all along. I still struggle to get past *that* night. Actually,

I don't struggle with it. It's very simple. What he did to me was unforgivable.

"Well, not exactly, but I would still like someone to—"

"I know. Someone to choose you." She wrinkles her nose like the very idea leaves a lingering smell of rotten eggs.

"Yeah." I shrug off and ignore her fundamental difference of opinion.

"Well, what about these guys? No dating necessary, they just want a wife." She spins her laptop to face me. I don't bother to look up.

"Yeah, because that doesn't sound creepy. What do you mean, guys?" Then I do look up and swipe to enlarge the image.

"It's got to be a joke, but this advert is flying around Twitter and the rest of social media. Dream come true for someone like you, someone wanting the whole marriage thing. But four guys? Jeez, you'd have a bucket fanny in a week." She belly laughs at her own joke.

"Yeah, but what a week." I snicker and start to read the advert.

"Shame there's no pictures." She draws her lips down in an exaggerated pout of disappointment I happen to share.

"Navy guys? Hmm, well, that counts me out. The lucky girl would have to super fit to handle that amount of—"

"Cock," she cries out, fanning herself and mock fainting flat-out on her bed.

"I was thinking about stamina, but yeah. Still, it does sound good, don't you think? I mean four guys worshipping your body. It feels like forever since I've—"

"Your punani got a pounding." She's so unbelievably crude, but I love her filter-free expressions which frequently make me pee my pants. She has been my lifesaver this last month since I moved out and ended my ten-year relationship with the newly titled Dave the Dickhead. *He hasn't even called.* "Finn, baby steps, don't you think? This would be a monumental change for someone like you. I don't think you're quite ready for this, honey. You haven't managed to pick one guy yet, and to go from having fucked one guy to gangbang central? We're probably talking DVA or maybe DVDA. Now that's gonna make your eyes water." Her salacious tone and deviant grin makes me ask, when I really should know better.

"DVA?"

"Double vaginal and anal or DVDA is double vag and double an—"

"Okay! I get your point. Maybe I need to get one date out of the way first, eh?" I wave my hands frantically to interrupt and rush my words to stop her from finishing her sentence and my mind from flashing to a full visual.

"Never going to happen." She chuckles, and her tone is slightly mocking.

"A girl can dream." I flash her a wink. She may have been trying to shock me, but I don't need too long to warm to a new idea.

"Come on! You promised to be my wing woman." One week later, I fight to pull the covers from Hope's death grip. She has the duvet tucked over her head and is resisting any attempt I have used to try and rouse her lazy arse for the last fifteen minutes. She groans, and I snatch the covers and whip them back so far, her flailing arms are useless at trying to capture them back.

"You don't need a wing woman. It's the gym," she grumbles and flips onto her tummy, pressing her head into her pillow.

"I do, and you said you'd help." I wait patiently for her to flip back around. A few short seconds is all it takes. Her face is still like thunder, but at least she's now sitting up.

"Why couldn't you eat your body weight in ice cream like any normal woman does after a break-up?" She squints one eye open, the other scrunched shut, then smiles when she meets my gaze.

"Because I might have a date, and I have a feeling I'm going to need to be fit." I tempt her innate curiosity and abundant nosiness.

"Not another Dave, because I can tell you right now I won't let you go down that road. You are gorgeous—every inch, curvy or trim. You don't have to change for any man." She clicks her fingers in a sassy little air curve.

"I agree, and this isn't about that. It's just he's from California and he's in the military. We bonded over our love of jogging." I motion a little jog. I'm already dressed for the gym so I look the part, at least.

"No one *loves* jogging." Hope shivers and an expression of complete horror flashes over her sleep-crumpled features.

"Exactly, that's how we bonded." My smile is as fit to burst as I am with the weight of the secret I have to keep. *I have to.*

"Hang on a minute? You're going on a date? In the States. Isn't that a little—"

"A bit of a trek," I interrupt.

"A bit fucking crazy is what I was going to say, but okay, let's go for the practical element here. Yes, it's a bit of a 'trek.'" She air quotes and lays the sarcasm on nice and thick.

"Get up and I'll tell you all about it." I clap my hands to hurry her along, there's so much to do.

CHAPTER SEVEN

Present Day

I DIDN'T LOSE ANY WEIGHT WITH THE FITNESS REGIME I started in the two months since answering the advertisement and setting the date to visit, but I'm fitter than I have ever been. A nervous smile creeps across my face, and I can feel my cheeks start to burn. *Am I going to be fit enough? As Hope said that's a lot of—*

"Cocktail menu?" The flight attendant's bright, friendly voice interrupts my wayward thoughts.

"Oh, no. Thank you. The champagne at dinner went straight to my head. I don't want to be smashed when we land. Which will be when?" She informs me with a dazzling smile, we're just forty minutes out, I sit back and let out a satisfying sigh. I could get used to this, luxuriating in first class courtesy of my men. *My men.*

That advert wasn't a joke.

Far from it.

Unfortunately, the few Skype conversations I've had, haven't been great for one reason or another: the connection was poor, the sound didn't sync, or the quality of the image was grainy and broken. But I have spoken daily to one, more, or all of them in some fashion: message, text, or long emails. I'm confident they are all…Hmm… What? What is it I am confident of? The closer I get to landing the less confident I actually am. My mouth has been dry for the last hour despite ample refreshments, and the butterflies in my tummy need an extension built, there are so many of the critters. I take a calming breath and repeat the mantra that has kept me on this crazy path for the past few months, and ultimately made me board the plane.

It's for one month. What's the worst that could happen?

I struggle with my last bag, which happens to also be the last remaining piece of luggage on the carousel. The trolley is loaded, and I lean into the handle with my shoulder to gain enough leverage to make the thing move. Not too fast, or I'll never be able to stop it, and I'd most likely mow down anything in my path: kiddies, little old ladies. No one would be safe. I groan as I round the corner, just through the automatic doors of the exit and that's when my jaw hits the floor and I let the trolley drift from my hands, not caring what damage ensues. *Holy Fuck!*

The airport is crammed, but it's like someone has put the soft focus filter on my peripheral vision because all I see is *them* and a massive neon sign with a flashing arrow at the end of the walkway, which says: "World's Hottest Men Here". The residual images from the few Skype calls we managed to make, wage an almighty battle in my mind, trying to identify who is who from this distance. Oh my God, they can't be real. The blond guy on the left of the group is in jeans and a crisp white T-shirt. But the others? They are in uniform, which, I have to say is… There are no words to describe how unbelievably hot that is. I'm a liquid mess below the waist and my throat is parched dry as a desert.

I struggle to swallow, because the icing? The actual icing is they're each holding a separate sign with the words: Welcome Home Our Wife.

So it begins.

I had wondered if this little set up would be very on the down-low, but there it is, bold as anything for all to see. No going back, signed, sealed, and delivered. *Now why won't my feet move?*

Deep breath, Finn, come on, move! And nothing. If anything, I think one of my feet lifts to take a step backward, but it's way too late. They spot me and are moving my way in unison like a wall of muscle.

The blond in the jeans I know is Brady; they call him Pink. He is sporting the widest grin and breaks free of the formation and rushes toward me. His strong arms reach out, scoop around my bottom, and he lifts me high, then spins me in a slow, dizzying circle.

"Girl, you came!" he calls out, turning us to face the others, still holding me flush against his solid frame, my feet dangling a good few inches from the floor.

"I did. I really did. I'm just as shocked, I can promise you." I let out a nervous laugh.

"Aw, and you have the cutest accent. Doesn't she have the cutest accent?" he calls back to the others who have now closed the gap and are flanking Pink and crowding around us.

"You *have* heard her speak before, Pink. Don't go acting all crazy and frightening the girl." The tall, dark-haired one on the end speaks with a deep rumbling voice, and his lips curl with a warm, friendly smile.

"Oh sorry, ma'am—" Pink's tone is deeply apologetic, and

I'm about to forgive the nonsense when I recognize the oldest, Aarón, who starts speaking again.

"And maybe you could put her down so we can all say hi." Pink bites back a cheeky grin, his pale blue eyes sparkling with mischief as he slowly slides me down his body. The lump in my throat is going to be a permanent feature, and I stifle an audible whimper when he finally releases his hold.

They're all of similar build, like brick shit houses, big and super fit. Aarón is much taller, maybe six-five. He is the one who just spoke and the one they call Charge. I wait for someone to speak, but they are all staring. Four pairs of eyes, all different shades, but intensely curious and piercing. *Okay, I'll go first.*

"Hi!" I give a little wave and then laugh when they all seem to exhale a sudden breath filled with tension and visibly relax. Stunning smiles now dominate their features, and I make my best guess at identifying them because those profile pictures did not do them justice.

"You must be Enzo." I hold my hand out to the one nearest to me. He takes it and pulls me into a hug. He has very short, black hair, dark tan coloring from his South American father, and light brown eyes from his mother's side. He lets me go and leans in to kiss my cheek before completely relinquishing his hold. I have sent multiple messages to each of them over the last three months, so I have a vague and spotted history.

"Tug, my friends call me Tug." He flashes a wink, and I return an easy smile.

"Right." I tip my finger in acknowledgment. None of them seem to use their real names, but then, neither do I.

"I'm Toxic, or you can call me Marlon, if you like." Marlon has light brown hair, just as short as Tug's, with floppy spikes at the front. It's still no more than a few inches, but it softens his cut jaw, strong brow, and penetrating hazel eyes. He steps up to me in favor of pulling me to him, and his arms cover me like a shield; his hug is firm and gentle. *It feels so good.* He stands back and points to the others. "You've met Pink, and this is Charge." I turn and tilt my head back to gain eye contact, because Charge is now standing very close.

His wide shoulders seem to block out the daylight, and my entire field of vision is filled with the most beautiful man I have ever seen. Glossy dark brown hair, almost black, and those eyes? God! They are the deepest clear, piercing blue and seem to scorch a path straight to my soul, searing me with heat and intensity. *I can't breathe.* He doesn't blink just devours every inch of my face, searching, but I'm not sure what for. I get a nervous knot in my tummy, which is unsettling. Maybe he sees something in me that he doesn't like? Maybe he sees *me,* and that's causing the deep line across his brow to deepen and his jaw to twitch. *Maybe I've made a huge fucking mistake.*

"You are much more beautiful in the flesh, Finn." The way he rolls the word around his mouth and lets it flow from his perfect lips with a seductively delicious tone makes my legs tremble and my core clench. He stretches his right hand out to take mine, lifting it from my side and placing it like some precious piece of glass in the palm of his other hand. His hold is strong and surprisingly sensual. His thumb traces the bump of my vein on my wrist across the pulse point, and I swear my heart stops beating. He leans down to place a kiss on the back of my hand, his eyes never leaving mine. The devil himself dances behind those long lashes, I have no doubt. This might be a mistake or heaven, but one thing I'm sure of, *I'm definitely going to burn.*

Okay, this is awkward. I'm wedged in the middle in the backseat between Toxic and Tug. Huge man thighs spread so wide mine are squished and literally stuck together from the sweltering heat. The old pickup truck is possibly the coolest thing

I have ever ridden in, but it has no air con and even with the windows fully down, I'm dripping. The guys all stripped down to their t-shirts when we started to drive and there's this musky man smell that is intoxicating, heady and fresh. Despite the hurricane blowing in from the windows, it's all I can smell and very distracting. Tug puts his hand on my thigh and squeezes. I jump and let out a nervous apology at the concern that shoots across his face.

"Sorry, darling, but couldn't hold off any longer, not touching you, I mean." His grip is firm and at a respectable place about mid-thigh, with no indication it's going to start wandering. His deep eyes and soft smile are as genuine as his words. I get a warm tingle inside.

"Oh no, that's fine. Just a little nervous I guess." I shrug and return his grin, but I jump again when Toxic does the same on my other leg. He flashes a smirk, though, when our eyes meet, and continues to hang his head out of the window, his aviator glasses protecting him from the glaring sun and bugs.

"You need to think of us a spiders." Tug's tone is completely serious, which makes me frown. Is this code? Am I missing a joke perhaps, because why the fuck would I want to sit in a car with four fuck-off-sized spiders. "We're much more afraid of you than you are of us." He grins, and I snort out a laugh, which makes him laugh outright. "You know, darling, you're just too damn cute. We're gonna eat you all up."

The audible gulp escapes from my throat, and they all turn around. Four pairs of hungry, demanding, deliciously dangerous eyes boring into me. *Like I said…dripping.*

I haven't paid much attention to the scenery, my eyes keep drifting to the swell of toned arm muscles lightly covered in sweat, the glimpse of a tattoo, or some occasional eye contact in the rear-view mirror from Charge that makes the hairs on my neck stand at full mast. We swing a sharp left and I fall against

Toxic, my hand reaching out to Tug for balance. I grip the material on his trousers a little too close to his crotch, and he tenses, but I release my grip quickly. Face on fire, I snatch my hand back. I'm pretty sure I grabbed his cock along with the material, but that would make him…I want to say huge, but looking at where my hand actually landed, I'm going to say deformed. He wiggles his brow, and a knowing grin spreads, wide and wicked, across his face. *Oh, shit.*

"Someone's in a hurry?" Pink calls out from the front and slaps Charge on the shoulder.

"There's a lot to get through." The curt response is matter of fact and not in the least playful. I wonder whose idea this was and if they're really *all* on board. I get a different feeling from Charge, which might be something or nothing, but I guess we have the whole month to figure everything out, to find out if we fit. I chance a glance at Tug, and my wayward thoughts make my thighs squeeze together conspiratorially. *That* is never going to fit.

The dirt drive turns once more to an automatic white five-bar gate that starts to swing wide as we roll forward. Evergreen trees line the road, and on either side are white posts and rail fencing, separating fields with horses and smaller paddocks, as far as the eye can see. Or for a couple of hundred acres Pink informs me with a pride-filled smile. This is his passion since he got out of the Navy.

Charge pulls the truck to a stop at the bottom of some steps leading to an expansive front porch, which seems to wrap around the double-story, wooden farmhouse. The boys jump from the car, and I slide slowly to the edge of the back seat to peer at my new home; it's stunning.

A large overhang is supported by white pillars along the front and around the building by the looks of it. The white, wooden boarding is pristine. Although I don't think the building is new, it's weathered and clearly loved. There are several steps leading up to a double-oak door, and I can see a swing on the porch. Is it wrong to feel giddy about a swing? *They have a swing.*

I jump when a hand appears in front of my face, but I grimace my apology when my eyes meet Charge's stern expression.

"Sorry, still a little nervous."

"Understandable, but I think we can help with that now." I hesitate, but at his commanding tone I grasp his hand, and I'm helped from the high truck. My knees buckle when I hit the ground. I don't know if it's from the long flight or the intimidating presence of this God-like man holding my hand, but he wraps his arm around my waist preventing me falling any farther. He steadies me, and once I have my footing, his arm falls away, making me slump a little at the loss. He still has my hand and tugs me to follow him.

"Okay, let's get this freak show started." Toxic barks out a laugh, but I freeze at his comment, pulling my hand roughly from Charge's hold, and crossing my arms. A deep and instant swell of sickness hits my stomach like a sucker punch.

"That's what you think I am? A freak?" I step back and watch the horror on Charge's face morph to pure rage.

"You asshole!" Tug thumps Toxic on his arm while Tug looks at me with confusion.

"What? No! Fuck no! Shit!" Toxic's eyes dart from me to Charge and back to me.

"You apologize now, Toxic or—"

"You don't need to threaten me, Charge. Of course I'm gonna fucking apologize." Toxic stands in front of me and waits until I meet his eyes. I draw in a deep breath and tip my chin up. His hazel eyes have tiny, gold flecks in them and hold my gaze but are crinkled with obvious concern. "Fuck, Finn. I'm sorry. I wasn't thinking. I mean…I think *we're* the freaks. Not you. Never you. We're so fucking lucky we found you. I just made the joke because, well, this ain't the norm, you know, and I think that makes us freaks, but in a good way. Fuck, darling, you've saved us from a life of one-night stands and tired right arms, so don't go thinking you're anything other than the best thing to happen to a bunch of freaks like us."

"Did you have to focus on the sex, asshole?" Pink groans, running his hand down his face. I look over to see both Charge and Tug roll their eyes.

"What?" Toxic holds his hands up in defeat, and I can see the genuine frustration and anxiety that he might have upset me. I step up to him and take his hand.

"It's okay, Toxic, and thank you for explaining. This is an *unusual* situation, but I'm also a little tired, so not in the best frame of mind to take a joke." He gives me a tentative smile, and I squeeze some more reassurance into his hand. "And it's okay to mention the sex. It's not like I came here to bake cookies."

"What? There aren't going to be any cookies? Dammit, I want a refund." Toxic jokes and pulls me into a side hug.

"No refunds, but you do get the four week trial period before you send me packing," I reply with a half-teasing tone.

"Never gonna happen, sweetheart. Never gonna happen." Toxic kisses the top of my head as he steers me up the stairs and through the door Charge is holding wide open. Charge's deep voice washes over me as I cross the threshold.

"Welcome home, Finn."

CHAPTER EIGHT

"WOULD YOU LIKE A TOUR, OR DO YOU WANT TO rest before we get started?" Charge asks, and my instant gutter mind flashes the deepest pink hue across my cheeks, making his lips twitch with amusement. "I thought we could go through the binder," he clarifies.

"The binder?" I frown, then understanding hits me. "Oh, yes, the binder. Of course. How about a quick tour? I'm surprisingly not that tired. I feel like I've been mainlining coffee straight for the last three months," I snicker.

"Adrenaline, which again is understandable," he states.

His face is so handsome but impassive. We've chatted a lot over the past few months, now I'm here, and I can't get a read on him, at all. "Would you like some chamomile tea?" he asks.

"Oh, yes, that would be great." He never breaks eye contact, even when he addresses the others.

"Pink, why don't you show Finn her quarters, and we'll bring her bags through. Then we'll do the tour together."

"Cool beans." *Oh, ground swallow me now!* Did I say that out loud? What am I, twelve? I cough to hide my embarrassment. "That would be perfect, thank you. Oh and I need to call Hope. Just to let her know I haven't been abducted." I chuckle awkwardly.

"What makes you think you haven't?" Charge replies deadpan, and I force out a stilted laugh which falls flat, until Tug speaks.

"Man, did you not hear the girl say she's not up to jokes yet?" Tug winks at me, and I laugh a little lighter now, even if Charge has yet to crack a smile at his own 'joke'. *Jeez, that guy is intense.*

Pink tilts his head for me to follow his lead, and I do, catching Charge's nefarious smile and piercing stare when I chance a glance behind me. The goosebumps dance like a flash mob across my skin, and I give a full body shiver once we are at the top of the stairs and out of sight.

We are a good way down the long corridor before I ask.

"Is he always so…?" Pink stops midstride and faces me with a wide, knowing grin as I search my vocabulary to describe what Charge is making me feel. Nope, I've got nothing.

"Oh yes." Pink chuckles and motions for me to carry on to the end of the hallway. "He's a good guy, Finn. The best." Pink opens the door and steps aside to let me through. All troubling thoughts and confused feelings dissolve when I enter this picture-perfect, show-house master bedroom.

The room is massive, easily as big as Hope's entire one-bedroom flat back home. It has a sloping roof with exposed beams and French windows, which open up onto a balcony. The chiffon curtains billow with the slightest breeze coming in from outside, and the sweet aroma of honeysuckle drifts in with the warm air. The hardwood floors have a shine I could see my reflection in, if I could take my eyes off the massive four-poster bed. I must have gasped because Pink is laughing.

"You like it?" He takes my hand and leads me over to another door. "Then you'll love this." The en suite has a bath big enough for five and a huge open shower. I do love it, but the bed looks fabulous. I think I might weep, it looks so comfortable, with the thickest mattress, pure white covers with intricate lace edging, and hundreds of pillows.

"This bed looks amazing." I sigh and run my hand over the softest cotton sheets. His face is the picture of puzzled amusement. "I've been mostly sleeping on Hope's sofa for the last four months, with the occasional night sharing her bed when she wasn't *with* some random stray," I clarify so he doesn't think I'm *that* crazy; it's not like some weird bed fetish. I just like my sleep.

"This is your space so no sharing, unless you want to." Pink searches my face, but I have nothing to add. I knew I would have my own space, I didn't think it would be so utterly enchanting. The bedroom door opens, revealing Toxic and Tug as they enter with their arms full of my suitcases. They each look like they are barely carrying a bag of groceries, and I know each case weighs a ton. I had to pay a fortune in excess baggage charges. They place them at the end of the bed and then stand in a semi-circle of awkward silence, casting furtive glances to one another.

"Okay!" I clap my hands together with a sense of purpose. It's going to be a long month if we can't break the ice. "Let's get to know each other properly."

"Really?" Tug takes an eager step forward before he's hastily pulled back into line by Toxic.

"I think she meant the binder, dipshit." He slaps the back of Tug's head and looks to me. "You did mean the binder, right?"

"Um, yeah, I did." I shrug an apology to Tug for his misunderstanding. But seriously? He thought we were going to get down, gangbang style right now? I chew the inside of my lip to stop the thought from creating a telling smile. *I'm a slut.* Then again, if the purpose is breaking the ice, I do believe *that* would not so much break it, as smash it to smithereens.

We meet up with Charge at the bottom of the stairs, and he proceeds to take over the guided tour. This was his grandparents' place. The boys moved in when Pink left the Navy and needed something to do. He's always loved horses, so was happy to take over the stud farm. There's an open-plan kitchen, which leads into a sprawling dining and lounging area. The back of the house has several sets of French doors, which open up to a terrace and the glorious views over the land and down to one of two lakes. The second is farther into the land and much more private, according to the boys. There's a game room, study, and gym. The garage leads to the pool house, and all the bedrooms are on the first floor. We walk a slow loop around the entire house, and I can't quite take in just how beautiful it all is or how quiet.

The stables are set away from the house down at the other end of the drive, but they have a different entrance, so the main house is completely private. This is clearly important as it's mentioned twice in the space of five minutes, but I don't ask why, since there's plenty of time for questions. I'm just trying to take everything in without either my jaw dropping or drooling. We arrive at the back of the house and I'm taken into the laundry room, which is overflowing with sheets and shirts, uniforms and heaps of underwear.

"And this is the laundry room," Charge states.

"So it is." I smile tightly.

"Since you won't be working we thought you might get bored and you'd want something to do," he elaborates, and I respond just as matter-of-factly.

"When I'm not doing one of you guys, you mean?" I can't

help my snarky tone, because this has just gone from my dream deal to my worst nightmare.

"Um, not exactly. We just thought—" I hold my finger up as a warning and interrupt.

"Look, you are clearly looking for a maid who fucks, because who in their right mind would want to do laundry to stave off boredom?" My voice gets a squeaky high-pitch when I become agitated, which tends to make me sound a little unstable. They all look a little shocked at my outburst.

"I like to do the laundry." Toxic holds his hand up, and I snap my mouth shut, because he's completely serious. He takes my finger, still pointing in an accusatory manner, curls the digit into my palm and holds my fist in his. "We don't need a maid, Finn. We already have one, but we all do chores we like to do, and I happen to find it relaxing. You can just switch off. We didn't mean to offend you." I feel a wave of embarrassment, tinged with shame that I was so quick to assume. But seriously, how was I going to put those things together when I was barely able to convince Dave to pick up a takeout menu, let alone clean up after himself.

"You will help with the chores, Finn, but only pulling your fair weight. Like Toxic said, we don't need a maid; we have one. What we do need is a wife." Charge's tone is a soft reprimand, but his smile eases the sting. "How about we go over the details, to avoid any more misunderstandings."

"Yeah, that's a good idea," I mumble, backing out of the room. *At least I didn't say 'cool beans'.*

We all take a seat in the living room, although this now feels like an interrogation because the men are all seated facing me on a long and low leather sofa and I'm in an armchair. Charge has handed me the most enormous 3-ring binder. It must be three inches thick and I have only flicked through, and each page is printed on both sides. The sections are subdivided with their names. I lean forward and take a sip of the chamomile tea.

"Why the nicknames?" I take another sip before putting the cup down on the coaster.

"It's all in the binder," Charge answers and the others nod.

"Hmm, okay, but maybe you could just tell me?" My question seems to cause some confusion, and I bite my lip to stop from smirking.

"I'm Pink because of my surname, Pinkerton." Pink is happy enough to answer, even if Charge is scowling.

"And because you're so pretty, you could pass for a girl," Tug jokes, and Pink punches him on the arm.

"And you? Why are you called Tug?" I open the file and slide my finger to his section, but there's so much on the page I couldn't pick out the answer, not unless it jumped from the page and bit me on the arse. I look up at the sound of rustling material and see that Tug has dropped trou and is holding himself in hand. Not *all* of himself, because his cock is fucking enormous and roughly the size and width of a barge. "Oh! I get it. Tug… yep, okay." My eyes must be like saucers, and I physically try to rein in my shock. I swallow back a squeak and let out a lungful of air that's filled with heat. My cheeks are on fire, and a nervous chuckle escapes with the exhale. "And Toxic? I'm a little nervous to ask now," I joke, causing him to laugh.

"No, my junk is fine. Nothing toxic about that." He cups himself but, thankfully, keeps his pants on.

"No, it's just your ass that's toxic." Pink hold his nose and a light punching match ensues. I start to turn the pages and the room falls silent.

"You're funny, pretty boy." Toxic blows Pink a kiss, and I snicker. "I got mine when we were kids, and I'd mess around with household chemicals, trying to make my own fireworks and shit," he clarifies, and I nod happily in understanding and relief, that he isn't actually called Toxic because he farts.

"How about you, Finn? Do you have a nickname?" Pink asks, and I sniff out a strange, flat laugh.

"Yeah, sort of. My boyfr—Dave." I correct myself. "Dave used to call me RP." I cringe a little, because it really wasn't my favorite.

"RP? What does that mean?" Tug looks confused, they all do, when they look at each other and then back at me for an explanation.

"Oh it was just a joke, really. Only it stuck. RP stands for Roller-Pig," I mutter, feeling a pinch of humiliation.

"Excuse me? What now? Your boyfriend used to call you Roller-Pig?" Pink says, his brows raised with shock.

"Yeah." I try and pull a faint smile, like it isn't a big deal. "It's not as bad as it sounds. It's from a film with Matt Dillon, when he goes to investigate the girl, Mary, then he comes back and tells all these lies about how she's this really gross girl now to put Ben Stiller off." I can't for the life of me remember the name, but that doesn't look like it would help any, because they all look dumbstruck. "It was one of the words Matt used to describe her, and Dave thought it was funny because I had started to gain a little weight. I lost most of the weight, but the nickname stuck." I shrug.

"Jesus, what an asshole!" Tug shakes his head. They all share the same expression, which is a mix of disgust and concern.

"So it would seem." I shrug again and fall silent. I can feel their eyes on me, but I focus on the binder in my lap.

"Aren't you going to ask me?" Charge speaks, breaking the quiet, a wolfish grin tipping the side of his mouth, and his eyes darken.

"Oh, that one is *not* rocket science," I retort, and don't look up. I try to focus on the pages, even as I can feel his stare. After several minutes of not really taking anything in, I close the book and look up.

They all look to one another with deep, almost comical frowns.

"Sorry. You want me to read this now?" I slap my hand on the closed binder.

"Yes," they reply as one.

"You're kidding, right? It's a tome. It will take me weeks." I sniff out an incredulous laugh.

"How are you going to know what we like?" Toxic asks.

"Oh I don't know…I could ask?" I offer, but keep my teasing tone.

"If you read it, you wouldn't need to ask, you could just *do*." Charge's tone is more resolute, and it kind of gets my back up.

"Really? Because I think I would still need to ask." I open the binder and pick a section that catches my eye. "Hmm, okay then. Who is it that would like me to work my tongue nice and slow around their taint?" Pink and Tug cautiously raise their hands.

"Right, then. That would be my first question. What the hell is a taint?" I barely finish the question when Tug has once more dropped his trousers, his underpants, and is lifting his meaty cock high. His other hand is pointing.

"This bit here, sugar. This is the taint." He winks at me and shrugs at his friends when they groan. "What? She wanted to know." He stands and grabs his fallen trousers.

"I did. Thank you, Tug. Very helpful. Words are fine, too, by the way." I wrinkle my nose, but he laughs at my observation.

"But a visual is better?" He playfully wiggles his dark brows.

"Okay." I exhale slowly and run my hand through my hair, lifting it high for some cool air to hit my neck, and dropping it. "I get that you've all spent a lot of time compiling this, and I think it's great, because if anything, you have given some serious thought to what you want from me. But all I want is to get to know you in a normal way. This is not a *normal* situation by any stretch of the imagination. So this might be the only *normal* thing we do together." I've pled my case, and there's a rumble of mutterings as they sit back and confer.

"How would we do that?" Charge asks.

"Date. I mean we have a schedule, yes?"

"Yes, it's in the binder." Charge raises a brow, and I ignore his condescending tone. My idea is much better; he just doesn't know that, yet.

"Great! Then on the day each of you have me, we go on a date." I smile brightly but falter when they all still do not respond. I huff. "I can try and read the pertinent points in your section in the binder before the date, and then we can go from there?" My compromise is a hit.

"We could do that." Charge agrees with accompanying nods of approval, and I give an excited little clap. "But maybe we should talk about what you want sexually together."

"Um, yes, we can do that." *Did it suddenly get really hot in here?* I pull at the collar of my T-shirt and quickly take another sip of the now cool tea.

"You've only had one sexual partner, is that still correct?" Charge asks, his gaze fixed on me.

"Yes." I give a short nod.

"Anal?"

"Excuse me?" I'm glad I don't have tea in my mouth or they would all be wearing it.

"Do you enjoy anal?" he repeats without inflection.

"Who doesn't?" My flippant remark is taken as an answer, and I'm seized with utter panic. I rush to clarify. "Sorry, I was joking. Honestly, I don't know. I have only ever had like a thumb or finger in *there*, but I enjoyed it." He frowns and I feel a cold chill wash over my body. For the first time since I answered the advert, I think I'm wholly out of my depth. My hands shake, and I grip them together to hide the fact. "Look, I'm sorry if you were expecting someone more experienced. I'll understand if you want—"

"You're perfect, Finn." Charge stops me in my tracks with his words and sincerity. "And if we can't make anal pleasurable for you, then we shouldn't be doing it. Simple as that." He drags his bottom lip through his teeth and tilts his head, his tone filled with utter carnal confidence, and I squirm in my seat. He notices—they all notice. "So multiple partners at one time would also be negative?"

"No. Yes. Sorry." I shake my head because I'm still lost in those lips. "No, I haven't had multiple partners at one time, but I wouldn't be here if I had a problem with that, now, would I?"

"Very true." His lips carve a sweet, sexy smile which, for the first time, truly puts me at ease.

"I think what you need to understand is, as much as this is a fantasy for many women, I actually really like you guys, and I want to make this work. And I really liked the idea that you wanted a wife." My voice is quiet, but my tone is completely sincere.

"We do want a wife, but more than that, we want to make sure you are happy. We will do everything in our power to make you happy. We have no limits, no shame, and we will never say no to you. We are here to please you. No judgment and no lies." Charge pauses, and I crumble under the intensity of his gaze.

"I'm twenty-five. No, sorry, I'm really twenty-six, not twenty!" I blurt out. "I'm sorry I lied, but you have no idea how much I wanted this, and I thought with a bit of time at the gym I could—"

"We know." Pink calls out over my confession.

"You said no lies, so I needed to tell ... Wait! You know?" My hands cover my mouth but the truth is out there now.

"Yes. Tug works in intelligence, remember?" Toxic ruffles

Tug's non-existent hair.

"I do, but it wasn't the Enigma Code, you had it on your Facebook account." He winks at me, and I want to slap myself for being an idiot. Not sure for which bit in particular. Just general all-in-one total idiot.

"Oh."

"We're glad you told us the truth, because I meant what I said…no Lies, ever." Charge repeats, and his heavy emphasis on the last word is noted.

"I can live with that." I nod my agreement.

"So we alternate days and you get one day off after every four." Pink offers up my schedule with enthusiasm and an adorable sparkle in his eyes.

"What about my period?"

"What about your period?" Tug asks, but their faces are screwed up with my use of the P-word.

"Well, I know some people are okay handing out red wings, but trust me, I'm *not* one of them. I go from either dying in agony and wanting to be held all night, to hunting down the sharpest blade in the house and wanting to kill anyone who crosses my path." I snort, because it's a complete lottery which side will surface.

"Then whoever's time it is, will hold you all night," Charge states and shakes his head like I had set a task that was simply just too easy.

"And if I try to kill them?" I ask, because I'm only partly joking.

"You can try, darling, but we're all trained killers. I think the odds are against you doing any damage." Tug lets out a low belly laugh.

"Oh, I think she's capable of doing considerable damage." Charge's cryptic comment is too much for my jet lag and this biblically large, life-changing day.

"Do you not want me here, Charge? Because I thought this was *all* of your idea, and I get the feeling you're not very happy with the situation." I stand up and my hands fly to my hips, clenched into tiny fists. The three others all stand, but Charge remains seated for a moment—a long moment—before drawing himself to stand. His full height and frame are impressive, but the way he looks at me has me reeling with mixed feelings.

"Then you're entirely mistaken." He holds my gaze with such intensity I know he isn't lying. But there's something unsettling, and I know he feels it, too.

"If you say so." I break the contact and shake my head, muttering my words.

There's a silent standoff when everyone is looking at one another, heated glances and thinly veiled desire where propriety fights with raw need and lust. The tension is palpable and sexy as all hell.

"So who's first?" Tug asks the question I was definitely thinking, and all eyes point to me.

"I think Finn might like the first day to herself," Charge states but it hangs in the air like an unanswered question. I look at the expectant eyes of the other three, wide, easy smiles, and desire radiating off them in waves. I stand and tuck the binder under my arm.

"Might as well get this freak show on the road," I say with a teasing smile, moving my head to motion for them to follow, which three of them do. I reach the bottom of the wide-open staircase with Toxic, Tug, and Pink racing over themselves to join me.

"Are you not coming?" I ask with a level tone, but feel the hit of disappointment in my chest.

"Read my section." Charge's gravelly tone and deep timbre sends an electrical charge across my skin, I tingle with a million prickles and liquid heat mainlines straight to my core. I quickly flick to his tab in the binder. It isn't as thick as the others and the page with the heading sexual preferences is almost blank—almost. I look back over after digesting the words.

Sex: my way.

My whole body shivers, but I don't get time to take in what that might mean, just that those words have an effect on me. *He* affects me. Pink has scooped me into his arms and is climbing the stairs two at a time, Toxic and Tug hot on his heels.

No time to dwell. Baptism of fire coming up.

CHAPTER NINE

"Condoms?" Pink kicks the door to his room and walks in, but before I can respond, he drops me from a height onto the plush comforter and deep soft mattress of his bed. I fall back with a cry of surprise and instantly start to pitch up onto my elbows. He crawls up my body, not touching, but so very close, his mere presence pushes me flat. Heavy-lidded eyes drag slowly up my prone body until they rest on my lips. My tongue darts out to wet the dryness so I can speak, but his mouth is on mine before I do, his tongue diving in to give chase. Firm and deep, a light, twisting duel that tastes divine, with a sweet scent of apples and a heady helping of lust. His body is still hovering, and the connection feels all the more intense because it's just his mouth working mine.

I'm aware of the bed dipping with additional weight, and I catch my breath when Pink finally breaks the kiss. He sits up and pulls his T-shirt over his head. Either side of Pink, I can see that Tug and Toxic have done a little more than remove their

T-shirts. Their trousers are gone and really there's very little point keeping their underpants on, because the thin material hides absolutely *nothing*.

My chest feels tight, and I'm not sure if it's the beginning of a panic attack, or the fact that I'm faced with this glorious sight of toned muscle, carved and sculpted to perfection within touching distance. These men are regarding me with a hunger so raw it leaves me a trembling mess, balanced on a precipice of my ultimate fantasy and my darkest desires. I hope it's not a panic attack, because falling either side of that peak feels like a win-win to me.

"Condoms?" Pink repeats and jumps to his feet. He unhooks his belt and drops his jeans, tuck jumping high enough to snap them free of his legs. He balls them up and throws them into a basket in the corner. Swift, impressive, and precise movements, and although the bed has bounced and wobbled he maintained perfect balance before once again dropping to his knees, his thick thighs on either side of mine. I'm speechless, which seems to be a problem as they are each frowning and exchanging worried glances. Then I remember he actually asked me a question. I slap my forehead. I'm like a magpie and they are the shiny objects, very distracting.

"Sorry. Condom. What about condoms? I didn't bring any." It's my turn to frown with concern; I can't believe I forgot.

"No, darling, we have condoms. I'm just asking, do you want us to wear them? We all have clean and clear medical reports in the binder, but since you haven't read—"

"Oh I see." I blurt my interruption with a wide smile filled with relief. "Um, no that's okay. If it's in the binder, I'm sure you're all fine, and I'm on birth control. Oh, but I don't have my medical records with me. I didn't think. Sorry." I start to bite down on the inside of my cheek, and my arms creep across my tummy for protection. Tug pulls the hand nearest him before I can take hold of my waist. His fingers entwine with mine.

"You're clean, baby. Your medical records checked out just fine." Tug's words of comfort do the opposite.

"How did you…? Should I be worried about that level of intrusion?" I narrow my eyes, but I'm unsuccessful at retrieving my hand. With a wry smiles he pulls my fingers to his lips and kisses the tips.

"You can if you like; however, you can also be reassured, you're now under *our* protection," he adds, peppering each word with a soft kiss. When my expression remains unchanged he lets out a sigh. "For your peace of mind, this wasn't intrusion." He raises a brow and suppresses a grin. The comment takes moment to sink in.

"I posted that on Facebook, too, didn't I?" I grimace.

"You did."

"I don't normally air my dirty laundry, but I was a little upset with my ex." I let the wave of hurt wash over me, and it still stings enough to halt my train of thought and take me back to the eye of the shitstorm. That night caused so much turmoil and doubt, my trust was shattered, and I questioned *everything*. The best way to ease my mind was to get tested, something I'd never considered in the ten years we were together.

"His loss, baby. I might even buy the guy a drink." Toxic takes my other hand, bringing me back to the now. "After I beat the shit out of him for hurting you, but I am—no, we *all* are more than happy he fucked up."

"Me too." I bite my lips to temper the shit-eating grin, because happy isn't the only thing I'm feeling.

"So?" They chorus.

"So…no condoms." I giggle.

"Thank fuck for that." I don't know who said that because I'm covered with kisses, hands, and tongues, and manhandled and adored to distraction.

I had dreamt about this. I'm pretty confident I'm not the only woman who has, but my biggest worry when this scenario actually became more a *very* likely reality, was that I would feel used and be passed from pillar to post. *Yes, that's a euphemism.* I needn't have worried at all.

Pink pulls me up to a sitting position and then there are hands helping me out of my clothes, reverent, strong, and gentle. Caressing touches, light and sensual kisses on my cheek and my neck. My jeans are pulled loose. I look down to meet Pink's scorching gaze as he hooks his fingers into the edge of my panties. He draws the material down my legs, never taking his eyes from me. Heavy hands on my shoulders lay me back on the bed and my eyes roll to the heavens as the first set of lips kiss my skin, then the second, and oh God, Pink's mouth is right *there*. Hot breath and firm pressure as he spreads my legs wide and drags his tongue along my core, which must be dripping by the sounds he's making. Sexy groans and so much sucking, my toes start to curl and one hand flies to his hair, which is long enough to grip and pull.

My other hand is still being held by Tug, who has lain along one side of me, holding my arm high and pressed flat to the bed. His attention is focused on my neck, nipping and grazing with his teeth. He bites down and pleasure sizzles and shoots straight to my core like a high jolt of electricity through my veins. My back arches and I can't keep my body from moving and writhing from their ministrations. Toxic's mouth is tracing a path of feather-light kisses to my breasts. He circles my nipple with his tongue, teasing and tantalizing, the puffs of cool breath making me ache for more. More of his touch, more kissing—just *more*. I whimper when he pulls away and shuffles to change position with Pink.

They move as one: a slick, pleasure-giving machine. They seem to anticipate each other's moves, but their focus is me.

Only me. My body is thrumming, alive, and the one word that comes close to describing how I feel is worshipped.

Toxic's lips cover my core, his tongue flat and rough against my most sensitive flesh. His mouth works and moves, massaging my folds and sucking the tender skin. His tongue teases my clit, and I cry out when he slips a finger inside me.

"Oh God!" I gasp, and my thighs clamp tight around his head. He chuckles when I release my grip but looks up with a brow arched high in curiosity. "Sorry," I gasp, and my cheeks must be the deepest red, flushed with a mix of pent-up arousal and slight embarrassment.

"Please don't tell me we're the only ones to put our heads between your legs, because that would be a fucking crime." His lips tip with humor.

"Oh, no. My waxing lady gets right in there, but she's more about giving pain than pleasure." I let out a light breath as I try and calm my racing heart.

"Your ex didn't go down on you?" Pink chokes out a cough with his skepticism.

"High days and holidays, but he wasn't a fan." I shrug it off. "I can't come like this. It's not a big deal."

"Hmm…" Toxic's grin widens, and my eyes flick to Pink and Tug, then back to Toxic nestled between my legs. They are each sporting similar nefarious smiles.

"Did I say something amusing?" I ask Toxic.

"No, darling. But you did set us a challenge and, boy, do we love a challenge." His head drops and his tongue swipes a long, languid stroke from my entrance to my clit. I flop back onto the bed, and a groan of frustration leaves my mouth eclipsed by a deep sigh of carnal satisfaction. I didn't mean to make it a challenge—or did I? His fingers slide inside me and do this soft, pumping action that has my muscles clenching, and I get a deep tingle at the base of my spine. His tongue slides along my soaking flesh, and he starts to pick up the pace.

My heart pounds hard in my chest, but the noise is drowned out by my ragged breaths. I tense at the first wave and panic, trying to crawl away from the onslaught of pleasure, or curb it at least, as it hits me full force, but it's useless. Hands from all angles hold me in place, and all I can do is endure, bearing the mind-blowing sensations which start at the tip of my toes and rip through my body like a freight train. I soar for those endless, blissful seconds that feel like hours, where my breath freezes in my lungs, and my eyes see nothing but shooting stars and hazy light. Every nerve ending in my body crackles with life and energy.

When I land back on this planet from the most unbelievable high, my body starts to tremble. I've never...I mean, *that*...that intensity has never happened before and I'm a little stunned. Tug pulls me into his embrace, and Pink and Toxic crowd me with their warmth and...I don't know what...I know it's not love—I'm not that ridiculous—but they make me feel safe, cherished and really, really *liked*.

Tug eases me back and starts to crawl down my body, kissing along my tummy, multiple hands squeezing and stroking my skin. They seem to always be touching me.

"My turn, darling." His lips brush the landing strip of hair above my clit, and he grins. "I like this little piece of hair here. It's cute. You might even get to keep it." His finger strokes the line of hair and he wiggles his brow playfully, but before I can ask what he means, all breath leaves my lungs as his tongue dives deep inside me. His large hands cup around my bottom pulling me to his urgent, demanding mouth. My shoulders are lifted and Toxic slides behind me so he can wrap his strong arms around my waist, my back to his chest. Pink is now laying tender kisses along my side as I start to quiver and moan, feeling the build-up like a massive explosion waiting to annihilate me with one more skillful touch from one or all of these sexy as sin men. *My men.*

I barely regain consciousness from my second high when Tug positions himself to tease another climax from my sated and completely exhausted body. I'm confident it was as magnificent as the previous two; it's an assumption though, because I don't remember it. And I don't remember falling asleep, either.

My eyes spring open to a dark and unfamiliar room, a mass of limbs crisscrossing my body, and I get a flash high-definition recall of my *challenging* evening. I suck my bottom lip, which still feels puffy from all the kissing. My *foof* must have the worst case of trout-pout, given the amount of kissing, sucking, and unbelievably amazing, but unreciprocated attention, it received. I get a flash of guilt and berate myself. I'm not sure if there's a list of wifely duties in that binder of theirs, but slipping into a coma during oral sex probably isn't one of them.

CHAPTER TEN

I'M WIDE AWAKE. I CLOSE MY EYES AND TRY TO FORCE myself back to sleep, but it's useless. I'm not used to all the bodies, the total darkness, or ignoring my rumbling stomach. I can't get out of the bed without crawling over someone, and I don't want to add a broken night's sleep to my list of failings. I slink under the covers and slide all the way off the bed and quietly onto the floor. I fumble around in the darkness for any items of clothing and find one t-shirt; it's better than nothing. Slipping it over my head I squint around the room, cloaked in utter darkness, searching for that telltale thin strip of light indicating the door and my escape. It's faint, but I crawl in the direction of the glow and silently creep out of the room.

The stairs creak a bit as I land on them, and I hover at the first audible groan, my breath tight in my chest, my head tilting upward, toward the bedrooms. Waiting a few moments to hear any signs of movement and satisfied I haven't disturbed anyone's sleep but my own, I carry on and finally release my held breath when I reach the kitchen. I figure this is far enough away from the bedrooms, and I can try and find something to eat without waking the household. I open the massive, silver refrigerator door, squinting at the bright light from within. Well, I suppose at least it's full, but maybe, not a great day to be a chicken, I snicker to myself. Every shelf has some form of chicken: sliced, whole birds, drumsticks, and packs of uncooked breasts at the bottom. Spoilt with the lack of choice, I pull out one of the cooked drumsticks and step back from the door.

Letting the door swing shut under its own weight, I turn and drop the food and open my mouth to scream blue fucking murder. A hand presses hard against my mouth, and I'm stepped flush and firm against the now-closed refrigerator door. The tall, strong frame towers above me, and my hand is trapped between us, so I can feel his heart beating just as fast as mine. My wide eyes relax with recognition, though Charge just scared the shit out of me.

"If I take my hand away, are you going to scream?" He dips his head so his eyes meet mine. His face is searching, but I relax against his firm hold and nod.

"Why the hell did you do that?" I snap in a hushed whisper.

"Do what?" His voice is deep and loud enough that his whisper is simply mocking my attempt at stealth.

"Sneak up on me and slap your hand over my mouth like some mugger." I swallow the lump in my throat, because although his hand has moved from my mouth, it's now resting curled around my neck, his thumb stroking my collarbone.

"First, I don't sneak. I made plenty of noise, but you were too busy foraging to notice." His mouth twitches with amusement. "Second, I didn't slap. I placed my hand to stop you from screaming and waking the others, and third, you honestly think I would let a mugger anywhere near you?" He tilts his head slightly, and his piercing stare meets mine. His crystal blue eyes look almost black, like inky pools, and they bore right through me, rendering me a little lost for words.

"I…I…" My tummy tightens with the sincerity of his words, and the way he holds my gaze does crazy stupid things to my insides. I snap myself from his trance. "Sorry I was foraging because I'm hungry and—"

"This is your home, Finn." His tone is sharp, and I tense because, if anything, he sounds angry about the fact. He exhales slowly and the air from his lungs washes over my lips, and I can almost feel the burn of whiskey from the rich aroma in his warm breath—intoxicating. "You can eat the whole damn contents of the freezer, if that's what you want, if it makes you happy."

"It's full of chicken. I think you're safe from me eating it all." I wrinkle my nose.

"You don't like chicken?" His brows shoot up like I have offended his great ancestors.

"No one likes *that* much chicken. Well, except maybe Colonel Sanders," I reply with a straight face and a tight lip.

"You're funny." He frowns when he says this, but his face softens with a wide smile, and then he lets out a deep laugh. It's a nice sound and his fleeting expression of carefree pleasure suits him. *He should laugh more often.*

He still hasn't stepped back, and when the laughter dies, there's just us…looking at each other. I swallow the recurring dryness in my throat and ask the question I didn't really get the answer to earlier.

"Why didn't you want to come to bed with the others?" I tip my chin when he doesn't answer and keep my eyes fixed on his. He takes his time but gives me an answer, of sorts.

"You've read my page."

"Which doesn't really say much."

"It says enough."

"Okay. So, sex *your* way and your name is Charge. Are we talking full-on Dominant with whips and chains and shit?" His lips quirk and his left brow arches high at my question.

"You'll find out, little one. You'll find out soon enough." He leans down and traces his nose on the skin of my neck, and I tilt to give him better access. I have a full-body shiver from the slightest contact. He groans his approval but pulls back, and I sag at the sudden loss of heat, though it feels like so much more.

"But not with the others?" I push for clarification.

"I don't share." He states flatly, and I scoff.

"Isn't that an oxymoron given our little setup?"

"Not at all." His reply is deadpan and completely serious. "On my days, you will be mine and mine alone."

"Why?" We've talked and messaged each other for weeks, but this is completely new information and sounds like a restriction fraught with complications.

"I want to know I'm the one inciting the reactions I desire from you, and *just* me. That can't happen in a group situation. Call it a control thing." His tone borders on stern.

"Hmm, okay. What about on the other days? Does that mean you won't touch me on those days?" I'm surprised that I don't like that idea at all.

"Do you want me to touch you on those days?" His hand slips from my neck, and his index finger now traces the loose scoop neck of the oversized tank top, from my shoulder to the swell of my breast. My nipples are hard, angry peaks demanding attention, and his light touch is like a raw charge touching my sensitive skin.

"Yes, I would like that." I draw in a steadying breath as I can feel my knees weaken. I'm glad the fridge has my back, or I would be on the floor.

"Then I will." His teeth pull his bottom lip right in, and he lets it out tortuously slow. I'm so wet right now, I squeeze my legs together to find some kind of relief.

"And the others won't mind?" With enormous effort, I drag my mind back to his question. "I mean, surely they could have the same 'no touching' rule."

"They could, but they don't. It's all in the binder, Finn." He flashes me a knowing smile, and I puff out a breath of frustration.

"Gah! Okay! I'll read the damn binder, but I still want my dates." I place my hands on my hips with my demand. The tank dips perilously low, and I snatch the neckline back up, gripping the material close to my chest. He takes my fist and unclenches it, making the shirt swing low and loose. My pert nipples are like beacons to his hungry eyes.

"Oh I know you'll read the binder." His thumb traces the outline around one nipple, and my breath all but freezes in my throat on a sharp inhale. A deep rumble vibrates low from his chest. He continues to talk as if we both aren't off the charts horny and unaffected by what he's doing. *Okay I can play this game.* "And we are all looking forward to the dates. They're an excellent idea."

"Well, at least I have done something right." I shrug and let out a little laugh to try and ease the rocketing sexual tension.

"What do you think you have done wrong?"

"Oh…I…We didn't…Um, you know, we didn't actually…" Why can't I say the word? *For fuck's sake, I just had a gangbang with three unbelievably hot guys, and I can't say the word fuck in front of the other hot guy. Get a fucking grip, Finn.* "Earlier, I mean, we didn't fuck. I fell asleep after I came. In fairness, I came *a lot,* but I didn't , you know, return the favor." My cheeks feel like they are on fire, but I did it.

"You have trouble saying the word fuck?" His tone drops about two octaves with that last word, and I stifle a whimper.

"Not in the past. Seems to be another new experience for me," I joke.

"Nothing wrong with new experiences. Besides, I doubt they would've gone to fourth base without a date." His tone is teasing. "And I happen to know you did nothing wrong whatsoever." He says as matter-of-factly.

"Do you guys have a weird telepathy thing going on, or—oh, God, please don't say you have cameras." I slap my hand over my mouth in horror.

"Calm down. No cameras. We're close, which you'll see soon enough, but no telepathy. Pink came down for a drink and to get you some water."

"And he told you?" My hands are still supporting my jaw from hitting the floor with mortification.

"No, he didn't have to." His statement is expressed with an incredulous tone, like I don't really get how close these guys are. I don't, but it's very early days and as Hope always tells me, "Every day's a school day."

"Oh." I don't bother to question that connection, not tonight, not right now. I'm just a little confused with how he makes me feel and a *lot* tired.

"Would you like me to fix you something to eat?" He switches the subject and finally steps further away, out of my *very* personal space.

"Actually, I'm not so hungry anymore. I'll just sit down here for a while." I point over to the low sofas. Even though it's pitch black inside, the crescent moon is bright enough to cast a little light, sufficient to keep the nyctophobia at bay.

"Aren't you tired?"

"I am. I just"—I run my hand through my hair, I can feel the exhaustion in the follicles—"I'm shattered, but I can't seem to keep my eyes closed. I spent ten years sleeping with the same man. I think it's going to take a little time to get used to the multiple bodies." I sniff out a soft laugh. "And I'm still not great in an empty bed either. I used to sneak in with Hope when she didn't have company." I smile softly.

"Would you like me to sleep with you?" I turn to face him and see that there's nothing salacious in his eyes; if anything, he looks a little concerned.

"I bet you say that to all the girls," I tease.

"When I share a bed, I don't tend to use it for sleep, Finn," he retorts with a low rumble.

"Oh." I swallow the lump but hold his gaze, which heats my skin and melts my core with every passing second. His dark eyes hold me spellbound, the magnetic draw like a physical tie pulling me closer, and I'm powerless to stop it, even if I wanted to. This is my choice, and I don't want to stop whatever *it* is. He blinks and breaks the connection.

"But for you I will make an exception, if it'll make you happy." A wide warm smile splits his handsome face, and I stumble over and ignore any internal reservations and agree.

"It would, thank you." My tummy does this little flip that makes me light-headed when he flashes a heart-stopping, supernova-bright smile.

"The pleasure is all mine." He grabs my hand and strides off, making me physically stumble just to keep up.

CHAPTER ELEVEN

Charge

△

I HAVE THE WORST CASE OF BLUE BALLS. MAN, I WISHED I'D at least jacked off before I climbed into her bed. I wasn't thinking. I know *why* I wasn't thinking. From the moment she appeared from behind that mountain of suitcases at the airport, I knew we'd struck gold—*solid fucking gold*. We'd been looking long enough, but there was something about her answer to our advertisement that struck a cord. She was funny, for sure, but honest, too, and I'm not being naive. We don't do naive, given our collective backgrounds and training. We delve a little deeper than your average amateur stalker on social media. What we found was *her* truth. We spent the last three months, each of us peppering her with questions disguised as conversation, not trying to trip her up, just a full-scale reconnaissance in order to compile our own Finn binder. We never got to the binder stage with the others.

If she makes that sexy sleepy sigh one more time, I might have to break my blindfold rule and just pin her down and slide myself into what, I can only imagine, feels like fucking heaven. My arm holds her close, her head tilts up and one ear is pressed to my chest, her lashes are so long they rest on her cheek, and her plump, pink lips part just enough to let her soft breath escape. Her platinum-blonde hair is a mass of tangles and curls and falls over her shoulders to fan out on the pillow behind her. She looks like a fucking angel. Isn't that what Toxic said her name Seraphim meant? Angel or cherub or some shit like that? Well, that's *on fucking point*.

Ah, shit! She moves her leg so it's resting over my thighs, curled around me, and if it moves just a fraction further north she's going to feel exactly what has kept me awake all damn night.

"I don't miss you, but I miss this, so much." She sighs out clear as day, but her eyes don't open, and her breathing is unchanged.

"Miss what, angel?" I know I shouldn't have asked as soon as I let the question slip from my mouth. People can't lie when they sleep talk, they can't tell what's real depending on the dream, but they don't lie if you ask them a question. It can be a gross invasion of someone's innermost thoughts, but… *There's no but.* I know this, and I ask anyway.

"Feeling wanted." Her arm starts to loosen across my abdomen, but mine tightens around her back preventing her withdrawal. I know she's talking about that shithead ex of hers, but the fact she feels wanted in my arms, makes my chest swell, and I want to hold the feeling for as long as I can. The tension in her body resists my embrace at first then softens. Her hand fans out and her palm lays flat and soothing on the skin of my forearm.

Her head turns, and she kisses my T-shirt, and for the first time in forever, I wish I didn't have to cover myself. But I'll feel her lips on my skin soon enough—my way.

Her body curls against mine as she stretches and grumbles against the pull of the dawn. The room has a soft glow of pink light filtering through the pale drapes, and just when I think I should perhaps kiss those lips and rouse her gently, her leg sweeps up my body, hitting my erection and causing us both to cry out—me in pain and her in shock. Although the look on her face screams of terror rather than surprise.

I cup my cock as she scrambles to the other side of the bed, so far and so fast, she scoots right off the edge of it and lands with a thump then squeals from the hardwood floor. I stretch over to see her sprawled on her back, her tank top dropped low and exposing a sweet expanse of boob, and her pajama shorts so loose I can see right to her…*shit*. I'm staring at her pussy. Dammit, my balls couldn't ache any more if they were in a vise, and my cock is in absolute agony. I force my eyes to meet hers and away from that too tempting sight, while trying to adjust the hard-on from hell into something more manageable. I pull the comforter into a pile and drape it across my crotch. Thankfully, she can't see any of this from her position.

"My eyes are right here!" She snaps her fingers and points to her beautiful, aquamarine blue eyes.

"Oh, I know they are, angel." My voice is a low rumble I can feel deep in my chest, rough and raw like my burgeoning desire for her. "And they are almost as mesmerizing as your—"

"Finn! Are you okay?" Tug interrupts when he crashes through the door. His bedroom is next door, and he must have heard Finn fall. I take comfort that his response is quick, with Toxic close behind, and he's right down the other end of the corridor, his bedroom near mine. "Oh, Charge, is Finn okay?"

"I'm fine." She pops her head above the bed and gives a little wave, which is cute, if a little formal, given how intimate these guys have already been. "Forgot where I was, and had a little fright, that's all."

"Little? Sounded like a massive scare, what with the crash landing and all." Tug frowns, his arms crossed like he doesn't quite believe the simple explanation.

"Little, hmm? Tug, I think I'd have to agree with you. Finn definitely had a massive shock." I wink at Finn and bite back a throaty laugh as her cheeks burn bright red. She flashes a narrow glare my way, but her tongue peeks out to wet her lips, and my eyes lock on that little movement. *Yeah, massive is about right.* I stretch my hand to help her up but she shakes her head and hops to her feet without my assistance.

Pink wanders in, dragging his hand through his bed hair and yawning. There's a surreal moment when we all fall silent and just take in the scene: four half-naked men and one mostly naked, smoking-hot, super-cute woman. But more than that, and I see it in my *brothers'* eyes as I hope they see it in mine, this woman is going to be *our* wife, and that makes her exceptional.

"So what's the plan?" She claps her palms together, and the confidence breaks our trance-like state, but her clasped hands belie her composure. We glance to each other, and four pairs of hungry eyes fall on her. She must feel the weight of it like an anvil. "How about I go to the little girls' room and you guys decide what you want to do with me. I mean, what the plan is…Okay, maybe stop looking at me like you're gonna eat me." Her laugh is too high to be easy and is tinged with nervousness.

"We've already done that, but I'm up for round two." Tug's voice drops low, and his intention is as clear as his eyes are penetrating. *So much for easing her nerves.*

"Fuck, Tug!" Pink punches the top of his arm, but Tug doesn't flinch. If anything he looks confused.

"No. Look, I get it. It's fine." Finn steps up to them to stop any further horseplay. "I know why I'm here. Believe me I do." She takes a moment to draw in a steadying breath and meet each of our gazes before she continues, once she's sure we are all listening. "We've spent the last three months getting to know each other, but now I'm here, we have a relatively short time to make this very serious decision. And you guys are all hotter than hell, so it's easy to get distracted and just devour one another and never get out of bed for the whole month." I hold my breath, waiting for the *Hell yeahs* and *Sounds goods,* but they don't come, because this isn't a game, and we're all deadly serious about wanting this to work. So we listen and she goes on, "But, we're all going to need more than that if this is going to work."

She has certainly left me speechless, because that's exactly what I wanted to say. I know I'm not alone in wanting to explore her tight little body, but we have just over four weeks to really get her to know us, which is no time at all when it's got to be split four ways. Her bright smile dazzles as she spins and dashes to her bathroom, leaving us all grinning like idiots and more than a little dazed.

"Man, those pictures on Facebook don't do her justice." Toxic launches himself on the bed and Pink and Toxic come and take the remaining space.

"Or the ones I got for her binder, and that shit took some finding," Tug adds.

I jump in. "And that's the last time you're gonna mention it, dipshit. She doesn't need to know how detailed our recon was, okay? It might freak her out." I didn't think I would need to state the fucking obvious; however, by the look on his face, set deep with frown lines, perhaps I did.

"So we're gonna lie?" Toxic's dubious tone is echoed with an expression of disbelief from Pink and Tug.

"No, we're gonna make sure she won't care by the time we *do* tell her about her binder," I clarify, though that doesn't seem to have eased anyone's concerns.

"And what about the rest?" Pink asks

"The rest?"

"Yeah, man, what if she asks about your folks?" Pink's words hit hard, but I keep my face impassive, my mask fixed. But I'm happy for the information to be shared. No, happy isn't the right word. I'm more resigned.

"Then tell her," I state flatly.

"Really?" They all chorus together.

"She's going to be our wife. I don't have a problem her knowing us. Most of it is in the binder." I try to shrug off the magnitude of this declaration. The people who know what really happened are sitting on this bed, my chosen brothers. But even they don't know what *I* went through. The fact that I want to share some of it with Finn is huge. I know it, and I can see the importance of it on their faces.

"If she reads it." Tug arches a brow.

"Oh, she'll read it." My tone is laden with sensual warning.

"You gonna tell her *everything*?" Pink cuts in, and my burgeoning grin disappears.

"No!" I snap.

"You said so yourself, she's going to be our wife. Shouldn't she know about—"

"No!" I cut his conversation for the second time.

"Dammit, Charge, don't blow this for us. If she asks—" Pink's pleading tone is ineffective, and I bark my interruption with more aggression than I intended.

"You distract her." My jaw clamps tight, and I take a moment to rein in my temper. I draw in a deep breath and look at each of them. They clearly feel as hopeful as I do, or they wouldn't dream of applying this sort of pressure. "Look…I can't, okay? The best I can give you is maybe, one day."

"Then we'll take that." Pink slaps my back now that we are

all sitting on her bed. "Besides, I think we can distract her easily enough for the time being. Notice how she squeezes her legs when she checks us out?"

"And her mouth? She sucks on her bottom lip like I want her to suck my—"

"Oh, man, those lips." Toxic thankfully cuts Tug's crude musings off, or I might have to nutpunch him. This isn't some chick we're going to be comparing notes on; this is Finn.

"I know it's still early, Charge, but I got a real good feeling about this one." Toxic's grin is wide and hopeful.

"You said that about Chloe." Pink shoots him down, killing his smile like he did mine. He's on a roll this morning.

"Yeah, well, Chloe slipped under the radar, and she never got this far, so she doesn't count." Toxic bites back.

"She's special for sure, but taking us all on is a big deal, so let's make sure we get it right and not scare her off." I look over at the closed bathroom door, and when I turn back they are all looking at me with wry grins.

"Right," Tug says, elongating the word so it has a heavy dose of sarcasm in the mix. "If anyone's gonna scare her, Charge, it's you and your kinky shit."

"Fuck off, Tug. She knows about that and she's still here, so how about you keep your mouth shut about my private fucking business." I raise my curled fist to hit right between his legs, but he scoots back out of my reach.

"I was only fucking with ya', brother. Calm the fuck down." He chuckles nervously. "Look, we all know each other's boundaries, and you're pretty much the only one who has them. The not sharing, and we are all cool with that, so how about we move on and figure out a timetable. Charge, you've got this week off, but I'm not happy waiting a whole damn week before I can touch her again."

"Me, either." Pink and Toxic agree.

"Understandable. How about we alternate as we would normally, and when she's here permanently we can sort out how we share during leave periods. It's not like we have much annual leave, anyway. It's just that I was the one who could get this straightened out at the last minute."

"So who goes first?" Tug asks with obvious enthusiasm.

"Who goes first with what?" Finn walks out of the bathroom, towel drying her hair, and my stomach drops. Damn what I wouldn't give to share a shower with her, watching the droplets of water she failed to dry trickle down her neck, along her collarbone, down her thighs. All the way down her toned legs. She freezes in the doorway, transfixed, and I watch as her mouth struggles to deliver the necessary moisture to her throat. Her legs twitch, and I know she isn't struggling where it counts. She flashes a quick smile, and her cheeks are a beacon of instant color.

"On a date," I add quickly before she concludes we are in fact a bunch of animals. "We were deciding who gets to have the first date with you. You can choose if you'd like."

"No way am I making that choice. No, you guys sort that one out, and I'll just do as I'm told."

"Good to know," I state and watch her jaw drop and her eyes darken.

CHAPTER TWELVE

Finn

THE SHOWER I JUST TOOK WAS QUICK, BUT I THINK I need to go back in and switch the dial to ice blast. The way they all look at me could scorch my panties right off, and it hasn't gone unnoticed, judging by the heat in Charge's stare, that I'm not wearing any.

"What about flipping a coin?" I blurt and instantly cringe at my own suggestion. I don't want the selection to be the result of a coin toss. "No, wait. How about you each put your name on a piece of paper and I pick one out. That's fair."

"We could just go by rank." Charge grins wide, the others groan, and there's a good deal of eye rolling.

"Or you could suck my balls." Tug punches Charge just shy of his groin, and I suck in a breath for him. A small tussle ensues while I fetch some paper from my bag.

"Here write your names on these pieces of paper." I hand out the torn chunks and one pen to share.

"Why don't you write and just pick?" Pink takes the pen but holds it back for me.

"I don't want to influence the draw." I shake my head.

"And you writing our names might do that?" His face crinkles with confusion and amusement.

"It might. Don't argue, just do it," I sass, placing my hand on my hips for effect. I even drop a hip to emphasize my attitude.

"Oh, I like sassy, Finn." Pink grins.

"At least one of you does." I chance a glance at Charge, and, sure enough, his lips are curling in a wicked sexy, knowing smile. I can't wait to learn what that grin means. "Okay, put them in here." I hold out a small carved wooden bowl I took from the oak dresser which dominates the far wall. Once all the papers are in, I give it a little shake and hold it up high. I stretch my other hand out, but before I can grab a piece Tug coughs an interruption.

"I think you should give it another shake, darling." His face is the picture of innocence, wide eyes and cute smile.

"Really?"

"Just to be sure." He nods energetically.

"Okay." I start to shake when I catch a sly fist bump between Tug and Toxic. "Really? What are you, fourteen?"

"No offense meant, darling, but damn, when you shook that sweet ass of yours just then, I did feel like I was fourteen, and just as horny." He tips his head and lifts his shoulders but doesn't look remotely apologetic, and it dawns on me, why would I want him to apologize?

"You know what? It's a little strange for me to be looked at the way you all do, but I'm gonna take it with no offense, because I know this whole new shiny toy thing will wear off. I just hope I can get that look once in a while, when it does." I laugh lightly, though it changes quickly. I get a sick twist in my stomach, because I don't remember when I lost that look from Dave, but I haven't seen it in so long, this just knocks the air from my lungs.

I didn't see them move—I must have closed my eyes with the painful memory—but they are all instantly around me. Charge lifts my chin with his finger, and the tingle in my nose means I'm seconds away from big, fat tears clouding my vision. I blink and blink again.

"Hey…If someone stopped looking at you the way we are now, then he was a fucking idiot. Trust me when I say we know exactly what we have here and how fucking lucky we all are." His soft, deep voice and beautiful words penetrate every raw nerve and soothes me.

"Damn right." Tug agrees

"Absolutely, sugar." Toxic's smile is so big it distorts his handsome face.

Pink adds, "So fucking lucky, darling," with such heartfelt sincerity, I crumble, and they close in for the best group hug, ever.

"We couldn't be happier he fucked up. We also know you're still hurting over what he did. Just know he will regret it and come for you again," Pink warns, and I scoff with a sharp laugh and a runny nose.

"He didn't want me, Pink, and he won't come for me." I sniff and rub my face dry.

"Good, because you're ours now," Charge declares like it's a done deal, a fact that ignites a warm spark deep inside my chest; it's little, but it's there. "Now, pick a slip of paper, angel, and put one of us out of our misery."

"Pink." I unscrew the paper and squeal as Pink dips and thrusts his shoulder into my tummy, lifting me high and spinning me around and around. I grab his boxer shorts for stability but the material isn't nearly robust enough, stretching and coming away in my fists. His dark tan lines highlighting the white, firm globes of his arse. *Something utterly biteable about a firm butt.* He stops after a few spins and slides me down his body.

Charge holds the bowl out, and I take it, but I must look puzzled.

"You need to pick the rest, so we can fill in the timetable," he clarifies.

"Oh, right, of course." I pick the next piece. "Charge, then Toxic, and that would mean Tug, you get—"

"Don't even think about saying anything derogatory, or I just might not go gentle on you tomorrow." Charge's deeply commanding, gravelly tone goes straight to my lady parts.

"I was going to, but I won't now." I mutter and shrink from his sexy but intimidating glare.

"Shame." His eyes fix on mine for long, sensual seconds before he blinks and turns away. "Okay, I'll get breakfast on, and we'll leave you to get dressed."

"Do I have time to unpack?" I call out as they all head for the door.

"I don't know, do you? Breakfast will be in twenty minutes." Charge looks at his watch as if starting the countdown.

"Shit. Well, I will if you all bugger off and leave me alone." I start to push and maneuver the muscle mountains out of my door, which happens because they are cooperating. "Oh, what should I wear, Pink? What are we doing today?"

"Riding, darling. I'm going to show you the land, the only way it should be seen." He flashes a bright smile, all straight white teeth and dimples. His blond hair long enough to hang adorably over his deep blue eyes.

"Oh I didn't bring jodhpurs, and I don't have a riding hat." It's only a fluke I have jodhpurs at all; they were part of a fancy dress costume and I didn't think to pack them. There isn't much call for horse riding outfits working as a hairdresser in the city.

"Jeans will be fine. Although I would pay good money to see your sweet ass in some skintight jods." He gives a playful wink and drops his eyes to my bottom.

"And riding hat?"

"We don't wear riding hats, darling, but I will have something that will suit you just fine." He tips his head and starts to walk backwards down the corridor.

"Okay." I wave him off. He flashes the widest smile, and I return it tenfold. I'm more than a little excited. I have only ever ridden a donkey on the beach when I was tiny. I barely remember, but it must have been before my Gran became sick, and I was taken into foster care. Horses and hobbies were something other kids did. I close the door and I look at my stacked suitcases. Now, where did I pack my jeans? And more importantly where did I pack my sports bra?

I have a light tan, but I burn easily, so I wear a thin, long-sleeved, striped blue and white top with my skinny jeans. It's possible I'll be too hot, but better that than third-degree burns and sunstroke. I have no idea how long we're going to be out today, but after breakfast, Pink packs us some provisions, a couple of towels, and a blanket. He throws the bag in the back of a different pickup truck and opens the door for me to climb in. I wasn't waiting for him to; I was just standing there, staring, a little awestruck at the house now I have time to really take it in. The spot is stunning with rolling fields, woodland in the distance—isolated but homey. The sun is already bleaching the color from the ground and the nature that's trying to thrive under this heat.

"You ready?" Pink starts up the truck and the whole cab vibrates with the noise. I smile and nod, grabbing on to the door as the truck launches forward.

We pull up to the stable block a few minutes later. We could've walked. In this heat, though, I can understand why we didn't. Pink takes my hand as soon as I jump down from the cab and leads me over to a large steel and wooden barn.

"Let me introduce you to the other ladies in my life. They should all be tacked-up and ready, but don't get used to that." His tone is a light mock warning. "If you wanna ride, you have to do that shit yourself, and muck out the stalls too. It's just 'cause it's the first time, and this week is more like a vacation, if that makes sense."

"Oh, absolutely. I don't know how to tack-on, but I'm a fast learner." My wide smile is making my jaw ache; I'm *that* excited.

"Tack-up." He grins.

"Right…tack-up. Anyway, I don't have a lazy bone in my body, quite the opposite. You have to tie me down to keep me still." I snicker, and his mouth twists in a suppressed smile.

"Not my thing, darling, but Charge will be happy to help you there." His eyes meet mine, and I know my cheeks must be inferno red, though he doesn't say more, just throws me a knowing, wicked wink. He pulls a massive sliding barn door open enough for us to squeeze through and the scent of warm hay and horses hits me like a perfume counter at a department store. The aroma, however, is farmyard fresh and just as pungent. I wrinkle my nose in disgust.

"You get used to the smell. Well, you might not, but I don't smell it anymore." He chuckles.

"Really, you don't smell that?" The mix is heady: hay, shavings, sweat, feed, and definitely shit—not muck heap strong, but still…

"Yes, I can smell the horse crap, but it doesn't bother me." He laughs as I pull my top to cover my nose and try ineffectively to block the smell. "Come on, princess, let's introduce you to Lady."

There's a long line of stables with metal grills above wooden half walls, and each doorway has a horse head peeking out. The one Pink leads me to is gorgeous: a light cream color with a bright white long mane and fringe—forelock. I drag up some basic horse knowledge from God knows where.

"She's pretty." I reach up and stroke her soft, wide cheek. Her bridle is already on and so is her saddle, which looks like a sofa, it's so wide and padded.

"She sure is. She's a Quarter Horse, and this color is Palomino. She's having a year off but she's the main brood mare. We'll see her youngsters when we ride out." He pulls the door wide and leads Lady from her stable. "Here, hold her while I grab Tramp."

"Tramp?"

"Yeah, he's my stallion." Pink beams with obvious pride.

"Stallion. Is he all right to ride out with a lady horse? I mean isn't he going to want to…um…" My pause is enough for Pink to chuckle his interruption.

"No, darling, he's more than safe to ride out with…I mean he might want to, but he can control himself." He winks at me, and I feel my cheeks heat once more, this time with the double meaning. "Here, put these on, and this hat should fit." He hands me some soft, suede legs that dangle from a thick belt and a cowboy hat.

"What are these?" I put the hat on my head so I can hold up the legs for closer inspection.

"They're chinks. They'll protect your jeans and stop you from getting sore against the stirrups."

"Oh cool." I give myself an internal high five, since I managed to drop the ever embarrassing 'beans' from my expression of understanding and pleasure.

Pink introduces me to Jake, the farm hand in charge of tacking-up, and Jake's grandson, Mason, who comes to help out on weekends and holidays. They are both polite and friendly enough, but I get an odd feeling, and I wonder how much, if anything, everyone will know about our situation. Before I can dwell too much, Pink hoists me into the saddle and secures some saddlebags across the withers, and rolled one of the blankets behind the seat.

We set off at a leisurely pace, keeping to the shade of the trees that line the edge of the fields. After about ten minutes we have crested the brow of a long incline, the house and stable block are now nowhere to be seen on the horizon.

"Do they know?" I ask after a long breath.

"Does who know what?" Pink has these deep dimples when he smiles and deep furrows in his forehead when he frowns, like now.

"Do Jake and Mason know about me?"

"Sure they do." His face softens and his beaming smile makes my chest warm and tighten at the same time.

"Oh." I flash the best smile I can, and his frown deepens.

"Is that a problem? Because we sure as shit ain't keeping you a secret, so you better get used to it." His tone is light but serious, too.

"I guess…I just—"

"Look, darling, people who we care about know. They've known us a long time, so they're happy for us. No judgment whatsoever, and people who don't know us, well, yeah, they'll judge, I'm sure. But the thing is, they don't matter. Their opinion doesn't matter. The only thing that matters is you being happy. Now, if you're going to have a bit of trouble managing with this, you need to let us know. We can help, but you need to be okay with this. I mean *really* okay with this, because then you *really* won't give a flying fuck what anyone else thinks." His words sink in, and shame hits me.

"No, you're right. And I *am* happy." My eyes search his as he holds my gaze. I barely blink because I mean what I say; I just hope I'm getting that across. "It's different, is all."

"I'll say. The same guy for ten years and no one before you met him. Hell, you're practically a virgin." He grins.

"Bit of a turnaround for me, that's for sure, but…" I hesitate, not sure how to phrase the question I've been skirting around since I answered the advertisement.

"Spit it out, darling. You know you can ask us anything." he cajoles.

"Why? Why one wife? I mean I've chatted online with each of you and you're *all* great. And smoking hot, seriously. I just don't understand why one wife and why me?" I rush my garbled thoughts in one breath.

"Shit. That really was a mother lode of a question." He sucks in a sharp breath but chuckles too. "You know Charge is better at explaining this, but since you asked me, I'll try." He turns in his saddle and drops his reins. I tense, thinking Tramp will now bolt given the chance, but his head just droops lower, and he plods along, his gait unchanged. I don't risk doing the same. "We met in juvie what feels like a life time ago. We had all lost our parents at some point, although I never knew mine and Tug still has a granddaddy. The rest? Well, we had no one. It was just us four. We enlisted when we got to the right age, except Charge. His guardian wouldn't let him. He's got this fucking massive trust fund, and it was expected for him to go into banking or some shit. He fought that and got to go to the Officer Cadet School, then flight school. But it meant we were mostly together. Same career, same leave and shit. You see, when you go through shit at a vulnerable age you make some seriously strong bonds. You don't want to break them, like *ever*, and you figure a way to stay together. Sounds really gay, don't it?" He chuckles, and I raise an ironic brow because looking at his high-cut cheekbones, strong jaw and crystal eyes, he's beautiful, but not in the least bit gay. I'm a hairdresser, so my gaydar is off-the-charts accurate.

"I think it's kind of beautiful, but that doesn't make it gay. It's nice when you have someone like you guys have each other. Family isn't always what you hope it would be, so the fact that you've made your own, I understand why you'd want to protect that. But, it wouldn't stop each of you from getting married." I point out.

"Actually, that's exactly what started to happen. When any one of us started to date, there was always friction between the girls. It just didn't work in the long run. We've tried this situation with slightly more success over the last two years. One came close and she didn't really want the whole package. She thought we were kidding."

"Who was that?"

"Chloe, but she never moved in. We tried a few weekends. It was pretty obvious she wanted just one of us."

"Which one?"

"I don't think it mattered. She was playing us off against each other, but we don't keep secrets. She messed with Charge pretty bad, and he doesn't trust people at the best of times, so don't freak out if he asks a shit ton of questions but is also a little closed off." He shrugs this off, like it's just Charge's way. "He's a good guy, Finn. The best, actually. Anyway, that's why it has to be one wife for all of us. Unfortunately, you can't legally marry all four, so you'll have to pick just one." He drops his head to one side and pulls a soppy, sad face with his curved down lips and exaggerated pout.

"If you still want me after a month." I point out with a cautionary tone.

"We all want you." Pink states emphatically, and I get a warm burst in my chest again.

"Is that why you chose me, because I'm an orphan too?" As

soon as he spoke about it, I made the connection.

"It probably struck a cord, having a similar background, but no, we chose you because you were honest." He levels his steely blues at me, intense and serious. "See, there are two ways you can go with an online relationship. One, you can lie and soft filter the shit out of your life, just showcasing the good stuff, or you can be balls-out honest."

"And I was definitely balls-out honest." I groan, because he's right. I didn't see the point in hiding who I am, what I want, or pretend to be someone I'm not. I did that for ten years and it got me a big, fat rejection with a side helping of gut crushing humiliation. If this was to work, I had to be honest with myself and with them, warts and all. *Hashtag no filter.*

"I could've been lying?" I tease.

"Ah, darling. You could've, but you didn't, and now you're here and we're not letting you go." He beams his bright, dazzling-white smile and lets out a deep and happy laugh that's all kinds of infectious. "So, want to blow the cobwebs away?"

"Hmm?" I query.

"Wanna lope?"

"Lope?" This is code, and I feel I should know it, but I know my face must be registering a big fat blank.

"A fast ride?"

"Oh, yeah! Sounds, um, great." I clench my jaw and force a tight, tense smile.

"All right, then. Hang on tight, and tuck in behind me. Lady likes to race but once she gets in front, she'll turn tail and head straight for home."

"Oh, okay. Maybe not that fast then?" I'm hesitant, but Pink just chuckles.

"Nah. Where's the fun if you're not screaming my name." He kicks Tramp who seems to squat back on his haunches only to launch himself forward like a rocket. I notice his speed as he disappears ahead and then feel the whiplash as Lady does the same. My hands clamp round the lump at the front of the saddle, and I hold on for dear life. I would scream his name and a slew of other profanities, if my jaw wasn't locked in terror.

CHAPTER THIRTEEN

Pink

I HEAR HER SCREAM AND CAN'T HELP LAUGHING OUT LOUD. Lady is the safest ride I have, but she's fast. I turn around and watch her face quickly change from absolutely petrified to euphoric. I know that expression, because I saw it just before she came all over my tongue. Now, I'm not saying she's about to come, but she's at the very least enjoying herself. Lady lengthens her stride and pulls up alongside me, the thunder of hooves on the firm ground mean I have to shout to be heard.

"Having fun?" I call out, and she chances a quick glance my way before snapping her head back to keep her eyes wide open and looking straight ahead.

"It's…it's unbelievable!" She cries out, and her smile rivals the midday sun for glare and shine. I know Charge will probably pull out the money card to try and gain an edge on his date, but we all have our little tricks, and I doubt Finn is the kind of girl to be dazzled by a flashy night out. *We'd be disappointed if she was.*

"Ease her back gently, Finn. You don't want her taking the lead." Finn's eyes widen as Lady stretches her neck, two more strides and she would be doing just that, and then it would be like the Kentucky Derby in a race back home. I want her date with me to be memorable but not nightmare inducing. She pulls gently on the reins, and Lady slows down to a more comfortable lope. We ride for an hour or so, changing gait and chatting. She's easy company, asking questions that are all detailed in the binder, though she's right, this is much more fun, and I can flip whatever question back on her. She's cute and funny, and the way her tits are squeezing out the top of her tiny sports bra, since she took her long sleeved top off, has made my ride so fucking uncomfortable I can't wait to get to the lake.

We have been winding our way through the forest for about twenty minutes when the trees start to thin, and although its heavily shaded, the sun breaks through the canopy like a spotlight that strikes the water and casts a million shards of refracted light back into the cove. The lake is small and surrounded by high rocks and trees; it's very private and quite perfect. I jump from my horse and go help Finn down, but she's already on her feet with an enormous, awestruck grin on her face.

"Pink, this—God, it's so beautiful here. Look at that water. I don't think I've ever seen that color before. Can we take a dip?" Her voice is breathless with excitement, and a warm feeling spreads in my chest that she's so animated about a place I love.

"Thought you might like some lunch first. You should probably drink some water at least. You've been in the sun a lot today already. The others will fucking kill me if I bring you back all fried to a crisp."

"I'm fine. I covered myself in factor 50, but I'm hungry." She nudges me playfully over my concern.

"Great. I'll tie the horses up, and you go lay a blanket out on the sand."

"Cool. Do you want me to take the bags too?"

"Nope, I've got them." I lead Tramp and Lady over to the lake to let them have a drink first, then tie them up in the shade. Joining Finn on the blanket, I unpack the bread and cheese, some chicken pie Charge made, and a small container of sliced fruit. I chuck her a bottle of water, which she catches with one hand, snapping it right out of the air. "Nice catch."

"Thank you. I have some talents you guys probably don't know about," she teases. Her breathy voice and loaded statement make my cock swell.

"I doubt it." I scoff and watch her brows knits together.

"It's a little unnerving that you've been investigating me. I know you had to, but it's a little creepy all the same." Her sexy playfulness evaporates, and I'm eager to get it back, but she looks genuinely concerned.

"We did some, but honestly, most of what we know, you've put out there on one platform or another. Believe me, the sections we've compiled on each of us is way more detailed than yours," I joke.

"You have a file on me?" Her voice is pitched high and anxious. *Shit.*

"Sort of…yes." I mumble. *Dammit.*

"Really?" She tries to soften her voice, but I can see worry etched in the tight features on her face.

"Yes, but like I said, it's mostly what you've put out on social media. A little background checking but that's it."

"So I could see it?"

"Sure." I wave it off like it's no big deal. *Fuck.*

"Then that's all right. As long as I can, I really won't want to.

It's bad enough Charge is gonna make me read all of yours. I'd die of boredom if I had to do the same with my pathetic life."

"It's not pathetic." I correct with a stern tone.

"It's hardly life-changing or lifesaving like you guys." She sniffs out a dismissive laugh.

"You change those homeless people's lives when you go out and give them free haircuts on the street."

"You know about that?" She gasps. I nod and hold her gaze, searching her face for any sign of uncertainty or disquiet. "I didn't tell anyone about that, Pink. How did you know?"

"Why didn't you tell anyone?"

"Answer the question." Her tone is sharp, and her arms are now crossed across her tummy. *Shit, shit, shit.* I draw in a deep breath.

"Just before we invited you to stay, we had a friend tail you for a few days." Her eyes widen like saucers, and I rush to try and limit the damage. "It was a trusted friend. We wouldn't hire a stranger. We had some gaps in our recon and this filled in the blanks. So why didn't you tell anyone?" Her eyes scrunch as she absorbs what I have said, taking her time before she replies. I'm so relieved when she does.

"It was something I wanted to do. I lived on the streets for a while and small acts of kindness in a world that pretends you don't exist, if you're lucky, or is downright disgusting, if you're not, well, they make a difference. But, the minute you tell people, it becomes something else. I don't do it for a pat on the back or to make myself feel better. I do it because I can."

"I can understand that." Reaching over, I'm glad when she lets me pull her hand from around her waist and hold it in mine.

"Don't think I'm completely okay with the investigation, by the way. That's still fucking creepy to think I had someone following me." She narrows her eyes but her tone has lost its fire.

"I know, but if you weren't the one, you'd never have known."

I pull her closer, and she nestles into my chest, her arms wrapping around my waist. I kiss her hair, which smells like sunshine.

"Still doesn't make it right," she grumbles.

"Swim?" I ask.

"Are you changing the subject because you have no defense?" she quips.

"Yep. Swim?" She snickers into my shirt, melting into my hold.

"Sure." She shakes her head in defeat, and I breathe a huge internal sigh of relief. Charge would have my balls on the grill if she'd freaked out, or worse packed right up and gone home. "I didn't pack my bikini. Is it okay to swim in my underwear?"

"Absolutely not." I grin and pull my shirt over my head. Jumping to my feet, I take no time at all dropping my jeans, kicking my boots off, and screwing all the clothes in a ball then throwing them into the undergrowth beside the blanket. Finn's jaw drops comically, her eyes flit between my solid erection, the wide smile on my lips, and my carnal gaze.

"Oh." She manages to choke out on a cough. I turn and stride into the cool lake; three long steps and I push off the soft sand bed and dive in headfirst. When I surface, I flick the wet hair from my eyes and tread water, watching and waiting. She's kneeling on the blanket and even from this distance I can see her worrying the inside of her cheek.

"Come on, darling. The water feels great!" I call out and splash my arms swimming backwards.

"It looks great, but what if someone comes?" She calls back, even looking nervously over her shoulder.

"Finn, we rode for nearly two hours to get here. Unless Charge gets his helicopter out, no one is going to see us. I promise."

"Charge owns a helicopter?"

"He's a pilot, and yeah, he does. Now, get your butt in here, or

I'll drag you in fully clothed." I'm only half joking.

"Okay! Fine." She stands up and unbuckles her chinks and wiggles free of her jeans. Her boy shorts are low and the white of both her bra and panties will be completely see-through if she isn't brave enough to strip down completely. She hesitates for a moment as if thinking the same thing before she shakes her head and sucks in a deep breath so loud I can hear it from halfway across the lake. Her clothes are in a pile next to mine and she's taking her bra and panties off lightning fast, throwing them onto the ground, and dashing into the water with a squeal and a splash. She disappears under the surface and emerges a few feet from me, all glistening, pink-cheeked, and breathless. I close the distance and pull her to my body, her legs wrap around my waist, and all the blood in my body surges to my cock when her heat presses against my abdomen.

"Hmm… You were right, the water feels great." Her breath kisses my lips, hot and sweet like honeysuckle. She feels so damn good.

"Oh, darling, that's not the only thing that feels great." I swim us closer to the shore so I can get my footing. I'm going to need leverage. My erection is swaying just below her ass, and I know every time it brushes her soft skin I feel it like a shot of pure electricity to my balls. Her arms grip around my neck and her hands slide up into my hair, where they make tight little fists and pull. Her eyes lock on mine, her lips a millimeter from my mouth and already wet from the lake. Her breath catches, and I chase that breath with my eager lips.

Her grip tightens, her legs and her arms lock us together, and her lips are soft, full, and taste so fucking sweet. My tongue dips inside and tangles with hers until we are both breathless and grinding on each other like feral animals. She moans into my mouth when my hands drop to cup her ass. My fingertips sinking into the soft, firm flesh. Her hips roll against me, and her mouth is just as eager and desperate. I break the kiss.

"Finn, if you're not ready, we have to stop right now."

"I'm ready," she gasps.

"Really? Because there's no rush, darling. I'm happy to make you come with my mouth or fingers. We don't have to fuck." My voice is level but strained.

"We really do." She whimpers and pushes her body a little further down on mine, so my cock is nudging at her entrance.

"You completely sure? Because I'm hanging on by a thread here, darling." I hold back the moan that's rumbling deep in my chest.

"I'm sure…I'm so sure…Please! Please, fuck me." She pants her plea, and it's too much.

I surge up and slide deep inside her with one strategically placed thrust. Her head drops to my chest and her sharp little breaths make me stop for a moment.

"You okay, darling?" One hand cups her cheek, stroking her silky skin and sweeping her hair from her face.

"Yes! Yes, just, um, give me a second." She lets out a slow breath, and I can feel her tight muscles around my cock flutter up and down, making room and acclimating to the intrusion. She lifts her head, flushed cheeks and sexy-as-all-hell smile. "Okay. Sorry, it's not been that long, but you're…well, you're really big." She sighs, a shy smile curling her lips.

There's not a guy in the world who doesn't want to hear that, but she's in for a wake-up call when she gets with the others if she thinks I'm big. Her hips give a tentative roll, and I clench my jaw because that feels like fucking heaven—tight and hot, slick and so fucking smooth. I grab her hips and move her along my shaft, at my speed and my depth. She throws her head back and cries out. The sound almost makes me blow, but she's nowhere near ready. With her head tipped back, I cover one of her breasts and work her nipple with my tongue until it's hard like a pebble, while she's furiously grinding against me with the help of my hands. I switch breasts and work the other nipple before my lips work their way up to her neck, kissing and sucking. I'm careful not to mark her, even if I want to suck down so hard the mark I leave would be more like a tattoo than a love bite, but I don't. It would be a dick move when she belongs to *all* of us.

Her hands pull at my hair, and she tugs me close so our lips crash together. Her tight little body is pumping hard, up and down, and then again, a little grind every once in a while when she's feeling brave and relaxed enough to take my full length, but she bites back a squeal every time she does. She draws my tongue into her mouth and sucks slowly then releases it. Her eyes are dark pools of lust, and her lids are so low she looks dazed.

I shift her legs so they are both on my shoulders, she dips low but the water supports us both and she doesn't go under; she just goes deeper—I go deeper. Her whole body tenses, and her muscles around my cock clamp down tight and start to ripple. She gasps, eyes wide, and a silent scream escapes her open mouth. Her whole body starts to convulse, and it takes all my balance to keep us both upright; it's enough. She starts a reaction that my cock is too eager to follow. I feel the pinch and ache deep in my balls, the tingle in my spine, and my hips start to piston, relentless and fierce. Water swishes and splashes around us like a whirlpool until we both cling together at our mutual peak, cresting that euphoric high as wave after wave crashes through our bodies. We cling together, breathless and limp, and for me at least, barely standing.

CHAPTER FOURTEEN

Finn

HOLY FUCKING SHIT! MY LEGS TREMBLE SO MUCH, He allows me to shift them from his shoulder so their grip is now around his waist and it starts to loosen, but his strong hold prevents me from slipping further into the water and drowning. I suck in large gulps of air since it was stolen from me by that most amazing climax. It takes long minutes before I can pull my head up from his chest, which, I'm pleased to notice, is heaving just as deeply as mine. Or maybe that's because of the extra weight. I hate that the self-destructive doubt is always lurking because of Dave. I never used to feel this way about my body. I try to wriggle from his hold all the same.

"Hey, darling, where do you think you're going?" His deep chuckle resonates, and there's an echo from the acoustics in the cove.

"Your arms must be aching. You can put me down now." I try and ease myself from his grip and off his still hard cock.

"Do you regret what we just did?" His quick and first response crushes me, and I hate the look of sadness that settles on his face.

"Oh, God, no. No! Not at all. " I rush to quell his ridiculous and wholly erroneous conclusion. "It was amazing! God, how could you even think that? I haven't *ever* come that hard." I chew the inside if my cheeks as I start to feel them burn at my confession.

"You're trying to get away from me, darling. What else am I supposed to think? I should've waited. I'm sorry. I just—" Cupping his face, I bring it close to mine.

"I'm so sorry, Pink. You did nothing wrong. You did what I wanted…what I *desperately* needed, and you were incredible. It's just…I'm heavy, and I thought you would be—"

"You're shitting me, right?" he interrupts, his astonished tone mirroring his expression. I choke out a laugh with no humor. His handsome face is the picture of utter confusion.

"Um…I'm not as thin as I used to be," I mumble apologetically.

"Christ, woman. How thin were you? I don't know what shit is going on in your head, but I can guess who put it there… that asshole." He spits out the words with venom but his eyes soften when he continues. "You're perfect, drop-dead-gorgeous, end of conversation. You fucking weigh nothing at all, darling. Hell, I carry more weight than this"—he squeezes my arse playfully with both hands while still buried deep inside me, and I have to close my eyes at the toe-curling sensation—"when we run with weighted balls."

"If you say so." I let out a sigh mixed with a moan.

"You don't sound convinced."

"Let's just say, it's easier to believe the passive-aggressive, bad stuff when it's drip-fed for years. It tends to take hold." I twist my lips flat.

"Then it's our job to break that hold." His hand sweeps from my arse to my brow and around to hold the back of my neck. We are nose to nose. His breath flutters across the dampness of my skin, sending a million tingles to flash over my body in waves. His blue eyes are deep, crystal-clear wells holding my gaze with such intensity, I struggle to breathe. "Finn, you're so damn beautiful, we couldn't believe our luck when you walked through the doors at the airport. You're *it* for us."

"I don't know what to say," I whisper, and the warm glow I feel inside swells with his tender words. His adoring smile twists into something playful and a little wicked.

"You don't have to say anything, darling. Unless you want to say, 'Fuck me again, Pink'. You can definitely say that." He tilts his hips and loosens his hold, so I drop further down on his rock-hard cock.

"Ah"—I moan, and my eyes roll right back to the heavens—"yes, do that. That would be perfect." I sigh.

"Just. Like. You." He times each word with a delicious, deep thrust and roll of his hips that instantly has me climbing. My fingertips grip the hard muscles of his shoulders and our lips crash together with an animal urgency, and each time he pounds into me he pushes me farther, higher, until I'm floating in an erotic euphoria that consumes my mind and body. I have never come so quickly, or so hard. *Dave who?*

We lay together, air-drying our sated, naked bodies on the blanket in the shade, though we must have both fallen asleep for some time, because I wake up and feel the telltale, sun-stroked tightness on my skin. The late afternoon sun has now dropped low enough that our protective canopy has been pushed back and we are now bathed in glorious sunlight. It might not be the power of the midday rays, but I know I'm still burnt. *Shit.* Pink stirs as I crawl over to the edge of the blanket where there's still a little shade. My skin tingles as I move and reach to grab my underwear from the undergrowth.

"Wow, we really slept, didn't we?" He stretches, and all those taut muscles on his abdomen ripple. I let out an appreciative sigh.

"We did, and I think I might've caught a bit of sun." I scoop my boobs into the sports bra and shimmy into my panties.

"Oh, darling, I'm sorry. Are you okay?" His voice is thick with concern, but I wave it off.

"I'm sure I'll be fine."

"Here, drink some more water, and I'll start packing up." He hands me the last bottle, and I sip while he quickly slips his jeans, boots, and shirt on. He stuffs the remaining picnic in the saddlebag and rolls up the blanket. All the time, I'm staring, mesmerized by the beauty of this place and him. He flashes me a wolfish grin, having caught me blatantly ogling him.

"You gonna get dressed, darling, or are you planning on riding back like that?" He wiggles his brows mischievously. "Not that I'd mind, but you'd get some epic chafing to go with your sunburn if you did." He chuckles, and I shake myself from my stupor.

"Oh, yes, sorry. " I scramble to my feet and pick my way across the bushes to retrieve my clothes. I must've thrown them with my pitching arm because they are deep in the bushes.

"I'll fetch the horses." He walks off to untie Lady and Tramp. I reach for my jeans, but as I lift them, something big, black, and wiggly brushes my arm, and I scream bloody fucking murder. I drop my jeans, and my heart is in my throat, beating so hard, my panic consumes me. *What the fuck was that?* I stumble back, catching my footing on the undergrowth. I fall back, leaves and branches scratching my skin in my flailing attempt to distance myself from whatever the hell that was. The next second I'm lifted in the air, and I hear the thunder of hooves disappearing into the distance.

"Fuck, Finn! Are you all right?" I can hear the fright in his voice.

"S-s-snake." My whole body is tingling with nerves and raw panic. I try to suck in some air, but my chest won't move. Pink carries me over to a rock and sits me down carefully, his hands brushing and sweeping across my skin. The look of worry in his eyes is not doing anything for my rising anxiety.

"Did you get bitten, Finn?" he asks, still moving over my body, checking for any signs of a bite mark or any other injury.

"I…I don't know." I press the pain in my chest. I think my heart is going to explode.

"Think, darling. Did you feel a bite? What did it look like?" He tries to keep his voice level and calm, but I can tell from the look in his eyes he's anything but.

"Black and um…" I try and think. Everything is a blur and I still can't breathe properly.

"Red? Yellow? Black and white? Please, Finn, talk to me, darling."

"White…it had white rings. It was huge, Pink." He lets out a deep breath and his face relaxes.

"Okay. It was probably a kingsnake and, yeah, they can get pretty big, but they ain't poisonous." He is still inspecting my skin, but his expression is much less fear-stricken. "You scared the shit out of me, darling."

"Sorry," I whisper, feeling a wave of relief, which washes over me but seems to make my body shake uncontrollably. Pink scoops me into his arms and holds me, peppering my hair with soothing kisses and stroking my skin lightly.

"It's the adrenalin, darling. You'll be fine in a little while. You want me to go and get your clothes?"

"In a minute, you know, when I've stopped shaking." I let out a strangled laugh.

"Sure thing, darling." He continues to hold me, and once my heart stops trying to break free of my chest, I let him retrieve my clothes.

"The horses?" I look around, and it sinks in that my scream must have scared them away.

"Ah, yeah. Lady will probably be halfway home by now, but Tramp will be waiting on us at the edge of the woods." He holds out his hand, which I am happy to take.

"Oh, God, I'm sorry, Pink." We start to walk in the direction of the newly trampled ground.

"Don't be silly, darling. I'm relieved you didn't get bitten, or it wouldn't just be you who would need to be buried." He chuckles, and I freeze at his comment.

"What? You're telling me there are snakes that could kill me out here?" I shiver.

"This ain't the UK," he mocks.

"No kidding! The worst you'll get in London is a nasty wasp sting." My eyes are wide as we make our way through the forest, but Pink laughs and pulls me into his side, dropping his heavy arm over my shoulder.

"You normally have to go looking for them, darling. They don't tend to look for us. You got lucky." He's joking, but I'm not quite ready to laugh about it. It might not have been a poisonous snake, nevertheless, still nearly died of a fucking heart attack.

We reach the end of the wooded path and, sure enough, Tramp is standing there. Pink climbs on first and offers me a hand to haul me up and onto his lap.

"It's gonna take a bit longer to get back. We have to walk since it's the two of us, but at least you'll get to see the sun set over the farm." He clicks his tongue, and Tramp starts trotting forward.

"Oh, well, there are worse things than riding into the sunset with a gorgeous cowboy." I smile up at him as he looks down.

"Just remember to tell the others that. I have a feeling they're going to chew my ass out once they see your scratches and you tell them about the snake."

"How about I don't tell them about the snake, but do let them know that I've had the best day ever." He beams at my words.

"I want you to always tell the truth." He holds my gaze, the golden sunlight makes his blond hair look almost white, and his blue eyes are so clear I could dive into them.

"I do, always." I pause for a moment, his gaze drifting over my head, and I whisper loud enough so he can hear. "Thank you, by the way. I have had the very best day." I snuggle into his hold, feeling very, very tired.

"Hey, darling, you might want to be awake for this." Pink's soft words rouse me from my slumber, and my lids flutter open just in time. The horizon is a blaze of orange flame, a sizzling, brilliant light that's slowly melting into the darkness as it sinks below the earth. I can almost hear the hiss as it scorches the ground. With not a soul around, surrounded by miles upon miles of open land, the raw and natural beauty of the moment is utterly breathtaking. Pink pulls Tramp to a halt, and we watch in reverent silence as the last of the light loses its battle with the night sky. Surprisingly, it's not that dark when the sun completely disappears. The sky seems to quickly light up with too many stars to fathom and there's a strong beam of light which seems to bathe us in an unnatural glow. I think the sun got to me, and I'm hallucinating. The beam of light gets stronger and there's a loud roar of an engine. *I don't feel so good.*

I hear voices and force my eyes open.

"You okay? Jake came and got me when Lady came back without her rider." Tug calls out from the jeep. He kills the engine and I can see that the others are all in the car.

"Yeah, we're fine. Had a little fright with a kingsnake, and Lady took off," Pink explains.

"You sure it was a King?" Charge asks.

"Pretty sure. She didn't get bitten, but she's scratched up a bit from when she fell."

"And she can answer for herself. I'm fine guys. I caught a little too much sun, that's all." I interrupt, and my tone has the required amount of attitude to silence everyone.

"You wanna come back with us?" Tug asks.

"Do you mind, Pink? I feel a bit queasy." I look up to see him already nodding.

"Sure, darling. Are you going to be okay?'

"Yeah, I need to sleep it off and drink a gallon of water." I wave off his concern with a light laugh.

"Okay, darling. I'll check on you when I get back." He helps me off the side of Tramp and I fall straight into Charge's arms. He doesn't let me touch the ground, and carries me into the jeep and holds me on his lap.

"You need to be more careful, Pink!" Charge admonishes with a deadly serious tone, and I stiffen.

"He didn't do anything wrong. I had the most amazing day, Charge. Really." I try to argue, and Charge flashes me a tight smile.

"I'm glad you had fun, angel, but that doesn't negate the fact you got hurt, and that's unacceptable." His tone brooks no rebuttal, though I can't help myself. I had a great day, and I'd hate for Pink to think he did anything wrong.

"I think you're being a bit harsh." I mutter.

"No, he's not, darling. He's right, but I'll make it up to you on our next date." Pink answers, and I shake my head with frustration. Wincing as I feel the first stab of pain behind my eyes, I know one killer headache is coming up.

"There's nothing to make up for." I sigh and pinch the building pressure in the bridge of my nose.

"I'll see you back home." Pink tips his hat and nudges Tramp into a trot, quickly disappearing into the darkness.

"Okay, but really, you don't have to wrap me in cotton wool. I can take care of myself," I call after him.

"But you're ours now, so you don't have to." Charge expresses a sentiment they all seem to share with the synchronized nodding from Tug and Toxic.

"Yeah but…" I pout.

"Nuh-uh." Charge puts his finger across my lips, silencing me. I purse my lips against the light pressure and frown. "It's my date time now, and that means what?" he asks.

"We do things your way," I grumble, but my lips twitch with pleasure at his response.

"Good girl."

CHAPTER FIFTEEN

Charge

△

S HE PRETTY MUCH PASSED OUT AS SOON AS I LAID HER down in bed when we got back last night. She wouldn't eat anything, but did down a tall glass of water. We all took turns checking on her throughout the night, but today is my date, so I decide to let her sleep in and bring her some breakfast before we get started. *She's going to need her energy.*

Since it's a first date, I knock on her door, and there's no answer. I wait a minute, knock again, and open it in lieu of a third unanswered knock. The bed is empty, and her bathroom door is closed. I place the tray of coffee and pancakes on the bedside table and sit on the bed. After ten minutes of no audible noise, I walk over and tap lightly on the door too.

"Go away!" Finn's voice is soft and muffled.

"Date day, Finn. I've made you breakfast," I reply, ignoring her request.

"I'm not going on a date." She sniffs, sounding like she's crying. My guts clenches, and I fight the hurt that swells deep inside. She doesn't want to spend time with me. I know Pink won't have told her about my past; however, maybe she knows. I swallow the pain, because, dammit, I deserve a chance.

"You don't want to go on a date with me. May I ask why?" I keep my voice as level as I can, but it sounds clipped and gruff.

"No! Not you. I don't want to go on a date, full stop. I can't." She sobs, and I can hear she's clearly upset, but I smile in utter relief.

"Okay, angel. You wanna, tell me what's going on?" I coax, my tone more soft and encouraging, now that I know I'm not the problem.

"I…I'm…I don't want you to see me like this," she mumbles, and I have my ear pressed to the door in an effort to hear her.

"Like what, Finn?" I push the handle down and press my weight against the door, and it snaps back and clicks locked as soon as it closes. *Dammit.*

"Charge, can you maybe…um…Can we postpone our date?" Her tone is pitched high, and there's an underlying panic which worries me. "I'm sick and want to hide under a rock. Trust me, you'll thank me for this."

"I doubt it, angel, and no, I'm not postponing. If you're sick then I need to take care of you. Now open the door." My tone is stony and uncompromising.

"No! Please, can't we take a rain check? That's a thing, right? Rain check?"

"Sure, it's a thing, but at the risk of repeating myself, which I *really* don't like to do, no." My voice is clipped. "Now open the door, or I'll break it down."

"Can you at least close your eyes?" she pleads.

"Finn!" I warn with a deep and deadly serious tone.

"Fine, but don't say I didn't warn you." She swings the door wide, and I have to bite my lips to stop from laughing. The mortification in her big, blue eyes makes me think she isn't in the mood to join me in a chuckle.

"Oh, angel, come here." I hold out my arms and she shakes her head. Her smooth skin is dotted with dozens of bright red blotches. Every inch of skin is sprinkled with angry-looking, raw spots from her toes to a huge one on the end of her nose. "So in addition to the snake incident, you didn't happen to roll around in poison oak by any chance?" I clamp my mouth tight as soon as I speak, because I want to snicker, but her sorry-looking pout and soulful eyes are adorable.

"I fell over, but I didn't roll around. I look hideous, Charge, and it itches like crazy."

"It really isn't *that* bad. Whatever you do, though, don't scratch, angel. It will make them worse." Her bottom lips trembles, and big fat tears burst from the saddest eyes I've ever seen. "Come on, angel. I promise you don't look so bad." Not the right thing to say, apparently as she falls forward in a wail of sobs. I wrap my arms around her back and knees, then scoop her up and carry her back to bed. She snuffles and sniffs back the tears, and after a little while, she tips her head up as I look down.

"Better?"

"Not remotely. I feel wretched. How can you even look at me? I'm a hideous freak!" She cries, and I stiffen.

"You think a few marks on your skin bothers me? Because it doesn't," I state.

"Well, it bothers me."

My stomach drops at her words, my jaw clenches, and I draw in a deep breath to steady myself and fix my mask.

"Understandable, but it doesn't last long." I keep my voice

level and push my gut-wrenching feelings aside; this isn't a deal-breaker. I don't expect anyone to be okay with my scars. I'm certainly not fucking okay with them, so I won't hold that against her. It's not like she will ever see them, anyway.

"How long?" Her wobbly voice interrupts my nightmare reality.

"A few days, sometimes longer. The key is not to touch them." I narrow my eyes in warning.

"You know that's going to be impossible." Her hand twitches, and she reaches out to her leg. I take her hand and thread my fingers through hers. She needs distracting and so do I.

"How are you feeling other than the itching? Any sickness, diarrhea?"

"Oh, God, kill me now." She slinks down the bed, pulling her hand from mine to cover her face. "We're really having this conversation?" she mumbles into her palms.

"Finn, I'm serious. I can't take care of you if I don't know what I'm dealing with." I pull her hands away, and I see that her cheeks are bright red, and her eyes are screwed shut.

"I'm fine, other than the itching." I can hear the mortification in her voice.

"Okay, good." I slip off the bed and stand. "Right, drink this water and see what you can eat of the breakfast I made. I'm going to get some lotion that will help and some cuffs."

"Cuffs?" Her brows shoot up, and her mouth drops; it's comical and this time I do laugh.

"Date day, remember?" I continue to chuckle when she snaps her jaw shut.

"You can't possibly want to *do* anything sexual with me looking like this?" She waves her hand up and down her still-hot-as-hell body.

"Angel, your beauty is soul-fucking deep. So, yeah, as long as you're not *feeling* sick, I most certainly can."

"Won't the friction from fucking be like scratching?" Her brows knit together, creating a deep crease at the bridge of her nose. Everything she seems to do I find ball-achingly cute.

"Who said anything about fucking?" My lips creep to form one perfectly nefarious grin.

"Oh…Sorry. I thought with the cuffs…" She blushes, and her eyes drop to my crotch, which deepens the hue of her cheeks before she snaps her eyes back to meet mine.

"They are to stop you from scratching," I clarify, watching her throat contract in a slow swallow.

"So no fucking?"

"Now I didn't say that, either, did I?" I keep my face impassive, which is a challenge when she throws her head back heavily onto the pillow and lets out a huff of air.

"Gah! You're frustrating," she groans.

"You have no idea what frustrating is…*yet.*" Her eyes meet mine and darken just before I close the door and turn to leave her bedroom.

"How is she this morning?" Pink asks, as I rummage in the medicine cupboard for some calamine lotion. I place it on the counter and level a glare at him he rightly flinches from.

"She got sunburned, hmm?" He nurses his espresso and shifts uncomfortably on the kitchen stool.

"No. She got poison oak," I state flatly, and watch his brows lift with surprise. "She locked herself in the bathroom and wouldn't come out. I had to threaten to break down the fucking door before she would come out."

"Shit. I didn't notice any vines, but I'm not allergic, so it probably didn't even register. Sorry, man. Bummer it's your date day and all." He pulls an apologetic half-smile.

"I thought she didn't want to spend any time with me when

she said she didn't want to date. It stung, but not as much as her reaction to a few damn spots on her skin. She freaked out, Pink!" I can't hide the hurt in my voice, and he stands and walks around the island counter and faces me. He looks concerned and deadly serious.

"She won't have meant it like that, man. Not the way you're taking it...not at all. The ex did a number on her self-esteem. Trust me, the same thing happened yesterday when she thought she was too heavy for me to hold."

"Hmm." I huff dismissively. I hear what he's saying, but I can never share his certainty. This is different. I walk past and grab a couple of water bottles from the fridge.

"How she could look in the mirror and see anything other than fucking perfection is beyond me." Pink pats my shoulder in an attempt to divert my downward-spiraling thoughts. His question makes my mind flash with her image, and I have to agree.

"Preaching to the fucking choir, brother." I nudge him out of the way.

"So whatcha gonna do today?" He slides back onto his stool.

"Talk." I reply and hold his stare.

"Talk?" His intonation is urging for more detail.

"Talk," I repeat, and he tips his head in understanding, knowing he'll get nothing more from me. "She might want to postpone the dates with Tug and Toxic until the spots have gone. So if you see them before I do, you might want to warn them."

"She didn't get to postpone with you?" he counters. I raise a brow at his question, as if he took a stupid pill for breakfast.

"She didn't get the choice," I clarify flatly, making him grin.

"I'll tell them. If you need help sharing the care, yell." He offers without any salacious undertones. I take the lotion and add it to the water already in my arm.

"I got this."

"Yeah, I know man, but I kinda feel responsible."

"You are responsible."

"Thanks for making me feel better."

"It's not my job to make you feel better, Pinkerton. It's my job to make Finn feel better, and this is going to help with that." I shake the bottle of lotion and lightly punch him on the arm as I pass. I'm not mad at him, but I'm not all that happy either.

Finn's eyes widen when I enter and throw the cuffs and a spreader bar on the bed. It's not how I had intended to introduce her to *my way,* but they will work. She's surreptitiously smoothing her palm across the bumps to ease the itch, but even that's a bad idea.

"Um, so this is 'your way'?" She snorts out a laugh.

"No, angel. This is to stop you scratching. My way is…well, you'll find out soon enough." I draw my bottom lip in slowly and enjoy the way her eyes fix on my mouth, and she absently mirrors my movement.

"Wow, you keep your cards tight to your chest, don't you?" She shakes herself to regain her focus, and I fight not to chuckle at the obvious effort.

"How so?" I step slowly around the edge of the bed.

"You don't like to give much away." She's chewing on the inside of her cheek, because the indent is a dead giveaway, I don't know if it's due to nervousness or the rash, which must be driving her crazy.

"I will answer any questions you have, Finn. I don't intend on keeping anything from you, which isn't to say you get all the gory details right away. After all, we don't want you running for the hills, do we? Not now that we've found you." Her smile is tentative at my compliment, but her brow is still crinkled.

"There are gory details?"

"There are *always* gory details." My tone is far from light, but she looks unfazed by my assertion.

"I don't mind, and I won't go running for the hills. If you all are serious about wanting me, all I ask for is honesty. The wife thing is important to me, but..." She hesitates and looks reluctant to continue.

"But?" I encourage her openness; it's one of the things we all fell for; she's been frank, honest, and open, right from her very first email.

"I think choosing is going to be an issue." She purses her lips with the troubling thought, but they're so soft looking, the perfect shade of pink, and begging to be kissed. I blink to regain my focus.

"We don't want you to rush your decision. Take as much time as you need."

"I worry that the dates might not be such a great idea. I think maybe I'm not getting to see the real you. Everyone puts on their game face for a date."

"You think you aren't seeing the real us?" My grin widens at her astute observation.

"We all put our best foot forward when we want to make a good impression."

"True, but the real you always shines through to those observant enough to look." Her eyes never leave mine, searching for my truth with such intensity I fight to hold her gaze. Regardless of my secrets, the heat between us crackles like a live wire, and the sexual tension is palpable. She breaks first, her smile sweet, and her cheeks pink right up. She lets out a steadying breath, but when her hand reaches to scratch her arm, I catch it in mine and clip the cuff around her wrist.

These have a soft leather layer inside so they won't chafe or be abrasive at all if she pulls against them, *which she will*. Her breath catches and her pupils dilate; it's going to take all my self-control not to fuck her, because she's right, my body grinding against hers is as bad as her eager little fingers when it comes to scratching. I pull her hand up to the center bar of her wrought-iron bed frame and hold my free one out for her other. She complies instantly, and my cock twitches, swelling uncomfortably in my jeans.

I crawl down the bed and secure her ankles to the spreader bar, before sitting back on my haunches and surveying the sight before me. I tap my finger on my lip and hum my concern.

"Problem?" she asks, already trying to bend her legs at the knees in a fruitless attempt to bring her wide-open thighs closer together.

"I should've taken off your clothes before I cuffed you." I internally berate myself for the rookie mistake, which I blame on her being all kinds of distracting.

"Then I'd be naked!" she squeals and the sound goes straight to my already aching balls.

"That would be the idea. You're going to want the lotion all over your body, trust me. Clothes are going to be a hindrance."

"Hmm…really, if that's a line, I'm not buying," she scoffs.

"I don't use lines." I jump off the bed and turn to leave the room.

"You're going?" she shouts, utter terror in her voice, draining the color from her face.

"I'll be back." I calmly state, trying to keep my expression impassive given how adorable her stunned expression is.

"But what if…" she pauses.

"No one will come in, Finn. This is my day, and I don't share." I finish for her, ending the conversation.

"Don't be long," she says, her tone tinged with an edge of hysteria. I raise a brow and hover by the door. "Please," she adds with a nervous smile.

I disappear without responding. I can imagine how hard her

little heart is pumping, or how very wet she is by the ever-darkening, damp patch on the silky material between her legs.

I return a short while later and smile when her whole body relaxes. I dump my gym bag on the floor next to the bed.

"You're going to the gym?"

"Not that kind of gym bag, angel. This is my tool bag." I hold her gaze and wait to see if she's following me.

"Tools as in…um."

"I can't fuck you today, but if you're very good and beg me nicely, I might keep you distracted some other way." It must be eighty degrees in this room but the hairs on her arms stand to attention as her skin prickles with goosebumps. Her breath catches and her hips grind into the bed as best they can, given her new restrains. Her whole body shivers and quickly tenses when she sees the flash of the blades in my hands.

"You're going to cut my clothes off? Isn't that a little extreme? I kinda like this outfit." She rushes out her objection, which I brush off.

"I'll buy you a new one."

"It's skintight, Charge, you'll cut me!" she yelps.

"Only if you don't hold still." I slowly crawl onto the bed, my eyes never leaving hers. Her tongue peeks out and drags across her lips. Her cheeks are a deep shade of pink, and her pupils are so dark that the crystal blue part of her eyes looks black. *Perfect.* I wouldn't dream of doing this, if she wasn't responding like she is. She's covered head to toe in an itchy-as-hell rash, which she needs distracting from. She's also excited, intrigued, and really turned on. I can smell her aroma, a thick sweet scent that's completely intoxicating. I straddle her, taking care not to rub my thighs against her and place the blade against her skin, avoiding any of the red marks. I pull the material of her shorts away from her body and start to slice. The material falls to the side, and I do the same with her top. Her breath is deep and slow as she tries to control her racing heart.

I swallow the thick, dry lump clogging my throat. She's spread wide and naked, so aroused she's dripping onto the sheet, and I can't fuck her. I'm not sure who is in more pain at this precise moment. Her, with a mild case of poison oak, or me, with a major case of blue balls.

CHAPTER SIXTEEN

Finn

WHAT IS WRONG WITH ME? I SHOULDN'T BE GETTING turned on like this, because I'm sick. Well, I don't feel ill, but I look horrible, which doesn't seem to bother him, not in the slightest. Jeez, Dave wouldn't come near me if I had a slightest sniffle. The way Charge's bright blue eyes darken and his lids droop makes me melt. It's shocking the effect he has on me, with his glare, his presence, and, oh, God, his touch. I can feel wetness pooling like a well, and with my legs spread like this, I'm a hundred percent sure he can see it, too.

"Better." His raspy voice does strange things to my insides.

"For whom?" I arch a brow. He's not looking at my face. His heated stare is fixed and unwavering between my legs. I squirm with wanton need, and groan when I get the unbearable urge to scratch.

"Problem?" His lips are curved in a wicked smile, but the expression on his face quickly drops to worry when his eyes meet mine.

"Itchy," I whimper.

"Allow me." He picks up the lotion bottle and a wad of cotton wool. Very carefully he tips the bottle and soaks the material with the pale pink liquid, then I'm in heaven. I mewl at the first ice cool and delicate touch. The itching vanishes, and all I feel is bliss. Charge looks up with a wry smile.

"It doesn't last too long, angel, unfortunately, but I can apply more anytime you want." He continues to dab soothing spots all over my skin until I'm more lotion than not.

"Oh God, that feels good." My sigh makes him chuckle. I close my eyes and sink into a dream-like state, enjoying the respite from the relentless irritation. I have spots everywhere, and he's very, *very* thorough, flipping me over to cover my back and easing my legs up so he can get to those hard to reach areas at the very top of my thighs. I think I should feel embarrassed—my cheeks certainly burn—but I feel cherished. His fingertips brush my folds, and all the air leaves my body in a rush, cool lotion and hot breath against my core. My thighs start to tremble with the stretch and extreme angle of the hold. The building need within me seems to start at my toes and blazes a path through every fiber, nerve ending, and tiny cell; it's making it hard to think about anything else, other than wanting his touch and *more*. I bite my lip to stop me from begging. *What would he think of me wanting sex, when I look like an extra in a horror movie?*

"There. You look pretty in pink." He screws the lid on the bottle and drags his eyes slowly up the length of my body.

"I look gross, but thank you for saying that and for the magic lotion. I don't even feel the itching. I think I'd be safe out of the cuffs." I jangle my arms.

"The lotion doesn't last, and you'll find yourself scratching without even realizing it. If you scratch, it makes them worse and prolongs the recovery time." He lies beside me, blowing puffs of cool air across my skin.

"Are you saying that because you like me all tied up and helpless?" I raise a cheeky brow.

"Oh, angel, I don't need an excuse to keep you tied up." He flashes a devilish wink, and I shiver. "So what do you feel up to doing today?"

"I don't want to leave the bedroom," I blurt out. "I'd rather the fewer people who see me like this the better."

"I have postponed the cookout over the weekend because I thought as much, but Finn, the others won't care. They'll want to come and see you, take their turn in caring for you—in sickness and in health, I do believe." His fingertip traces a pattern on my skin, but not playing Join the Dots.

"But we're not married." I point out the flaw in his statement, which he's quick to dismiss with a wave of his hand.

"A formality, angel. So, do you want me to bring in a TV so we can put a movie on or—"

"We could chat?" I offer as a much more interesting alternative.

"Sure, we could chat. Let me go wash my hands. I'll fix you something cold to drink." He leans back over the bed and plant a kiss on my forehead. "I'll be right back."

"Don't leave! What if—"

"Finn, it's my day, angel. It's just you and me." He stands at the door and fixes me with his sexy-as-all-hell stare, stealing the breath from my lungs and all sense from my brain. He's dressed in a white T-shirt, which fails to hide the strong curve of his toned torso, the material tight against his flexed bicep. Charge has tattoos on both arms I haven't been close enough to look at, to see what the exact designs are, but one peeks out from the edge of the sleeve. His loose, worn jeans hang from his trim waist, and his large frame blocks the whole damn doorway. Short, dark hair that looks almost black makes my fingers twitch to run through the spikes, because I know they will feel soft to the touch. His eyes seem to change color with the light, and right now, they are deep blue with a flash of emerald green and they pierce right through me. His smile dazzles, all wide with bright, perfect, pearly-white teeth, and his face looks stunning when it lights up with joy. He looks so happy—truly happy—with me. I get a warm feeling in my belly, which radiates and feels good in all my other parts, straight through to my soul.

It feels like he's gone for days, when I know it's only minutes, but I've never been left like this, tied up and naked and so un-believably turned-on. The one time I mentioned adding some spice to Dave, he shut me down. The pain of his rebuttal was surpassed only by the monumental humiliation that followed on his birthday. At the time, I thought it might be fun, and the way every nerve in my body is now on high alert, I know I was right. Even more so because it's Charge.

He walks back into the room looking like an irresistible mix of delicious devil and drop-dead-gorgeous god. I see raw desire when his eyes meet mine, making his jaw clench; the little mus-cle below his high-cut cheekbone ticks like crazy. My eyes dip to the sizeable bulge in his jeans, and I comfort myself with the thought that I'm not the only one who's off-the-charts horny.

He pushes the door wide while holding a tray of drinks in one hand and a different bag in the other, and he chuckles at my audible gulp. *Jeez, how many toys does he have?*

"Relax, angel. I brought some books, a checkerboard, and a pack of cards." I let out a relieved breath and join his laughter.

"I was a little worried. I mean, how much kinky shit would you need to fill two bags?" I joke.

"Hmm…" His enigmatic smile is utterly devious, and a chill

dances across my skin in waves, making my hairs prickle up-right. He doesn't elaborate and it takes me only a moment to understand why.

"You have more than would fit into two bags, don't you?" His lips twist with a knowing grin before he answers.

"Yes, but I think it's cute that you think I would have just one bag."

"Why do you need so much…stuff?" I can't fathom why he would.

"It's not a question of *need*. It's a question of want." He states this matter-of-factly and then elaborates. "I like sex, Finn, and this is just a part of me. I don't see the point of hiding it or being coy about my kink, not when we have a short time frame to really get to know one another."

"Oh, I'm not complaining. Just curious." I try to shrug, but my cuffed hands and outstretched arms make it a little awkward.

"That's very good to know. I can work with curiosity." He drops the bag and prowls around the bed, his piercing eyes not leaving mine for a second. I get a liquid instant spark in my core, and it spreads like a burning flash flood through my body. "Would you like me to put some more lotion on you?" His voice is so deep and throaty, it makes my toes curl.

"Do you mind? I'm a little tied up." I jangle the cuffs with my cheeky comeback.

"For your own good," he admonishes lightly.

"Hmm…the jury's out on that one, Mister," I retort, and he grins but doesn't argue my point. He unbuckles his belt and slips his jeans down his strong, thick thighs, and if I wasn't hot before, I'm a molten mess now. His black, fitted boxer shorts are like a second skin, and his huge cock is outlined in such detail, I swear I can see the thick ridge running its entire and impressive length. My tongue darts out with excited anticipation, and I wonder what perfection must taste like. He cups himself, blocking my view, and stalks up the bed, a deep furrow set in his brow, but his face is inscrutable.

"What are you thinking?" My mouth works without the filter, because I'm not sure I want know the answer, but my brain is otherwise occupied.

"I'm thinking if you lick your lips one more time, angel, then poison oak or not, I won't be responsible for my actions," he growls.

"Oh." I fail to hold back the whimper.

"I'm trying to be good here, Finn, but damn…"

"I don't want you to be good." I'm panting, and if I could put my hands together, I would be pleading. I hope my tone is enough to tip the balance. I'm not above begging. "I'm kind of in agony here. I need…" I blow out some of the heat from my body in a puff of air mixed with my embarrassment at sounding so wanton.

"Tell me what you need." His voice drops an octave and feels like tantalizingly smooth velvet across my skin.

"I…I…" My face burns as the words stall on the tip of my tongue, but I shake my head. I can't ask for what I desperately want. What if he says no? I'll be mortified—humiliated. "Some lotion, please. I'm burning up." I chicken out and hold my breath, waiting for the recoil. His face softens, and there's not a hint of anger. If anything, he looks a little disappointed.

"Of course." He picks up the bottle and starts to meticulously cover every inch of my body. He flips me to do my back first. I drift off at his tender touch and the feel of the blissfully cool liquid on my skin, but I wake when he turns me onto my back. Once he's finished, I'm again on edge from the intimacy of his ministrations.

"I'm sorry." I whisper my apology.

"What for?" His brows pinch together, and his expression turns stern.

"For not…I…" I draw in a breath for courage. If I can't speak now, this is all going to be pointless, and I so want this to work for all of us. "I…I'm not great at asking for what I want."

"I gathered as much. But why?" His tone is coaxing.

"Oh, you know, the usual." I start to nibble at the inside of my cheek, his gaze intense and searching.

"I'm sorry, I don't know. What's usual? I don't see what is to be gained from not asking for something you want. Something your body clearly craves. Or am I mistaken, Finn?" He arches a brow, his expression anything but uncertain.

"God, no. Definitely craving…I guess it's a mix of embarrassment and fear." I try and explain feelings I have never had to articulate before. *No one's ever cared enough to ask.*

"Fear? I won't hurt you, Finn. I want to make you happy. This is only ever about pleasure for me—for both of us." His hand rests between my breasts over my heart, which beats a strong, staccato rhythm at his touch.

"Not that type of fear, Charge. More fear of rejection, I guess. You know, of being embarrassed and laughed at." I close my eyes at the rush of mortification as my flashback hits me right where his hand lies.

"Fuck, Finn. I can't even get my head around that statement." He sits upright, a heavy cloud darkens his features, and his jaw is clamped shut. He breathes in heavily through nostrils which flare then relax when he slowly releases the air. He seems to need to gather himself before he speaks. "You have nothing to *ever* feel embarrassed about, not with me or the others. I want you to feel absolutely free to ask of me for *anything* you desire, *anything* you think might give you pleasure. There are no limits, Finn, to pleasure, and for anyone to ever make you feel anything other than like a goddess, well, they are a fucking fool." The tingle in my nose is instant as is the trickle of tears from the corners of my eyes. "Angel, don't cry. Talk to me, Finn. Please." His hand moves from my chest to cupping my cheek, catching the tears with the pad of his thumb.

"I...I have never felt the way you guys make me feel, and I want to let go, I really do. I wouldn't be here if I didn't, but it's easier said than done when..." My voice breaks, and a fresh rush of tears falls unchecked. *Dammit.*

"When someone's made you feel worthless for years." Charge draws his own conclusion on the scraps of information I have given him, and sadly, it really isn't too far from the truth.

"Not years, but certainly the last year. I don't want to mess this up, but it's hard, you know?" I offer a genuine smile even if it sticks on my teeth with the residual sadness I can't seem to shake.

"I understand, but it isn't possible to mess up, Finn. I promise." He holds my gaze, and his eyes tell so much. I don't know what exactly, but I like it. "Do you trust me?"

"Yes," I say without hesitation.

"Good girl." He leans over the bed and pulls some objects from his bag. He's careful to lay them beside me in full view: a blindfold, a glass dildo, a small silver gem plug, and a flogger. Dave may have rebuked my attempt to introduce some spice, but I still did the research all the same.

CHAPTER SEVENTEEN

Charge

△

HER BREATH DOES THIS LITTLE HITCH, AND HER tummy muscles clench as she checks each item I place beside her. It breaks my fucking heart that some asshole would temper her passion, her desire, her innate sexuality. *Fucking coward.*

I pull the blindfold out and carefully tie it over her eyes, securing it at the side so she doesn't have a knot digging into her head.

"Comfortable?" I whisper. My lips are below her ear, and I take delight as her whole body shivers. She nods, so I ask again. "I need to hear the words, angel."

"Yes." She sighs, and I press a kiss against her cheek, the curl of her smile widening under my lips.

"Good girl. If you want me to stop at any time you say so, okay?"

"Yes. Do you want me to call you Sir?" My cock surges with blood at her breathy question.

"Normally, I would like that very much, but for now, I would mostly like to hear you say *my* name when you come." She whimpers, and I know I beam. She can't see it, which is why I can finally pull my shirt off. *Time to get dirty*.

I lie on my side next to her and trace my finger down her skin, the red marks are already starting to fade, but I still have to be careful not to touch, or irritate them. I follow my finger with my mouth, kissing a path from below her ear, down her neck to her collarbone. She sighs, and her sweet breath washes over me; she's intoxicating. I shift up and over so I'm hovering above her and trailing kisses down to her breasts. Her nipples are puckered tight, and I flick my tongue out and tease the tip. Her back is arched up from the bed, and she's now millimeters from touching my skin. I suck in a breath, my eyes flick to the blindfold, and I let out a calming breath.

I refrain from using my whole hand to massage her soft flesh, even though it's killing me. With my lips and fingertips I can be more precise and easily avoid any sore spots, and still drive her to where I want her to be. I cover her nipple with my mouth, sucking and swirling my tongue, pulling the peak, then releasing it with a slight scrape of my teeth. She writhes and undulates beneath me, and I repeat the process several times, alternating my attention equally, until her breaths are ragged, and her hips fruitlessly grind into the comforter.

"Need something, angel?" I rasp out the question and swallow against the dryness in my throat.

"Mmm mmm." She shakes her head and bites her lip into a tight, thin line.

"Words, angel. I need to hear the words," I demand, my tone a soft rumble.

"No, I'm good thank you," she whispers.

"So, you don't want me to try and ease this ache right here." I blow a cool breath of air on her pussy, which glistens from her arousal, causing her to cry out. *Damn, her scent is driving me crazy.*

"Oh, God! Please." She sighs, and I smile, but I want more from her—much more.

"Please what, angel?" I ask, my intonation innocent.

"Oh, God, Charge. Don't make me say it, please." She scrunches her face up with adorable annoyance.

"Angel, I will give you everything you ask for. But, you have to ask." I tap her nose lightly, and her face relaxes.

"Ugh. Hmm…" she moans, tipping her head right back like she's seeking divine intervention. *She'll get it, once she asks.*

"Well?" I place my lips at the top of her little strip of hair, which points a clear line to all that heavenly goodness. My nose circles the gold stud piercing, then dips into her belly button, making her giggle, which eases some of the tension.

"I want your tongue," she mutters.

"I like the sound of that. Go on." I pepper a line of kisses from her belly button down her landing strip, but not quite to her clit.

"Oh God," she moans.

"Charge. Oh, Charge," I correct and grin, because her head snaps up. I can just imagine her narrowed eyes and fiery stare. She flops back with a loud huff of resignation.

"I want your tongue on me—in me. Ahhh, Charge!" She cries out as I drag my tongue slowly with just the right amount of pressure from her clit to the entrance. My lips cover her, and I don't draw breath, sucking and licking, stroking and devouring every drop she gives me. I'm relentless, and I don't ease up for a second, not until I feel the first wave of contractions and then everything stops. I pull back, and she sags like her bones have suddenly lost all rigidity. She lies limp on the bed, and once she catches her breath, she snaps at me.

"What? Why did you stop?" Her incredulous tone would be comical if not for the deep frown on her face. I ignore her question and pose one of my own.

"What did you want me to do, angel?" I keep my tone even.

"I thought it was pretty obvious. I want you to make me come." Her head is raised, and she's staring right at me. I can almost see her deep, crystal-blue eyes through the silk. Her lips purse between each sentence, and I can feel her frustration, nearly a palpable, quite angry entity.

"How would you like me to do that?" I punctuate each word with more kisses. I can't stop touching her. I can't get enough, and as much as this is a lesson for her, it's also torture for me.

"Again with the obvious questions." Her flip tone is clipped and bordering on hostile.

"There is such a wide range of possibilities. I'll need you to be more specific." I'm trying to soothe her down. My purpose is not to rile her up and get her angry; my intention is to rile her up so she lets go.

"Really? Because you were doing just fine. All you truly had to do was *not* stop!" she shouts.

Okay, maybe my plan isn't quite working the way I had intended.

"Would you like some time to cool down? I can sense you're a little *tense*." I emphasize the last word but keep a playful note in my voice.

"Oh you can *sense* that, can you?" Her legs twitch, and I know if she wasn't spread wide with restraints, these gorgeous, long legs would be clamped so tight I'd need a crowbar to gain access.

"You also might want to adjust your tone," I warn, my playful tone is losing its lightness.

"Oh, might I? If I'm a little snarky, it would be because your wicked, talented tongue has kind of left me hanging! What? Wait! Where are you going?" she calls out as soon as the bed dips.

"I said, I think you need to cool down." I slide off the end of the bed and take deliberate steps toward the door.

"You can't be serious?" I hear her incredulity as the door clicks shut, with me still standing inside.

"Oh, my fucking God!" She screams after me, or so she thinks. "I can't believe he did that!" She pulls at her cuffs and tries to shuffle and squirm to ease the pressure I built. "That was so fucking hot!" She exhales a light laugh, and her face pinks right up. She looks so fucking sexy, spread out, hard-peaked nipples begging for my touch and her pussy, all wet and wanton. I need to get her to push past her reservations. She needs to fully trust me and trust herself. *She needs to let go.* She has it in her; I can feel it under my fingertips. I know she'll be spellbinding when she lets go, when she really gives herself to me. I can't fucking wait.

It's another ten minutes, before I pull the handle and watch her jump to attention.

"Charge?" Her head snaps toward the door, and as much as it might be fun to tease her a little longer, this is our first time, so I'll go easy.

"Yes, angel."

"Oh, thank God. Please don't leave me again." Her plea is soft and a little anxious.

"That will depend on you, angel. I didn't want to leave the last time, but you left me no choice." I walk back over to the bed, her head following my movement, her cheek twitching as she chews the inside of her mouth and mulls over my words.

"I'm sorry," she says quietly after a moment.

"And why are you sorry?" I gaze down at her as she looks up at me.

"I was snippy with you, but in my defense, I've never done this before, and I thought you were being cruel," she argues, but all her fire is gone. Her tone is defensive, and there's an underlying sadness that fucking kills me. I quell the building rage, which burns from understanding why she might feel sad at a time like this. *Asshole ex.*

"Angel, I would never be cruel." I place my hand on her ankle and stroke my finger slowly up her leg, over her hip and along her stretched torso. "You need to understand I would *never* be cruel. I may be a little inventive, but what I do to your body is for our mutual benefit. I want to push your boundaries, Finn, but first I need you to let go."

"So you're not being mean?" Her tone is more hopeful—happy even.

"It might feel that way, but no." I chuckle, and her smile widens, and her body softens. "I know this is taking you right to the edge of your comfort zone, but I need you to understand: When you embrace that space, you will be able to fully enjoy *everything.*" I pause a moment to let my words sink in, then continue. "So I will ask you again: Do you trust me?"

"I do." Her shy smile and instant answer make my chest ache with warmth and something I have never felt before. I don't know what to call it, but the feeling is so damn good, I want more.

"Good girl." I climb onto the bed and rest my hands at the apex of her thighs, pushing them a little bit wider. She smells divine, and even after her enforced time-out, I can see she's unbelievably wet. My thumbs trace her folds and open her fully so I can use my tongue to gorge on her arousal. I groan into her sweet center when she cries out my name. I pull back before she really starts to climb, because I need her cognizant and receptive.

"Tell me what you want me to do to you, angel. You saw the objects at my disposal. " She sucks in a breath and holds it, even as her legs begin to tremble with the surging desire clearly coursing through her body. "I want you to tell me what you want me to use to make you come."

"Oh, God!" She pants out on a rush of air, and I drag my tongue slowly around her clit to push her a little closer to the edge. "Charge, I…I—"

"Tell me!" I demand in a low growl, my eyes darting to her face, which flashes a dark red just before she speaks and leaves me speechless and so hard it's a miracle I don't explode in my boxer shorts.

"I want you to fuck me with the dildo and stick the plug in my arse, and…and I want your tongue. I want your tongue on my clit." She bites her lips together, and I can see by the pinch of her face, even under the blindfold, she's screwing her eyes shut. *My brave girl is so fucking hot.* "Please!" Her plea is a rushed afterthought, which makes my chest tighten and spurs me into action.

"That I can do." I place my mouth over her scorching core, swirling my tongue elaborately over her clit and along her silky flesh, dipping inside before I sit back up and make good on her request. I pick up the glass dildo first and palm the plug for later. The glass is cool to touch and slides easily from her clit to her entrance. I apply a little pressure and watch it slowly sink inside her. Damn, that's the sexiest fucking thing I've ever seen! My cock is in agony. Nevertheless, this is for her, and she really isn't up to me fucking her, because there's no way in hell I could be *this* restrained if my cock was buried to the hilt in heaven.

"Oh, God, Charge. That feels amazing." She sighs and tilts her hips up to encourage me to move. I push and pull, twisting and working the glass deep and deliberately, touching the parts my cock is literally weeping to feel. Her tummy clenches, and I ease back so as to penetrate shallowly. She lets out a steadying breath, her fingers curling up into tight little fists.

"You ready for the plug, angel?" My voice is a barely-audible whisper.

"Yes!" she puffs out on a laugh.

"You've never had nothing bigger than a thumb in there; is that right?" I look at the silver, cone-shaped plug in my palm; it's small but still bigger than any digit.

"Yes, but I liked it." I can't hide the grin spreading across my face at her welcome burst of enthusiasm.

"Okay, then. Let's try, but if it's uncomfortable in any way, you need to tell me. Understand?"

"Yes."

"Good girl. Now, open your mouth." She drops her jaw instantly, and my balls tighten at her obedience. I place the small, silver plug on her bottom lip and push it into her mouth, keeping a firm hold on the gem-encrusted end. "Make this wet and warm for me."

Her lips wrap around the plug, sucking it in, eager to please. I pull it out, and with some slight resistance, it plops from her mouth. In lieu of some extra lube, I pull the glass dildo free and drag the plug through her wetness and down to her tight, puckered entrance. Her legs begin to tremble at the first contact, and I use my voice to soothe and calm her. "Tell me to stop, Finn, at any time, and I will. But trust me, I'm going to make this worth that pounding in your chest."

She gives a rapid little nod, and I growl my disapproval at her silence.

"Sorry. Don't stop. Please don't stop!" She flashes me a sweet smile, then sucks both lips into her mouth, biting down as I very slowly push the tip of the plug against her tight ring of muscles.

At the same time I reintroduce the dildo, sliding it all the way inside her soaking pussy. She moans, arching her back, pushing against my hand.

"Oh, Charge! God, yes! *Yes!*" With the deep penetration of the dildo, I managed to distract her enough to ease the plug all the way in with very little resistance. Her cries of pleasure are visually represented by the glorious flush of color and glow, kissing and covering her skin. I start to move the dildo, leaving the plug to keep her with a delicious, full feeling. Judging by those erotic little moans and pants, she loves it all.

"Oh, Charge, I'm…I'm really close. Please don't stop. *Please!*" she begs breathlessly.

"Wouldn't dream of it, angel. Not with this front-row seat to perfection." She gasps, sucking in a loud and shocked breath when I start to pump and push her higher, harder, and farther than I believe she's ever been. I lean down, covering her clit with my lips and I suck, pressing my tongue flat and firm, letting her grind against my mouth with wild abandon. Her legs tremble, and every muscle in her body freezes, tenses, and she screams so damn loud, I think she might startle the horses. *Absolutely fucking incredible.*

CHAPTER EIGHTEEN

Finn

I DON'T REMEMBER FALLING ASLEEP. I THINK THE LAST climax was too much. *As if that's a thing.* But I must have really passed out, because it takes me a few minutes to orient myself when my lids do flutter open. My arms and legs are free to move, and the thin, soft, cotton sheet drapes my body lightly as I'm wrapped around Charge. *I can't believe I did that!*

I can feel the heat in my cheeks at the thought and the un-stoppable pull of my lips into the widest motherfucking smile. Amazing, utterly mind-blowing.

I tip my head on his chest so I can see his face, mindful not to wake him. He has a rich, golden tan, strong jaw, and his dark lashes are so long they fan onto his high-cut cheekbone. He is possibly the most beautiful man I have ever seen. This isn't to say the others aren't handsome, because they are, but there's something ethereal about this man, which tugs at more than my libido. He coaxes and cares, demands and delivers, pushing me to explore myself, all while cherishing me and making me feel safe and *wanted*. My eyes drop to his full, soft, extremely talented mouth, and I feel a bubble of heat like a direct hit between my legs. *God, I'm insatiable.*

"Keep looking at my lips, angel, and I will never let you leave this bed." I jump at his deep, rumbling voice, and look to see his wickedly wide smile and soul-piercing eyes gazing at me.

"And leaving the bed would be a bad thing?" I quip with a cheeky, full smile.

"Not at all. But I have to feed you, and I thought you wanted to chat," he reminds me with a light tap on my now crinkled nose.

"We can chat in bed?" I pull a playful pout, which makes him laugh.

"Not if you keep looking at me like that, we can't," he admonishes, though his tone is teasing.

"Sorry, I'm being selfish. You must be…I mean, you didn't… do you want me to…" I stutter.

"Finish a sentence? Yeah, that would be good." He leans over to kiss my hair, chuckling at my sudden awkwardness.

"No need to go back to being reticent, Finn. Not now. And I'm in the Navy, remember? There's not much you could say that would shock me," he points out with a serious arch of his brow.

"Okay," Sucking in a breath, I force myself to say the damn words. What's the worst that could happen? I have to remind myself he's not Dave. "You didn't come earlier, would you like me to"—I close my eyes and soldier on—"to suck your cock?" I rush the rest of my thoughts, preventing any interruption that might make this even more awkward. "I know we can't have sex, although there are probably some positions that would work, but I can definitely go down on you." I bury my face in his

T-shirt, and the hard muscles beneath feel like granite.

"I love it when you talk dirty." I can almost feel his smile; it's warm and playful. He hugs me to him, planting a litany of tender kisses on my hair, making my heart swell. "I'm good, angel. I want to wait until you're a hundred percent, but if you're up for a repeat, I'm more than happy to oblige." I look up from my hiding spot to see him wiggle his brow, and I laugh and choke at the same time.

"Only if you want to put me in a coma."

"No coma. How about I fix us some lunch, and you can start reading this." He pulls the large 3-ring binder, which is taking up most of the surface area, off the bedside table. He holds it out for me to take, and although I mutter and grumble, I shift back on the bed, pulling the sheet to cover myself and take the damn binder. "I'm sure it will give us something to chat about." Scooting off the bed and pulling his jeans up, he walks out the door, barefoot and glorious, with a quick backward glance, which makes my heart beat just a little bit faster.

I manage to read quite a portion of Charge's section, and he wasn't wrong about me having questions. It is crammed full with facts, but little detail. Charge returns and barely gets one foot in the door before I pounce with my first question.

"What were you in juvie for?" I close the binder and flash a smile at his shocked expression.

"Wow! You're a fast reader."

"I may have skimmed the kindergarten years," I confess with a sheepish shrug.

"Shame, some of my fondest memories are from those years." He walks over to the bed, and I move over to make room and flatten the comforter.

"I'll go back and read that, I promise." I pat the bed for him to have a seat.

"Arson," he states flatly.

"Oh! That's pretty serious." I suck in a sharp breath, and he shrugs.

"My guardian certainly thought so." He calmly places a tray with two bowls of sweet-smelling tomato and basil soup, crusty bread rolls, some sliced fruit and a large jug of water. "I had gotten into a lot of trouble before that, and it was escalating. This was the last straw, and Donald, my guardian, decided he wasn't going to bail me out. My sentence was set for eighteen months, but I should've served much longer, so I know I was lucky. I didn't think so at the time. I thought he was a piece of shit for abandoning me like that, especially after everything, but it turned out to be the best thing to ever happen to me." His eyes soften, and I recognize his affectionate expression.

"You met the others there." I match his smile, which is un-ashamedly bright.

"Yeah, I did."

"How old were you?"

"Fourteen."

I take one of the rolls and pull it apart, using the motions to give me a second to think. I was in foster care at fourteen and having just met Hope, my life was turning a corner. I started working at one of her mum's salons and spent most of my time either there or at Hope's house. I don't like to dwell on the years prior to meeting Hope.

"What were you caught burning?" I finally ask.

"My parents' house." His derisive tone startles me.

"Really? Why?" I can't hide the shock in my voice.

"When they died, I hated everything, everyone and anything that reminded me of them. The house was one big mausoleum, and I hated that it was still there when they weren't. I was living with Donald, but I snuck out every chance I could. One night I found myself there."

"Your parents were in a car accident." It's a statement, having read the little snippet in the file. He gives a curt nod.

"Yes, along with my grandparents and my brother." His body tenses, his shoulders straightening, and I worry I may have asked one too many questions. Pink warned me he might not be open to scrutiny, but he's quite the opposite, and I find myself hungry for any and all information he wants to share.

"Sorry, Charge. We don't have to talk about this. " Any story that involves a child being left an orphan is not going to be pretty. *I know mine isn't.*

"It's fine. I mean it's not fine, but it happened. I loved my parents; however, they lived for the limelight and appearances. Don't get me wrong, they were always there for us, gave my brother and me all their time when we needed them, and we never wanted for anything. Nevertheless, they did love to show us off when the cameras were there, and I really fucking hated that. Hated them for it." His distain drips from the words like tar, black and ugly. "My father co-owned a film production company with my guardian, and my mother was an actress who gave acting up when she had my brother. Anyway, it was a big premier night, and I wouldn't go, flat out refused, but my baby brother was the peacekeeper, always cheerful and wanted to make others happy. He told them I was sick to stop a big fight and to keep my father from punishing me." His eyes close, and agony distorts his handsome face as his thoughts cause him physical pain. He falls silent. I reach for his hand. It's no comfort, I know, but I can't *not* touch him when he looks so unbearably sad.

"I'm so sorry, Charge." His fingers thread through mine, and he lifts my palm to his lips.

"It was a long time ago." His features slowly lighten as the somber cloud of devastation drifts way, and after a short time, he lets out a long breath, lifting his eyes to meet mine. His earnestness catches me off guard. "This arrangement is important to *all* of us for the same reason, Finn. We don't want to lose anyone again. We've all lost enough. I know it's a challenge, taking on four guys. It's definitely going to take an exceptional woman." He fixes me with the most intense, soul-searching stare, and he's utterly mesmerizing. After a long moment, I'm able to speak.

"You can't know that's me. You barely know me, Charge." I hate the uncertainty in my voice, especially when he sounds so confident, seems so sure of everything.

"True, and I'm not going to rush you. You can take all the time in the world, but me, I'm going to trust my gut." He flashes the most brilliant, heart-stopping smile, stealing the breath from my lungs, leaving me a little dazzled. He's certainly an assault on all my senses.

Picking up my spoon, I absently stir the steaming hot soup, mulling over his words and the heartfelt sincerity. I don't doubt he believes and means what he says, which is both flattering and scary as hell. I try to divert the heavy conversation, at least until I've been here for more than forty-eight hours.

Has it really only been that long? It has been longer in my head and my heart; in my mind it's been three months of daily free and honest conversations with four of the most amazing men I've ever known.

"Tell me about the tattoo on your arm." I point to the ink peeking out from his white-capped shirt, his bicep flexed in an impressive bulge of hard muscle under smooth skin. "You all have them, but I noticed they are slightly different." He grins at my change of topic, but he humors me and answers.

"The anchor with USN is pretty self-explanatory, United States Navy, and the rope dangling from it with the four stars represents the four of us. This symbol underneath is fire." He pulls the sleeve up on his right arm and twists so the whole tattoo is now visible. "When we were kids in juvie, we banded together and gave ourselves each an element. We needed something to make us feel like we were one, a unit, stronger together, you know?" I nod, though I don't think he expects me to answer, and I'm too eager to learn to risk interrupting. "It felt like this was us against everyone else, against the world. And what is stronger than the four elements?" He shrugs and takes a big bite of his bread, chews slowly, swallows, then continues. "Might seem silly, but it helped, and when we were old enough, we all got inked together."

"It isn't silly to want to belong. It's nice that you found each other." He gives a tentative smile and rolls his cuff back down, the bottom of the three curved flames peek out, the middle part of the flame is like a spiral. I notice that regardless of which element, the spiral pattern is common in each of the tattoos.

"So what would that make me?" I ask, and his brows shoot up, and a deep frown furrows his forehead. "I don't think there's a fifth element, other than the film." I snort out a little laugh, and he grins. Stiffening, I drop my spoon and then scramble off the bed. I tug the sheet from the bed as I move across the room, keeping it tight around myself to cover my body as I rummage through my drawers. I pull what I was looking for free from the cubicle and hold it up against me with a triumphant smile. My T-shirt with the letters Ah in an element square from the periodic table, and the words underneath printed 'The element of Surprise'. Charge barks out a laugh and continues to laugh when he stands and walks over to me. His immense frame covers and cloaks my body as he holds me carefully, but close enough I can feel the strong and steady thump of his heart; it's a great sound and I love the comfort it brings me.

"See, my gut is never wrong." He kisses my hair, and I melt.

CHAPTER
NINETEEN

Finn

THE FIRST WEEK DIDN'T GO TO PLAN, SINCE MY SPOTS took ages to fade. and while I felt fine, I was still reluctant to venture out into the big, wide world. It wasn't a huge problem considering Charge had the week off work. So I spent most of days with him either reading the folder or exploring the countryside. I helped him cook, and when the others came back from work, I split my time with them, though it was fluid, not forced. Pink would take me up to the stables and teach me the basics; not that shovelling shit needed a degree, but grooming and handling the horses wasn't particularly intuitive to this city girl. Toxic liked the outdoors; he kept the garden smart, and the woodpile fully loaded, but also liked to play pool and was happy to teach me when we were together. Tug is quieter when it's just the two of us, and he's most relaxed while holding me in his lap as we watch old films.

I still wasn't able to sleep on my own, and, because Charge didn't seem to sleep at all, he would lie with me, stroking my hair and back until I drifted off. Most mornings I woke to an empty bed, but I wasn't sure if he left during the night or was just an earlier riser. One night we all stayed in my bedroom, chatting until the wee hours, and I woke up to a human Jenga constructed of all four men, fully clothed and fast asleep.

This is like the best vacation ever! A hedonist's wildest fantasy come true.

I spoke to Hope during the week, but I wasn't comfortable giving her salacious details. I know she's eager, but I feel it cheapens what's going on and what we have, which, although it is off-the-charts sexy as all hell, it's also pure and beautiful.

I haven't had my date with Toxic or Tug, because I haven't been a hundred percent, and although they all continue to care for me, and are attentive, affectionate, and playful, I haven't had sex since I was with Pink at the lake, and I haven't *come* since I was with Charge.

I'm surrounded by perfect alphas, inside and out, assaulted every waking minute by a tsunami of testosterone, hot sexy bodies, sweet affection, and the constant touching. Oh, my lord, the constant touching! It's the understatement of the year that I'm a little relieved when the last spot finally fades. *I'm literally panting.*

My full recovery is declared halfway through the second week, and Tug and Toxic decide they want to share a date. I get all shivery thinking what that might entail, but whatever happens I'm more than ready. *Did I mention panting?*

I had strict instructions to have an early night because it was going to be a full day. I also agreed to join them on their morning run. I have used their gym on occasion, but I prefer swimming or just walking around the farm for exercise. It will be nice to get out, though, and they said something about training on the beach which, for a city girl, sounds amazing.

I wake with a start, my heart racing and my eyes wide, though I can't see a damn thing; its pitch dark. There's a noise outside my door and I panic with the ridiculous notion that we're being burgled. The door opens and, of all the things, I pull the covers over my head. After a while there's a hushed whisper I recognize.

"She's sleeping?" Tug speaks softly.

"No point whispering, Tug. We're here to wake her up." Toxic booms and I pull the cover back to take a peek, my eyes squinting to adjust to the lack of light. Their shadows block the glow from the hallway, but even the soft light filtering past their collective body mass, is too bright, causing me to retreat back under the blanket and groan.

"We heard that. Come on, sugar. You said you wanted to train with us," Toxic coaxes, his volume adjusted to indoor level.

"In the morning," I grumble, my voice muffled by the comforter.

"It *is* morning." Tug laughs and I feel the first pull of my cover, which I snatch back and clamp tight around my body. In a flash the comforter is gone, and I scream.

"What the hell, guys!"

"Oh! Someone's not a morning person," Tug jokes, and I scowl at him, but with the darkness I doubt he can see my fiery glare.

"It's not morning!" I huff, pulling a pillow to cover my scantily clad body. "It's still dark…that means it's nighttime."

"It's 0400 hours, sugar, and that's morning," Toxic states flatly. "Come on, sunshine, up you get." His voice softens as he tries to coax my cooperation. He attempts to pry the pillow from my vice-like grip. I growl, and he snatches his hand back like I have bitten him.

"Whoa! Now I know why Charge is always first up," he teases.

Frowning, I say, "It's the middle of the night, guys. You can't be serious?" I resort to a childish whine. "Who gets up at this time to go running? Crazy people, that's who?"

"Crazy people and Navy Seals. Now shift your...what do you call it?" Tug looks to Toxic for assistance.

"Arse." Toxic makes an admirable attempt at a British accent and adds a great roll of the letter R, which makes me laugh. Tug takes the opportunity to lift me from the bed and wrestle the pillow from my grasp. I'm awake now, so there's little point pretending otherwise.

"Did you pack a change of clothes?" Toxic looks around the bedroom.

"I packed what you told me to pack." With that flat response and a huge exaggerated yawn, I point to my large yellow tote bag. "Give me twenty minutes and I'll be ready."

"You'll be ready in five, or we'll take you out naked." My brows shoot up at his remark. Tug is fighting a grin, but Toxic looks deadly serious. I scuttle into my bathroom and in record time, I'm clean, dressed, and fully awake.

"Just so you know I hate you both right now," I grumble and take my bag from Tug with an aggressive swipe. He chuckles.

"Ah, sugar, you couldn't hate us if you tried." He pulls an adorable full fat bottom-lipped pout.

"It's four o'clock in the morning, and I'm not even going on holiday...trust me, I don't have to try that hard right now." I start to follow, and although I'm in a daze, I don't mean to drag my feet. My body just doesn't respond at this ungodly hour. I grunt as Tug hauls me over his shoulder and speeds along the corridor.

"Come on, slow poke, we'll never get there in time, if you're gonna' do that snail pace." He jogs down the stairs.

"Tug, I can walk!" I drop my bag to grab his sweatpants for stability. Hard arse muscle twists and flexes beneath my fists. Toxic scoops up my bag, chuckling at my futile, disgruntled indignation.

Tug drives the open-top jeep and I sit in the back with a thick blanket and Toxic's strong arm wrapped around me. I'm sipping on a protein smoothie the guys insisted I drink but it's the wrong temperature for my morning drink and is severally lacking in caffeine so I barely manage more than a few mouthfuls. The cool breeze dampens as we near the ocean, and the stars are just beginning to fade. The inky sky has the faintest bright light on the horizon, and any grumpiness I harbored dissolves as we pull up to the deserted beach and park. There's a steady rumble of waves crashing in the distance, and although the sun hasn't broken the surface of the earth yet, there's enough light to see that this place is quite stunning.

Wild, sandy beach, as far as the eye can see; it stretches for miles in both directions. Uninhabited and desolate, it reminds me of a science fiction landscape and, certainly at this unearthly hour, it feels like we're the only three people on the planet. Tug kills the engine, and Toxic leaps over the side and offers me a hand. I jump down and shiver; the breeze still holds the chill of the nighttime and without the blanket and his warm embrace, I'm freezing. I rub my arms vigorously and start to jog on the spot.

"Come on, sugar. Let's get you warm." Tug grins and for a moment I feel the trickle of heat between my legs at his possible meaning. But he simply holds my hand and starts leading me down the slight sand dune to the flattened sand of the shoreline. *Jeez, get a grip, Finn, not everything has to have a sexual connotation.* He pulls his sweater off exposing his bare chest with ripped and cut muscles, just like Toxic's, though he has more hair. A dark spattering that gathers in a thick and heavy line down to his...*for the love of God, Finn, stop it!*

I shake my head lightly and feel my cheeks burn when my eyes meet his, and he glances over to Toxic with a telling smile.

"Right, what's the plan?" I clap my hands together and rub, desperately trying to divert my wayward thoughts.

"The plan is we run." Toxic kicks off at a slow lope, followed by Tug who is jogging backwards, tipping his head for me to follow.

"No warm-up stretches?" I call out but race to catch up. Even at a slow pace their long strides eat up the beach.

"This *is* the warm-up." Tug chuckles, and both men fall on either side of me as we power along the shoreline. I'm not unfit, but there are levels of fitness and I'm nowhere near these guys' stratospheric heights. Although running on sand—even compact sand—is really fucking hard on the pins.

The guys drop back as I start to fall behind, and I fight for a bit longer, but at the risk of my lungs exploding, I concede defeat and collapse on the sand. I suck in large, ungainly gulps of air and think perhaps I should've stopped about twenty minutes ago. I cough and splutter on my hands and knees.

Toxic and Tug both crouch down on their haunches, concern etched on their faces, and Tug offers me a bottle of water. I pull an apologetic smile and grab the drink.

"Steady. Don't gulp, or you'll get cramps." Toxic strokes my back as I sit upright. I feel embarrassed, not that I couldn't keep up, because frankly only an Olympian could, but that I didn't listen to my body and stop when I felt the first real wave of exhaustion. At least then I would be gracefully bowing out, rather than collapsed into heap of dripping sweat and Lycra.

"I'm sorry," I pant out, one word at a time.

"Hush, don't be silly, sugar. We got carried away. Kinda' liked having you alongside. It's our fault, we knew you were getting tired. We just wanted to make it to the headland before the sunrise." Tug flops down onto the sand on one side of me, and Toxic does the same on the other.

"But it's just as pretty watching from here." Toxic tips his head toward the horizon and I follow his gaze. *Now, that's worth waking up for.*

"Wow!" My second understatement of the year, and both are on the same day.

The sunlight bursts so bright over the horizon, I have to shield my eyes with my hand. The glow quickly saturates the sky, and the rays illuminate the azure-blue sky. It's spellbinding, breathtaking, and all those words that completely fail to capture this humbling sight. I start to lean but hesitate with which direction. I want to rest against one of them and soak up the wonderful dawn vista, but even that choice is too hard. *How on earth am I supposed to choose among the four?*

Tug lifts me into his lap, making that decision for me, and I sink back into his hold. My heart still struggles to regain a normal beat pattern, but his steady *thump, thump* is strong and comforting—a little like him. A few minutes pass, and Toxic stands, pulling me from Tug's lap and lifting me high onto his hips. My legs automatically wrap around his body, and his gaze falls on my lips. Tug is at my back and I'm cocooned within a warm wall of muscle. Toxic's lips brush mine, and my tongue dips out to taste him. His wolfish smile widens and he looks over my shoulder at his friend.

"We can't, man. We might be the only ones on the beach right now, but not for long." I can feel Tug shake his head. I sag and whimper, pent-up lust coursing through my veins, almost as rapidly as my frantic heart pumps my blood.

"We can," I gush, my slut filter on mute. A tinge of shame flushes through my cheeks at my overt, wanton plea, but I push it aside. We all chose this and I have absolutely no reason to feel anything other than adored, desired, and wanted. Because that's exactly how I feel when I'm with any one of these guys.

Oh, and horny as hell.

"Oh, sugar, we are definitely going to have to rain check until a little later. I don't know about Tug, but I won't be able to stop if we start something now, and this beach is the closest one to the largest military base on the West Coast. There's likely to be a hundred soldiers running this shoreline soon, and I, for one, ain't about to let *anyone* see our girl in action." His tone drops low, and the rumble in his chest vibrates through my body. His playful tone has vanished, along with my libido.

"Oh, God, when you put it like that, no!" I stiffen, and the horror in my voice makes them both laugh.

"Relax, sugar. We might share with each other, but we don't have any intention of letting anyone else have even a peek at our little piece of heaven." He squeezes my bottom, and they both crowd me protectively so I'm fully enclosed and closeted.

"Abso-fucking-lutely!" Toxic echoes Tug's sentiment.

"Oh, good," I squeak out on a relieved breath of air. I trust them all, but we are still very much in the early stages of exploring each other's boundaries.

"But back home, sugar, all bets are off." Toxic grins, and Tug gives an audible, "Hell, yeah," before stepping back, letting me find my feet back on the soft sand. My legs wobble because my muscles are the consistency of jelly after my overexertion. Grabbing Tug's wide bicep to prevent myself from hitting the deck, I'm grateful when his arm secures my weight against his body.

"Okay, sugar, looks like we're carrying you back," he chuckles.

"You can't!" I cry out in protest, worry about my weight and the distance prompting my outburst.

"Sure we can." He scoops me into his arms and starts jogging back the way we came. Strong strides quickly consume the distance back to the jeep, the pace much faster than the one I had tried to keep up with, and yet, he moves like I weigh no more than the bottle of water in Toxic's hand. Part way back they break stride just to switch who's carrying me, but not because Tug is tired, but because Toxic feels left out. I manage to protest and make a case to run the last quarter mile, but I collapse when I reach the jeep.

"Need coffee," I gasp.

"Jump in, sugar. We know just the place. Breakfast time!" Tug climbs in the front seat and starts the engine.

"My legs won't move," I groan, dropping my head to my knees. Before I take another much-needed gasp of oxygen, I'm lifted high and carried into the back of the jeep. The sun warming the sea breeze, we pull away from the desolate beach and head off, back towards civilization, pancakes, and java beans.

CHAPTER TWENTY

Toxic

△

FIST BUMPING CHARGE AND PINK, I SLIDE INTO THE LONG booth seat opposite. Finn beams a bright, stunning smile at the others, slipping in beside me, and Tug locks her in. *Perfect.* She looked so fucking hot running between us, her soft, tan skin glistening as she worked up a sweat made running, for me at least, a challenge. Dressed in skin-tight, black shorts and bright pink crop top, showcasing her killer curves, she's making my fucking balls ache like there's no tomorrow. I felt bad that she pushed herself, but pleased too; it was impressive that she kept the pace like she did—until the moment she collapsed.

I shift in my seat, a painful surge of blood rushing to my cock, the sudden flashback stretching my shorts. Thinking about her in my arms, that sexy-as-hell sigh and lust-filled gaze nearly ended me. I don't know where I found the strength to stop, but I gladly listened to Tug, who was the voice of reason, because I know for a fact Finn was on exactly the same page I was. *Man, I can't wait for later.*

"Hey, darling. How was the early start? Did you enjoy your run?" Pink grins, and Charge chuckles. I scowl at them both, because they thought our idea was dumb, and Charge warned us that Finn didn't appear to be a morning person.

"Oh, laugh it up, guys, but I had the best morning." She flashes her gorgeous smile at Tug, kissing him lightly on the cheek, then turning to me, she leans in for a quick embrace, her slim arm wrapping around my tummy. Her hold makes me feel all fucking warm inside. Straightening, she continues to enlighten my best friends. "I was glad they woke me up at sparrow fart. That sunrise was the most beautiful thing I have ever seen other than you guys," she teases with an exaggerated wink.

"Sparrow what now?" Pink barks out a throaty laugh.

"Fart—at sparrow fart. It means really early. " She giggles lightly at the confused look on all our faces. It must be a British thing.

"How are her fitness levels?" Charge asks, sipping his espresso.

"Pretty crappy," Tug answers, and Finn twists round and slaps his stomach in indignation.

"Hey! I kept up," She argues, causing Tug to lift his hands up in surrender at her irked tone. "It's abnormal the speed and distance you run," she protests.

"You kept up, sugar, because we slowed down, and you nearly needed an iron lung after the first stretch." Tug smiles indulgently, and I arch a warning brow over her head, because I can feel her hackles rise. He hangs a heavy arm over her shoulder, pulling her into an affectionate hug. "I'm teasing, honey. You did good."

"First stretch?" she queries, her irritation seeming to evaporate with his praise.

"Yeah, sugar. We do that run several times but since we carried you back, we didn't think you would be that happy to wait on us. Beside you said something about coffee." Tug kisses her hair, and she snickers, pulling upright and away from his embrace.

"Oh, God, yes! Coffee and food," she groans, looking enviously at the two empty cups on the table.

"How are my favorite boys?" Marilyn appears, swilling a jug of the steamy, black liquid, which makes Finn perk up.

"We're good, thanks, Marilyn. How's Rodney?" Marilyn and Rodney own this small diner we've used for almost ten years—ever since we enlisted. It's a great pit stop for breakfast most days when we train at the beach and the occasional evening meal when Charge doesn't want to cook. It's nothing fancy, but feels like a second home, and Marilyn thinks of us like the sons she never had.

"Oh, you know, same ol' same ol'. Hello, there, sweetheart." Marilyn smiles directly at Finn, who is quick to offer her hand, but before she can introduce herself, the shit hits the fan. "So you're the latest dream girl? Well, give it to my boys to pick the pretty ones, that's for sure." Finn retrieves her hand and visibly shrinks a few inches in size. We all outwardly flinch, and Charge and Pink fire the stink eye at both Tug and me. *Fuck.* "The usual for you boys, and how about you, sweetheart?" There's an awkward silence, and Marilyn's eyes flit between four grown men holding their breath and panicking. "Oh, darling, I didn't mean anything by that. I gotta learn to keep my mouth shut." Marilyn tries to brush off what she said; nevertheless, the damage is done.

"It's fine." Finn waves her hands like it's no big deal, but her body is rigid next to mine. "I'll have some pancakes please, and coffee—lots of coffee." She lets out a stilted laugh, which does nothing to ease the tension.

"Sure thing, darling." Marilyn scurries off hastily, leaving the scene of her verbal crime.

"Finn—" Charge tries to speak, but she's quick with her interruption.

"Would you excuse me? I need to use the ladies' room." She nudges Tug, who jumps up like her fingertips are firing high-voltage electricity.

"Finn?" Charge repeats, and she pauses to turn and face us with a forced, bright smile that's like a kick in the nuts.

"I'm fine, Charge. I just need to pee." She again tries to smile, but she gives up and hurries away.

"Dumbass! Why the fuck did you bring her here?" Pink fires across the table, his narrowed eyes nothing compared to Charge's dark scowl.

"Fucking idiots." His voice is barely above a whisper, and I know that's when he's at his most furious.

"Hey, calm the fuck down." I use my hands, waving, downing the rising animosity. "We brought her here because she wanted coffee, and we always come here. It's nothing special, Charge." I try to justify our error. It wasn't a strategic fuck-up; at worst, we just didn't think.

"No, but she *is,* and now she probably feels like another notch in four fucking bedposts!" he growls, and I take the hit—we both do.

"Shit, I'm sorry, okay? I wasn't thinking, Charge." Tug rubs his hand across the back of his neck, his shoulders bunching near his ears, and we all feel the same.

"This won't fuck it up, trust me," I state, my stern tone a reflection of my own frustration, but I genuinely think this is a minor hiccup compared to what could potentially end this deal.

"And what's that supposed to mean, exactly?" Charge rises at my provocation, but I know lashing out is his first line of defense.

"*We* don't have the secrets or the hang-ups, Charge. I don't mean anything by it, you know that, man, but it's the truth." He stiffens at my statement and nods, acknowledging the truth of what I said.

"I told her about my folks." Charge's fingers grip his cup, oozing tension from every pore.

"You did?" Pink exclaims, his tone as surprised as the expression on all our faces. Charge is as closed off as they come, with good reason, so this is unprecedented.

"Yeah. Didn't think twice either. It felt right, so cut me some fucking slack. I have no intention of fucking this up any more than you all do." He glares at each of us.

"And the other stuff?" I push, instantly kicking myself for doing so, feeling the wash of shame that I should level any accusation at this man, my brother, and the man who saved my life.

"It's the second fucking week, Toxic, give me time," he snaps.

"I'm sorry, man, I was out of line." I'm quick to set things straight, but Charge still gives me a death glare. It's not like him to hold a grudge, so I can't help thinking this conversation troubles him more than he's letting on.

"All right, guys. Just calm the fuck down. We have all the fucking time in the world, because none of us want this to end. So how about we stop pointing fingers, and make sure Finn makes the right choice," Pink jokes, trying to kill the tension.

"Which is?" I ask with a curious quirk of my lips.

"Me, of course." Pink sits back, puffing his chest like an ass.

"You gave her poison oak," Tug points out flatly.

"And you brought her here," Pink retorts

"And I'll explain. I will sort this, okay?" My voice is level and certain as I attempt to soothe the undercurrent of rage that's flying at me from all corners.

"Explain what?" Finn comes back, and, surprisingly, she does look brighter, the edge of sadness gone, and that killer smile is back to full-strength, giving the brightness of the California sun a run for its money.

"That he's a dumbass." Pink offers me up, and I kick him under the table, not hard so he doesn't move, but hard enough.

"Finn, we're sorry. We didn't know Marilyn would say something like that. This is our normal hangout and it didn't occur to me *not* to bring you here."

"I'm glad you did. I don't want you hiding me away, and I need to not be quite so sensitive. It's not like I'm the first girl you've tried out." She shrugs lightly, and I can see in her eyes this little bit of trouble has already passed.

"But you're the last." Charge took the words right out of my mouth. A splash of pink colors her cheeks as she takes her seat beside me.

"I bet you say that to all the girls," she retorts.

Quick to disabuse her of this thought, we all say, "No," at the same time.

"Oh!" She chews on her cheek but can't hide the smile from splitting her face.

After breakfast, which we managed to finish without further incident, we head off to the harbor, agreeing to meet the others at the bar after dinner. A friend of Pink's is the lead guitar in a local band, and it's their final night of a small tour. We thought Finn would enjoy a night out and a chance to meet some of our other friends. This last week has been great, but as much as we'd like to keep her all to ourselves, we know we should mingle more—No. Actually, after this morning's debacle with Marilyn, keeping her locked away is exactly what I'd like to do. We walk down the pontoons, with some of the most impressive sailing boats in the world moored on either side. The musical chime of the rigging running against the myriad of masts gets my heart thumping. I love the sea, and a strong wind is like mainlining crack for a sailor. *I hope Finn feels the same.*

We arrive at *The Four*, our very own lady of the sea, a Jeanneau 58 that has just the right amount of luxury. She is a serious sailboat, and the absolute best place to be on a clear and windy day. Jumping over the gap between the pontoon and the boat, I hold my hand out for Finn to follow. She kicks off her shoes the second she hits the deck.

"This is yours?" Her eyes wide with wonder, she takes in the splendor of the blond teak flooring and gleaming stainless-steel fittings. The seating area in front of the steering console is covered with protective plastic, but still makes the boat look pristine.

"Ours," I correct with a proud grin. "There's a shower below in the master cabin, if you want to freshen up." I point to the center of the deck where an arched doorway leads down some steps to the interior of the vessel.

"It's amazing! I'm not being funny, but how on earth do four Navy guys afford something like this? You're not actually drug smugglers, are you?" she laughs nervously.

"No, sugar. That's sort of frowned upon in our line of work. Charge has this fuck-off trust fund. He didn't touch it for years. He hates the idea of money making him different from the rest of us. It doesn't; we don't give a shit, but he felt it did, so he just ignores it. He made us all trustees a few years back. Not that we'd spend any of his money, but he felt better that we could if we needed to, like if we were real brothers." I shrug off the only explanation I have.

"That's very generous." She exhales slowly, eyes still taking in every detail.

"That's Charge. Anyway, we all love the ocean. This wasn't a tough sell." I wink and start to unhook all the protective covers. Tug has loosened the spring lines and pulled in the fenders before he lands back on the pontoon to make one last sweep to make sure everything is good to go.

"It's really big." Her tone is filled with awe, and I bloody love that. *The Four* is impressive, and she flies like shit off a shovel in the right conditions.

"That's what she said." Tug jumps from the dock and lands heavily behind Finn.

"I meant the boat," she snickers.

"You really didn't though, did you?" He wraps his arms around her waist, picking her up and spinning her in his arms until she's perched on his hips. His mouth crashes into hers, for a fast and furious kiss, before he drops her slightly shell-shocked, tiny frame back on the deck.

"Um…wow." She exhales loudly, a huge grin illuminating her face. "Not kidding though, how can just two people sail this?"

"First, it's not *people*. We're two skilled sailors. Second, it's not just two of us, but three." I wiggle my brow playfully and laugh when her own brows shoot up in horror.

"I can't!" she gasps, placing her hand over her heart. "I've never so much as sat on a pedalo!" she squeaks, and I bark out a deep laugh at her sudden panic.

"Relax, sugar. Every day's a schoolday." I wink, but she doesn't look remotely convinced. Sighing I try to comfort her with further explanation.

"It's rigged so it can be sailed by one of us, sugar. Trust us. We have precious cargo right here." I step up to her and stroke her long, blonde hair that's whipping in the breeze, trying to tame it by pushing it behind her ears. "We just want to show you our *other* passion." I hold her gaze and watch her throat as she swallows. *Sweet.*

CHAPTER TWENTY-ONE

Tug

"S HE'S IN THE SHOWER," I CALL OUT TO TOXIC AS HE starts to maneuver *The Four* out of her mooring.

"And?" His face twists with confusion.

"And my balls ache so much I want to join her." I grab my package to try and ease the dull pain, though I know it will be a brief respite.

"You said you wanted to double up. That was your idea, remember?" he retorts with a wry smile.

"I know," I groan.

"Well, *The Four* won't sail herself, so you'll just have to stow it until later."

"Tonight?" I can't hide the slight panic from my tone.

"I was thinking when we get to the cove, we could take a little dip and eat some lunch, then…" His suggestion hangs in the air between us.

"Sounds fucking perfect. You really think she's up for it? For us both, I mean?" I look nervously over my shoulder, because she has a habit of walking in at just the wrong time, and the last thing I want her to stumble in on is *this* conversation. "She seemed keen on the beach, but this isn't some fantasy. This is high-definition reality." I grab my cock not for effect, but because it's straining painfully against my zipper and aching like a motherfucker.

"We won't push it, Tug. This is up to her and we'll follow her lead, okay?" Toxic says.

"Cool. Man, I hope she wants to." I can't fight the devilish grin that splits my face in two.

"Wants to what? I keep coming in on the tail end of you guys discussing me, and it's driving me nuts." I blow out a puff of air in relief. *Perfect timing, Finn.*

"Hope you want to have a go at steering." Toxic steps to the side but keeps his hand on the wheel. Walking over cautiously, her eyes narrow and flit suspiciously between us both.

"That's not what you were talking about." Her astute observation makes me think this *is* a conversation we should have with her. I look at Toxic and see from his expression he's drawn the same conclusion.

"It wasn't, but since there's no escape now, we didn't want to freak you out," I finish off, winching out the jib and walking over to the right of the steering console where Toxic is showing her how to hold the wheel.

"Oh, now I'm intrigued." She grips the curve of the wheel exactly where Toxic's hands were and her forearm flexes with the tension. She flashes an excited smile up at Toxic, who is hovering at her back.

"This is a double date, yeah?" I press on.

"Yeah?" She draws out the word like it's also a question.

"We were hoping you were—" I hesitate, and she interrupts.

"A little late in the day for shyness and euphemisms now, Tug. Come on, spit it out," she giggles.

"And, sugar, let's hope it doesn't come to that." Toxic grins, and Finn laughs loudly, though her cheeks couldn't be any redder if they were on fire.

"I'm not going to lie and say I'm not nervous, because I am. I've never done *anything* like this before. I think this situation is pretty unique. Honestly, there can't be many others who have." She flinches as she says the words, and I hate that I know why. I couldn't have predicted Marilyn would say what she did; still, I curse myself for taking her to the diner unprepared. That shadow of doubt wouldn't be there, if we had at least warned her. She shakes her head, clearly trying to push the image out of her head. *Good.* "I trust you all, and I wouldn't have agreed if I wasn't at the very least curious enough to try." She bites her lip, and although her reticence is there, it's hidden under her adorable modesty and hooded, sparkling eyes.

"I don't know what else is flashing through your head, sugar, but being with you is not to be compared with *anything* we've done before—*ever*," I state as a matter-of-fact.

"Light years apart, baby," Toxic confirms my sentiment. "And if you change your mind, whatever you want to do is fine with us. Honestly, Finn, if we can't make you *want* us both, then we don't deserve the pleasure."

I get a kick from the shiver going through her, which has nothing to do with the wind chill picking up. Her tongue peeps out to wet her dry lips, and her sweet tits rise ten to the dozen with her increased panting breaths. *Oh, yeah, we'll make her want us both.*

"You got the helm, sugar, so Toxic can grab a shower?" I ask, watching any residual color drain from her face.

"What? No!" she gasps, and her hands fly from the wheel. Toxic grabs them and puts them firmly back in place, before stepping away and quickly disappearing below deck.

"Relax, sugar. I'm here, and you're going in a straight line. It will be calm until we reach past the harbor wall, and I'll take it from there, if he's not back." She nods tentatively, and this half grimace freezes on her beautiful face. She's changed into some tiny, denim, cut-off shorts and a loose, wife-beater shirt with cut out sides and scoops low at the back. The top barely covers her black, string bikini that's tied around her neck with some beads. Her light-blonde hair looks almost white, reflecting the bright sun, absorbing the shine and magnifying it tenfold. She has it pulled up high in a twist, with wispy tendrils whipping around her face as the wind picks up.

Toxic returns, and I grab the shower next.

I'm back in time to help let the mainsail out, kick back and let this baby fly. Toxic has his hand either side of Finn on the wheel and steers us hard into the wind. The boat heels, and the angle is perfect, but it makes Finn scream and grip with white-knuckled terror to the wheel.

I'm winching the sails and making sure we can maintain this speed, or more, but keep casting a glance back at Finn. Her color may have drained again at the first tilt of the boat, but her grin is so fucking wide, I know she's enjoying the thrill. The spray from the waves we plow through drenches her and every squeal of delight and shocked cry makes my cock twitch and blood fire. *I can't wait to be the one pushing her to make those sounds.*

She relaxes after a while, enough to release her death grip on the wheel, and come and help me with tacking.

By lunchtime she looks like a natural, dipping under the boom and moving confidently from the bow to the stern, howling with laughter every time she gets drenched by a wave. After an hour or so, we lower the mainsail and drift into a secluded cove just north of La Jolla Cove. There are no other boats anchored in the bay surrounded by high sandstone cliffs. The place is peaceful and, above all, private.

Once I drop the anchor, Toxic starts to lay out the picnic lunch, and I hand Finn a couple of large towels. She's soaked through, and I know it's not just her attraction to us that has her all goose bumped and perky. Taking the towels, she walks off down the left gunnel to the bow and lays one of the towels flat on the deck. She peels her wet shorts down her toned, tanned legs, revealing the skimpiest bikini bottom known to man. A glance over to Toxic proves he's fixed on the same vision I am. *I need to cool off.*

"Do you want to take a dip before lunch?" I cough as I try to even out my voice. "We've got snorkeling equipment."

"Oh, yes, that would be great." She skips back over to me, bouncing excitedly on her toes.

"Okay, sugar. You're going to need to stop moving like that, if you want to do anything except fuck." My voice drops with sensual intent.

"Tug!" Toxic bites out, his gruff tone thick with warning

"What?" I lift my shoulders and hold up my palms in innocence. "She knows us well enough to know this situation isn't all about sex, but damn, Toxic, she has to know she's off-the-charts sexy as hell." I turn to Finn. "You know that right? It's not all about sex, but Toxic pointing my comment out like that makes me look like a douche, when I know for a fact his balls are just as blue as mine."

"Jesus, Tug." Toxic slaps his forehead and drags his hand slowly down his face.

Okay, tact might not be my thing, but I'm still speaking the truth.

Slapping her hand on my chest, she giggles, but I wasn't

joking. "Come on, sweetheart, this way." I adjust the stiffness in my shorts and see her catch my action.

"Oh, God, you were serious?" Her face screws up with disbelief.

"About the blue balls? Yeah, pretty damn serious," I confirm, watching her eyes flit to my hand-covered crotch.

"Please stop talking, Tug, before you put her off us completely. Just get in the water," Toxic admonishes with exasperation.

"Really? How could you not know that, Finn? We're trying not to be monsters here, but if we had our way, you wouldn't leave the bedroom. You're smoking-fucking-hot, sugar," I reiterate, shaking my head in confusion as her face draws a blank. She even casts a worried glance down her delectable body, and her arms creep across her middle, and a deep frown dims her light.

"Um…you said something about snorkeling?" Her voice is barely above a whisper as she changes the subject, and I look over to Toxic. *What the hell?* His confusion mirrors mine. It's like she's never been told how fucking sexy she is. Has never seen raw desire in front of her *because* of her. I don't know if Toxic is reading my mind, but I'm making it my mission to erase that self-doubt, starting today.

"Sure…we don't have fins that will fit you, but the mask and snorkel will be fine." I adjust the straps so it's a better fit to her size, and then I lower the ladder into the water. She climbs down and drifts out onto her back, treading water and swilling whirlpools around her, puffing at the change in temperature. The crystal-clear water does nothing to hide the fact that her nipples could cut glass.

I stand on the bow and dive in, surfacing flush to her body, and she gasps and turns against me. Her skin slick with suncream slides against mine, her nipples the only abrasive part of her body touching my chest. A loud, shrill whistle breaks my carnal thoughts.

"Hey, you forgot these," Toxic shouts, throwing my kit into the ocean. *Shit.* The snorkel may float but the rest sink right away. I twist round and dive, chasing the fins, and my mask, all the time mentally cursing my friend. By the time I have surfaced and managed to put everything on, Toxic already has his hand out, pulling Finn along and swimming off toward the rocks. I slice through the water and catch up, diving below them and turning upside down to wave, swimming beneath Finn for a moment. I can see her lips widen around the snorkel and, yes, that image did equate in my mind to her sucking down my cock. *I'm not making a great case for this being about more than sex, but, fuck, this girl is hot.*

After we spend an hour or so exploring the rocks off the cove, we make our way back to the boat. Toxic quickly prepares lunch, or more accurately empties out plastic boxes Charge had prepared: a fresh green salad, cooked chicken, olives, cheese, and some other antipasti Finn seems to love. Charge must be going soft; there was even a small, white baguette, and I know it's for Finn, because we haven't had bread in the house for years. *Damn that looks good.*

"You can have some if you'd like, Tug. Bread really isn't the devil food it's made out to be." Finn leans over to offer me a chunk of bread with a spread of soft cheese on it.

"Devil food?" I query, taking the food.

"Moment on the lips, Finn." She rolls her eyes, but it's like she's taking code.

"Sorry, I'm not following." I chomp down on the food, emitting an appreciative moan; it's been a while.

"Your fridge looks like a health farm. If you're anything like my ex wanting to eat white bread and pasta is akin to shooting heroin into your eyeballs." Her laughter is flat and short.

"We are nothing like your ex, sugar," I point out through clenched teeth, but soften my tone to clarify. "I thought you knew that by now. You can eat what you damn well like. We don't tend to eat bread because Pink has a gluten thing. Makes him shi—"

"Yes, I get the picture!" Finn interrupts with a slight gagging motion. "Oh, I thought because you were all so…" She waves her hand up and down, and in the general direction of our half-naked bodies. A shy smile creeps across her face.

"So?" We both ask, leaning forward with keen interest. She draws in a slow breath and her cheeks pink up.

"You're all really fit. I assumed you were crazy health freaks, and it would be only a matter of time before I'm squirrelling away tea cakes and crumpets." She laughs, but Toxic and I remain unamused.

"You don't get it, do you?" Toxic sits back, crossing his arms. I straighten but don't mirror his intimidating posture. I chip in, "We want you to be happy, Finn. That's all we want, and however you achieve it is fucking fine with us. One thing you never have to do is hide."

"I hate that this so hard for you to understand." Toxic drags his hand through his hair, sighing.

"Ten years of conditioning, guys." She shrugs lightly, trying to dismiss the dark cloud that has settled over Toxic and me; anxiety and tension radiate off of her in waves. *Damn that fucking guy.*

"Here, let me clear this up." She abruptly changes the subject and starts to stack the plates. Toxic takes them from her, and I raise my hand, halting her from touching anything else.

"No, we've got this," I confirm.

"What am I supposed to do?" Her face scrunches, and her bottom lip sticks out in the perfect pout.

"Relax," Toxic says at exactly the same time the word leaves my mouth. Giving a resigned nod, she flashes a sweet smile. Grabbing a bottle of beer, she walks off to the bow. It takes us no time at all to clear everything away. Having had her tight little body swimming around us, nigh on naked, for over an hour, we are both a little preoccupied, focused, and driven.

"Finn, sugar, we need to take this below deck." She has just lain down in the sun, stretching out in the rays and sighing is the absolute end. I look to Toxic and his carnal glare reflects my own desire. She flips onto her tummy to look at us. I'm shoulder to shoulder with Toxic, and we couldn't be more blatant if we both had our hard dicks in our hands. Her little tongue darts out, and her eyes widen. She jumps up to her knees, and I stifle a moan at her obvious eagerness. *She's so fucking perfect.* Toxic holds out his hand, and I step down into the galley.

Her bare feet hit the top step and I swoop her up, pulling her into my arms, my lips too needy to wait a second more. My mouth collides with her soft one, salty from the spray of the ocean. Sighing, she molds her body against mine. The floor shakes as Toxic jumps down behind her, and when he steps flush against her back, it causes her whole body to shiver. I break the kiss and grab her hand.

My voice raspy, I utter, "Cabin," and pull her to follow my long and rapid strides to the Skipper cabin. I open the door, tugging her inside and Toxic follows. Finn's smile is shy, sexy, and tempting, her soft, pouty lips tipped up at the corners. Toxic looks like the devil himself with a grin so wicked, I hate to think what mine looks like; it's a wonder she's not burning up from the incendiary glances we rake over her body.

"You're so damn beautiful, you know that?" I cup her cheek, pulling her toward my mouth again. Gasping at the force, she matches my urgency with the twists and turns of her demanding tongue. My cock feels like it's going to explode. I push my leg between hers and feel her tense against my rock-solid length.

"Shhh, sugar, we'll take care of you, okay?" I whisper against her lips. Her reaction isn't unexpected, but this won't be fun if she can't relax.

"He's not *that* big." Toxic rolls his eyes, and I chuckle.

"Hell, yes, I am, but this isn't about me." I brush my lips over hers, and she sucks in a little breath. "This is about making you feel fucking amazing. Okay, sugar?" I coax.

"Okay." She gives a tentative nod. We both have no intention of making her first proper threesome anything but out of this fucking world.

CHAPTER TWENTY-TWO

Finn

THIS IS IT, THEN? MY MIND RACES AS FAST AS MY HEART beats in my chest. I get a moment of peace when I feel four hands on my body, holding me to this point, this pivotal piece of time. I search myself and wonder if I should feel shame, regret, or guilt. I would never in a million years have dreamt that I would be lovingly cosseted between two hotter-than-Hades men in the Skipper cabin of a luxury sailing yacht. Not that the location has anything to do with it; we could be anywhere. I rack my brain and search my soul for any sign of those feelings I'm pretty sure Dave would throw in my face if he saw me now—if he knew. Even so, I try, and all I feel is wanted.

Strong hands guide me to the bed, sweeping my skin and leaving a blazing trail of tingles and desire coursing uncontrollably through my veins.

I run my hands down Tug's cut chest, through the mass of soft dark hair on his lower abdomen, and steady myself, holding his sturdy hips. Toxic maneuvers behind me, pressing his erection hard against my bottom as we all kneel on the bed. Toxic's mouth is on my neck as Tug's lips brush mine, his tongue sweeping out as I open my lips to grant him access. He needs no further invitation. One of his hands threads into my still damp hair, and he pulls me firmly into an urgent, demanding kiss. I can feel Toxic trail kisses across my shoulders and down my spine, his day-old stubble grazing the soft skin of my bottom as he playfully presses his mouth to take a bite of the round flesh. I shudder and moan into Tug's mouth. I feel the string on my bikini bottoms loosen and then fall away. I shiver and burn up at the same time, a riot of desire and emotions bombarding me, and I struggle to breathe through the reverent kisses.

Tug breaks our kiss and leaves me gasping; his arms surrounding my waist prevent me from melting into a molten puddle on the sheets. My heart pounds so loud, I'm sure they can hear it. Tug places a finger under my chin, his hazel eyes glowing with passion and promise, his smile tender.

"You okay, sugar?" His raspy voice is filled with so much concern and compassion, my heart skips a beat, and I take my hand from his hip to press it against the sudden surge of warmth.

"More than okay," I exhale with a soft whimper.

"Good, that's what we like to hear. Anytime you want us to stop just say so. Okay, Finn?"

Toxic shifts so he's more at my side than behind me, his eyes searching my face, looking for any telltale reticence he won't find. I want this *so bad*.

Tug steps off the bed and drops his shorts. I would be lying if I said my eyes weren't out on stalks, but I don't get time to voice any concerns about how the hell that's going to fit, because Toxic sweeps me onto my back and inches down my body, one playfully tortuous kiss at a time. Nestling between my legs and pushing them wide, he inhales loudly. I look down to catch his carnal gaze just before his tongue does this amazing swirling drag from my clit to my entrance. I throw my head back and scream. *Holy shit, that feels so good*! I try to clamp my legs shut, but his strong hold keeps them pinned to the bed, wide and open. I try inching away, because the onslaught is so intense, I can feel my toes twitch. He's relentless and divine, and I can't seem to get enough. My hips tilt, and I shamelessly grind against his mouth, even though with the next breath I try to clamber away. It's too much and not enough.

My head rests off the edge of the bed, and when I open my eyes, two thick thighs block my vision.

Tug is stroking his considerable length mere inches from my face, his large hand barely making contact around his girth, his dark gaze is fixed between my legs, but when my hand reaches for his leg, his eyes focus solely on me.

"Something you need, sugar?"

His voice is hoarse, and the roughness sends a shiver through my body. I lick my lips and smile, wide and welcoming, my fingertips squeezing harder on his thigh but barely making a dent on the steel-hard muscle. He steps closer, and one hand cups the back of my neck supporting the weight of my head, the other places the tip of his glistening cock against my eager open mouth. I think the angle helps, because he's massive, and I can drop my jaw really wide. My hand doesn't even come close to reaching round his thickness, but I use my other hand to help, and I think he likes that by the way his knees buckle when I suck him down, squeezing and working my hands to at least give him the impression I'm taking more in my mouth than would be physically possible—unless I had a flip-top head.

"Oh, fuck, Finn. Yes!" Tug chokes out as I swallow again and again, before I need to pull back for some air. His balls are tight just above me, and I switch my grip to hold and massage them as I pull and suck him deeper into my mouth. My jaw aches with the stretch, but the appreciative rumbles coming from his chest keep me going until I almost bite down with a surprising, sudden hit of unbelievable pleasure which crashes through me like a fucking tidal wave.

"Shit!" Tug pulls back just in time, as every muscle in my body spasms and contracts. Toxic has his devious tongue pressed hard against my clit and two fingers buried inside me, curled and pumping the very last ripple of my orgasm from my core. My legs are tense and locked around Toxic's head, and my fist is clamped tight around Tug's cock. Tug's hand is hovering over mine for his protection, judging by the concerned look on his face. My eyelids flutter open as I suck in some huge gulps of air and slide back onto the bed. "Thought you were going to bite my dick off, you came so hard." Tug exhales, and some color returns to his face.

"It wouldn't have been intentional." I grimace apologetically but snicker.

"Oh, well, that's all right, then." He climbs onto the bed, pulling me up and lifting me high so I'm straddling his waist. Toxic is kicking his own shorts off, his shit-eating grin still wet and glossy from my arousal. He crawls onto the bed, wrapping his arm around my waist, pulling me close and kissing me deep and slow. Tug eases me up onto my knees and positions his cock at my dripping, wet entrance. My eyes widen with panic at the first push, and Toxic deepens the kiss, cupping my cheek and murmuring sweet, sexy pleas as he helps me ease down. I sink lower but whimper and pull back from the kiss, placing my palm flat on Tug's solid, heaving chest, taking a much-needed moment.

"You're so fucking tight, sugar. Take me slow, okay? There's no rush." His strained voice almost makes me laugh out loud, but I worry what muscles would contract and where, if I did.

I'm not convinced he's right; however, I do know with his size, it feels fucking tight—fucking torture. I give a sharp nod and a tentative smile, and with that cue he rolls his hips, and I sink further down, my legs spreading a little wider, causing me to hold my breath a little longer. *Holy shit, he's going to split me in two.*

"Let that breath out, sugar, and kiss Toxic. Focus on him and just relax this sweet, tight, little body of yours. I've got you." His soft, encouraging words make my breath hitch. Before I do as he says, I push out the breath I was holding and will myself to relax. Toxic is kneeling beside me, his lips brush mine, and his sweet, minty breath washes over me. He pushes my long hair from my face and fists the length, hauling me in for a kiss, which will distract as much as devour me. My body relaxes with his ministrations, and inch by very careful inch my body slowly accepts Tug's massive cock—the human barge.

I take another moment when I have him fully inside me and sigh when he starts to roll his hips, which feels pretty amazing. His hands move from my hips to my breasts, and he wastes no time working my nipples into hard, aching points, which makes me frantic for more, not sure what *more* I'm yearning for, but I feel unbearably insatiable. Toxic stands on the bed and deftly slides his cock into my mouth, with no effort and a considerable amount of pleasure by the growl that escapes his throat and the way he drops his head back. I rest one hand on Tug's chest and the other on Toxic's tense thigh as he picks up pace, fucking my face. His thumb strokes my jaw and I look up to see deep, dark desire and a sexy curl of his lips, which makes my heart clench.

My tongue traces his length, and every time I swallow him to the back of my throat, I swear he gets bigger in my mouth.

"Shit, Finn!" he groans, and his hand moves from my cheek to my hair, his grip increasing as I pull him deeper. I'm ravenous and sucking him with a wildness I didn't know I possessed.

His deep growl fills the room as he fills my mouth and comes down my throat. His cock pulses in my mouth, and I lick him dry as he slowly pulls out. He drops to his knees and flops onto the bed, his hand resting on my thigh, as he sprawls out beside Tug and me. His dark tan glistens from the exertion and his cut chest rises and falls rapidly as he regains his senses. Tug pulls me against his body and rolls us so he's now above me and we are flush with Toxic. Tug starts to move his hips and I suck back a whimper.

Burying his head into my neck, he whispers, "You're so fucking perfect, Finn. How did we get so lucky?"

He kisses me below my ear and along my neck, and I ache to feel the bite, the draw of his mouth against my skin, but he keeps the contact light. Toxic is on my other side, kissing and nibbling, driving me higher with tender touches, while Tug pumps and pushes, chasing the high I can feel start to tingle at the tail end of my spine. I know he's being careful, steady and cautious, and I can see it's an effort from the pulsing vein in his neck and tension in his heavy brow.

"It's okay, Tug. You can let go. You won't break me," I gasp, but there's uncertainty in my tone.

"Ah, sugar, a little bit like you, I'd destroy you if I let go. I'm perfectly happy just being balls deep, baby. You feel fucking amazing, and I'd only end up feeling like shit if I hurt you."

"Oh, okay. You feel really good, too. I was just being polite. I don't think I could take any more." I let out a small breath of relief.

"Being polite?" He arches his dark brow, and his mouth turns up in a wry grin, clearly amused.

I snicker at the way he rolls his eyes and Toxic's incredulous expression and shake of his head. "I want to make you happy, too, you know. I want you all to be equally happy with your choice," I offer as way of explanation, and Tug's smile widens and dazzles before turning all kinds of erotic and sexy.

"Couldn't be happier, sweetheart. Right now, though, I'm going to make you come like a freight train." He pitches up onto his hands, his forearm muscles flex and the ink which spreads from his shoulder across his chest, dances beneath the stretch and pull of his muscles. His hips sink hard against mine, and I arch off the bed.

"Oh, God!" I cry out. Walking the finest edge of pain and pleasure is like standing at the gates of heaven while secretly praying for hell. In my heart it feels wrong, but I want it all just the same. He never increases his pace, depth or force; he rolls the pleasure around like it's a spinning coin, waiting to choose the right time to catch it before it falls. His grip on my body is the only indication he's close; it's tighter, firmer, and unrelenting. It's enough to trigger an explosion inside of me that goes off like the Fourth of July fireworks display.

Every nerve and fiber in my body sizzles with desire and need. My heart races, and blood rushing in my ears is making me dizzy with lust and so much sensation. It's mind-blowing and utterly intoxicating, crashing through my body. Their hold keeps me tethered, securing me to this place, and ultimately as I fall, floating and drifting from my high, their hold catches and cherishes me until I have no thoughts, no movements, just a deep and sated sense of happiness.

CHAPTER
TWENTY-THREE

Finn

"WHY ARE YOU FIDGETING?" TOXIC HOLDS MY hand as we walk toward an industrial-looking warehouse with a thick queue of people wrapped around the length of the building waiting to get in.

"I was sort of hoping I would get time for a shower," I grumble. I had packed a change of clothes because I knew we were going out this evening, but I wasn't anticipating an afternoon of wild sex and swimming in the sea. My hair is a riot of tangles, with a hint of dragged through a hedge backwards, and I'm sure I reek of sin.

"If you hadn't slipped into a coma, you would've had time for a shower, sugar. Besides, you look fucking stunning." Tug grins, draping a meaty arm across my shoulder.

"Still would've liked a shower. Look at my hair!" Tug's hand moves swiftly to my neck, and he attempts to thread his fingers into the mass of locks, the stiffness of the salt and general disarray making it impossible and completely proves my point.

"It looks sexy, Finn. Now stop whining. You didn't strike me as one of those high-maintenance girls," Tug goads.

"I think there's high-maintenance, and then there's meeting your friends for the first time smelling like sex and looking like I've been fucked six ways from Sunday." I feel the flush in my cheeks, and a smile forms at the delicious memory.

"You know you're even more sexy when you get all riled up," Tug chuckles, winking across at Toxic, who wisely flattens his lips in silence but grins wide.

"Gah!" I groan with exasperation, but I know it's nerves. I managed to have a hot towel wash so I really don't smell like sin.

The boys sailed back to the harbor while I was out for the count; however, they barely gave me any time to get ready, and patience is clearly not one of their virtues. I changed quickly into my lace cup, baby doll, white summer dress, which has a low V-cut front and tiny spaghetti straps and floats just above my knees in a swishy fabric, which is super cute. It's a little skimpy, but my worn, weathered, light-denim jacket covers most of the exposed skin. I have some tan, and suede gladiator wedges give me a little more height and dress it up a little. My hair, however, is a lost cause but I can always say it's a British, shabby-chic thing, if anyone asks.

Toxic gives our names to the fierce looking doorman, and we skip the whole queue and walk into a heaving bar. It's dark inside, as the high-level windows have been blacked out, and there's minimal artificial light except around the stage, which seems to have hundreds of spotlights focused on the empty set where the band will play later. Music is blaring from a wall of speakers dominating the far side of the room, but it's early and the dance floor is empty. Most tables are full, and, by the looks of it, food is still being served.

"They clear the tables before the band comes on," Tug shouts, and I nod in acknowledgment. I had wondered where all those people outside were going to go.

We reach a roped-off flight of stairs, and Toxic unclips it, ushering me up to the mezzanine. It's still noisy, but there's more room to breathe, and I don't think we will need to shout quite so loud to be heard. There's another bar up here and several long tables overlooking the stage. The one nearest to us is where I recognize two familiar faces in a sea of strangers. Pink stands the second he sees us, and his face brightens, his eyes crinkle with the widest smile, those delicious dimples and straight white teeth on display. Charge is sitting back with his arm resting on the back of an empty chair but leaning in to speak to a woman. She's not an ordinary woman; she's a drop dead gorgeous, stunning, might-just-make-you-swing-the-other-way kind of woman.

My heart stops. Her perfectly straight black hair is slicked back into a high, tight and immaculate ponytail. Her skin seems to glow with a shimmery, golden tan; it's absolutely flawless. Her plump, pouty lips are sucking down on a straw, making even my mouth water. I can just imagine what that front-row view to this goddess is doing to Charge. I feel sick and have obviously frozen to the spot, because Tug crashes into me, sending me flying forward and into a tray of tequila shots.

Skidding to my knees, I instinctively cover my head with my hands as sticky liquid and shot glasses rain down on me.

There's an unholy, loud roar of laughter that stops almost as instantly as it starts, though I'm too mortified to look up to see why. *Ground, swallow me now.* My skin is dripping wet, my dress is all but see-through with the amount of liquid it absorbed, and my knees sting like a motherfucker.

"Wow, you really do know how the make an entrance, angel."

Charge's deep timbre makes me jump. His hot breath is at my neck, and his eyes search mine. I try to force a smile, but it's weak, and I give up when my eyes pool with tears. I blink them away and snap with a painful memory.

"Unfortunately, it's not the first time I've been humiliated in a bar full of people." He doesn't say a word, but I feel his strong arms scoop under my knees, lifting me as if I weigh nothing and carry me away from the carnage and prying eyes. I feel like a sorry-ass mess and bury my head in his chest. Kicking open a door marked private, he places me carefully on the counter top. He walks back to lock the door, and I jump down, sucking back a sob when I stare at my sorry-looking reflection. Half of my hair is soaked and slicked to my face, my dress has more splashes than a dry cloth, and I think I actually sliced an artery, judging by the blood streaming down my left leg.

"Perfect," I mutter as I angrily twist the tap to get the hot water flowing. I yelp as I'm once more lifted and placed next to the sink.

"Stay put," Charge growls. His dark eyes make a quick inspection of the pathetic sight in front of him. "I'm going to get the first aid kit. Do not move from here, understand?" I nod at his demand, and he flashes a quick smile. I'm so embarrassed. I don't want to stay here. I just want to go home. I don't want to be remembered for this, and I really don't want to meet Miss Perfect, not like this—actually not ever. My heart drops, and a swell of sickness hits me that I might have to spend a night watching Charge look at someone else the way he just looked at me. I hate this; I hate any little hiccup, which cripples me with self-doubt and insecurity.

I straighten when I hear the door handle click, trying desperately hard to trample my anxiety into the ground. Or am I just plain jealous? That would at least be a *normal* reaction.

Returning with a small box with a big red cross on it, Charge sets about cleaning up my legs. The cut isn't as deep as I thought, but it won't stop bleeding all the same. I keep a wad of cotton wool pressed on it, while he does his best to clean up the tequila from my dress, hair and skin. I jump when I feel his tongue on my shoulder, and I tip my head to allow him the access to drag it all the way up my neck to my ear. I shiver when he pulls back, mourning his absence with a soft exhale.

"Hmm... you taste like salt and hard liquor. Not quite as sweet as you normally do, but just as sexy." His deeply sensual voice seems to drop an octave. His eyes darken, eyelids drop, and his impossibly long lashes frame an incendiary glare. Even so, I can't shake my residual self-image, which is looking like the very poor relation to Missy Fucking Universe he was cozying up to moments ago.

"Oh, yeah, I feel so sexy right now." I cross my arms, and my attempt at humor falls flat as my laughter dies in my mouth.

"You want me to prove how sexy you are?" He arches his brow high and confidently pulls a wolfish grin.

"No." I lean away from his draw, because I don't quite believe the conviction of my words and need the space.

"No?" He leans into my retreating body, closing the distance and then some. I swallow the thick lump in my throat and cough to clear it enough to speak.

"You know how on our dates you want to know it's just you who's turning me on?" I watch his eyes take in every detail of my face, curious and searching.

"Yes?" he responds.

"Same goes for me, Charge." I tip my chin defiantly even as my stomach tightens with knots and nausea.

"I'm not following you. You think this"—he spreads my legs, making my heart jump and all the air leave my lungs in a shocked gasp, and steps up, pulling my ass forward so his rock-hard erection scorches my panties and melts my core—"is for someone else?"

"I don't know, Charge. You tell me." My voice wavers, though I'm pleased I can speak at all, because my heart is thumping so damn hard, I can't hear myself think. The way he's staring into my eyes, into my soul, is utterly mesmerizing.

"No, angel, I'm going to show you," he growls.

His hands dive under my dress, and he roughly pulls my panties off, bunching them in his hand and pushing them into his pocket. Then his mouth is on me, his hands gripping my bottom, lifting me high and hard against his body. My legs wrap around his waist as his demanding tongue devours me, stealing my breath and shattering my sanity. Is this really happening?

Charge is always so in control, and at this moment, his eyes are feral, his breathing is ragged, and his touch is wild and wonderful. He crashes us against the only flat wall, and his lips draw back, his teeth raking my bottom lip, and a low, gruff grumble vibrates through his chest. When he bites down, I cry out. His eyes never leave mine, and I can barely breathe for their intensity. His damn gaze sears right through me, so raw, filled with so much emotion, desire, and passion. My heart blazes, and my blood is on fire. I feel like he has branded my soul.

I can feel him fumble with his zipper, and in an impressive, swift, and perfectly positioned lunge, he buries himself so deep I choke out a cry. I'm starved of oxygen, and my open mouth hangs open from lack of air.

"You're so fucking perfect," he groans against my lips, and I sigh with a smile, feeling a warmth I've never felt before, like being enveloped in the world's biggest blanket. His hips start to move, grind, and pump slowly in and out of my body. He feels so good—*so* damn good. My hands rest on either side of his face, holding him as much as he's holding me, rooted. I drop them to his shoulders and begin to travel down toward his chest. His reaction is instant, as with one hand he snatches both of mine and pulls them high above me, slamming them against the wall as he pulls back and starts to pound into me. I feel like I'm falling, and I need to hold on to him. His grip is not just firm and forceful; it's fucking painful.

"Charge, my wrists…you're hurting me," I pant out between his brutal but exquisite driving thrusts. He stops and looks up to his hand and then back to me. His face clouds with something I don't recognize, pain maybe but something unsettling, though he shakes it away, and it's gone so quickly I think it might have been in my head.

"Sorry, angel." He loosens his grip, but keeps my hands in place when I really wanted them free so I could run my fingers through his glossy, dark hair, grip his broad, built shoulders, and dive beneath his black, button-down shirt and touch his skin. My fingers twitch to feel his skin. My body aches for that too; skin-on-skin contact would be so damn perfect, but not right now, not in a public toilet.

He steps closer, as if he wants to be a part of me; he's so close, so deep, I can feel him everywhere. His gaze is too much, and I feel the explosion deep inside, a small rumble that flashes through my body like a wildfire, sizzling my nerves and rolling through me with wave after wave of pure, unashamed ecstasy. His mouth covers mine to stop the scream from escaping my lips, but my climax keeps pounding through my body with every pump of his hips. He keeps me soaring, prolonging this unbelievable orgasm, until with a deep grunt and sudden push of air from his mouth, he stills and comes inside me, so fucking deep, my eyes are trickling with tears.

"Angel, did I hurt you?" he asks with concern etched on his handsome face. I shake my head because I still need a moment before I can speak, but when I do, I can't stop the most enormous smile from spreading wide across my face.

"No! God, no. Ruined me? Yes. Hurt me? No." I suck in large, unladylike gulps of air, and my legs begin to tremble uncontrollably and only stop when Charge eases me onto my feet. "That was unexpected." I let out a nervous laugh as I notice Charge stiffen and his face change from relaxed and sated to stern.

"I didn't want to do that." His brow furrows, and he runs his hand round the back of his neck. I feel like I've taken a bullet to my chest.

"You didn't?" My voice catches, and I don't even try to hide the hurt his words caused.

"Fuck! No, that's not what I meant," he snaps, then softens his tone when he continues, his hand now cupping my cheek. "I didn't want our first time to be in a goddamn bathroom, but you looked so… I couldn't *not* touch you. You have no idea what you do to me, angel, but I'm sorry I lost control. I will make it up to you tomorrow. You deserve better than this, Finn. I'm truly sorry." His words soothe away the sting, and his pleading eyes obliterate any residual pain.

"You're forgiven." I lean up to kiss him on the tip of his nose, and he smiles with my playful gesture. "And you have nothing to make up for. Having someone who is unable to keep their hands off me is not only a first, but it has to be the sexiest fucking thing ever."

"Even if it means having sex in a bathroom?" He cocks his head in disbelief.

"Yes, because this wasn't just sex. This was phenomenal sex. There's a *big* difference." I hold out my hand for him to return my underwear. I can see his brows knit together as he weighs his options.

"This dress is way too white and way too short to go commando, unless you really want everyone to think I'm a—"

He growls his interruption.

"Do *not* finish that sentence." He hands over my panties, which I quickly slip on. "Not even as a joke."

I straighten my dress and check my reflection. I look a hot mess, just not quite for the same reason I came in here. My eyes meet his in the mirror.

"You know this encounter didn't really prove I got you hard." I scoop my hair up into a band, and turn to face him.

"I know, but until I can introduce you to Flick, it's the best I could do. I wasn't going to wait until tomorrow to prove how *very* fucking wrong you are." He takes my hand and leads me back out into the main room.

"Flick?" I place my hand on his chest to stop him. He twitches under my touch, and his eyes close. I don't know why, but he answers my question so it certainly wasn't that.

"The woman you jumped to all the wrong conclusions with earlier. I take it that's who you thought I was thinking about?" I drop my hand and avoid his gaze, fisting the hem of my dress with my now free hand.

"Maybe." I bite down on the inside of my cheek. I feel incredibly embarrassed, because I was so quick to assume the worst.

"Maybe, my ass. First off, she's a lesbian, and second, it's only *you*, for all of us. So how about we go over there so we can show off our girl." He beams the sexiest damn smile, but I glance nervously over to where he's about to lead me.

"You think it's a good idea? I mean with all of you, won't that look bad?" He steps closer, his arm a protective shield, calming my worry right away and making me feel safe.

"These are close friends, angel. They all know us, and there's no judgment. Trust me?" He dips so we are nose to nose, eye to eye, and a breath away from our lips touching.

"I do." I whisper.

I meet so many people I know I won't remember a single name, but I'm deeply ashamed of my judgment of Flick, who happens to be the sweetest woman on the planet. She takes me under her wing from the get-go, and gives as good as she gets when the jokes and teasing comments come flying her way. There must be a hundred people in our section alone, and they all seem to know each other really well. They've either all served, trained, or worked together in some fashion. By the time the band comes on, I'm relaxed and having a great time. Flick drags me to the front of the stage and we scream and dance like lifelong groupies. Throughout the night, each one of the boys dances with me, offers me a drink, or just hovers, in the case of Charge, attentive and watchful. No one gives us any trouble or comes close enough to be a pest, despite the throngs of mostly male revelers.

I motion to Flick I need a washroom break, and she follows me. We are chatting whilst we stand in line, and I get the feeling I'm being watched. At the end of the corridor stands a skinny blonde wearing a tight pink dress, which leaves little to the imagination, strappy gold heels, and a thick layer of make-up I can see from here, who is definitely giving me the stink eye.

"Flick, do you know that girl?" I nod. Flick turns and then snaps her head back to me, her soft features hard and troubled.

"That's Chloe." Flick searches my face for any reaction. Due to the alcohol, it takes a little while for the name to register.

"Chloe. Chloe? *The* Chloe who was me, before me?" I frown because even I don't understand what I mean. "The nearly-chosen Chloe. *That* Chloe?" I try to clarify.

"She wasn't nearly chosen, Finn. She's a manipulative bitch who blindsided them and fucked Charge over. But yes, that's the Chloe." Flick almost spits the name.

"If looks could kill, Flick…" I can't help but shiver.

"She's all mouth, and she'll be so damn jealous. I've seen the way the guys are with you, and they were *never* like that with her." Her encouraging smile is heartfelt, and I reciprocate until my cheeks ache.

"Really?"

"Oh, trust me, honey, they are smitten." She puts her slender arm over my shoulder and pulls me forward, aggressively kissing my cheek. "And I don't blame them."

"You're sweet, but they hardly know me." I love and hate that I do this to myself. I want so bad to believe it, but the realist in me fights the ideal every step of the way.

"I don't know about you, but I can get a good feel for someone pretty damn quick. How long does it really take to fall in love? I get that it can take years, but it can also be an instant wham type deal." She gives a light shrug and a knowing smile.

"I guess." A surge of warmth flows from my heart to every nerve in my body at her words.

The queue isn't moving fast enough for Flick, so she heads straight into the men's restroom. I'm British, so queuing is in my DNA, but I chuckle at her balls-out demeanor. When she exits the men's she waves at me with a smug expression as she disappears to join the others. All I can do is cross my legs and curse my reserved manners.

I emerge from the ladies' only to come face-to-face with a condescending scowl and the tightly pursed and perfectly pink-glossed lips of Chloe. She crosses her arms, pushing her ample breasts a little bit higher and right in my face. I go to step around her, politely saying, "Excuse me," as I do, but she blocks my path with a side step.

"Whore!" she spits out the word, loud and acidic. It stings and hits me like a slap to the face, but as shocked as I am, I won't let her see that. I let out a bored puff of air and arch my brow.

"Is that all you have? Because really, Chloe, we both answered the same advertisement, so that would, in fact, also make you a whore."

"I was *trying* to make them see the error of their damn, sinful ways. You...you're just a dirty whore." She points her finger in my face, her sharp nails too long to be real and only millimeters from my nose.

"Adding unimaginative adjectives is not helping your case, sweetheart, and judging by that frown, neither are my long words, so I'll make this really simple. You don't know me. You know nothing about me, and yet you think it's your duty to spout your opinion from your glass house, when, let's face it, we know we're *both* sinners in this scenario. I can only assume, again, because I don't know you, that you think this is okay because of some disjointed sense of self-righteousness and moral high ground, which is arbitrary at best." I slowly lower my hand on hers, moving her accusatory digit from my face before I continue. "Just because we don't conform to your perfect box of ideals, doesn't mean ours are any less valid." She scowls, and I can see the cogs turning, trying to cobble together some witty retort, but she's taking her sweet time, so I carry on. "If I have to be more like you to enter the pearly gates, then I'm more than happy to burn. The company will be more fun."

"You're disgusting," she splutters. I smile, thinking that perhaps she needed more time to think of something better than another dumb insult.

"That's flattering, but really, it's early days, and I'm just getting started." I give an exaggerated, playful wink that makes her jaw drop. *Just the effect I was hoping for.*

"You're going to burn in hell for what you're doing," she sneers down her nose, her venomous tone perfectly matches her glare.

"Chloe, sweetheart, I already burn. Every. Single. Time." I let out a sigh, and a slow sensual smile creeps across my face. "And let me tell you, if that's hell, it feels an awful lot like heaven." Her eyes widen, and she takes a step back.

"Chloe, I suggest you back the fuck down if you don't want

to be completely ostracized from the group." Flick is at my back. I don't know how long she's been standing there, or how much she heard, but I'm grateful when her hand slips into mine and gives me a squeeze. My chin might be high, but my stomach hit the floor when she threw her first insult. My strength is seeping out of me with every strained breath, but I won't break in front of her. I have no intention of making her day, when she's ruined my fucking night.

CHAPTER
TWENTY-FOUR

Charge

△

I KNOCK ON FINN'S DOOR AS A TOKEN COURTESY, BECAUSE I don't wait for her to answer before I walk in. I left her sleeping when I woke in her bed in the early hours. I know she had a long day yesterday. But today is my day, my second date, and although she wasn't a hundred percent healthy for our first date, it was still good enough to count. No, that's underselling it on a biblical scale. Just because we didn't fuck, it was still the best day I've had in a long, *long* time. We spent the whole day talking about nothing and everything as I tended to her skin when she couldn't concentrate for the itching, but the best damn thing ever, was making her come all over my tongue when I wanted to distract her and hear her moan. Something I plan on doing several times over the day and into the evening. I too have a busy day planned. *I have a lot to make up for.*

It's not that last night wasn't fucking amazing. I knew she'd feel like heaven wrapped around my cock, the way her sweet, sexy body molded to mine. Still, I curse myself for losing it like I did. I couldn't help myself. From the moment she stood at the top of those stairs, all wide-eyed and fearful, looking like a fucking goddess, I knew the night was going to be fucking torture. My chest pinched so tight, I had to turn away, or I would have been up and over there, crowding in on her so no other fucker could get a look in. It took everything to hold back, trying to take in a single fucking word Flick was telling me. Then Finn crash-landed. She felt so timid in my arms when I picked her up. Her face was burning up for all the wrong reasons, and I had to make it stop. I had to make her forget whatever flashback she'd had that brought so much pain and clearly had little to do with her tumble.

She looked like a goddamn angel in my arms—my angel. The moment my lips touched her skin I couldn't get enough, couldn't stop.

Today will be different. Today she'll understand exactly what *my way* entails, and I have to regain my control.

I pull the curtains back and smile when she curls into a tight, supposedly impenetrable ball, moaning and throwing in a colorful curse word or two she fails to muffle with the pillow pressed against her face.

"I let you sleep in, Finn, but it's time to get up now!" I lay out the clothes I have chosen on the bed, along with some lube and her first surprise of the day.

"Mmm, what time is it?" she grumbles.

I ignore her question. "I have something I would like you to wear," I announce, my tone brusque, and my request clearly piques her interest. Whipping back the covers, she sits upright.

Blinking rapidly against the bright sunlight illuminating her like the angel she is, all soft-focus filter and glowing.

"You do?" she beams.

"Yes." I stand at the end of the bed and block the beam of light from hitting her, so she doesn't have to shield her eyes and can focus on my gift. She shuffles down the bed, keeping the sheet against her chest. My mouth waters because I know damn well she's wearing the skimpiest silk top and French panties under that cover. Her lips pull up into a brilliant smile when she recognizes my white dress shirt, though she quickly loses her gorgeous, flushed coloring when she spots the silver butt plug.

"You want me to wear this?" Her hand lays flat on the shirt, her fingertips touching the plug.

"I do," I reply, keeping my tone level, my expression impassive.

"Your shirt and…" She leaves the sentence unfinished, and I quirk an eyebrow high. "This seems a little bigger than last time?" She picks up the shiny plug and rolls it in her palm. My cock twitches, and my balls ache like a motherfucker.

"For good reason," I clarify.

"What reason?"

"So many questions, angel." I shake my head slightly and let out a low, soft chuckle. "Let me just say, I'm looking forward very much to being your first, and this will help." Her eyes widen with understanding, but her lids are heavy, too, and her tongue darts out to wet her dry lips.

Her swallows are a comically loud sound, which makes her nose scrunch up with embarrassment. I place my finger under her chin when she drops her head.

"I want to make you scream but only in a good way, understand?" She nods her understanding, and I know she's nervous. It's written all over her face, but she's also pushing her own boundaries, and that makes me so fucking hard. "Good girl.

Now, get dressed, we'll have some breakfast, and then I will begin your training."

"My arse, you mean?" She worries the plug between her hands, her eyes searching mine though I have no intention of revealing all my plans. *Where would be the fun in that?*

"Among other things." My face matches my inscrutable tone.

I hear her soft footsteps pad down the stairs and watch as she pokes her head tentatively around the door.

"Pink is at the stables, and Tug and Toxic have left already, angel. You're quite safe." I chuckle when she breathes out a huge sigh.

"I don't know why I'm hiding," she snickers, skipping lightly across the bare oak floor as if it's cold. "It's not like they haven't seen me naked." She blushes from her roots to her tips, and I find that completely fucking adorable. She also rushes her words when she's nervous, which she clearly is because she doesn't draw breath. "I mean they've all seen *all* of me, but I feel exposed. I know that sounds strange, but I guess it isn't really when you think about it. The human body is sexier with clothes, I think. Well, some clothes, but even with some, a person can certainly feel more vulnerable like I do right now. You didn't leave me any panties or a bra!" She cups her perfect breasts, too late to hide her arousal.

"Didn't I?" I reply deadpan, pulling an expression of mock confusion, which makes her smile flash wide and bright, and she lets out another nervous laugh.

"Hmm… Okay, Charge. So what's the plan? Not that I have done anything like this before, but I've read books. What are we talking exactly? Do you have a dungeon with a St. Andrew's Cross and a spanking bench? Am I going to be clamped and pin-wheeled? Or is it more red room of pain?"

My fixed expression cracks, and I bark out a laugh. Her list has made her face turn the darkest hue of red, and if I didn't know better, I would think she was about to hemorrhage.

"I don't have a dungeon. I don't need one," I reply, drawing in a slow breath. My eyes fix on her, and I make sure there's no longer any trace of humor, which might lead to misunderstanding. I level my gaze on her, and she holds it with a mix of strength and curiosity. "Anything we do, we do because *I* want to bring you pleasure the likes of which you have never experienced before. I want to make you come, screaming my name so fucking loud I will hear it in my dreams."

"Okay." She exhales, and her whole body shivers.

"Good. Now, do you have the plug?" I inquire and she thrusts her arm out, the plug resting flat in her outstretched hand.

"And I brought the lube too." She holds out her other hand, her expression pleased and hungry for approval. *Perfect.*

"Good girl, but I wonder whether we'll need it." I drop my tone to a deeply dominant timbre and watch her pupils dilate and her breath hitch. I step around the kitchen island and tower above her tiny frame. I take the plug from her hand and place the lube on the countertop. With one finger I motion for her to turn, which she does, very, *very* slowly. Her chest freezes on a deep rise where she's holding her breath, but she squeaks and expels all the air when I place my hand firmly on her lower back and exert enough pressure to tip her forward. She bends at her hips, and my cock swells so much the ache is almost unbearable. I fight the urge to grind some of that pressure away between her ass cheeks. The curve of her backside sweeps to her long legs, which are taut and defined from the stretch.

Just before she reaches the point of no return, she blurts out,

"We're in the kitchen!" Her pitched tone is filled with panic and potential mortification. My smile widens, thankful she can't see my amusement.

"I don't share, Finn," I confirm.

"Yes, but—"

I interrupt her with a light slap on the ass. She stills, tensing, her cheeks and her skin prickle with an instant pattern of gooseflesh.

"I…" I grit out though a clench jaw, deadly serious, emphasizing each word. I press a little more weight on her back, and she drops her head to her knees. "Don't." I place the tip of the plug against her clit, and her legs clench, but she holds her position perfectly. "Share." As I finish my last word, I sweep the tip along her slickness and dip it into her dripping entrance.

"Mmm…" she moans, tilting her hips for more. I swirl the plug and sink it in a little farther, gathering all her essence. Her arousal is dripping onto my fingers, and I can almost taste her sweetness. I gently stroke the toy along her glistening flesh, repeating the movement several times before coming to rest, with crystal-clear intent, at my desired destination. She lets out a forceful breath, and I can see she's trying to relax, her fingers wiggling with agitation against her legs where she's holding for stability. My free hand sweeps and soothes as it moves over her ass cheeks. She has the softest fucking skin next to a newborn baby, but she tenses against my touch.

"Relax, angel." Her tension releases at my soft command, but the tight ring of muscles around her rosette isn't so cooperative. I ease the plug against the tight band, and the muscle resists every bit of gentle pressure—but then this plug is bigger than the last one. It *has* to be. "Bare down, angel. Let out that breath you're holding and push back onto me," I groan, closing my eyes on the wave of pleasure washing over me when she does exactly as I command. Her legs may shudder, but I sink the plug smoothly into her ass.

I help her stand up and have to bite back a laugh when her brows shoot up and her mouth drops open at the new and startling sensations assaulting her body.

"Comfortable?" I ask, still holding her steady. She takes a

moment but gives a cautious nod and an even more tentative smile, as if even moving those muscles is a cause for concern.

"How long do I have to have this…wear this…keep it…you know?" She stumbles for the appropriate words, which is too darn cute, given the last shared five minutes.

"In your ass?" I take her hand and motion for her to sit on one of the kitchen stools.

"Yes…that. How long?" She eases up, and I walk around to carry on preparing breakfast.

"I think today should be fine." Placing the pan on the heat, I nearly catch my hand on the flame when she cries out.

"All day! Oh, oh, *oh!*" She hovers back up off the stool, having obviously frightened herself sitting down a little too hard.

"Problem?" I arch a curious brow but keep my smile to a minimum curl.

"Other than a huge plug in my arse? Nope," she quips, and her eyes narrow and aim their humorless glare in my direction.

"It's not huge…*I'm huge.*" I flash a wicked grin and chuckle at her pouty lips and furrowed brow. "Now, what would you like for breakfast?"

"Apart from a cushion, you mean? Pancakes would be good." She seems to check her attitude halfway through her retort, but even her slight grumble leaves an unpleasant taste, and I know just the thing to take it away. I switch the heat back off, walk to her, and lift her in my arms. She's quick to wrap her toned, luscious legs around me, but I can feel her tummy tighten, and she puffs out little steadying breaths with every step I take. I carry her over to the sofa.

"Hold on to the back of the sofa. If you let go, I stop, understand?" My voices sounds raspy and urgent.

"What are you doing?" Her cheeks flush, and the sexiest damn smile splits her face, but her eyes are wide and hold a trace of discomfort. *Even a trace is too much.*

"Making you appreciate just how good this can feel." I push her legs up her body until she's almost doubled over, her sexy, round ass exposed and perfect. The gem of the plug is soaking wet from her dripping pussy, and she couldn't be more open if I had the spreader bar at maximum extension. "Hold the sofa, Finn," I grit out. My temper is frayed because once again I'm breaking my own protocol, but dammit, I can't stop. She's intoxicating, all-consuming, and today she's completely mine.

CHAPTER TWENTY-FIVE

Finn

"**T**HAT WAS *SO* GOOD," I MOAN, RUBBING MY TUMMY, which is now full to bursting.

"You did seem to enjoy it. Oh, you mean the pancakes." He tilts his head, placing his hand in the center of his broad, built chest. "I'm hurt."

"Really? Because you seemed pretty bloody pleased with yourself earlier, when I screamed your name so loud, I lost my voice for a good five minutes," I quip, as a warm glow spreads through me when his wicked smile morphs into something almost shy.

We clear away the breakfast mess, and I sip my cappuccino, shifting from one arse cheek to the other. Charge was relentless in the pleasure-giving department, but since the tingles and euphoria have ebbed, I'm still acutely aware I have a piece of stainless steel in my butt.

"Do you have an elegant evening dress you can wear?" Charge's question stops me mid-sip, foam resting on my top lip. I swipe my tongue over it, and think through the mountain of clothes I packed, furrowing my brow with the effort.

"How elegant are we talking? I have a few cocktail dresses but nothing long, if that's what you mean. I didn't think to pack the ball gowns." I snort at my joke; Charge is unimpressed.

"That will alter my plans slightly, but it's still doable. Come on, you need to get dressed," he clips his retort, more to himself by his impassive expression. His mind is clearly racing ahead of the information he has shared with me.

"What's doable? What plans?" I jump up and wince, but race to catch him as he strides out of the kitchen, like he's on a mission. "You mean, I get to put more clothes on, other than just your shirt? Do I get panties and a bra?" I tease.

"Reluctantly, yes." His eyes narrow, but darken too, as they rake slowly from my bare feet to my hooded eyes. He stops moving at the bottom of the stairs. Turning, he steps up to me, so close I have to tip my head back to keep the searing eye contact. "Maybe not the panties and wear a dress." His demand is gruff and curt. I raise my brow at his tone, and he holds my gaze for a long, heated second. "It would give me great pleasure if you don't mind."

I bite my lips tight to stop the smirk I feel pulling at my mouth. I think this is his way of asking and saying please, while trying to remain all dominant and not coming off as a complete arsehole. *Nice save.*

A ten-minute turnaround, and we are sitting in Charge's truck, kicking up a dust trail and heading away from the farm to God knows where. I wear a knee-length, pale-blue summer dress, which hangs from one shoulder and is made up of masses of floaty material, cinched at the waist with a wide, tan belt, which matches my satchel and sandals. I brought my denim jacket, too, though it's too hot to wear it at the moment, even with the wind howling through the open windows. My hair is braided down one side, but with the breeze whipping like a tornado inside the cab I will need to retame the beast once we stop moving.

We pull up another dirt track about a ten minute drive from the farm and park outside a large, industrial hangar. Charge leaps from the cab and briskly walks to my door before I get the chance to open it. He holds my hand as I jump down and takes my bag from me, pulling me against his side for a big warm hug. I nestle into his strong hold as we walk around the building to the far side. My step falters.

"It's a helicopter," I exclaim.

"Smart and beautiful, we really did hit the jackpot," he teases, and I respond with a narrow-eyed stare.

"Funny," I quip. "I meant, shit, it's a helicopter. I've never been in one." I wave my hand at the sleek, shiny, black machine, with imposing and unnervingly-thin blades.

"Another first today. Aren't I the lucky one?" Charge wiggles his thick eyebrows and flashes a killer bright smile, all wicked and sparkling white teeth.

"You can fly this?" I hesitate, but I don't resist when he tugs me closer to the bird that shouldn't be able to fly.

"I'm a pilot," he replies flatly.

"I thought you flew planes?" I argue. My heart rate just kicked up a gear and is affecting the pitch of my voice; even I can hear my concern.

"I do. Fighter planes, but I learned to fly this as a hobby. They're a lot of fun. Come on." His enthusiasm and excitement are infectious, and I return his bright smile while my stomach flutters with fear. There's a reason I've never been in one; they have no wings. My knowledge of flight begins and ends with the fact that the only things which *should* be able to fly have wings. He straps me into my seat and adjusts the headphones so they are a snug fit. I can feel the color drain from my face, and now I'm challenging the wisdom of eating all those pancakes as my stomach rolls ominously.

"Trust me?" he mouths, his voice muffled by the cans on my ears.

"Always." I force a smile, which he crushes from my lips with a shockingly breathtaking kiss. *He's really good at distracting me.*

We start to hover and every muscle in my body tenses, making an odd and pleasant effect emanate from deep inside. I glance over and see a telltale knowing and wolfish grin tip his lush soft lips. I shake my head, because smugness is so unbecoming. Though speaking of coming...ten minutes into the flight and every dip and swerve, I feel deep inside. The scenery is amazing; ragged cliff tops with sporadic palatial properties, the wild ocean crashing onto deserted stretches of miles and miles of soft, white, sandy beaches, and in the distance, the cluttered colors of a dense city. I try to take it all in, fighting the building ache, because this is thrilling in every sense, but equally, I can't wait to land. His deep voice crackles in my headphones.

"That's Hollywood right there. You'll see the sign any minute."

"Really?" I twist and turn, my eyes scouring the horizon.

"And the Grand Canyon?" I crane my neck left and right looking for more. The cityscape isn't nearly as enticing as a natural wonder.

"We're about a two-hour flight from that, angel." He grins.

"Oh, yes, of course. Geography isn't my specialty." I let out a light laugh and shrug.

"I'll take you. The guys like hiking there, so we could make a weekend of it."

"That would be amazing." I beam, but quickly turn back to

press my nose against the door window and ask again, "Where are we going?"

"Beverly Hills—dress shopping." I bite my lip into a thin line and my hands grip together nervously. Geography may not be my thing but I do know Beverly Hills. I also know my hairdresser's salary is no match for couture and premium brand shopping. "My treat." His large hand leaves the stick for a moment to cover my clasped fingers, squeezing some comfort and reading my mind. I'm not sure I feel much better, but I appreciate the gesture. I have always hated charity, especially since, as a child I had no choice but to accept it.

Charge lands the helicopter on the top of a swish apartment building, and we spend the next two hours visiting some of the most expensive boutiques I have ever had the misfortune to feel both awkward and embarrassed in. I shake my head at the gorgeous, silver, floor-length Amanda Wakeley gown, and Charge's eyes narrow; it's the fifteenth dress I have rejected for no good reason and for my *own* best reason.

"Right." Charge replaces the gown and, ignoring the assistant with her next selection, he grabs my hand and hauls me out of the shop. Striding down the street, I have to jog to keep up, and now I feel like complete shit. Here he is, giving me my very own *Pretty Woman* experience, and I must be coming across as the ultimate brat—an ungrateful brat at that. We enter the first restaurant and he asks for a private table. An uncomfortable silence falls after we sit down, and I wish I could have a redo. He doesn't deserve this shit—*my shit.* I don't know how I can make this right. Even if I explain, I doubt I will make much sense. Not to someone like him. His childhood was charmed, struck by tragedy but still a world away from mine. How could he possibly understand? And my biggest fear? What's actually worse than revealing all my ugly? Is the thought that after I tell him, he will look at me *that* way. Doubt will rear its insidious head. I don't want to give him a reason to ask himself why I wasn't wanted.

We place our orders, though food is the last thing on my mind.

"I'm sorry." My hands in my lap are sweaty with my fingers twisted together.

"I can see that," he clips, his tone flat, but he looks more upset than angry.

"I just…" I drop my head. Even as I rehearse the words, they sound trite.

"Yes?" he pushes, and I draw in a deep and calming breath. He deserves more than this, but I'm not sure I can give him what his deep, dark eyes are imploring.

"I can't afford to shop here, Charge." I tip my chin, because I'm not ashamed, but I am out of my depth.

"I said this was my treat. I didn't bring you here to spend your money, Finn."

I sigh, his soft-spoken response completely disarming me.

"I don't like charity," I say, but the words burn my throat as the years of unwelcome memories bombard me.

"I'm not offering charity. I'm buying my girlfriend an outfit, because we have a premier to attend tonight, and I want her to feel comfortable. You could turn up in sweat pants and a hoodie and still be the most stunning woman on the red carpet, but that would create another entrance situation I don't think you would appreciate." His warm smile softens the sting of the reminder of my utter embarrassment last night.

"That's very sweet, but I would prefer to buy my own clothes, Charge." I twist the napkin in my hand, and he places his heavy hand over mine. He loosens my death grip and interlocks his fingers with mine, before looking into my eyes with his searching gaze.

"Why?" And here it is, his serious, deep frown, and piercing-dark eyes bore through me. I slowly draw in a deep breath.

I really don't want secrets, but some things are just so hard to share. I have no idea how much I'm going to download so I just open my mouth and pray my filter kicks in before I ruin everything.

"When my grandmother reluctantly took me in, she wouldn't spend her money on me. She got some benefits from the state, but she had her own money, too, and the money from the Government was supposed to be for me. It wasn't much; still, it never came my way. Anyway, she had friends who would come round and she would make a big show of how benevolent she was, providing me with a roof and food. Her friends would bring sacks of clothes, and she would make me go through the bags in front of them and pick out what I wanted. They were always awful, old lady clothes, but I didn't have a choice. I hated it. *God, I hated it.* It was bad at primary school but it got so much worse when I hit my teens. I would save every penny I made doing odd jobs and go to the local charity shops, just so I could buy my own clothes. I still got ripped into at school for looking like a charity case, but that's what I was." I press one hand to my burning cheek and feel the trickle of a tear. His hand covers mine, and I lean into his hold, his thumb catching the drop.

"This isn't the same, angel. Not by a long fucking way." He shakes his head, and his handsome features are shaded with darkness.

"I know." I suck in a stuttered breath, as a riot of emotion threatens to turn that trickle into a torrent, which I really don't want. *The memory isn't worth my tears.*

"You said reluctantly. Your grandmother didn't want you?" His soft words still slice open a lifelong, weeping wound, and I fold with the unbearable pain.

"I'm sorry, I didn't mean to upset you. I'm just trying to understand." He shifts in his chair, pushing to get closer, but the stuffy seating arrangement makes it impossible. He stands, and in one swift move has me in his arms, sits back down, and cradles me like I'm the most precious thing on the planet. I look up as he gazes down.

"I know. I do, but I can't." I suck back the building sobs, biting and swallowing down the bile and sorrow. When I speak again, it's through gritted teeth and a tense jaw. "No, my grandmother didn't want me, and she wasn't the only one." That's all I can give him, and I know from the look in his eyes it isn't enough—nowhere near enough. I close my eyes. The memories come thick and fast, as, one more time, I relive and endure every single, hateful word as if it's *real time,* and I'm helpless to save my little, five-year-old heart from shattering.

"I'm sorry, Finn." His deep soothing voice washes over me on a sweet, whispered breath.

"Yeah, me, too. But hey, what doesn't kill you makes you stronger, right?" I physically shake myself, and as I have always done, I brush it off and brave it out.

"Right." His brow knits together, his tone not remotely swayed by my sudden switch.

"So premier. You mean a film premier?" I power through the treacle of unanswered questions, ignoring the plea for more in his eyes. I have to ignore it, and I'm so damn grateful, regardless of his disquiet, he has let me change the subject.

"I do. We have a new film out, and tonight is the red carpet deal. I don't normally attend, as it really isn't my thing; however, I thought you might like a night of glitz and glamour." He tucks some loose hair away from my face and cups my cheeks, planting a small kiss on my lips when realization that I'm not able to give him any more finally sinks in. He helps me up, and I return to my seat.

"I would like that!" My genuine excitement makes him smile, and I sigh with relief that the moment has passed. *My mouth-to-brain-to-heart filter is intact.*

"I'll be able to introduce you to the stars," he boasts, and I sniff out a derisive laugh. I have met stars, cut their hair, massaged their scalps and their egos.

"Oh, I'm good, thanks. Unless they shit gold, they are just people, after all. They put their trousers on one leg at a time just like the rest of us." He barks out a belly laugh, and I smile at the happy sound. It suits him; his whole face seems to lighten. He always seems to hold a seriousness, but now that it's gone, even briefly, I can see the difference. *Utterly heart-stealing*.

We enjoy the light lunch, and I have a few glasses of wine, which makes the afternoon much more relaxed. I pick a stunning black Gucci floor-length, halter-neck dress; it's backless, with a scoop so low, the no-panty request is a must. I pick out some plain shoes, but Charge bulldozes over my decision and insists on some classic, black-patent Louboutin stilettos. *I don't put up much of a fight!*

We even fooled around in one of the changing rooms, before Charge warned me he will fuck me where I stand if we carried on. The gasp from the assistant just outside the curtain was like an ice bucket challenge, and we ended the afternoon *copping a squat* in the private garden next to the low-rise apartment block where Charge parked the helicopter.

"Shouldn't we be getting home?" I sigh as his hand creeps up my thigh to the very apex, and his fingers stroke languidly along my folds. He seems especially pleased that I have obeyed the no panty request—or was it a demand?

"Hmm?" He isn't listening, and I snicker. I'm sitting across his lap, and the ample material of my dress is thankfully hiding his forearm. His hooded eyes move down as I look up.

"Unless you want me to change in some toilet, and you intend on going in jeans and that sexy black tee, we'll need to go home." I roll my eyes at having to state the bloody obvious.

"My apartment's just up there. I thought that might be more convenient." I sit up and clamp my thighs, trapping his hand.

"You're kidding, right?" I crane my neck to look around his wide and imposing frame to the building directly behind us.

"Why would I? I have an apartment here." He nods over his shoulder to where my line of sight is fixed.

"The others weren't kidding when they said you were loaded then?" The block of pristine-white apartments looks like something from a movie set, immaculate and not quite real, or lived in. The design is a pastiche of Art Deco with crisp lines and elegant detailing on the balconies. The entrance, though, is ultra-modern, with floor-to-ceiling glass, and even from here I can see into the pure white marble reception area with a concierge desk and security guard. I let out a low whistle. I can't imagine how much it costs to have a place here.

"They weren't." His frown deepens like the whole notion makes him hugely uncomfortable.

"It's okay. I'm not interested in your money, Charge. I'm interested in how many ways you can make me scream." I wrinkle my nose and reach up to kiss his downturned lips.

"Oh, good. Because we haven't even begun to explore the pleasure of *pain*." The way his tone drops an octave on the last word sends a sizzle of electricity racing up my spine. I shiver in his arms, and his smile widens. I love that my reactions please him, not that I can control them, because they're innate and I really can't help it.

"I thought that's why I have this little plug inside me, so as not to experience pain." I arch my brow quizzically. His impossibly dark eyes turn liquid, swirling with promise and intent.

"That's true." He sinks two fingers inside me and the surprise escapes my mouth in a suppressed cry. He croons, dipping his head so his wicked, warm breath scorches my skin and makes my heart flutter and my breath catch. "I don't want your first time with anal to be anything other than *pleasant*." His voice drops to a low rumble I can feel in my toes. "I'm talking other forms of pain." He ripples his fingers inside me, pumping in and out, curling and twisting slowly. My whole body ignites—thrums. The way the salacious words drip from his sensual lips makes me whimper.

"I like the sound of that," I mutter. My heart rate kicks up a gear, already beating a strong staccato, and the hairs on my necks spike.

"Good girl." His soft, full lips cover mine, and I lose myself in his dreamy, dexterous tongue, which engages mine in a delicious duel. His fingers curve and press down on the sweet spot inside me, causing me to both melt and explode. I bury my head in his neck as a waves of pleasure and embarrassment creep up my neck and settle on my face like a beacon. I'm a breathless, gasping, trembling wreck in his arms when he releases me. "But that will have to do for now." He taps my nose, and I sag as my bones buckle with disappointment. *I know he was just getting started.*

CHAPTER TWENTY-SIX

Charge

△

S HE GRIPS MY HAND SO TIGHT WHEN SHE TAKES HER FIRST step on the red carpet, I chuckle and then mock groan as if in pain.

"Ease up there, Iron Man. I'm going to need that hand to fly us back tonight," I tease.

"Sorry, I really don't want to fall flat on my arse in front of the world's press." She tries to flash a smile, but I can see the panic in her eyes, and even the tiny curl of her lips looks like a huge effort.

"I would never let you fall, angel." I dip my head so I can meet her worried gaze. She needs to see me and, I hope, understand I don't just mean tonight. I wrap my arm around her waist, and we walk the long, red carpet. Each tentative step she takes seems to get easier as she finally starts to trust my secure embrace. A long line of golden rope separates an army of suited photographers and news crews that line the walkway from the curb to the main entrance of the movie theatre. The flashing lights and volume of cheering from the crowd gathered just beyond the rope and barricades, can be unnerving, and I sense Finn's reticence, so I pull her in tighter to my side. In fairness we slip past almost unobserved; there are much bigger fish to catch than a silent partner in a major Hollywood production company, although Finn certainly could give any leading lady and Goddess of the Silver screen a run for her money.

I get accosted by a few reporters. I'm polite but brief, responding with a very firm, "No, I will not be leaving the Navy anytime soon to join Donald's production company."

Once we reach the door, I notice Finn exhale a huge a sigh of relief.

"Will your guardian be here tonight?" she asks. Her eyes are wide, though not with wonder at the glitz and spectacle, but for me, gazing and searching my face as if we are the only two people in the room. She's utterly mesmerizing, and for the first time, I doubt myself and my choice of date location. *We don't need all this.* I also don't get the chance to answer her question.

"Charge, what the hell?" A loud, booming voice from across the foyer makes me both grin with pleasure and roll my eyes.

I lean down to whisper, "He's here. Brace yourself." It's not necessary; I just want to be closer. I brush my lips just below her ear, and her whole body shivers. *Perfect.*

I turn and spot my guardian, Donald, a round man barreling through the gathered VIPs. The crowd parts like the Red Sea at his request. He's almost as wide as he's short, with no hair to speak of, but with a very broad, warm, genuine smile. He barely nods at me before focusing his attention on Finn, who presses her body just a little bit closer to mine. I continue to chuckle as her evasion tactic is steamrolled, and Donald manhandles her into a personal-space-invading, crushing hug, and a very show-biz kiss on both cheeks. He releases her and pushes her to arm's length. It's only because I know he's utterly harmless that I allow him to touch her at all.

"You must be Finn. You know, he said nothing about your beauty." Donald tsks and shakes his head with his mock reprimand.

"Donald." I say his name with a warning tone that sounds much more like a threat. *Good.*

"I'm lying. He told me you were exquisite, and he wasn't lying." He waves off my scowl, and I scoff.

"Like I would say 'exquisite' any day of the week, but I certainly mentioned how goddamn beautiful you are." I pull her back tight to my side and out of Donald's overeager embrace.

"It's very nice to meet you." Finn looks to me for guidance, but before I can help her out, I'm interrupted.

"Call me Don, and the pleasure is all mine." He takes her hand once more and kisses the back of it, but there's a glint in his eyes, which is more rogue than chivalrous. "I can't believe you're here. I can't count the number of invitations to these events you have turned down, but at least I can understand why you came this time." He holds Finn's arm out, appraising the vision. She's *my* girl. Her pink cheeks darken under his scrutiny.

"You don't like these things?" she asks me, a tight little frown creasing her flawless face.

"He hates them, even as a child." Donald's face pales, and I grip Finn's hand a little harder, involuntarily, but she squeezes me right back. The comfort in that small gesture hits me hard, straight in the chest. My eyes dip to her, and I search the deep-blue pools. My heart continues to pound at the look she's leveling at me, searing right through me. Compassion, yes, but so much more, and right now, with all these reminders, I'll take everything I can from her.

Smiling down at her, I reply, "I still hate them, Donald, but at least tonight I can be guaranteed the very best company." My forced bright tone and Hollywood smile quash the sadness and the sorrow-filled memories before they can take hold.

"You're coming to the party." A statement rather than a question.

"There's a party after the film?" Finn's question is laden with hesitancy, which fuels my doubt about being here.

"We don't actually *watch* the film, my dear. That's for the tourists." Donald chuckles and gives an exuberant high wave above our heads at some people behind us, his focus having already moved on. He shakes my hand warmly and offers a string of fatuous platitudes to Finn that make me cringe. Judging by the tension in her jaw, she's feeling equally nauseous by his insincerity.

"So, no film?" Finn gazes up at me, but I can't make out her tone.

"We can watch the film, if you'd like." I take a best guess and am happy to luck out when she answers and makes my fucking night.

She whispers conspiratorially, "Actually, I'd rather be with you, somewhere we won't get kicked out for chatting." She beams, tipping up on her toes, and making my cock twitch when she brushes her soft, full breasts against my arm.

"Me, too." I grab her hand and briskly lead her through the foyer and out the rear of the theatre.

We lasted twenty minutes at the party, a room bursting with bullshit and Botox. Finn nursed her champagne and took sips through her clenched jaw. One look in her eyes revealed all I needed to know; she hated this as much as I did.

"Do you want to get out of here?" I smile at her instant response.

"At the risk of sounding ungrateful, I really do." She fails miserably at hiding her pleasure at my suggestion, her smile bursts onto her face, lighting it up brighter than the Hollywood searchlight.

"Thank God." I pull her hard against my body, relishing the full body shiver and sinful smile playing on her lips. "I don't know what I was thinking, but then, when I'm with you, I frequently seem to lose my train of thought."

"Is that bad?" A mischievous light dances in her deep-blue eyes and her smile dazzles.

"No, angel, that's not bad at all, but let me take you home and show you what *bad* really is." She bites her lips flat, stopping a whimper from escaping, though I still hear the sound muffled in her mouth. Her lids drop to half-mast, and her skin just fucking glows. *I can't wait to get her home.*

Finn wanted to come back to the farm, rather than stay the night in the apartment and although the extra travel was a pain in my balls, it was the right choice and I'm glad we're here, in my room. I have never been able to really explore this part of my nature, nothing beyond more than the odd blindfold or playful handcuff scenario, which only became a necessity after my *accident*. But even so, one-night stands are too brief to develop the trust needed to really enjoy the possibilities when someone truly gives themselves: their body, mind, and submission. I feel about ten-fucking-feet tall looking at her: open, bare and bound—just for me. *Perfect.*

She's kneeling on the deep, soft rug at the end of my bed, hands tied behind her back and her ankles cuffed together. Her pleading eyes nearly made me cave when I placed the blindfold over them, but I so desperately want to feel her skin on mine, it's the only way. I can't bare her eyes to look at me any other way— the way she looks at the others and the way she looks at me is no different, and I'm not ready for that to change. Despite what I told Pink, I'm not sure I ever will be.

My scars are ugly and not just disgusting distortions on my back and left side, they run so much deeper than the twisted skin. I shake the barrage of tortured images away and focus on the beauty before me. So damn stunning, she makes me ache all over in the best way possible, and I intend on satisfying that need. I'm as naked as she is and standing just in front of her, my painfully-hard length in my hand. The dull throb in my balls and unbearable stiffness don't ease off with my attention, but I know what will help.

"Tell me what you're thinking, angel." My tone is low and sensual. Her body sways forward toward the sound, as if she needs a more physical connection. I want her *need*.

"I want to touch you." I can feel her desire like a force field glowing around her; it's intoxicating.

"I understand." I watch her mouth purse. Clearly chewing on her cheek, she keeps wetting her lips with sweeps of her tongue.

Breaking the sensual silence, she states, "I want to see you."

"I understand that too, angel. Now, tell me how you feel?"

"I'm…"—she puffs out a frustrated breath, her back arching subtly to push herself closer to where she thinks I'm standing. Her breasts look heavy, her nipples perfect, pink nubs, which are begging for attention—"hot and achy."

"Wet?" I gravel out, low and throaty.

"Oh, God, yes." She exhales with a needy groan.

"Have you read the binder?" My question obviously takes her by surprise, and her head tilts with confusion.

"Yes…most of it." Her brow furrows.

"Did you read the others' sections about oral preferences?" I continue, watching her features soften as she starts to follow my thought process.

"I did, but you didn't have anything in your section about it or sex. It only said, 'My way.'" Her voice drops to mimic my deep tone.

"Correct." I step closer, and she straightens her back, feeling the heat from my body like a palpable wave thrumming with sexual tension. "I want you to show me what you've learned from the files, and if you remember every preference, I will tell you mine."

"And if I don't remember?" She raises her brow enough for it to peek above the silk blindfold.

"Do you want to please me, angel?" My tone drops an octave, but I keep it impassive. I don't want her to know how much I *need* to hear her answer.

"Very much so," she says without faltering.

"Then, as much as I'm sure I will enjoy your mouth around my cock, you and I will both know it won't be as good as it *could* be."

"Hmm, I understand." Her shy smile at repeating my words makes my heart swell, causing my cock to drip excitement onto my thumb. I place the tip on her bottom lip and give her the first question in the form of my best friend's name.

"Pink?" She purses her lips for a moment then flicks her tongue over the sensitive tip, circling the crown, with light delicate and fluttering licks. Her lips barely touch me; it's all tongue work, along the shaft but mostly concentrating on the tip until my balls tighten and my toes curl. I caress her cheek to get her to ease up, before I blow out a slow, steadying breath to gather myself before I speak.

"Toxic?" I manage to say in a surprisingly level tone. It's odd that once I mention my friends' names they are gone from my head. I don't think about her lips on them as she works me, which is a good thing. Nevertheless, I'm struggling to think of my own name, she's *so* damn good. Her lips push over the crown, and I let out an agonizing groan. *Good lord, that feels fucking amazing.* I cup the back of her head but refrain from moving her, holding or guiding. She does all of it by herself, sucking along my shaft and dipping her head to take my balls one at a time into her wet, hot, talented, and sexy-as-hell mouth. Pulling each one with a gentle tug and releasing with a soft plop. *Fuck, my knees feel weak.* I tap her cheek, and she pulls back, her chin tipped high and her pouty, pink lips all swollen and wet.

"Tug?" I choke out, and she grins but then frowns. I see her wiggle her fingers.

"Um… I'm going to need my hands."

"No, you won't," I correct, and her brows move like she might be rolling her eyes.

"Okay." Shrugging, she drops her mouth wide open and waits. Damn, I could die a happy death, because there isn't another sight in the world that looks quite as heavenly. I lift my cock and pull my balls up so she can drag her tongue exactly where Tug showed her on the very first day. Her tongue is tentative at first, clearly getting her bearings. Once satisfied she's in the right place, she drags her hot, wet, and dexterous tongue slowly from just the side of my ass to the underside of my sack— the taint. It's all I can do to keep my own position, when she moans and repeats the torture. Her tongue feels like a scorching hot ribbon, teasing pleasure from the very depths of my spine. I step back, and she manages to steady herself, before actually hitting the deck. I wouldn't have let her fall, but I couldn't let her continue.

"Is there something wrong?"

"Not at all, quite the opposite."

"So you can tell me now. What's your preference? What do

you like?" Her tongue draws her bottom lip into her mouth; the anticipation is hell—for us both.

"You might not like what I'm going to say," I grit out, tension in every fiber of my body, coiled and ready to explode.

"But I've earned the privilege to hear it all the same." She tips her defiant chin, and I hold back a chuckle, like I would actually be crazy enough to deny her anything.

"Yes…yes, you have."

"Tell me," she pleads. I curse inwardly and pray at the same time.

"I want to make you gag. I want to stick my cock so far down your throat you're choosing to swallow me rather than take your next breath *and* I'm not giving you the use of your hands to stop me."

"Oh."

CHAPTER TWENTY-SEVEN

Finn

"**O**H." I REPEAT, GLAD HE CAN'T SEE MY EYES, because with closed lids and the blindfold, I'm saved the embarrassment of him realizing how much his words turn me on; how much lust and desire is coursing through me and likely dripping onto his super soft rug. I'm wanton and filthy and so fucking happy. "Okay."

"Okay?"

"Yes, please, Sir. Is that better?" I quip with a cheeky grin.

"It's a start." His finger traces the edge of my jaw, coming to rest on my swollen plump bottom lip. My tongue darts out and then disappears. I beam up at him, and my heart thumps double time when I hear his breath hitch. I open my mouth and stick my tongue out as an open invitation no man will decline. His cock is heavy, and it throbs against the corners of my mouth when he slides the tip along the flat surface of my tongue. I have to stretch my lips wide to accommodate his size. He fills my mouth with just a few thick, solid inches. I start to ease back and forth, in and out, my tongue doing crazy things along his length, my eager lips pulling him in and sucking. When I moan, the vibrations travel though me, and judging by the pinch of his grip in my hair and ragged exhale, I think he feels them from the tip of his cock to the base of his balls.

His hands are threaded in my hair, and he starts to push deeper, slow and steady. I try to keep my teeth sheathed, but he's so fucking enormous, it's impossible. Luckily the pace is deeply delicious, not feral and frantic, so I can take him deeper the way he wants. I don't just want to please him and give him the best blowjob of his life; I want to rock his fucking world.

He lets out a gravely, rough moan and curses under his breath. His hips lunge forward as he holds my head firm. My airway is cut off, and my breathing stops. The seconds drag, and my throat makes its first instinctive attempt to swallow him down. *God, that feels amazing, making him moan like that. Best feeling ever.* I can picture him coming undone. Unfortunately, that's all I can do, picture it, I can only imagine his chiseled cut chest, toned defined torso with dips and lines in all the right places.

Strong thick thighs flexed and taut, adding to the power his fine arse is putting into each thrust, and his ridiculously beautiful face distorted with the pleasure he's receiving. His thumb reaches round and strokes my throat, little encouraging touches that make all the difference. A feeling of calm and adoration envelops me. I swallow again and take him a little deeper before I feel the first judder of rejection at the back of my throat. He eases back to let the air flow.

"So fucking good, angel. *So fucking good.*" His voice is breathless, filled with wonder, and I feel invincible. I lap at his length as he pushes through my lips again, and each time he does, I take more of him, a little deeper and for a little longer. I can hear his labored breathing, and I know he's close; I can taste it.

"I'm going to come, angel." His gruff tone is tight with the effort to maintain control. I moan around his cock, and it's like I've lit the powder keg without the fuse. An animal roar escapes his chest, and he can no longer help himself. He thrusts deep and hard, holding me tight against his abdomen as my throat contracts like crazy, and he empties himself, his throbbing cock pumping streams of hot liquid down my throat. I freeze for a long second, sparkling dots flitting over my tightly squeezed lids, and the first sways of dizziness prickle my skin. But he pulls back before that takes hold, or I come close to gagging. He lifts me from my position and right into his arms, his mouth on mine before I take a much-needed gulp of air. An urgent but quick kiss, then he breaks away and gives me space to steady my own breathing with deep and necessary pulls of oxygen. Even with the blindfold, I can feel his eyes bore into me, his arms embrace me and his words undo me.

"Mine," he whispers, but then corrects himself. "You're extraordinary, you know that?" My chest is tight and bursting at the same time. My head spins with new and wondrous feelings I can't vocalize, but I try, because I can sense the intensity of the moment, and his voice is thick with concern.

"That was amazing. You felt…" I shake my head and let out a puzzled laugh. "I felt powerful and powerless at the same time. It was…God, I want to see you." I struggle against my restraints, feeling them for what they are for the first time, a hindrance.

"I understand." He sweeps his hand over my face, to soften what I know is going to be a rejection to my plea.

He kisses my mouth, gently, teasingly light and moves to my neck. I tip it back to give him better access. He could do that for days, and I wouldn't complain; I'd melt. I'm unbelievably wet, considering he has yet to lay a finger on me, just the odd touch, caress, and tender kiss. It's enough. My heart rate is spiking, and I squeeze my legs together, acutely aware of the unbearable building ache and only occasionally aware of the butt plug residing comfortably in my arse.

"Something you need, angel?" His breath scorches and cools my skin in equal measure. I'm coated in what must be a sheen of perspiration that reacts with his breath like a jolt of electricity, and I can feel the trace of gooseflesh where his breath touches my skin. His kisses blaze a trail, leaving me panting for more.

I know there's no point pleading again to touch or see him. I'll get the same infuriating response, and I have a much more urgent, building need, demanding attention.

"I want you." I try a different tack.

"Hmm…I understand." I can almost see the wicked turn of his lips as the low, rumbling words fall from his mouth, in-between the tortuous trail of kisses he's pressing onto my skin as he makes his way down my helpless body.

"I *need* you." It's not a lie, and I'm so far beyond begging, it's only because my hands are still tied behind my back that they are not clasped together in prayer.

"Good," he croons, flipping me swiftly onto my front. I can feel his strong thighs trap me as he moves to straddle my legs. His mouth is still working its way down my back. I hold my breath when his hands cup and squeeze the "not as firm as I'd like" flesh of my bottom. His appreciative groan eases my insecurity, and then he obliterates it with his words and actions.

"You have the fucking sexiest ass I've ever had the pleasure of devouring." He sinks his stubble-dusted face between my cheeks, and as much as my instant reaction is to clench in a what-the-hell moment, his strong hands pull my cheeks apart and massage in sensual pulls and squeezes that quickly make me forget his face is right *there*. He lifts my hips up and sinks his face lower so his tongue is working its way beautifully from my clit to my entrance and back again. He's so slow and deliberate, firm and relentless, I can feel the spark of raw pleasure light in my very core. My toes wiggle with anticipation, and I hold my breath, waiting to die from the ecstasy I know is on the tip of his tongue. His teeth graze me in the most delicious way, and I want to grind myself against him, and he pulls right back, giving me none of the friction I need. I turn my head to the comforter and let out a howl. I can feel him chuckle, the vibrations rippling through the bed from whatever body part he has pressed against it.

I yelp when he pulls my legs off the bed so I'm kneeling on the floor, my tummy flat on the bed, my hands still tied behind my back. My legs are secured at the ankles but not so close I can't open them a little. I shiver from top to toe when he slides down flush behind me, his legs straddling mine, his heavy chest sinking onto my back. It's like I can feel every curve of his taut muscles, and his skin on mine is both rough and smooth, but always searing hot. He feels so damn good I melt from the inside out. His mouth is at my ear, and he rumbles out a husky whisper that even to my lust-addled brain is strained.

"Where do you need me, angel?"

"Oh, God," I whimper and feel his lips smile against my neck.

"Do you want me here?" His lips cover my mouth, his tongue diving, swirling, teasing mine with too delicate strokes. I'm so on edge, I want him damn well *everywhere*. He breaks the kiss and moves so swiftly, I sag at the loss of contact. His large hands sweep down my body and rest on my hips. Once again I can feel his burning-hot breath so close to my core, *I* can almost taste me. "Or here?" His tongue circles my clit, and my hips jerk, though his fingers grip tightly to stop me moving away. My jaw is clenched, and I'm wound so tight, I doubt I will be able to answer him. "Or how about here." He tugs on the plug in my arse that I have been blissfully unaware of for some time, but not anymore. *Holy hell.* The moan that escapes the back of my throat is raw and desperate, and the sound surprises me, but it's a perfect reflection of my current state. I nod with my head buried in the comforter, thankful for the coverage as my cheeks flame. *You're utter filth, Finn.*

"Oh, angel, I'm going to need more than a shake of your head." He's still moving the plug inside me, but he has also slipped two fingers inside my very wet center and is working me in tandem. *Oh. My. God.* "Finn?" His deep tone registers on the periphery of my erotic haze.

"Oh, God, you're going to make me say it, aren't you?"

"Own it, Finn. You want it. Now tell me." His tone is demanding, and I don't hesitate.

"I want you to fuck my arse." I suppress a squeak as my mouth tries to retract my wanton words. Too late, they are out there, and I don't care. This is my decision, for me, I'm off the charts horny with the sexiest man on the planet, who wants *me*, every last filthy piece of me. I will own it. "Please," I gasp, shuddering when he pulls the plug free, replaced smoothly with his thumb, and I can feel him move the head of his cock along my slick center.

Cool lube is worked with his thumb in ever-increasing larger circles. The pressure is unbelievable, but after a short time, he removes it and positions his cock where the removal of the plug had left me wanting more, wanting him. I take in a deep breath and exhale slowly as I will every muscle in my body to relax. He's gentle and insistent. The building pressure as he breaches me spikes to a point of pain, though he keeps his movements gentle so the edge is there but no more. His hand slides around the front of my body and his fingers glide with heavenly precision over my clit and dip inside me. I feel nothing but full and fabulous, every nerve in my body zings to life, tingles and dances like the little hairs all standing to attention across my skin. My head drops, and my eyes roll skyward, not that he can see them, but he can hear the effect he has on me, my sighs, my moans, my stuttered breathing, which catches with every roll of his hips. He sinks in further, inch by careful inch until he rests, hips flush to my bottom and he's buried to the hilt. Tension radiates through his tight grip on my hip, and his taut thighs encase mine. I know he's in as much sensual agony as I am. He pauses a moment, and I'm glad for it, because I *so* need a moment.

"You okay, angel?" His voice is surprisingly even, but he growls when I nod. I clench at the noise, because I feel that rumble everywhere. I feel *him* everywhere.

"So good." It's a pathetic adjective to describe the indescribable; nevertheless, it's all I have. Every nerve is on fire, and every brain cell is occupied elsewhere.

"Perfect," he declares, ending our moment. His hips start to move, his fingers curl into my flesh, and all hell breaks loose as my body takes over. It's had enough waiting; it has seen the goal and is ready for the mother of all prizes.

"Charge?" I pant out an unasked question, desperation with a tinge of panic in my voice. I hope to God he doesn't stop this freight train I feel in my toes, my fibers, my soul.

"I understand."

I screw my eyes tight with disbelief, but before I own it in the name-calling department, he becomes my hero, saying the only three words that matter at this moment in time.

"Come for me." He keeps the pressure exactly right, fingers curled inside me, hitting the perfect spot, driving hard and relentless, pushing me to heights I didn't know existed. My climax is a slow rumble of pleasure, which builds and builds, and like a tsunami-strength wave, it crashes through me, wrecking my body and my mind. I can't breathe. My whole frame trembles with aftershocks, and dark spots and flashes of stars burst over the inside of my tightly-shut lids. I'm gone, out for the count.

It might be seconds or it could be hours, but I'm vaguely aware I have the use of my arms and legs. It's dark, but I know my blindfold is gone, too, because I'm gazing at the most beautiful, deep-blue, sapphire colored eyes I have ever seen. My arm drapes across his T-shirt-clad chest, and I can feel the steady, strong *thump, thump* of his heart.

"I didn't know if you wanted a shower?" His fingers are stroking through my hair, and it feels divine.

"Will you join me?"

His body tenses, but his smile is warm, his voice soft. "Maybe in the morning." He kisses my hair.

"Hmm…okay." I snuggle into his hold. I didn't really want to move. I start to drift, and dreams, sweet happy dreams, dance in my mind as I hover on the edge of consciousness. "I've never been so happy or so scared." I tell the dreamcatcher I can see swinging in the sunlight in my bedroom window. *Keeper of all my dreams and nightmares.*

CHAPTER TWENTY-EIGHT

Charge

△

ER FIRST TWITCH WAKES ME. HER HEAD IS NESTLED somewhere between the crook of my shoulder and my chest. We both crashed after the best fucking night of my life, and she feels so damn perfect lying next to me. Her body has tensed, and her soft breathing picks up. The moonlight casts an ethereal glow against her creamy bare skin, but when I delicately brush away the hair that has fallen over her face, I'm cut to my core. I freeze, can barely breathe, and feel fucking sick at the same time. Tears. Rivers of tears trickle down her cheek. Why the hell is she crying? Did I hurt her? She said she's never been so happy before she fell asleep, though she also admitted to being scared. Does she regret what we did? Does she regret coming here?

Her shoulders start to shake, and my hand strokes her skin to try and soothe her. My mind is racing, and I need to know what she's thinking. I have to know why, when I have the best thing in all our lives in my arms, she's fucking crying.

"I thought it was my grandmother being mean," she says, clear as day, but I know from her breathing and the dead weight of her head she's still asleep. Her eyes are moving rapidly behind her closed lids, and she's dancing on the edge of consciousness; however, she's definitely still asleep. "I never get to eat chocolate." She lets out a bitter laugh and falls silent again. Just when I think she's drifted off, she sniffs and speaks again.

"My mother came to see me when I was seventeen. I didn't realize she was still alive. Whenever I asked, my grandmother always said she was probably dead." I stroke her hair and let her carry on. I know I should probably stop her. I should wake when she's clearly reliving a painful memory, but the thing is, people will tell the truth when they sleep-talk, and I want her truth.

"What did your mother want?" I ask softly, ignoring the rising guilt clawing at my stomach.

"She left me with my grandmother when I was five. Took me there and told my grandmother she didn't want me, never wanted me. That she should've had the abortion, but my grandmother wouldn't let her, so here I was. She tried to walk away, leaving me on the doorstep. My grandmother shut the door in our faces." She pauses, and my breath catches, mindful that any movement could end this monologue I'm so desperate to hear. I can feel the wetness on my chest from her free-falling tears, but still I don't wake her. "I remember crying, but not because of the words. I didn't really understand the words, not until I was older, and my grandmother explained what they meant. No, I cried because of the loud bang from the door slamming. My mother took my hand and dragged me away, swinging my little body to a stop in the front garden where she told me to sit. She said she would be back." She falls so quiet, I feel her breathing rather than hear. "I asked if she would bring me back a chocolate bar." She sniffs out a derisive sound that changes to a sob. "She didn't even lie, she told me no and to just wait. She never came back."

My fucking heart breaks for her, and I feel like a total shithead for eavesdropping on her private hell. I'm just about to end this and wake her when she starts to talk again.

"My mother found me and wanted to make sure I wasn't looking for her. It would be ironic if it wasn't so fucked-up. She had a new man, but she'd lied and told him she didn't have children. She wanted to make sure I wasn't going to show up and mess things up. She sought me out to reject me all over again. I was surprised I had the courage to tell her bluntly how that would never happen. She fucking broke me and thought I'd want anything to do with her."

"She didn't deserve you." I press my lips into her hair and pull her close, not caring if I wake her.

"I still want her to want me. I still want someone to want me enough to keep me." That's too fucking much. How can she not think we want her? But even as I think the words, I know. She just fucking told me why, and her asshole ex compounded her fears. I twist and roll her onto her back, my urgent mouth covers hers as she wakes with a gasp. A second of hesitation, then the most dazzling yet sleepy sexy smile moves against my mouth, and she opens, accepting my tongue and threading her hand into my short, spiky hair, gripping as best she can. I nudge her legs wide with my body and ease myself into her. Every inch I push into her slowly and deliberately, making sure she's with me and not still stuck in her nightmare. She sighs and shivers, all the while smiling against my mouth. I sweep my hand down to scoop her ass, and I roll her onto me rather than me thrusting into her. Once I know she's with me, and I can feel her warm, wet, and willing muscles ripple against my cock, I don't hold back. I power into her, marking and claiming, pushing her higher and higher with every proprietary pump of my hips. I growl the word "*Mine*" into her neck, and she explodes.

I wake with a raging thirst and a rock solid erection wedged against Finn's sweet ass. I unwrap myself from the spoon and with considerable effort leave the bed. I pull a pair of boxers on and stealthily leave the room. My bedroom door creaks like a motherfucker, but I must have left it open, so I'm silent in my escape. Waste of fucking time, as the hall is pitch black, and my eyes don't adjust in time to stop myself from tripping over a crouched body slumped against the wall. My bulky frame crashes to the floor, and I bite back a curse. Pink doesn't.

"Fucking hell, Charge!" He rubs at his jaw that I must have caught with my knee. I scowl at him, and even in the low light I know he can see me. He nods and follows me downstairs without further noise.

I hit the kitchen and instantly feel his hand on my shoulder. He spins me and is right in my face.

"What the fuck do you think you're doing?" he snaps, his face inches from mine. All I can see is fury. I don't think I've ever seen him so mad; a dark scowl clouds his face, flares his nostrils, and his jaw is clenched so tightly, the muscle on his cheek is bulging. I wrack my brain but come up with one thing. I marked Finn last night with my mouth. I couldn't help myself, and I know she fucking loved it. She came like a fucking train at the first bite, but he can't possibly know that unless he was in the room. *The door was open.*

"I don't know what you're talking about," I grit out, straightening to my full height, a few inches taller than him.

"Really?" He doesn't back down, and the tension builds.

"I'm tired, Pink. If you have something to say, say it." I tip my chin and hold his glare.

"And why are you tired, Charge?" he goads, his chest almost touching mine.

"Fuck off. I'm not telling you that," I snarl, and I'm itching to step away before I hit him, though I won't back down.

"Not what I meant, asshole," he snaps.

"Then enlighten me." My patience is on its last tether, but I know my rising anger is a defensive tactic.

"Finn…sleep-talking," he states, knocking the fucking wind from my lungs. *Shit.*

"How did you know?" My voice is impassive even if my stomach has dropped, and I know I have no color left in my face. I felt it drain away.

"Yes, because that's the important question." His derisive tone is thick with sarcasm and disappointment. "Why the fuck didn't you wake her?"

I step back and run my hand through my hair, gripping the knot of tension in the back of my neck. He has every right to be disappointed, disgusted even. *I know I am.*

"I was going to. She started to speak, and I…She was crying, and I thought I'd done something wrong." I start off calm, but with my rising guilt comes agitation and a rush of excuses.

"You did do something wrong." He fires the accusation with pinpoint accuracy. I'm too late to brace for the impact, and my chest caves. I shake my head as her words replay in my mind. The sadness, the unbearable hurt. That little girl carrying the burden of such a cruel rejection from the one person who was supposed to protect and love her.

"Did you hear what she said, too?"

"Yes," he states, and I see the first flash of understanding in his eyes. The silence is choking as we both process what we heard. He isn't finished with me, though, and the silence doesn't hold for long. "It's fucked-up, but it's still *her* story to tell, if she ever wants to. How would you feel if she did that to you?"

"I don't sleep-talk." My flip remark is low.

"But you do cover up." He ignores it and is intent on pushing. I know he's angry; moreover, he knows better than to walk this path.

"That's different," I say, harshly and with an air of finality. He lets out a long, slow sigh, and the tension seems to dissipate with the air he expels.

"Keep telling yourself that, brother, and she'll walk right out the door. We understand, Charge. We love you, but think about it, okay? Don't fuck this up for us." The accusation in his words holds no strength, and his tone is more of a plea than any type of reprimand.

"I won't, but I need more time," I offer, hoping my resolution is justified.

"Remember: You're the only one of us who does," he warns.

"Is that a threat?" I don't like the turn of the conversation or the returning tension in his statement.

"Never, Charge. Not ever." He pushes away my suspicions and pulls me into a hug. He slaps heavy fists against my back and releases the connection, his eyes conveying only concern, and maybe hope and something else that binds us as brothers. "Love you, man."

I make sure I shut the bedroom door tight when I return, although the damage is done. I fucking hate the fact Pink is right. I should've woken her. I had no right to intrude on her private thoughts. It's possible she was dreaming. However, even as I think it, I know that's bullshit. From the information she *has* shared about her past, I know in my gut what she said was the painful truth, and that's why it's buried so deep, it takes the blanket of darkness to coax it out.

I'm a fucking idiot.

I have to pray she trusts me enough one day to tell me herself. I know I don't deserve it, but that doesn't mean I don't want it.

CHAPTER TWENTY-NINE

Finn

I T'S THE TAIL END OF MY THIRD WEEK ON THE FARM WITH the guys, and I have had several full-on, fantastic dates with each of them. Even so, I can't deny I do love my days off.

The sun is past the full intensity of noon, and its rays are still beating down and warming my body. I'm expecting a call any moment from Hope. I texted her earlier to arrange it. It's been a strange couple of weeks, and after spending some time with Flick the other evening in the bar with the live band, I find I'm really missing some female company. I have had the entire morning to myself, and apart from a kiss at breakfast time from the boys, I have been completely left to my own devices. I don't know if they can sense that I needed a little space, but I did. These last few weeks have been wonderful, intense, and a little overwhelming.

I have my iPad perched on the edge of the hot tub, a chilled glass of crisp fruity white wine, and I'm reading some seriously sexy dark romance novel, intermittently watching the sun slowly crest the midday high. It's so beautiful here, peaceful and stunning, perfect.

I know Chloe said I was going to burn in hell, but I can't help thinking this feels a lot like heaven.

The ringtone shrills against the quiet backdrop of chirping birds and nothingness. I swipe the screen and see Hope's sleepy face. It's only eight in the evening in London, but she's clearly already crashed, her alarm to prompt her to call me has probably just woken her up. She yawns and shuffles up her bed, plumping pillows and trying to position the screen so we can FaceTime without having to hold the tablet. Her fiery hair is tamed into two braids, and wearing her superman T-shirt and goofy grin, she looks no different from when I first laid eyes on her.

"Hey, Hope! God, it's good to see you." I blink back a well of tears that hit me hard and out of nowhere. *What the hell?*

"Hey, babe. How's the cock-fest? Cockwork orange all you dreamed it would be? Or are you chafing like a speed walker in the desert?" She grins, and her shoulders shake with her rapid-fire one-liners.

"Cockwork what?" I ignore the rest, but this one confuses me.

"Orange. You said you were in Orange County, and I can only *assume* with four guys there would be considerable cock-working going on," she snickers.

"Clever. Did that take you all day to think of?" I arch a brow, unamused.

"Nah, half a day, max." She shrugs off her lame joke and beams her brightest smile at me. I've missed her face. "So, what's up, baby girl? I miss you like crazy. So if they're not treating you right, I'm ready to come whoop some arse and drag you back."

Her tone is light, but her narrow, searching eyes are completely serious. I sniff out an incredulous laugh.

"Oh, God, nothing like that! The complete opposite," I gush. My dreamy tone makes her eyes roll, and I can feel the creeping heat on my neck, spreading quickly to my cheeks. "It's been amazing." Her eyes soften at my sincere tone.

Shaking herself, she retorts, "Ah, don't say that. Tell me they're all gross and have tiny dicks." Her pale brows hardly register on the screen, but the deep furrows of disappointment do.

"Why?"

"Two reasons. One, because I'm jealous, and two…" She hesitates, and her eyelids blink rapidly. Her voice drops when she speaks, and I find myself leaning in to hear her whispered words. "And two, it means you might not come home." I tilt my head, dropping it to my shoulder, knowing if she was here, I'd pull her into a hug.

"I have another week to make my decision." I offer as a sop, but it really isn't.

"And?" she pushes.

"And nothing. There's no way I can make that kind of decision. This month has gone by too fast." I lift my shoulders like it's not a big deal, but I feel the frustration and panic arise in my belly, something I get every time I think about my looming deadline.

"I thought your visa was for three months?"

"It is, but we only agreed one month."

"Can you stay longer?" Even if her tone is filled with reluctance, she still wants me to be happy.

"I haven't been asked." I hate the insecurity and pain acknowledging this brings. I feel it like a hard hit in my chest, although it's the truth. They all tell me every day how lucky they are, how perfect I am, and how much they want me. But not one of them has asked me to change my ticket.

"Hmm…" Hope mulls over my words and doesn't offer her opinion. Her mind has raced beyond or back to the gutter. "So tell me: How is it?"

"I'm not giving you details." My tone is a warning she chooses to ignore.

"Are you walking like John Wayne all the time?" She pouts, and I snort with a dirty laugh. I'm still not going to spill. "Okay, tell me what they're like?"

"They're pretty amazing, actually. I mean, they are each very different, yet the same in many ways. It kind of feels like I'm dating one guy with split personalities." It's not a great explanation, but it fits.

"Hmm… kinky." She wiggles her none-existent brows, but I get the idea.

"You have no idea." I shake my head lightly and get that flutter in my tummy when I think of them—*all* of them.

"I know, and you won't fucking tell me." She scolds me, but it doesn't hold. "So, there isn't one you prefer?"

"I like them all," I answer, instantly and truthfully.

"Oh my God, you've fallen for them, haven't you?" She bounces on her bed, and the screen slips. I'm dizzy from the movement, but she quickly rights her device and looks intently at me for confirmation.

"I really like them, but I don't know them. Not really, not all of them, at least." My mind can't help zeroing in on the one I feel is holding back—Charge.

"Are you happy, Finn? I mean really happy?" Her stern tone is coming from a good place, and I return her serious stare with a warm and completely sincere smile.

"I am." Another instant response.

"And you're being yourself? Not trying to impress, because you know that shit will bite you in the arse." She doesn't need to elaborate, and I berate myself for ever letting someone tarnish my shine.

"I think so. I mean I'm being honest. I was from the get-go. All the emails and Skype calls. I never lied, and I was always me." I do a mental scan of information I exchanged on a daily basis, and I'm happy I have been true to myself. I know when I'm ready, I will share the hard bits too—one day. "I know Charge is still hiding something from me, but I don't know how significant, and to be fair, I haven't shared all my dark and scary."

"You don't have dark and scary. You have fucked up and unbearably sad, and I understand why you don't want to share. It's hard enough to hear, it must be agony to tell, but what do you mean, hiding something?" Hope is the only one who knows *everything*—well, her and Dave. He was amazing when I told him, even if it did take years. I can't fault him for that. He said everything I needed to hear and just let me tell my story when I was ready. It all went downhill from there, but I trusted him enough to share the most painful part of me.

"Have you seen Dave?" I ask, the memory of him burning more urgently than answering her question.

"He caught me at your salon. Carlos said he had been popping in on the off chance he would—"

"Did you tell him where I was?" I interrupt.

"Oh, yes, and gave him plane fare to come and visit. Give me some credit, Finn," she bites out, and I can see in her eyes, my faith or lack thereof has hurt her.

"I'm sorry, I didn't mean anything by it. I just know how persuasive he can be." She tips her head, and I know she's accepted my apology. She's all-forgiving, and, besides, she loves me. "So how did he look?"

"It's Dave. How do you think he looked?" Her tone filled to brim with derision.

"Good. *Really* good." I drag my hand around my neck,

squeezing the instant tension even the constant bubble and heat from the hot tub can't ease. Hope interrupts my wayward and unwelcome thoughts.

"What do you mean hiding?" She repeats the question I failed to answer earlier. I let out a slow, heavy sigh as I try and pinpoint in my head what my concern really is.

"He's never taken his shirt off, and every time we've been together, he makes me wear a blindfold." The examples don't really help define what's missing, I just feel there's more. Ultimately I want to know what he's keeping from me and why.

"Oh, kinky." She grins and I sniff out a laugh.

"You said that already." I roll my eyes, and she leans in conspiratorially.

"So you think he's all deformed and gross? Maybe he has a hump?" Her nose wrinkles with distastes and my eyes go for a second round trip in my sockets.

"I'd see a hump, Hope."

"Ah, good point. So he's hiding something under his shirt. You said he was hot, so it can't be that bad." She taps her fingers on her cheek as if she's weighing up possibilities. I have done the same, and all I can conclude is he doesn't trust me enough to share. Why would he? He doesn't really know me.

"Oh, he's *so* hot. God, I can't even. And I can't think there would be anything to make me think any different if he was scarred. I hate that he would think I was so shallow, but the fact he doesn't trust me enough, kinda hurts." I confide my fear to my best friend and she does what she does best, she comforts me.

"It's only been a few weeks. Some people carry deep scars they *never* want to show. Give him time." Her earnest sentiment makes me feel a little shame. He has been to war. I can't even imagine what it might mean. It's unbelievably selfish of me to put pressure for full disclosure for my own peace of mind, especially when I still hold my own insecurities. He must have his reasons, and I need to respect that.

"When did you get so wise?"

"I'm all-wise and all-knowing. So, you love him, this Charge guy." She states this as a matter of fact, and if I'd had a mouthful of wine, my iPad would be wearing it. I cough and splutter all the same.

"What? No, I never said that." I shake my head vigorously, and she simply returns my protestations with a wry smile.

"Hmm…All-knowing, remember? So this is the real deal, then. You're going to marry one of these hotties?"

"That would be the plan." I trace the rim of my glass absently. The gravitas of the situation hangs, but it isn't heavy; it's just unprecedented.

"You don't sound so sure?" she coaxes.

"I am, but…" I hesitate, and her penetrating eyes bore into me. I try and shrug off my doubt, but the bottom line is like a big-ass red flag. "They haven't actually asked me to stay, and they know I have a three-month visa. I even told them Carlos said I could go back anytime." I hate the way my voice wavers, and my nose prickles with pent-up tears and pathetic insecurities founded on nothing more than a lifetime of rejection. Justifiable, but I still feel wretched.

"And instead of asking them, you put two and two together and came up with them just fancying a month of English muffin?" Her tone and flippant retort are full of sass and sweet kindness.

"Something like that." I shrug off her passive compliment.

"That's your self-esteem talking. So stop right now and tell me, do you honestly feel like they are playing you?"

"Um…" I chew the inside of my cheek, but she doesn't give me time to draw comfort from my worrying tick.

"No ums. Hand on heart, tell me what your gut says." She's

relentless when she has my happiness and the bit between her teeth.

"My guts says I need more time," I lie. I know I'd stay in a heartbeat *if* I was asked.

"Then ask for it." She throws her hands up in frustration and, for the first time, I'm glad I'm nearly five and a half thousand miles away. She would be beating sense into me right about now.

"Maybe…" I squeal as a splash of water covers my back but somehow misses my iPad. "Don't say a damn word." I hiss under my breath and watch as Hope's eyes transform to roughly the size of saucers. Charge rests his head on my shoulder. I'm kneeling facing away from the water, but I know it's him. I felt him before he even touched me. He kisses my cheek and I hear three more bodies hit the water.

"Who's this, angel?" Charge's dark T-shirt is clinging to every bump and bulge on his perfectly defined chest, but he's still wearing that damn shirt. I shake off the questions clouding my mind, weighing heavy elsewhere in my chest. *Be patient.*

"Like you don't know from your super stalking," I scoff but decide to make the formal introduction all the same. "This is my best friend, Hope," I say with a bright voice, and then giggle, because something very, *very* rare has happened—my best friend is speechless.

"Oh, hi, there, Hope. Gonna need to steal my girl away. We have a cookout this afternoon and people will be arriving anytime now." He drops his mouth to my neck and nibbles all the way to my shoulder. I'm a little speechless myself.

"Hi, Hope!" Pink, Tug, and Toxic gather around, and all our faces squish together to fill the screen. She still hasn't spoken, although her mouth is wide open.

"Hope, this is Pink, Tug and Toxic." I point, and each of them in turn flash her a megawatt smiles. Still no response. "Would you like me to send them away, Hope? You seem a little—"

"Holy fucking shit, Finn!" She finally breaks her stupor. "You did *not* say they were *that* fucking hot. That's why you have your days off, isn't it? So you can reintroduce your legs to each other?"

"Hope!" I cry out, mortified, but the boys all belt out deep, throaty laughs.

"There's no fucking way I'd want a day off. Just saying…" She fans herself, pulling the top of her T-shirt away from her body to seemingly let out the steam. She's hilarious, or at least she's trying to be.

"Really? I'm right here, and you're flirting with my boy-friends. Do you have no shame?" I tease, and she levels an in-credulous glare at me.

"None whatsoever," she quips, her tone straight and dead-pan. I drop my head in my hands, but a huge smile begins to stretch my lips at her response. *Yes, I'm that lucky.*

"So Hope, you gonna come visit us?" Pink asks.

"Depends. Does Finn plan on sharing?" She tilts her head with hopeful expectation that I quickly shoot down.

"Finn really doesn't," I answer instantly and am rewarded with hot heavy hands all over me, possessively squeezing and stroking my body.

Charge kisses the skin below my ear and whispers, "No shar-ing, angel."

"I'm only teasing. Well, half teasing." Hope gives a little shrug and sniffs with a snicker.

"You'll come for the wedding though?" Pink asks enthusias-tically, and the mention of the W-word renders me mute.

"Oh, I wouldn't miss that." Hope's eyes widen, and she claps her hands excitedly like a demented seal pup. I pick up my wine glass and suck down a large, unladylike gulp. How can he men-tion a wedding when they haven't even asked me to stay?

Finn

I TAKE A PEEK OUT OF MY BEDROOM WINDOW, WHICH overlooks part of the porch that isn't covered, the back garden, yard, and pool. A long table has been set up beside the rustic, brick-built barbecue from which thick grey plumes of mouthwatering smoke rise into the clear sky. From here I can hear the sizzle as the coals react with the juices from the various meats charring under Charge's attentive hand. *Oh, lord, those hands. Stop it, Finn, for God's sake, stop thinking with your clit for one bloody moment.*

People have been arriving in a steady flow for the last half an hour, bringing large plates of food, baskets with home-cooked pies and bread and beer—lots and lots of beer. Pink and Tug brought some extra tables down from the stables earlier and some hay bales for makeshift seating. They said a *few* friends, but there's at least fifty out there, and people keep coming. I wonder if they've invited the whole damn Navy. I have changed about twenty times, and I know one of them will be up any moment to drag my nervous arse out to meet everyone. The friends I met a couple of weeks ago at the bar were nice enough, very friendly, but the venue was loud and bustling so not really a great environment for chatting or interrogation. There's a loud pounding on my door, but the handle doesn't move, and the door isn't instantly opened, which means it's not Charge.

"Hey, darling, you coming out anytime soon?" His voice is softly coaxing, and it makes me smile, even if my tummy is in knots.

"Come in, Marlon." I prefer his real name, and he lets me have it. "I can't decide what to wear."

"I can see that." He grins. "Do you have the ball gown from the other night?" he asks flatly, and my brows shoot up in horror.

"Yes. Why? Do you think I should...? For fuck's sake, Toxic, not helping." Happy to use his nickname when he's being an arse.

"Darling, it's a cookout not the Oscars. We don't care what you wear as long as you get that cute little *be-hind* downstairs, stat." He points at the open door with a tilt of his head.

"Don't care what I wear? So I could go like this?" I wave my hand with frustration and exasperation up and down my skimpy-bikini-clad body.

"Ah, no. That would *not* be a good idea. We really don't want World War Three breaking out or the MPs to turn up and haul the four of us off to jail."

"You're funny." I sniff out a light laugh

"I'm not joking." His deadpan retort makes me stop mid-chuckle.

"Oh." I look down and back at his warm hazel eyes. "Well, I don't want to give people any more of the wrong idea."

"Wrong idea?"

"Me being a slut." I shrug off my flip insult, but it's a nig-gling nub of real concern in the pit of my vaguely conservative stomach.

"What the hell, Finn? Why would you say something like that? You don't think that, do you? Christ!" He sounds utterly mortified, and I wish I could swallow back the words along with the thick feeling of guilt now pressing on my chest.

"No, sorry. I'm nervous, and that was a bad attempt at a joke. Don't worry, I won't give up my day job for stand-up comedy anytime soon." *Wow, word vomit, Finn.* "Marlon, I didn't mean it. I don't think that. I mean, our situation is unconventional, but I didn't mean to disparage it."

"You didn't disparage, Finn. You insulted yourself, which is worse. A slut fucks around. You fuck us, your boyfriends. Consenting adults doing consenting things. Yes?" He steps clos-er, so I have to tip my head back to hold his intense, serious gaze. He's not fucking around, and neither am I.

"Very consenting. I'm sorry." I place my palm on his chest and offer my most heartfelt and apologetic smile.

"I know, darling. I fucking hate it when you put your-self down like that, even with a lame-ass joke. We all hate it." He steps back but still towers, his sincere, soul-searching gaze warming my heart and more. His lips press softly against mine, the long seconds of connection make my toes twitch and my tummy flutter. His innocent kiss is a little more heated, and his lips twist into a wide and wicked smile. "Now, my dilemma is: Do I let the others kill me for *not* bringing you down to the par-ty or for *not* letting you leave the bedroom?"

"Hmm… No murdering, thank you. Not today. I'm nervous enough as it is." I step away from his heat and instantly shiver and shake myself to regain focus. *It's a wonder I can function at all.* "Right, how does a short denim skirt and a tied cropped check shirt sound?"

"You had me at short." His voice dips, and I lightly push him out of my way. Time to face the music.

I grab a beer from the fridge but don't get a chance to blend in with the crowd, because Flick bounds over to me and hugs me like we are long lost friends. She's lucky she's not wearing the contents of the bottle, she's so damn rough and jiggly. She might have a slight frame, but she's all muscle.

"You look so damn cute, Finn. Why the hell haven't you called me?" she admonishes, pulling a mock reprimanding frown. I glance over to Toxic and Pink, my eyes meeting theirs then flitting to check for Tug and Charge. My cheeks heat and the smile dominating my face is both involuntary and from my heart. "Yeah. Okay, girl. Little bit of vomit right there," she teases, tugging me away from my men, intent on introducing me to some female company.

The afternoon is filled with fun and fabulous food. I was blissfully ignorant of the hard work that must have gone into preparing for such a spread. They wouldn't let me help when I offered, and I didn't argue. I do start to collect up the empty beer bottles and dirty plates when the crowd starts to thin, though. The sun is melting into the hazy heat of the evening horizon, and the amount of alcohol consumed is starting to surface. The laughter is getting louder, the jokes dirtier, and there's some rough play and harmless fighting breaking out. Flick is more than happy to take on a few of the guys in an arm wrestle. Then, as I skirt the edge of the pool with both hands full of dishes, I'm knocked in the side and sent flying.

The dishes crash and in a mix of shock and pain, a blur of bodies hit me full-on, and the next second, although time feels distorted, I hit the water and sink. I get a slow, heavy kick to my shoulder as someone pushes off me, which sends me deeper. A rush of bubbles escapes as I try to kick my way to the surface, but I can't seem to fight through the bodies. *Jeez, how many were in that bundle?* I feel a hand actually push my head, and I start to panic. The pool isn't that deep, but it doesn't matter if these arseholes won't let me up. Darker spots appear behind my tightly shut lids, the pressure behind my nose is sharp and painful. My lungs are burning me up from the inside, and my whole body is fighting for its next breath.

I can finally gasp for air as I'm lifted free and into strong arms, against a tight, T-shirt-clad chest.

"Get them out of here!" Charge yells out, his tone dark and deadly. I continue to cough as he carries me through the kitchen and into his study.

He sits me on his old leather sofa and sweeps his hands over my hair, my face, down my arms, speedily, meticulously checking every inch of my body.

"I'm okay." Little choking coughs still sporadically burst from my chest, even as I try to offer a relieved smile.

"They caught you here; you're not okay." He traces his thumb over a red bump on my shoulder; it's big, but I doubt it will bruise. I'm more shocked than hurt.

"I'm fine, but you look—you're soaked." I'm not thinking. I don't even realize what I'm doing until it's too late—far too late. I grab the bottom of his shirt and pull it up. Only a little bit, I don't see anything, I really don't. Not his abdomen, not his chest or skin. I see nothing except blind rage and fury. He has my wrists in a move so fast, I don't see it, but I feel it. His grip hurts, and by the look in his eyes, it's supposed to. It doesn't hurt nearly as much as the pain he's holding back, not a fraction of it. *Why are you holding back?*

"Please show me, Charge. Please tell me." My voice is soft, because right now he looks like a caged and cornered animal.

He releases his hold like my skin is acid to his touch, and I would be hurt if it wasn't for the turmoil racing across his tortured, handsome face.

He stands and steps back as I rise and mirror his move, preventing his retreat and closing the gap. He shakes his head, but I ignore him. I tentatively place my hand on his chest, over his heart, it's beating so damn fast I swear my fingers bounce from the pounding. His hand covers mine, but I feel it's to prevent any wayward wandering, and I can see any hope I held that *this* might be the time die with a sad shake of his head. A wave of unease swirls in my stomach, and my heart hurts for him—for us. If he can't trust me, then this is a deal-breaker.

"I can't," he states, his tone resolute and tinged with utter sorrow.

"I know." My other hand rests against the sexy stubble coating his rugged jaw, and he leans softly into my touch, closing his eyes and relishing the contact. He's not broken, not completely. "You need time."

"I do."

"Thing is, Charge, I'm kinda running out of that, and if you can't trust me—"

"I do trust you." He's quick to interrupt yet offers nothing new.

"Not enough." I tilt my head, my own sad smile barely tipping my lips.

"It's not that, Finn. *Fuck!*" He turns away, and I can feel the anger roll off him in strong, unstoppable waves, but it's not me he's angry with. He snaps back around, confusion replacing the look of anger. "What do you mean running out of time?"

"My return flight is next week."

"So?"

"So?"

"You're not leaving. You have a three-month visa, Finn. Why

the hell would you think you were leaving next week?"

"Not to state the fucking obvious, Charge, but I haven't been asked to stay any longer. One month was the deal."

"But that's crazy. We assumed—"

"Is it?" I snap my own interruption, my temper hovering somewhere between unbelievable frustration and wondering if he's dumber than a bag of spanners. "Is it really crazy? From what you know about me, you have to know I'm the last person to make fucking assumptions. I'm done making an ass out of myself, so excuse me if I want a fucking invite!"

"I—*we* want to *marry* you, Finn. How have we not made that clear? What else do you need from us?" He drags his hand along his jaw, his eyes piercing right through me, and I hold his gaze for a long time before I answer. He needs to see me, he needs to hear me, and if this is really going to work, he needs to trust me.

"Not us—you. I need your trust, but for now an invitation will do." I take his hand, and he covers the hold with his other, bringing my fingertips to his soft, full lips.

"Stay. Please stay. Take the next two months to decide, but make no mistake, we want you."

"Is that going to be enough time?"

"Only you know that, angel."

"I don't mean me."

"I understand." His jaw tenses again, and I decide to let it go. Hope's wise words ring in my head: "*Give him time.*" Only it's not her words ringing, it's the damn doorbell. "Who the fuck turns up to a party just as it's finished?" Charge rolls his eyes. I shrug at his rhetorical question and follow him out to the hall. I'm about to go up to my room to change when I freeze. Charge has the front door wide open.

"Is Finn here?" *That voice.*

"Who wants to know?" I know from Charge's tone he knows

exactly who is asking.

"Dave?" I answer for them both, my jaw gapping like a caught fish. I haven't been caught, though. I got away, and he let me go, so why the hell is he here?

CHAPTER
THIRTY-ONE

Charge

△

S HIT, THIS IS BAD. NOT AS BAD AS IT COULD'VE BEEN IF, not five fucking minutes ago, I hadn't made it clear we wanted her to stay. This guy who's travelled over five thousand miles and is standing on my doorstep is definitely not good.

"I'm Finn's boyfriend." I clench my jaw so tight I nearly crack a tooth, though I don't have to correct him because Finn clarifies with a suitably clipped tone.

"Ex...*ex*-boyfriend, Dave. What are you doing here?" Her pitch is a mix of panic and shock.

"Thought that was obvious." He tilts his head like she's said something cute.

"Yeah, well, I don't make assumptions anymore, so you need to spell it out for me. You know, maybe treat me like the dumb blonde you took me for four months ago." She fires at him unleashing pent-up venom. *Good for her.*

"Finn, please." His shoulders drop, and his voice is pleading. I hate that I can see her resolve slipping. I know how much he hurt her, but she's struggling to hold on to the residual anger when he's crumbling before her. "Is this your new boyfriend, Finn? Am I too late?"

Yes, you fucker, you're too damn late.

"It's complicated." Finn looks with pleading eyes at me, and I fight the urge to stake my claim—for now.

"Right, I see." His eyes flit between me and her, trying to read the signals, maybe, but failing.

"I doubt that." Finn's tone makes me smile, because there's not a hint of regret, just a large slice of awe.

"Can we talk?" His eyes move from me to her, and he fixes her with a determined look she can't seem to shake. She doesn't answer.

"Come in," I offer, even if my instinct is to drop kick the asshole back across the Atlantic.

"I'll wait here." His snide tone does provoke a response though.

"Don't be a dick, Dave. You've been travelling all day. Come in, have a beer while I get changed, and then we'll talk." She pushes out a puff of air, and her arms are now crossed tightly around her waist, under her soaking, cropped shirt. She's starting to protect herself from him, and it twists my gut that she feels she needs to. I know he's never hurt her physically, but brute strength is not the only way to break someone.

"Fine." Dave steps inside, and I point the way to the kitchen. I don't get the chance to speak to Finn, all I see is her cute ass and sexy long legs scurry up the stairs.

"Beer?" I ask, nodding to the kitchen stools for him to take a seat. He's taking in the room and it's a moment before he answers.

"Do you have a light beer?" he asks, and I almost laugh, thinking he's joking.

"No, and I don't have a vagina either," I reply flatly, suppressing a grin.

"Beer will be great, thank you," he mutters, his jaw twitching, and he now looks like he has a poker wedged up his tight, British ass. Lucky it's not my job to make him comfortable.

"Charge?" Pink comes in with Tug behind him. They've done a damn good job getting the stragglers to leave, but I can see Toxic is still chatting with the last few guys who won't take the hint or are too drunk to care. The instant scowls on my friends' faces are enough to signify they both recognize the lowlife sitting in our kitchen, but I make the introductions all the same.

"Dave, this is Pink and Tug." Dave holds out his hand to shake, something he didn't offer to me. But then I did introduce myself as his main threat, and unless Finn choses to enlighten him of our *situation,* that's how it will stay.

"You having a party?" Dave nods to the yard with all the tables, debris, and general aftermath of one of our gatherings.

"We were, but it's done," I state the fucking obvious, since the yard is empty.

"So you guys all live here together?" He purses his lips like he doesn't like the taste of his beer all of a sudden.

"Yes."

"Cozy," he mumbles loud enough to be heard.

"Meaning what?" I challenge. The smarmy asshole doesn't meet my glare, just shrugs.

"Nothing," he mutters into his beer.

"Oh, he means something by it. He's as homophobic as they come." Finn bounds back into the room. She seems to have recovered most of her composure and is dressed in one of my black T-shirts and some yoga pants. My heart fucking skips a beat, she looks so damn good.

"I'm not." His indignant tone is accompanied with a flash of red to his cheeks.

"No, of course you're not," she quips, full of sass. "But don't worry, your arse is completely safe here. Well, except from me." She ruffles his hair, and he stiffens, a dark, mean scowl crosses his features, and he roughly straightens the mess she made.

"Still rocking the 'yoga pants are all that fits me right now' look, I see." And just like that, her shine is gone. It's like the ass-hole punched her full in the stomach. He doesn't get the chance to rectify his mistake, because I have him by the throat up against the wall, and he's gasping for air to breathe, let alone talk.

"Say that again," I growl. "I dare you." I feel her hand on my forearm, but I can't hear her for the surge of rage rushing through my body. This is the passive-aggressive bullshit that's been undermining her self-esteem probably since their first fucking date. Lucky bastard like him, should've been building her up every damn day, not chipping away.

"Charge, please." I hear her plea, and I instantly release my hold, but not without giving him my most deadly warning glare. If looks could kill, this would all be over real damn quick. He coughs and splutters, rubbing his throat. I smile wide—*fucking pussy*—but the look in Finn's eyes as she flits her worried gaze between me and him is not what I want to see. She's hurting for him, dammit. I curse myself that I haven't done us any favors with my attack, because he's definitely playing up the injured party role.

"Finn, please, can we talk? *Alone.*" He turns into her body, effectively cutting me off and breaking her hold on my arm. She steps back, her eyes glassy, shaking her head.

"I'm really tired. I'm going to bed. We can talk in the

morning." She pinches the bridge of her nose, and her shoulders are nearly up by her ears, she's so tense.

"I'll come with you." He steps toward her, and my growl makes him freeze.

"Like fuck you will. I sleep with Finn, period." I couldn't stake my claim any more aggressively if I peed in a circle around her feet.

"She's *my* girlfriend." Dave turns to face me and snarls.

"Was…*was* your girlfriend. She's mine now, and she sleeps with me." If it's a pissing contest he wants…

"Stop! Just stop. I'm not sleeping with anyone tonight. I'm going to bed. On. My. Own." She punctuates each word with a fiery glare aimed at each one of us.

"Oh…Umm, Finn. I didn't book a hotel I thought you and I—" Finn holds up her hand halting him midword.

"Wow, please *do not* finish that sentence because I might just finish off that stranglehold I stopped a minute ago. And as crazy as this may sound, I actually think the least you deserve is for me to hear you out—actually scrap that." She shakes her head and gives a derisive, bitter laugh. "That is the *most* you deserve." She scowls at him, but softens when her eyes meet mine. She walks around Dave to kiss my cheek and then does the same to Tug, Pink, and now Toxic, who joined the after-party from hell just a moment ago and fell silent on seeing Finn's ex.

"Okay. Where shall I sleep?" Dave fidgets, calling after Finn as she disappears without a glance in his direction.

"Couch. There are three. Knock yourself out." I'm not exactly thrilled with her decision but I kind of loved the delivery.

Pink shows Dave to the guest room above the garage because that's as far as my manners can stomach. I don't want the asshole in my house. When he returns, we all sit around the kitchen island nursing our drinks from the rapidly decreasing contents of a bottle of Jack.

"Why is he here?" Tug asks the dumbest question that still needed to be answered.

"Why do you think he's here?" Pink's tone holds a mix of condescension and concern. I echo the latter sentiment.

"He can't have her, she's ours." Toxic grabs the bottle roughly, his petulant remark more suited to a spoilt child, though I echo the feeling too.

"It's not our choice to make, Tox. We all want what's best for her," I say, rubbing my hand down my face and around to my neck, dragging the tension to a different part of my body.

"We're what's best for her," Tug chips in.

"And we have to hope she chooses us, because the only thing that matters is Finn is happy. Whatever her choice, we have to accept it." I grit the words out, but I mean every damn one. I hope to heaven and hell she chooses us; ultimately, though, I just want her to be happy.

"And you could do that? If she chooses him, I mean. You could let her walk? Because I sure as shit can't." Pink narrows his eyes at me, and I fire the same look right back.

"Yes, you can," I state, my tone as cold as the glacial chill which runs through my veins at the thought. "We all could. Finn is what matters in this fucked-up situation, understand?"

"She won't choose him though, right?" Tug's voice holds all the certainty I wish I felt.

"She was with him for nearly ten years, Tug. She loved him for a long time. You can't just turn those feelings off, and, besides, all she ever wanted from him was for him to choose her. As grand gestures go, flying thousands of miles could only be topped by him giving her a fucking ring."

"Shit." All of them exhale the word at the end of my unpleasant theory.

I down the remaining amber liquid but don't bother to say anything. I would only be echoing that too.

I stretch my legs out, my boots hooked over the rail of the porch, feet crossed at the ankle. I suck in the sweet smoke of my cigar to the back of my mouth and hold it for long seconds before I let it drift in a thick swirl of white cloud. On any other night this would relax me. Not tonight. Then I doubt a horse tranquillizer would work I'm wound so tight. *Dammit.* I hold my breath when I hear the screen door creak open and tilt my head when I hear the soft padding of bare feet above me.

"Is that you, Charge?" Her soft voice is a mere whisper, and my cock twitches at her breathy, nervous tone. Not my proudest reaction, given the circumstances, but there's fuck all I can do about it. She does this to me—end of.

"Yeah, angel, it's me."

"I smelt your cigar." She shuffles and the next minute I can see her delicate toes dangling from the balcony, having threaded her legs through the spindles.

"Sorry, angel. I didn't mean to wake you."

"You didn't." She lets out a deep and heavy sigh, which raises my anxiety up a notch. She's struggling, and that's the last fucking thing I want. I need this decision to be the easiest fucking one she's ever had to make; not just a no-brainer, but the *only* fucking choice.

"Can I ask you a question?"

"Anything," I reply without hesitation.

"What happened with you and Chloe?" Her voice is barely a whisper, but I have to suppress a choking sound that rips from the back of my throat. *I did not see that coming.* But she asked, and although this isn't something I particularly like talking about, it's not a secret.

"I can tell you, angel, but I'd like to know where this came from first."

"Oh, I was mulling over thoughts about my past, you know? What with Dave showing up, I guess I got to thinking this could be Chloe sitting here and—"

I scoff with my interruption. "It was never going to be Chloe, angel; let me make that clear. We took a long time to find you, but it's *only* you. This isn't a list we're ticking off, you know." My tone is clipped, and I have to tamp down my rising irritation that she would even entertain the thought.

"Oh, I know. I didn't mean anything by it." Her tone is deeply apologetic, and it goes some way to lessening the sting of the misunderstanding. "Flick said something the other night about Chloe messing with you specifically, and I just…" She hesitates and then rushes a retraction. "Forget it, I'm being nosy. It really doesn't matter."

I shake my head, which she can't see, and I let out a heavy sigh.

"Angel, it's fine. There's no big secret with Chloe." I take a drag off my cigar and feel the heat trickle down my throat. I welcome the burn before I let it out in a soft curl of smoke. This is an unpleasant conversation at the best of times; tonight, it feels like a lead weight around my neck. I sigh again and answer her question. "She's a manipulative, gold-digging bitch, that's all. But since you've asked, I'll be specific. I was her brother's co-pilot, and we experienced a malfunction on a test flight. I was injured pretty bad, but not like Duke. He was in a coma, and Chloe would visit him every day. I did, too, since I was recovering. I think I liked having someone to talk to at the time, and I felt for her. She was very good at playing the heartbroken little sister. I'd lost my own family, and it was touch and go for Duke for a long time.

"We became close, and over the next few weeks we started

to explore the idea of our unique situation with her. It wasn't working as we had hoped, and there were red flags shooting up left and right, but even then, I still didn't think too much of it. A few months later, however, I was out drinking and ran into Duke. We started talking, and he told me he didn't have a sister. He had an ex-stalker girlfriend who wanted to marry a pilot. I just didn't see it at the time, but once he said that, all the warning signs made sense. It all clicked into place, the fact that she stopped visiting once Duke came out of his coma, and she was always busy when we were likely to run into him at the bar or at a social gathering." I let out a humorless laugh that falls silent in the dark night. I wait a moment to let that particular nightmare fade before I clarify in my most deadly serious voice. "But Finn, she never got further than a trial weekend. And trust me, she was never going to get any further than that."

She doesn't respond, other than to give a low hum, but I can almost see the furrows on her brow as she picks through the information I just supplied her with. I'm relieved when she doesn't ask any further questions about Chloe, since we have more important issues to address. Chloe is not worth a spare second's thought, and I'm glad Finn seems to be in agreement. Her next question certainly changes the subject.

"Are you okay?"

"No," I answer honestly.

"What's wrong?" She follows her ridiculous question with an apologetic scoff; I answer her all the same.

"Your face." I drop my head back and close my eyes, picturing her face, that cute wrinkle in her brow when she's confused, her soft pouty lips pursed, and her cheek moving as she bites on the inside.

"My face is wrong?" Her tone is an audible confirmation of her troubled mind.

"When I opened the front door, your face—your expression

wasn't of someone seeing a person they no longer had feelings for. You love him." I grind my jaw; I had to force the words out. They sound like they've been pushed out between my teeth.

"I met him when I was sixteen. He's all I've ever known until you guys. I was with him a long time, Charge." Her soft voice drops a little lower, trying to soothe, but I know there's only one thing that will. "I would have to be a masochist to stay with someone that long if they didn't have some redeeming qualities. You have to give me a little credit; he wasn't always an arsehole." Her lame attempt at humor in this dark time is appreciated, even if it's fruitless at lifting my hopes.

"He doesn't deserve you." I can't sound any more emphatic. My flat, serious tone holds nothing but the truth. In my heart, in my fucking soul I believe this.

"Charge," she says my name like a warning, but I don't listen.

"He doesn't, and you know it."

"And you do?" she bites out, and I can hear the hurt in her defensive tone.

"I do. We *all* do," I counter, trying to keep my control, though my chest is in agony with every broken beat her reticence evokes.

"He never lied to me."

"I never lied." I sit up, my boots crashing to the floor.

The noise shakes the silence of the night, but her whispered words are much more of a violation in this quiet night. "Semantics, Charge. Lying by omission is still lying."

"Low blow, Finn. You have no idea what you're asking." I drop back in my chair, my lungs empty all at once from the sucker punch and truth of her accusation.

"That's because you won't tell me. You're making this really hard, Charge." She is pleading, but my shields have already dropped into place.

"No, Finn, its real simple. I need a little more time, that's all. He had ten years, and how did that work out? I just need a little more than a few fucking weeks," I grit out.

"Touché with the low blow, Charge."

"Fuck, I didn't mean it like that, angel. I saw the way you looked at him, Finn, and that's something I have no control over." I rush my words out to try and stop this train wreck.

"I understand," she says, and I find myself letting out a flat chuckle.

"Man, it *is* frustrating when you say that." The tail end of my laugh dies, though, and she simply agrees.

"Yep."

The silence returns, save for the insects and critters in the yard, safe to scurry in the cover of darkness. "So what are you going to do?"

"I'm going to listen to him. He came all this way, and I want to hear what he has to say."

"I under—I see." I correct myself and relax when I hear her light chuckle followed by a sleepy yawn. It will be dawn soon. "Go to sleep, angel. You have a big day tomorrow."

"And you?"

"I hope not."

"No, I mean you should go to sleep, it's late.."

"I'm good here. You're not the only one who can't sleep alone anymore."

"I'm sorry." Her voice sounds so sad, it's like a fucking dead weight on my chest.

"You have nothing to be sorry for, angel—nothing. Whatever you decide, I only ever want you to be happy."

"I am happy."

"Then that's all that matters. Goodnight, angel." I try to end this conversation before I climb that vine creeping from the ground floor to her window, wrap her in my arms and never let her go. Especially not to talk to that douchebag.

CHAPTER THIRTY-TWO

Finn

THIS BREAKFAST COULDN'T BE MORE AWKWARD IF WE were all sitting naked with angry erections, me included. I twist my neck to the side and welcome the pop in the bone, releasing some of the ache from a sleepless night. Removing the palpable tension will take more than a mere muscle stretch.

Dave was already seated when I came downstairs, and Charge had made a mountain of pancakes and coffee. The aroma of the sweet treats lured me down, even if my tightly knotted stomach made me reluctant to leave the sanctuary my bedroom became last night. I hate having reacted the way I did when I saw Dave at the door. I hate it more because Charge saw it. I couldn't hide that I was happy he'd come for me, but that momentary high drifted off with flood of painful memories.

Nevertheless, nothing stopped my mind from hurtling, skipping and jumping to conclusions left and right. *He's here. He wants me. He wants me back. He's going to ask me to marry him.* I think that last thought actually deserves a full-on punch in the face for even entertaining the idea.

I push my plate away with the half-eaten pancake and stand.

"Moment on the lips," Dave jokes, and I have to reach over to stop Tug from knocking the comment back through Dave's teeth. My hand covers his clenched fist and my wide, panicked eyes ease him down. "Jeez, I was only joking. Does no one have a sense of humor here?" Dave scoffs.

"Sense, being the key word there, asshole, because passive-aggressive, shitty comments like that aren't funny." Pink shoots back, but I know from the display of dark scowls and hard glares they are all sharing the same level of animosity, and to be fair, Dave really isn't covering himself in glory. He's certainly not coming across as the guy I fell in love with.

"Let's go for a walk." I nod to the back door, and Dave is quick to jump to his feet. The tension in the room is both hostile and volatile, and I need to remove the dumbass detonator.

"It's nice here. I can see why you like it." His hands in his pockets, he looks as uncomfortable and nervous as I have ever seen him. His eyes barely take in the glorious view of the farm in the morning sunlight.

"Yeah, I haven't seen much of the state, but this part is stunning, and Charge did take me to Hollywood on one of our dates." The way the words rush out are an indication that I, too, am a little nervous.

"*Our* date?" His brow drops in a heavy frown with the question.

"Hmm… what?"

"The way you said 'our' was very strange," he clarifies, and it's my turn to frown.

"It's complicated, but I'm happy." I shrug off the opportunity to clarify, and he quickly fills the silence.

"We were happy once, weren't we?"

"Yes, Dave, we were." He takes my hand and my tummy flutters. He could always do that, but somewhere along the way he stopped. I look up, and my eyes meet his. His dark, thick brow is still heavy, but this time with uncertainty. His normally light brown eyes are almost black, but I can see the sadness; it's raw and honest, and it slices right through my heart. This man was the love of my life for most of it, and I remember most was good, at least. He was my reason to smile for so many years, and I'm winded by the surge of emotion that look and his tentative touch have resurrected. *Gone, but not forgotten.*

"I'm so fucking sorry, Finn. *So* fucking sorry." He steps in front of me and cups my face. His strong jaw is tense, and I can see the dark circles under his eyes. His voice cracks along with my heart at his continued confession.

"I've missed you so damn much. I tried to give you some space because I fucked up so bad, then I found out you'd left the country. I didn't know what to do. It was like a part of me wasn't there anymore. You're my soulmate, Finn." His words are heartfelt and hopeful. I slap that hope right off his face with my next question.

"Did you go?"

"Go where?" His brows shoot up and his expression darkens. He really can't think I'd forgotten. "Oh, yes, but only because I'd already paid for it." I step back and shake from his hold. "Shit, no, not the prostitutes—prostitute." He corrects. Doesn't it make me feel better that we're not talking in plurals. "I had paid for the *holiday*; I never went with a hooker. The others did, and I almost did. I won't lie to you, Finn, but I couldn't. All I could see was your face, your heartbroken face, and I fucking hate myself for that." He steps forward and I step back.

"So you were there the whole week?" I cross my arms, feeling a chill the sun's rays beating down can't warm.

"I got high, but that's it. I don't want anyone else. I just want you." He reaches for my hand, and then metaphorically punches me full in the chest with his next move. *I did not see this coming.* He drops to his knees and pulls a small velvet box from his back pocket. I'm breathless, my chest hurts, my stomach rolls, and I get a sudden urge to purge with the hideous sense of déjà vu, but he unclips the box, and this time it's perfect. It's a stunning solitaire diamond on a white-gold band. The sun catches the facets, and it shines and sparkles against the dark cushion. *He really does want me.*

"It's beautiful." My fingers twitch, but I don't reach for it.

"Please, Finn, you have to forgive me. I want to marry you. I've never wanted anything as much as I want you now." He pleads, and I feel it rock my very fragile core, but I hold firm, gripping my fingertips into my flesh to make sure this is real.

"I—I've changed. You might not like the new Finn, Dave." He sniffs with a playful laugh and tips his head.

"We were together for nearly ten years, there's nothing I don't know about you, Finn, however much you think you've changed. I *know* you, and I love *you*." He's saying all the things I would've died to hear just a few months ago, and at this moment, I have this unbearable pain ripping me apart that he's too fucking late.

"Charge isn't *just* my boyfriend." He stands but still holds my hand, and with his other, he awkwardly holds the ring I won't take.

"Sorry, but that's a good thing, then? I mean, if he's not really asked you out."

"They are *all* my boyfriends." His face is unchanged and still filled with confusion, so I lay it out. "I'm dating *all* of them at the same time, and I get to pick which one I'm going to marry."

"Marry?"

"Yes. I came here to marry one of them." I straighten my back and steady myself for the backlash of vitriol I know Dave is capable of when he's hurt, or worse, rejected.

"You're fucking four guys!" His confusion is replaced with a mix of intrigue and disgust—mostly disgust. "But he said you were *his* girlfriend."

"Yes, he was protecting me because, funnily enough, people are very quick to judge what is none of their fucking business," I snap, and he balks at the strength of pride in my retort.

"I'm sorry, Finn; this is a bit of a shock. Give me a minute." He drags his hand through his hair, and I watch as he tries to process what I've told him.

I feel an unpleasant claw and twist in my gut when the sadness and hurt begin to filter into his dark eyes. I hurt him, I can see it as clear as day, and I'm ashamed to say I knew I would when I spewed the words like I did. He's a proud man, but if he really wants me, he has to know the truth. I won't lie, and I may not be proud of the way I told him, but I'm not ashamed of where I am and who I'm with. He straightens his shoulder after a moment and inhales a deep, steady breath, and for the second time in almost as many minutes he renders me speechless. "I don't care, Finn. I want you back. I love you, every part of you. Please be my wife."

"Dave, I… How can you say that?" I shake my head at his nonsense. "I know you. You loved the fact that you were my first and only, and now you're just fine with me—"

"Don't…please. I get it, and believe me, the visual is cutting my heart right out as we speak, but I pushed you to do this. This is my fault, so I have to forgive you, and I do. Everyone deserves a second chance, Finn. Don't I deserve mine?" I can't look at him and see his tortured face, even though tears cloud my eyes and are streaming unchecked and relentless. I hear him calling my name, panic and pain in his voice, but I can't. It hurts too fucking much. My feet are pounding the rough dirt road, legs burning from a speed I didn't know I was capable of as I run blind, hopeless and heartbroken.

I crash through the back door of the house with the intention of seeking the sanctuary of my bedroom and a locked door, but I run into a brick wall of hard, hot, T-shirt-clad muscle.

"Hey, angel. You nearly knocked me out—what the hell?" Charge lifts my head with his large hands, making me feel so small and safe, protected and cherished. His worried eyes search mine, and my heart just about breaks all over again. *I don't know what to do.* "Angel, what happened?" His soft voice is my undoing, and I collapse against him, knowing he'll catch me.

His arms circle me like a shield, and after a brief and comforting squeeze, he lifts me into his arms and carries me into his study. He sits us back on the low soft sofa, and I just hold him right back, as if that connection is my lifeline.

My breathing steadies, and the sobs begin to subside, but he still hasn't pushed me to explain myself. I take an unladylike sniff and shuffle back out of his hold, mourning the loss of his heat, but I need to find my own strength to process this complete and utter clusterfuck. Pulling my T-shirt up, I pat my cheeks dry and wipe my runny nose. He chuckles, making me smile, though I can't quite laugh. I have too much shit weighing me down to do that.

"Would you like a tissue?" He arches a comical brow.

"Little late for that." I shrug, dropping my soaked shirt, opting for the back of my hand. *God, I'm a mess.*

"What happened? Because if he hurt you, angel, we have plenty of space to bury the body." His tone is teasing. He takes my hand as I try and wrap my arms around my curled legs, needing not only to become as small as I can but impenetrable too. *No such luck.* He tugs me back into his hold, his hands soothing my skin, his soft lips in my hair.

"He asked me to marry him." His breath freezes as his whole body turns rigid as rock beneath me.

"I see." He speaks into my hair, his mouth still not moving away.

"I told him about us…all of us. Why I was here." I explain.

"You wanted to push him away, so you didn't have to make that choice." Charge states his insight like its fact.

"What? No! Maybe. I don't know. I wanted to hurt him." I rub the fresh trickle on my cheek dry with my clenched fist.

"Did it?" His voice is a little clearer since he has lifted his head from mine.

"Yes, but he still wants to marry me. He still wants me." I look up as he looks down, his blue eyes like a stormy ocean, deep and dangerous.

"I understand." He holds my gaze, unwavering and penetrating. "We all want you, angel. I may not like the man, but he's obviously not a complete idiot."

"Not a complete idiot, no," I scoff.

"So?" He tips my chin high, keeping the eye contact, as it starts to drop.

"He said everyone deserves a second chance and…" I can feel the tears bubbling beyond my control and my stuttered breathing fails to contain the sobs.

"I understand—"

I snap my interruption as I pull from his light hold.

"I swear to God, Charge, if you tell me you understand one more time, I will kick you in the goolies so damn hard—"

"The what, now?" He coughs out a shocked short laugh.

"Goolies, nuts, balls, knackers, testicles." I go on.

"Right. Okay, angel. I don't want that, because if you choose us, I will definitely be needing them later."

"What? I didn't say—" My heart feels the icy slice of truth piercing the flesh with his understanding and kindness.

"Angel, I don't think for a moment you wouldn't be thinking about his offer. You loved him for a long time; you said so last night. All I will add, because I can see this is tearing you apart, is that just because we haven't known you as long, doesn't mean we don't want you just as fiercely."

"I…I don't know what to do, Charge. I can't breathe for the pain. I feel the same, but I've loved him for so long, and he *knows* me." I drop my head to my chest, and he lifts it again with a single finger.

"I *know* you, angel." Both his tone and his glare sear right through me, but I shake my head.

"No, he *really* knows me, Charge. Everything. Things I haven't had the courage to tell. All that ugly shit a person saves for a rainy day. All the shit someone keep locked in a dark corner in their mind… or under a T-shirt." I frown, because I don't mean for this to be about him. I don't want to push him like this. That isn't fair.

"I know, angel, and I hate that I can't give you what you want, but nothing you have in here is anything to be afraid of sharing." He places his large hand over my heart.

"I could say the same." I exhale a shaky breath, my eyes raw from the endless stream of tears.

"Maybe." He wipes the collection of drops at my jaw, but they are relentless.

"He knows me." I sigh, defeated.

"He knows what?" He slides from beneath me and walks across the room, agitation and frustration radiating off of him.

"Charge, I'm not meaning to push you. Really, I want to know, but not like this. I'm just struggling to feel my way through this, and my head's a fucking mess."

"I know, angel." He's swiftly back to sitting beside me, my hands clasped between his. "Don't let your mother leaving you on the doorstep make you settle for just *anyone* because you feel you're not worth wanting. Everyone who was supposed to protect you failed. Everyone who was supposed to want you—your mother, the abortion, your gran and how she treated you are all deplorable, but you're—"

"What did you say?" I stutter, and he freezes, his mouth making tentative sounds but his whole face is a picture of horror.

"That you're worth—"

"No, not that." I snap, and he flinches. "What did you say about an abortion?" His face pales as my world falls away. "Charge?"

"You knew we did extra research, a little above and beyond," he mutters, his eyes dipping away from mine.

"The binder...my file, you mean? Because what you just said is a bit fucking more than above and beyond, and you wouldn't look so fucking sick if it wasn't." I stand, and I'm shaking with rage. "Show it to me."

"What?" He obviously struggles to swallow.

"Did I stutter?" His eyes narrow at my callous tone, but not only do I feel like my heart has been ripped out of my chest, I feel as if *his* big heavy boots have left a big fucking imprint as they stomped down on it. He walks over to his desk and slowly pulls the top drawer. Lifting a slim lever-arched folder out, he hands it to me. I take it with shaking hands; my fingers grip tight to stop the visual display of my breaking body. I flick it open, my eyes scouring, dates, time, statistics summarizing my life. There are some pictures I haven't seen for a while, but my eyes start to glaze with a fresh flow of tears. I snap it shut and hold it out to him. "Show me. Show me where it says all that," I demand, my damn voice catching. He steps toward me and I can see the devastation in his face when I step back, away from his comfort. "Don't. Just show me, Charge."

"Finn." His plea makes my eyes screw shut as if that will block the sound of his voice, too. He grabs the folder, and I take no comfort in the fact he looks as broken as I feel. "It's not in here."

"How did you find out? Did you hypnotize me or something?"

"No, *no!* Nothing like that. You…" He lets out the heaviest sigh, dragging his hand through his spiked hair before he has the courage to openly break my heart. "One night you started talking in your sleep."

"And I just gave you an unabridged monologue of my child-hood and fucked up mother?" I ask, the words fall like acid from my tongue.

"Not exactly." His jaw tenses at my hostility.

"Oh, please, don't be coy now,"

"I asked you some questions, and you told me your story." His calm tone is ineffective.

"You did what?" I cry out, bending at the impact, I feel this like a direct hit in my chest.

"I'm sorry, Finn. You were crying, and I thought it was some-thing I had done. I needed to know you were okay. I should've woken you. I'm so sorry." He raises his hands and lets them fall as I level him with my disbelieving stare.

"You won't even show me what's under your damn shirt, and yet it's okay to delve into my unconscious mind and have a good old rake around."

"I didn't mean to pry." He straightens his shoulders, taking the accusations blow for blow.

"You didn't pry. You violated me, and the really sucky thing here, Charge, is I would've told you, if you'd asked. It's probably why my mind didn't shut down. Even in my sleep, I felt safe with you. Shame you don't feel the same."

I stand, dumbstruck and heartbroken. I can't even look at him because I know he reflects my devastation. I know he's sorry, but not as sorry as I am. I turn and leave the room. Dave is hovering in the hall, and I don't know how much he heard, but it really doesn't matter.

"Help me pack. I'm coming home."

CHAPTER THIRTY-THREE

Finn

D AVE REMAINS WISELY SILENT AS I THROW MY belongings into my suitcases. I know he must be pleased, but the tears haven't stopped streaming down my face, because I'm so far from sharing that pleasure it's unreal. I rush to the toilet for the second time to throw up my nonexistent breakfast.

"We don't have to fly today if you're not feeling up to it. We could stay a few days, maybe keep the car, drive down the coast to Mexico." His voice sounds light, optimistic even.

Jeez, the last thing I feel like doing is having a vacation.

"I just want to go home," I mumble, as I wipe the saliva from my chin. I'm a physical and emotional wreck. I'm probably not fit to travel, but I can't stay here. I need time to work out what I want, but I have never felt so betrayed, so exposed, so lost.

Five suitcases, packed in record time, but then there was little folding or care taken. I didn't bother with the toiletries, and I'm not going to bother going through the laundry for stray garments. Slipping my sweater on, I keep the hood folded as far over my head as possible and still be able to see ahead. Dave is on his second trip to the car, and I drag the last case along the corridor and thump it down the stairs. It's not like there's anything precious, or fragile; there's nothing left to shatter.

The boys are all standing near the door, and I bend at the sheer agony slicing me open at the looks they level at me. They are distraught and stoic, but their eyes are soft with understanding, which hurts the most. I start to drag my case, and Charge walks forward and lifts it from my hands without hesitation. He turns briskly and carries it to Dave's waiting rental car.

I shuffle over and fling my arms around Tug. He hauls me up his body, burying his face into my messy bun.

"I'm so sorry, darling." He holds my gaze and softens before my eyes, as they start to fill with more tears. He places me on the ground and Toxic does almost exactly the same—same hold, same gaze, and exact same words.

"So damn sorry, sugar."

"You change your mind, don't fucking hesitate, you hear me?" Pink states, his breath catching and he hides it with a wide, sincere smile. His hand sweeps away the damp tendrils sticking to my tear-stained face, and he leans down to kiss my cheek.

"I love you all. You know that, right?" I blurt, and it's a shitty time to say it, but I can't leave without them knowing.

"You gotta do what makes you happy, darling, and everyone deserves a second chance. Just know we love you too, *all* of us." His words are so damn kind, meant to ease my pain, I'm sure, but nothing will, because at this time I'm so fucked up I don't know what is causing me to hurt the most, *this decision or Charge.*

He's standing back from the rental, his arms crossed with taut, tense muscles and a stern expression that looks as hostile as the glare he had fixed on Dave. I start to walk to him, and he turns away. The last little beat of my heart flatlines. I swallow back the sob but can't hide the devastation. My face crumples, and I scurry to the car, slamming the door and burying my head in my hands. Dave gets in the driver's side and starts the engine. I nearly jump out of my skin with the loud bang against my door window. I turn and am faced with piercing, soul-sad, sorrow-filled eyes—Charge's. I press the window down and his hands swoop in to cup my face. His lips are on mine as if this kiss might just save his life; it just saved mine.

"You've already chosen, Finn, you need to listen to your heart. I know you're angry. I fucked up, but this is one assumption you should trust, and you know it." He grits the words out, his eyes boring through me, his jaw twitching with the effort to keep control.

"Damn right, she's chosen. She's in my car, so back off." Dave leers over my shoulder, but Charge doesn't break the gaze.

"I will fight for you, Finn. This *being wanted* goes both ways. Don't think for one second it doesn't. If this was the right decision, you'd feel better now. Do you? Do you feel better, angel?" His soft voice is like a balm to my soul and I lean into his hands.

"I...I don't—" I jolt in my seat as Dave floors the car, pulling away in a cloud of dirt and skidding tires. I snap my head to Dave, but then back round to where Charge was just standing. Large billowy clouds of dust settle, but the air fills with the hollow roar of Charge cursing to the heavens in a guttural cry.

"*Fuck!*"

"What the hell, Dave? You didn't need to do that. I'm in the damn car. I didn't get to say goodbye!" I choke out my words with a cry.

"Ripping the Band-Aid, Finn. You think he'd feel better with you wailing and crying and then still get in the car? Trust me; this is better." Dave's hand squeezes my thigh, at least I think he does, I feel so damn numb.

"It doesn't feel better." I turn and look at the retreating view of my home. *This is my home.*

"Maybe if you put this on, it will." He holds the engagement ring flat in his palm then wiggles it between his thumb and forefinger.

"I never said I'd marry you." I actually flinch back into my seat, away from his hand.

"But you came with me. We're going home." A harsh edge clips his tone.

"Because I need time. *We* need time."

"You're right, I'm sorry. I want to make this work. I want to be happy again, and *you* make me very happy." He palms the ring and slips it in his pocket, then places both hands on the wheel. Despite the lack of air conditioning in the car, I get a chill in my veins that makes me shiver top to toe.

"Yeah." I force my lips to twist upward, though it's an effort. *As long as you're happy.* Why do I get a tiny but intense feeling in the pit of my stomach that I have just made a colossal mistake?

Dave moaned about the weight of my cases but quickly offered a placatory smile when I narrowed my eyes and quite obviously bit my tongue. The tears may have stopped, but I can't seem to move forward from going over and over Charge's last comment. If this was the right decision, I *should* feel better. And what did he mean, I'd already made my choice? I chose Dave; how could that make him happy? It didn't make any sense. Unless… Have I chosen Dave, really? Or did I leave because I had to, because I was hurt. Because, let's face it, I didn't leave, I ran like the fucking wind, and one thing is absolute, I don't feel better; I feel like shit. I can't think straight, because my head is such a fucking mess. I just want to go home and then it hits me like a cartoon anvil.

I don't actually have a home.

"Hey, Finn, please don't cry. It's going to be all right, I promise." Dave pulls me into his firm arms, and I break all over again. He feels good, but not right. He pulls back, and his hand lifts my dropped head until my sore, puffy eyes meet his. "I've missed you so damn much. I'll do whatever it takes to make it right, baby. I want us to be a family." That's possibly the sweetest thing he has ever said to me, and he seals the sentiment with a soft and loving kiss. But it doesn't seem to make a toss of difference. I feel numb, like I'm on autopilot and it's only his guiding hand that's keeping me moving forward. Through check-in and security, through the departure lounge, every step farther away, every step feeling more final until I'm sitting at the gate waiting to board.

I'm not a great flyer, but I don't even feel my normal nerves. I feel empty. Did I really expect them to come charging after me, crashing through the airport to stop me from making a horrible mistake, declaring what they already professed, which I threw in their faces when I walked away.

No, I really didn't. Life doesn't work like that.

My time with them was wonderful, but maybe that's why I'm here now, because in my heart, I knew it wasn't real, and this is the only way I could walk away. I'm a realist.

Dave chuckles at something on his phone and hands me his passport to put in my bag. I take it, and for no other reason than it always makes me laugh, I open it to check his photo. I remember he must have taken at least a hundred pictures before he was happy. He still looks like a dork. The page opens, but not at the photo, and I stare, not at the picture but the Las Vegas stamp dated four days ago.

"Did you go to Vegas before you came for me?" I can hear the incredulity in my voice.

"What?" The look on his face doesn't require a repeat, and he fumbles and fidgets so much his phone slips from his hold and lands on the floor by my feet. In a comical slow motion play out of events he reacts too late. I have his phone and my eyes scan and read the damning evidence on that little screen as he tries to speak. "Finn, I can explain…" My palm jerks to just in front of his nose, but really, I should clench my fist and knock the fucker right out.

"Vegas?" I repeat, my voice a hostile and justified accusation.

"It was Eddie's stag do, and I thought…"

I let out a heavy mocking laugh as I interrupt before I have to listen to his pathetic explanation. I stand and take a step back.

"Oh, I doubt your tiny brain has room for such activity." Saliva is pooling fast in the back of my throat, and I'm really thankful I still haven't been able to eat, or I would be retching right now, when I need to keep reading this soap opera of texts. "Stacy. This is Stacy from *my* work, I take it?"

"Yes." He reaches for the phone and I twist from his reach.

"Well, it looks like congratulations are in order, Daddy." My smile is rightly sardonic.

"Finn…" He drops his shoulders, and his tone is a quiet plea, his eyes furtively looking at the attention we are drawing. I do not give one flying fuck who is looking at us right now. *Jeez, you're an idiot, Finn.*

"She got my address from Carlos, that's how you found me?" I shake my head, talking more to myself; he answers all the same.

"Yes."

"Why would she do that? If she knew you were coming to get me—Oh! Oh she doesn't know, does she?" I blurt out a hollow laugh, and my jaw drops in disbelief. *Wow.*

"I don't want her. I want you." He stands and tries to take my elbow, but my glare halts him. He snaps his hand back to his side but remains towering close, a mix of terror and confusion resting uneasily on his face.

"So"—I finger air quote to highlight the message I just read— *"I'll give you what you need, baby, just as soon as I'm home,'* is what? Code?"

"She's a little unstable. I just need to ease her down gently. I know it doesn't look good…"

"No. No, it looks great. I walk away from the best thing that ever happened to me, and you're still fucking someone else, who's carrying your baby! It's fucking perfect."

"Language, Finn!"

"Yes, because that's what's important here. You're fucking priceless!"

"I don't want to be with her, Finn, and I'll need help with my baby. I thought—"

"See, there you go again, *thinking*. And if that isn't the finest example of why you really shouldn't. You're a piece of work, you know that?" I throw his passport and phone down, turn and walk away.

"I made a mistake, Finn," he calls out, but really he doesn't need to. The whole room is silent, enjoying the show, like a disaster movie.

"No, Dave, *I* made the mistake. The biggest fucking mistake. I'm going to pray it's not too late, and they'll take me back." I feel a wave of torment twist my tummy that they might not.

"You can't leave me!"

"Can't leave you? Just watch." I wave without a backward glance, even his last insult doesn't make me falter.

"You're going to go be a slut for four men instead of becoming my wife? What kind of woman does that?" he snarls.

"A very, *very* lucky one." I flip him the bird and stride through the gate entrance way. I only manage one step when my dramatic exit is scuppered by protocol.

"Excuse me, Miss, but you can't just leave. Your bags are on the plane." The lady at the final check desk explains. I stop at the urgent tone of her voice but smile, because this isn't a problem.

"I don't care, I have to leave. I have to try and make this right," I urge, trying to convey the importance with clasped, praying hands.

"But your bags?" she insists, and I wave off her concern, as if that matters. The only thing that matters is that I have to make this right, now.

"Blow them up for all I care."

If I thought walking away from Charge, Pink, Toxic and Tug was *the* stupidest thing I'd done that day, it didn't even register on the scale of biblical idiocy I achieved with that throw away comment. Of all the things *not* to mention whilst in an international airport the top three would be, 'Man, this cocaine up my arse is chafing', or 'Yes, I'm carrying this luggage for a complete stranger', and 'My luggage is going to blow-up'. Now, in my defense, I never said it would blow up, I just said they *could* blow it up, because I didn't care enough about it to wait. However, Captain Hindsight excelled today. That's not what they heard, and it *is* the reason I was manhandled to the ground, cuffed— and not in a remotely sexy way—and have been sitting in an interrogation room for the last ten hours.

CHAPTER
THIRTY-FOUR

Charge

"**F**UCK!" DRAGGING MY HAND THROUGH MY HAIR, I storm back into the house. *What the fuck just happened?*

"You wanna tell us why we let her go?" Pink demands, leaning his hand flat on the kitchen island, flanked by Toxic and Tug, all glaring daggers at me. I pull the fridge door open and grab a beer, flip the top, and down the bottle before I answer. I need the precious seconds to gather my thoughts. *I don't fucking know.*

"I fucked up. I let the sleep-talking incident slip." I look at Pink when I deliver the blow, because he will get it.

"Shit." He does and drops his head back in a silent curse.

"What sleep-talking?" Toxic asks. Tug is frowning with equal confusion.

"She was talking one night and Captain numb-nuts here decided to ask her a shit -ton of intrusive questions." Pink enlightens them, and I cringe with the accuracy and sting of his accusation.

"Why? Shit, Charge, you of all people. What in the fucking hell!" Toxic slams his fist on the counter, and I don't think I've ever seen him so pissed, not at me at least.

"She was crying, and I wanted to know why. It's done now, and I'm sorry." I throw the empty bottle against the wall and get no satisfaction from the momentary release of anger. The frustration and fucking pain ripping me apart is magnified when I look at my brothers. *I really messed up.*

"She was so mad. She *had* chosen us. I know she had, I saw it in her eyes, even as she was debating giving that asshole a second chance. In her heart she was staying, but then I blew it, and she shut down. She had to get away, and I don't fucking blame her, but she'll be back. She chose us; she just doesn't know it. I doubt she'll even get on the plane."

"You better be right," Toxic warns, but it's not necessary. *I fucking know.* I take two steps toward my office and turn back. "Fuck it! Tug, find out what airport and flight she's on, and while you're at it, I want all the dirt you can find on Dave. We didn't look before, but I want to know every single thing that fucker has done since Finn left him. I want to know why he came back now."

"Why?" Tug asks.

"Because we're going to get our girl, and I might need more than my winning smile," I state flatly.

"You know exactly what you need, Charge, and there's fuck all point going after her, if you're not going to give it to her," Pink pushes, and my gut twists because he's right. This is in my hands now.

"I know. I still want that info, stat. We're leaving in T-minus five fucking minutes," I call out, as I take the stairs two at a time. I only need my wallet and we are leaving.

"Fucking hell!" I slam on the brakes as we hit a gridlock of cars and a never-ending line of red taillights all the way from the freeway exit to the main terminal. I punch the steering wheel and tilt my head back, hoping for some divine fucking intervention to calm my rage.

"Anyone want to tell me what the hell is going on?" I snap.

"I'm just checking. No traffic reports or accidents, I mean." Tug is scrolling through his phone when I catch a glimpse in my rear view when he looks up. "Wait, the airport's on lockdown. Terrorist threat. We're not getting in anytime soon, Charge."

"Yeah, I'm getting that much." I drop my head to the wheel and prepare myself for a long fucking wait.

The traffic hasn't moved in over an hour but at least the planes have started to take off again, which is good, even if it means we might miss Finn's flight. My phone starts to vibrate in my pocket, and I get a tight pinch in my chest that it might be her—fucking stupid thought, when we never actually spoke on the phone. It was always emails and Skype. I recognize the number. Just when I thought my day couldn't get any worse…

"Commander." I catch Toxic's eyes in the rear view mirror, but quickly look away and focus on the call.

"Yes, how long?" I clip, and my stomach fucking drops with the answer. *Shit.* "Very good. Yes, he is, I'll tell him." I end the call and close my eyes. I love my job, have always loved my job, but right at this moment, I wish I'd quit when Pink did. I hate leaving loose ends and not having Finn back in our home is one big fucking loose end. I wonder if leaving her at any time would be any less painful than leaving right now. I just hope I get to find that out, one day.

"Pink, you're gonna need to take the wheel. Try and find our girl and bring her back home. If she's left already, track her down, but wait till we get back. I want to be there when we get her. I need to tell her everything."

"How long you gonna be gone for?" Tugs asks from the back.

"As long as it takes. Commander's words, not mine. Come on Tox, he wants us at the base now." I slip my belt and jump out of the truck as Pink slides across to fill my seat. "I'm so fucking sorry I messed this up, guys, but I'll make this right. I promise."

"I know, man. We love her, too. She's—" Pink flashes an easy grin, and I interrupt with the only appropriate word.

"Perfect." He tips a brief nod, and patting his shoulder, I turn away. Toxic is beside me and we strike off at a steady jog against the stream of parked cars. The first taxi moving in the opposite direction has our name on it.

Finn

My bum is so numb, I feel like a polar bear at a marathon sit-down, and my back aches like a motherfucker from sitting in the metal chair that belongs to a child. I had one small glass of water hours ago, and I'm seconds away from dropping my jeans and peeing in the cup, or I might actually just piss myself to complete my humiliation. Not sure what else could go wrong to ruin my shitty day, but the door opens and a stern looking, beefy, grey-haired, ruddy-cheeked man is about to tell me.

"Right, Ms. Sanderson. I think you have some explaining to do?" He barks out like he's addressing an auditorium full of people. I jump at the boom of his voice, and maybe a little pee comes out—maybe.

"I'm sorry but I really need to pee first." Every muscle in my body is tense and crossed.

"Excuse me?" His enormously thick brows pinch together to form one intimidating unibrow.

"The toilet, I mean I'm going to answer all your questions, but unless you want a puddle on the floor…" I try for light humor, but it fails to penetrate the dark scowl and slightly disgusted look on his face.

"Fine, follow me," he grumbles, holding the door wide. I hurry as best I can with my thighs squished together, walking like I have a six foot pole rammed up my arse and just as uncomfortable.

I jump when I step outside the door. There are armed police everywhere. *God, I hope these aren't here for me. Stupid,* stupid *brain-to-mouth filter.*

I return several minutes later, with a lighter bladder and a breezy step, and am escorted back into the small, terminally dull, four-walled room.

"Right, Ms. Sanderson, as I was saying. Would you mind explaining why you thought it was funny to threaten to blow up a plane and shut my airport down for three hours?"

"Your airport?" I look at his badge, shiny, gold, official, but I didn't catch his name.

"I'm head of security here, so, yes, I consider this *my* airport. Answer the question, Ms. Sanderson?" His clipped tone belies his calm exterior.

"I didn't threaten that. I was upset and wanted to get away from my arsehat of an ex-boyfriend and at *that* time, and in a moment of complete and utter stupidity, I said something *stupid*. A brain fart, if you will, but not an actual threat. It was a misunderstanding as I'm sure you know by now," I plead, but avoid rolling my eyes. I need to show some degree of contrition if I'm to get out of here before I go gray. He sniffs out a derisive acknowledgment.

"There was nothing in your luggage to cause concern, but that doesn't mean we wouldn't take an act of terrorism seriously." He throws the last part of the sentence like a deadly accusation.

"I'm not a terrorist. I'm just an idiot who gave her ex-boyfriend a second chance, only to find out he's a cheating scumbag." I'm rushing my words because my nerves are getting the better of me. My stomach would be empty if it had anything other than my meager cup of water. I feel sick, and, honestly, I'm just a tad scared shitless. "I was trying to rectify the biggest mistake of my life before it's too late. Really, the worst I can be accused of is that my brain-to-mouth filter malfunctioned, but given that I chose to go with that arsehole I don't think my brain was fully functioning at the moment."

"I see." He's looking through my statement, which pretty much contains all my lifelong details other than who I sat next to in primary school. I actually remember the boy's name, but I think if I tell Captain Airport, he'll probably think I'm taking the piss.

"I'm not lying. I promise." I plead my innocence for the umpteenth time.

"Oh, well, that's all right then," he drawls, sarcasm dripping with a mix of contempt. I'm really not warming to him, but by the looks of it, the feeling is entirely mutual.

"If I can call one of the guys, they'll vouch for me." I offer in an effort to move this stalemate along.

"One of the guys?" He arches a thick and ugly bushy eyebrow.

"I have been staying with my boyfriend and his friends. They live the other side of Laguna. A beautiful farm, with horses and—" I fall silent at his darkened scowl.

"You have one call and twenty-four hours to get your story corroborated *and* for you to be picked up. If not, you will be deported on the next available flight, *and* you will be barred from entry back into the US." He shuffles the papers on his desk and screeches his chair across the tiled floor when he stands. He turns back at me, a smarmy smile spreading thin and wide when he adds, "For life."

He returns moments later with a phone. Not my phone, just a phone.

"Um, can I have my phone?" I ask with a hopeful tone.

"Um, no." He cuts me back, mimicking my accent with a condescending tilt of his lips.

"You know sarcasm is the lowest form of wit," I retort, and two for two he shoots me down, again.

"And incarceration is the lowest form of hospitality, so suck it up buttercup." He winks and part of me wants to scowl right back, but part of me wants to laugh. I bite my lips flat, because that was quite funny, and at any other time I'd probably laugh. I'm looking at a phone and searching my brain for any numbers, any fucking numbers at all.

"I don't know their numbers." I admit with a defeated exhale of breath.

"Ah, ain't that a shame." Okay, that did deserve a scowl, because now he's just being mean.

"What if I can't remember?"

"Then you get an even earlier flight." His voice has lightened at the thought of this being over sooner rather than later, for him at least.

"Shit! Okay, give me a minute. I haven't remembered a bloody number since the nineties. I mean, who does? Do you?" I snap.

"The important ones, yeah." His tone filled with self-importance, he's even looking down his rather crooked nose at my obvious stupidity.

"Well, you're lucky, then, not about remembering the

numbers, just having someone important." My voice catches, and all the sass and fire dies. Shit, I really don't know any of their numbers. I know Dave's, but I'm not calling him. I know my work number but I can't see how Carlos could help. The only one other number I know is my best friend's and I hope to hell she's not with a client. I dial Hope's number all the time silently praying and repeating the mantra, *Please don't go to voicemail. Please don't go to voicemail.*

"You've reached the sexiest bitch on the planet. Please leave...ah, I'm just shitting with ya'. Did you have your message all prepared in your head?" She giggles, and my whole body deflates with relief.

"Hope?" I gasp.

"Finn! Babe, what's with the private number? Did you like my—" Interrupting her, I clasp the phone with both hands like it's now my most precious lifeline.

"Hope, I need your help big time. I'm in trouble." I state, my voice calm but urgent, my intonation is completely lost on her.

"Shit, did they gangbang you into oblivion, and you can no longer walk without a bungee tie keeping your ankles together?" she snickers, but falls silent when I impress my dire situation with a little more gravitas.

"Hope, really not the time. Look, I need you to call one of the guys. Doesn't matter who, you just need to call them and tell them to come pick me up at the airport. Tell them I'm sorry, that I fucked right up, and that they might have to explain I'm *not* a terrorist."

"A what now?" she stutters, and I pinch the instant pressure at the bridge of my nose and squeeze the pain from my eyes with tightly squeezed lids.

"Please, Hope, it's really important. I have twenty-four hours or they're gonna, deport me, and I won't be allowed back, *ever*."

"Shit! Okay, babe. I'm on it." She hangs up.

She hangs up!

Nooo! Shit! She cuts the call before I can give her their real names, the address even. How the fuck is she going to call them? *I'm going to get deported.*

That was the longest night of my life. I'm still in the cell Captain Airport escorted me to last night, after my wasted phone call. They brought some food—and I use the term loosely—last night, this morning and again at lunch time. Other than the silence of the officer handing me my tray, I have been left to my own thoughts. They are getting darker as the minutes drag. I didn't sleep at all, and that little anxious knot in my stomach is now the size of the Indiana Jones boulder in *Raiders*. I jump when the door swings wide, and my breath catches, then releases with all the disappointment I have been harboring throughout the night.

"You're booked on the ten-thirty flight this evening, but since you're already through security we won't need to move you until an hour beforehand. You have one more hour here. I just thought I would let you know so you can relax and stop thinking Prince Charming's about to come to rescue your ass."

"Well, thank you for having my peace of mind so high on your priority list to take time out of your busy day. Dream squashing must just eat up the workday hours for you." I snip with thin lips and narrow eyes.

"Cute." He slams the door, his wide smug smile is the very last thing I see as tears fill my eyes, and I drop my head in my hands. I really don't know what I was expecting. I screwed up, and this is my Karma. I have my memories of the most amazing time in my pathetic life that will keep me warm at night with my cats. *I need to buy some cats.* I lie down and bury my head in my folded arms, the pillow barely rises above the thickness of the paper-thin mattress. I feel the touch on my shoulder and scramble to get away.

"Don't fucking touch me—"

"Hey, hey, darling." His soothing voice breaks me, and I fling my arms out wide at a startled and completely gorgeous Pink bending over me, grabbing him tight. Nestling into his neck and breathing in his earthy warm smell, my tears flow like a burst damn.

"Oh, God, I'm so sorry. I made such a mistake. I'm so sorry, Pink. I…"

"We know, darling. We know. We tried to come and get you, but the airport was on lock-down, some terrorist threat." He holds my shoulders as I sit back, while his soft teasing smile and the crinkle in the corner of his eyes fucking undo me.

"That was me, but I'm not…" I try to explain, but he shakes his head and laughs lightly.

"I know, darling, and so do they now. Come on, baby, let's get you home, where you belong." He takes my hand and pulls me to his body, there's absolutely no resistance. I throw my arms around his trim waist, and his big arms envelop me. *So, so good.* I lift my chin so it rests on his chest, and he looks down with a sweet and happy grin.

"Take me home," I whisper, and his mouth drops to swallow my words.

I had to sign some papers, and Pink already had my troublesome luggage in the truck. I actually only started to breathe easy when we hit the freeway. I kept thinking Captain Airport was going to change his mind and throw me on the damn plane regardless of my new non-terrorist status, as vouched for by an ex-service man and a currently serving Navy SEAL. Pink reaches over to take my hand, and Tug holds my other hand in his, as

I'm wedged between them on the front bench seat.

"How did Hope get hold of you? I couldn't remember any of your numbers. I don't think I even had them on my phone, other than Charge's, and she hung up before I could give her your real names." I ask once I'm sure we are headed home.

"Flowers." Pink's one word statement is pretty cryptic and his wink cute.

"Sorry?"

"She sent us flowers. She had our address but not much else. She tracked me down on Facebook, since the Stables has a page that I run, but I don't check if often, and when I didn't reply straight away she sent flowers. Got the delivery just after lunch."

"Flowers?" I repeat out loud.

"Yeah, the message said 'Check you're fucking Facebook messages, Finn needs you.'" He chuckles.

"Ah." I snort out a laugh. "That sounds like Hope."

"She put her number in the message, and I called right away," Pink informs me, and Tug adds his two cents.

"Smart girl." Tug nudges me and pulls me into a sideways hug.

"She really is. I owe her big time." I nestle into his hard chest and relish the warmth from his hold.

"We all do." Pink exhales the sentiment with a breath filled with relief.

"Is Charge very angry with me?" I ask after we've driven a bit further, and it's the only thing that's niggling a big fat hole in my mind.

"Angry?" Pink turns, and has a curious quirk to his mouth and tilts his head like he didn't hear me right.

"Well, disappointed. Is he disappointed I didn't choose you guys?" I clarify.

"But you did. He said you did. You just didn't know it," Tug offers, and Pink smiles wide and nods his agreement. "It's why we came after you because he was convinced you weren't going to board the plane and he wanted to be there for you."

"But not enough to come with you to get me?" My voice is soft and I can't hide my own disappointment.

"Darling, trust me he would be here if he could. Toxic and he got the call. They were deployed." Pink rests his hand on my thigh, but my head snaps round at his shocking statement.

"What! He never said anything about leaving." My voice pitched really high and squeaky with panic. I cough and try to regain at little composure.

"He didn't know. Got the call just as we hit the traffic." Tug shrugs, giving a tight apologetic smile.

"Is that normal? No notice, I mean." The panic has evaporated as quickly as it came, but it's replaced with a surge of unwelcome worry.

"For the Special Ops guys, yeah."

"Oh, God, I feel sick." I fold over and place my head between my knees, sucking in some steady deep breaths until the nausea fades.

"Hey, sugar, it's fine. It's the job." Two large hands sweep and soothe my back as I'm hunched over. I puff out some air and sit back. I can't quite manage a smile but I give a short nod.

"I guess. I just…I would've wanted to tell him, tell *them*, I'm sorry."

"You have nothing to be sorry about. He'll be stoked you're back. That's all that counts." Pink tries his best to reassure me, but it's really hard when we parted the way we did. And it being all my fault doesn't sit at all well.

"Will he call?"

"Depends." Tug looks over to Pink, but he just shrugs.

"Oh." I feel the weight of my unease press heavy on my chest and my heart. I know I won't feel any better until they are home. I guess I don't have a choice except to wait it out.

"It's the job." Tug shrugs again. It seems shrugging is explanation enough for this shitty situation.

"Yeah, okay." I slump back and find myself mimicking their shoulder movement in defeat. *If you can't beat 'em…*

CHAPTER THIRTY-FIVE

Pink

"**W**HERE'S FINN?" TUG IS POURING A FRESH POT of coffee, and I've just finished up at the stables. It's been three weeks since we brought her home and I know she's trying, but she's sort of drifting without the others. It hasn't helped that Charge didn't return my message, which meant he couldn't.

"Where do you think?" Tug rolls his eyes in the direction of Charge's study, Finn's go-to hiding place.

"Of course." Tug takes a sip of his steaming black drink and gives a wry knowing grin.

"I don't even want to think it, let alone say it out loud, but do you really think she's cut out for this life, and I don't mean us four, I mean the job?" I keep my voice low, even though the door to the study is shut.

"I asked her the same thing the other day; she's adamant it's because she didn't get to apologize. You know, she feels she didn't get to make it right, like she has with us," Tug explains.

"Yeah, that makes sense, but it can't help having all this time to mope either." I drag my hand through my hair and an idea starts to form. "She told me the other day she's never had so much free time. She's always worked." I spin the iPad that he's messing around on toward me and start to tap in some key words. It only takes a moment and I'm all set to pat myself on the back. "Right, well, I know just the thing to keep her mind off—"

"Yeah, me, too, man," Tug groans, and I punch him lightly on his shoulder.

"I didn't mean that." His crassness deserves another punch, and he ducks away, chuckling.

"Yeah, you did, but okay. What are you talking about?"

"The Ark Project down by the Bay." I tap the screen and swipe to enlarge.

"A shelter for homeless families?"

"Yeah, she can't work on her visa but she can volunteer, and she used to do that in the UK. I think she needs a distraction." I hold my palm up to halt the words I'm sure are crudely poised on the tip of his tongue as his free hand grabs his dick. "Other than your cock, asshole."

"I don't know; she was pretty distracted last night." His tone is playful with a touch of filth.

"Yeah, she was." I drag my hand through my hair again as the images flash in my mind and fire like lightning right through me, mainlining straight to my balls. Finn's sweet, sexy body cocooned between us, writhing and supple, hot and demanding. Those breathless pleas that fell from her lips when she exploded in our hands were like a choir of fucking angels in my ears, so damn good.

"You coming?" I start to walk in the direction of the study. Tug's eyes light up, and I want to throat punch him for his one-track mind, but when it comes to her, I'm not that much better.

"I'm taking her down to The Ark. Do you want to come with us?" I slow the words right down and am rewarded with a snarky scowl.

"I knew that, and, yeah, I'll come." He downs his coffee and jumps up to follow me.

I open the door and Finn looks up; a big, easy smile lights her face. She has her knees pulled up and is semi-snuggled in the corner of the worn and weathered sofa Charge won't throw out.

"Hey, darling. Wanna go for a drive?" I ask, leaning my shoulder on the doorframe.

"Oh, no, I'm fine. I'm good, reading." She waves her tablet at me as if that will stop me.

"Yeah…no." I step to her side and take the device from her fingertips. Her nose wrinkles in protest, but she doesn't resist. "Enough with the moping. We're taking you to do some good. So go get your scissors and shit, and meet me out front in five." My tone is as demanding as Charge's would be, and it obviously works, because she's sitting upright, ready to obey.

"What?" She jumps to her feet, eager but a little confused.

"Go. Shift that sexy little ass, and I'll explain on the way." I step back to let her move, which she does, even as her frown deepens. She reaches the door and spins.

"My visa won't let me work. I don't want to get into any more trouble."

"You're not working. You're volunteering." Her face shines

with happiness at my words, and I get a real kick that I made her smile.

"Oh, cool! Give me a minute."

"Take your time, darling. I've given you a full five of them."

Snickering, she dashes up the stairs, her bare feet thumping overhead like a mini stampede.

We pull into the industrial site and follow the signs to The Ark. It's a converted warehouse which looks bright and inviting against the backdrop of a rather dilapidated part of the city. The surrounding buildings are run-down, vacant, and should probably be condemned. My eyes flick to Tug, and I can see the concern in his expression mirrors the twist in my stomach. *Maybe this wasn't such a great idea.*

I made a call to the center and spoke to the director of the facility while Finn was getting her things, and I know they are excited and certainly sounded grateful for the offer. Finn is practically jumping in her seat, so I'm not about to tell her I don't think this is going to work for us. I barely get the key out of the ignition when she's pushing Tug to allow her out, slinging her satchel over her shoulder, and striding off to the door, leaving us both to gawk after her like idiots.

"We can't leave her here." Tug voices my concern, and I let out a resigned puff of air.

"I'm not sure we'll have much of a choice. You saw the look on her face. I'm not thrilled with the location, either, but this is just what she needs to get her mind off Charge and Toxic." Tug gives a light shrug; from his expression, though, he's far from convinced. By the time we've entered the building, Finn is already crouched down on her knees talking to a small girl with straggly, long, dark hair, clutching a panda with one leg missing. Finn looks over to us and the little girl runs in the opposite direction, straight into the waiting, welcoming arms of a man I assume is her father. Finn walks back to us and introduces us to Heather.

"Guys, this is Heather. She's the director here. Heather, this is Tug and Pink—don't ask." She grins, and I don't know whether she's referring to our nicknames or our relationship. It doesn't matter; Heather offers a friendly smile and shakes each of our offered hands.

"Nice to meet you. We spoke on the phone, thank you for dropping her off. So, how long have we got?" Heather asks.

"Excuse me?" I know I sound dumb, but I feel like I've missed a huge chunk of the conversation.

"Finn said she can stay, but she doesn't know how long. I just need to know how many people I can tell they are getting their hair cut today?" Heather smiles brightly, and Finn does the same.

"You're staying? Now?" Tug chips in, taking the words right from my mouth.

"That was the idea." She tilts her head, and a sweet smile tips her lips.

"Right, of course. I don't know, a couple of hours?" I offer.

"How about I call you when I'm done, and we can grab something to eat on the way back." Finn grins and rubs her hands together with uncontainable excitement.

"Sure." I reluctantly agree. "You have my number right?" I level an accusatory stare at her, and she rolls her eyes. Given her recent trouble with phone numbers, the sass has absolutely no justification.

"I do now." She waves her phone at me. "And it's fully charged." I pull her into a hug and rub her hair in a playful reprimand.

"Good." I kiss her cheek, and Tug does the same. We both cast a look back, but Finn is already being led away.

"She'll be fine." Tug pats my shoulder, and I groan.

"I need a beer."

We drive a little farther into town and hit a bar. Neither of us wanted to go back to the farm just in case Finn decides she needs us, so we shoot pool for a few hours, watch a game on the wide screen and check our phones every five fucking minutes. Five hours later, we get the call. She's waiting outside and that pisses me off. I floor the truck as soon as I recognize it's her, and I screech to a halt making her jump and drop her phone. I leap from the cab and am towering over her, as she picks up the pieces of her now shattered phone.

"What the hell, Pink! You scared the crap out of me," she snaps.

"What the fuck are you doing out here?" I snap right back.

"Waiting for you, duh!" She narrows her eyes just before rolling them at my question.

"Not outside, understand?" I drop down on my haunches to make sure she can see my eyes.

"No, not really. Dammit, Pink, look at my phone." I help her pick up the pieces at her dejected tone.

"We'll get a new one tomorrow, but no more waiting outside on your own, okay? It's dangerous, and you're too precious." Her face scrunches with a frown.

"Heather only left a minute ago." she offers, looking a little sheepish.

"It only takes a minute," Tug states from the truck, clearly hearing every word exchanged.

"I can take care of myself. I've taken classes." Her retort is feisty.

"Oh, really?" Tug chuckles, and Finn narrows her eyes. She pulls herself up straight and stands as tall as her five-foot-five frame allows. Stepping flush against Tug, who's now out of the truck. From over her shoulder I can see his eyes widen and his pupils dilate. His chest puffs with a sharp intake of breath. He's a big guy, we all are, and built too; at the moment, however, I'm not sure who I'd place my bet on in this impromptu standoff.

"Happy to show you, big boy." Her sultry tone belies some dark intent, and Tug's lips carve a deviant smile until she strikes. "But you might be needing these a little later." She slaps her hand hard into his crotch and he grunts out a loud curse, tensing and tipping away at the hips just enough to avoid none of the impact but all of the injury. *I felt that.*

"Okay." Tug chokes out a cough and massages his balls once we're back in the truck. "I'm still going to go over some other moves with you, just to be sure."

"That's really sweet, but I—"

She doesn't get to finish whatever she was going to say because I state emphatically.

"Not negotiable, darling. It's more than just your sweet ass on the line. Both our nuts would be on the chopping block if Charge found out."

"Have you heard from him?" she asks, sagging when I shake my head.

"Believe me, sugar, no news is good news."

"No news is fucking killing me. It wouldn't be so bad if I could speak to them, but okay," she grumbles.

CHAPTER THIRTY-SIX

Finn

I'M SURE IT GETS EASIER. I KNOW I'M FINDING THINGS especially hard to deal with because of the way I left. The fact that I never got to apologize, beg forgiveness for being an idiot, and tell them to take care, makes me ache. But it's been four weeks and I'm kind of going crazy.

Helping out at The Ark has been a lifesaver. The shelter caters specifically to families, and the massive industrial unit houses thirty, family-sized tents, which are sadly always full with a wait list as long as my arm. I cut all the children's hair on my first day and have worked my way around most of the adults. Heather then opened up for walk-ins, and word soon got out, so I have been kept super busy on the days I go in.

My nights aren't a problem either, and the notion I would get a few more 'days off' with there being only two of them was laughed off as ridiculous. But I do miss them as a whole. If I'm honest, I miss Charge maybe a bit more. My new phone buzzes in my back pocket, and I can't reach for it fast enough, even though it's crazy to think it would be him. I look at the screen and smile all the same.

"Hi Flick,"

"Hey, girl, how you been? What are you up to?" I snicker that she doesn't actually pause long enough for me to answer. "Get your ass down here. I haven't seen you in forever, and the band is killing it tonight."

"We weren't planning on—"

She draws breath, and I try to add my input into the one-sided conversation.

"Tell those boys to take you out. They can't keep you locked in a tower forever."

"Pretty sure they could," I snort. "But it's not them, it's me. I don't feel much like going out." I defend my men, because this really is my deal.

"You can't stop living when they get deployed, girl. It doesn't work like that," Flick protests.

I've heard the same argument from Pink and Tug, but I think this situation is slightly different.

"Oh, I know, but It's complicated," I mutter to deaf ears.

"Well, how about you come down here and tell Auntie Flick all about it. I'll bet your ass I can uncomplicate it for ya."

"I don't doubt—" I stop mid-sentence, and check my watch.

As if reading my mind, Flick says, "Finn, it's seven-thirty on a Friday night. Come and have a beer. Let your hair down. Those boys would be here in a shot, and you know it."

Her attempt to guilt me into coming is right on the money. I don't want to be this person. I don't want to stop them from doing what they would normally do, and I don't want to stop living. Even when it's hard not to feel their absence like a huge fuck-off hole in my chest, it's not healthy, and I have to be able to deal with this. It's their job for three of them, and I would no more ask them to stop doing what they love than they would ask me. *Man the fuck up, Finn.*

"Hmm... I'm sort of bringing the mood of the house down. Okay, I'll check with Pink and Tug, see if they want to—"

"We do! Whatever it is, we do. If it gets you out of the house and puts a smile on your face, we're in." Tug calls out in an overly loud voice so Flick can hear. I think the horses at the stables heard that holler.

"There you go," I laugh into the phone. I didn't even see them behind me, but they were obviously there the whole damn time. "We'll see you soon."

"Great, see ya' when you get here." She hangs up before I can double-check where she is.

"I take it you know where to go?" I turn to face two eager, handsome faces wearing bright, dazzling smiles.

"Same bar, sugar. It's always the same bar." Tug winks.

"Look, I'm sorry if I've been a killjoy. You know I wouldn't stop you guys from going out."

"Finn, stop. You're not, and we understand. It won't always be like this, but we get that this is hard." Pink steps forward and strokes my cheek, his large palm resting to cup my face.

"Sugar, we do not need to go out to have a good time. Been there, done that, and nothing compares to just having you." Tug comes up behind me, wrapping his strong arms around my waist, stepping flush against my back rather than pulling me away from Pink. I feel so damn protected and treasured with these guys, but Pink gets the wrong end of his stick.

"Jeez, Tug! Really? Does everything you say have to revolve around your dick?"

"What? It doesn't; that's not what I was saying." Tug sounds genuinely mortified, and I lift my hand up high, stretching to wrap it around his neck, tilting my head back so I can briefly kiss his pouting lips.

"Tug, ignore him, that was really lovely. Thank you. You both have been amazing, and if you're really up to it, I would love to go out tonight."

"Hell, yes!" They both call out, peppering me with a hundred kisses all over my face and neck. I squirm, giggle, and finally break free only because they let me.

"Great, give me ten minutes. I think PJs are a bit informal, even for a bar," I joke, running up the stairs to get changed.

I pull my hair back into a high ponytail and slick on some nude lipgloss and a swipe of mascara. I swap my PJs for a button-front, denim mini skirt, an off-the-shoulder white gypsy blouse, and some cute ankle cowboy boots. I'm good to go in under ten minutes.

"I love that you can do that, by the way." Tug opens the door to the truck, and I slide all the way over until I'm sitting next to Pink in the driver seat.

"Love what?"

"That you can look like you do without spending hours and shoveling a shit ton of makeup on your face." He looks me up and down with a mix of sexy appreciation and downright lust.

"Like I have a choice with the huge amount of time you guys always give me to get ready," I quip.

"You don't need a single second more, beautiful." Pink takes my hand, threading his fingers with mine in a secure hold.

"Well, that's lucky, then." I nudge Pink first and then lean over to do the same to Tug. I flick the radio dial on and turn the volume up high. "Let's rock!" I shout out above the instantly recognizable intro of Credence's "Bad Moon Rising". I won't ruin the evening by singing along, but I love this song.

There's a long queue around the building but, like last time, we stroll right through the roped-off doorway and into the loud, dark bar full to bursting with sweaty bodies. The band is on, and the crowd ebbs and flows with the swell of heaving revelers. Tug leads Pink and me in a snake of joined hands through to the back stairway and up to the mezzanine. I barely step one foot on the top step when Flick appears from nowhere and pulls me away from my men. She gives me a tight rib-crushing hug and grabs my hand to lead me back down the way we came. Turning briefly to wave and give the guys an apologetic shrug, Flick drags me through the crowd right to the front of the stage.

I don't know the words to the songs, which is probably a blessing, but I jump and dance like Tigger on speed. After an hour or so, I'm a hot, sweaty, dehydrated mess and I desperately need some fresh air. Flick offers to get the drinks and I head out toward the rear terrace. The dark corridor is narrow, and I have to turn to the side to squeeze past a hulk of a man with his back to me. He turns as I unavoidably brush past and he slams his tree trunk arm against the wall, right in front of my face.

"I know you." His voice is rough, and his breath is soaked with liquor. I don't turn but try to duck under.

"I don't think so," I reply with a vehement shake of my head. He drops his hand to prevent my escape and pushes me back against the wall.

"Yeah, I do. You're the new slut." He barks out a dirty laugh.

"What the fuck!" I snap, but he presses his hand against my mouth and lifts me with one swift move and backs us both under the stairwell. *Where the fuck is everyone?* I bite down on his hand so I can scream, but he doesn't flinch. I struggle and kick, only stopping when he slams me against the wall. I lose all the breath from my lungs and the capacity to fight. *It's useless anyway, look at the size of him.*

He removes his hand but keeps it hovering in case I venture

a scream. My heart is thumping like a jackhammer in my chest, but I'm trying to keep calm. "I tell you what." I suck in a deep breath that actually hurts, and I wonder if this arsehole didn't crack a rib. "If you back off now, I won't tell Charge and the others, and you might just live."

"Ah, but Charge isn't here, is he?" he sneers, peering down my top, sweat beading his top lip. His eyes are glazed black and his preternatural dark glare chills the blood in my veins. He looks high as well as drunk, but his remark actually makes my heart stop. *No, Charge isn't here. No one is.* I can hear people, lots of people, but the noise from the band will drown out any pathetic attempt to be heard, unless someone was standing within spitting distance.

"But Pink and Tug are and—" His ugly mouth crashes onto mine, and I bite down and catch his lips. He pulls back and rests his forehead on mine. He sucks in the blood, slow and menacing.

"I'm only helping you out, darling, no need to be like that." He grinds his filthy groin against me. I retch and try swallowing back the bitter pool of saliva in my mouth, but it just sits there, refusing to go down. "I know you're two cocks down with them gone, and your hungry little pussy must be starving by now." I'm now glad I didn't swallow, because I pull back a little and manage to spit full in his face. The shock makes him step back, which is all I need. I stamp the heel of my shoe down his shin and snap my knee up hard. He buckles, and his balance is gone—more to do with the alcohol than me, I'm sure, but I'll take it. I use the wall as leverage and kick his shoulder away and watch him topple like a not so mighty oak.

"Come anywhere near me again, and I'll ask the boys to hold you down while I cut your bollocks off with a rusty saw." He groans and tries to move. I don't wait around to gloat. I've seen way too many horror films, and I know I would be screaming, "Get the fuck out of there, you stupid bitch!" at the screen right about now.

Turning, I run around the corner of the stairwell into a group of people. *Oh, now, there are people.* Fighting my way through using panic and the adrenaline still coursing through my veins, I run straight into Flick.

"Shit, Finn! What happened?" She holds my shoulders, which are shaking.

"Nothing," I blurt, grabbing the beer from her hand. I down half the bottle before I have to come up for air.

"Wanna try that again?" She tilts her head and raises a suspicious brow.

"It's nothing. Some guy thought…" I swallow back a sudden rush of bile and wince as I force it down.

"Thought what, Finn?" she pushes.

"Thought…" I draw in a shaky breath as it all hits me, and I start to really shake. *Shit.*

"Jeez, honey, come on, let's go and sit upstairs." She wraps her arm around my waist and pulls me close.

"No, I can't let the guys see me like this."

"Why the hell not?" she exclaims, and I puff out a flat humorless laugh.

"Firstly, they'll kill him, and they would both end up in prison. Secondly, they'll never let me out of their sight again." My imploring tone helps, because when my eyes meet hers, she gives a reluctant nod.

"I don't think the latter is such a bad thing," she remarks.

"I wouldn't be able to hang with you without them," I clarify, and her eyes widen with understanding.

"Oh, right. Okay, let's take it to the ladies room." She turns us toward the restrooms, and I try to stop her, but she keeps her arm tight around me until we are secure in the cubicle. Her expression is so full of concern, I feel bad that I'm already over it.

"Really Flick, I'm fine. It was just some drunk guy trying

his luck. He said I needed cock because Charge and Toxic were away." I let it all out, because I really don't want to waste any more of my evening; it's done and dusted, and I dealt with it.

"What guy?"

"I dealt with it." I appreciate her caring, but I really just want to carry on with my night. I *was* having fun.

"You should tell them, Finn."

"I will, just not now. I want to enjoy the evening, please." Holding my shoulders and gaze, her eyes search mine. I'm pretty sure she's checking for any signs of trauma by her serious expression. "I'm fine, Flick. I promise."

"How about you tell me who he is, and I get him removed." She tips her head waiting for my answer. "He might try his luck with someone else not quite so feisty."

"Shit, I hadn't thought of that. Yes, let's go tell the bouncers." I straighten myself up in the mirror and am thankful he left no marks. I let out a fortifying breath and straighten myself right up. *Okay, let's do this.* I stand on the first step of the stairs to get a better view and I look around the edge of the room. If I'm honest the last thing I want to do is clock the guy again, or ever, but she's right. "Him. That one at the end of the bar."

"Hick?" I shrug at her question. "You took down Hick?"

"I took down an arsehole. He didn't give me his name, but that's him."

"I'm impressed." She blows a low whistle from her pursed lips. Looking me slowly up and down before nudging me playfully.

"Whatever. I'm going to go back upstairs and wait for you there, okay?" I wave her off and skip up the stairs, happy to put Hick and our horrible encounter behind me.

"Sure, won't be long," Flick calls after me, but she's already gone by the time I turn around.

The rest of the evening was fun. I danced with the guys,

drank too much, and was about to doze off in the truck on the way back, when Pink woke me fully with his question.

"You wanna tell me why Hick was being carted off by the police back there?"

"How would I know?" I answer way too quickly and a little too high-pitched to be remotely convincing.

"Well, I would've said you didn't, except for the look you exchanged with Flick when we were outside. The squeaky pitch of your voice isn't exactly crying out innocence, either, darling." He raises a knowing brow, and I twist my lips into an apologetic smile.

"Might want to point out, it's not a great idea to lie to us, sugar." Tug offers the wise words with a warm smile.

"Shit." I groan, and suddenly feel all the alcohol swimming in my tummy. I puff out a long slow breath. "Fine, but you're not going to like it." I pause for some witty comeback, but they are both deathly silent, only the engine and roll of the tires is keeping the heavy silence at bay. "Hick kinda said something about me."

"Said something?" Pink presses.

"Right, okay. So he grabbed me and pulled me under the stairwell. He basically suggested I needed more cock while Charge and Toxic were away, and he kissed me." I squeeze my eyes shut and wait for the apocalypse.

"Fuck!" They both yell, and I sink back into my seat. Pink's knuckles glow white from the grip on the steering wheel, and Tug punches the dashboard.

"And you called the cops?" Tug's tone is pure anger.

"What? No! Flick must have, but why is that a fucking problem after what he did?" I hope I'm getting the wrong idea with his tone and question, and they aren't about to put bros before me.

"It's a problem because we can't drive back and beat the

ever-loving shit out of him, that's why." Tug yells out through clenched teeth.

"Which is why I didn't tell you," I shout right back, my head turning between the two of them so fast I'm getting whiplash. "You would be the ones in the cop car if I did, and I can't lose you, too." My voice catches, and a surprising well of sadness mixed with a stupid amount of alcohol has tears bursting onto my cheek.

"Oh, sugar, don't cry. Please, baby." Tug pulls me onto his lap, and I can feel Pink's hand squeezing comfort into my thigh.

"You haven't lost them, darling. They'll be back before you know it." Tug loosens my hair and rocks me in his big strong hold. I tip my head up to see his light brown eyes smiling at me.

"Promise?" I ask, but he doesn't answer me and neither does Pink. I look at them both, but before I can berate them for teasing me, Tug stiffens beneath me, and Pink removes his tender touch from my thigh. I sit up and look out the front windshield as we near the farm.

"Why is there a military vehicle here at this time of night?" I hate that I know the answer before I even asked the question.

They don't answer me. They don't have to. I don't know how I know, but I feel it in the pit of my empty rolling stomach and my clenched heart. Pink pulls the truck to a stop nowhere near the military jeep and turns to me. His hands cup my face, and every nerve in my body freezes, and an icy chill washes like a wave through my soul. I start to shake my head. *No. No. No!*

CHAPTER THIRTY-SEVEN

Pink

"FINN, YOU NEED TO STAY IN THE TRUCK."

She's shaking her head before I get the damn words out. I look over her head at Tug, who's mirroring the gesture. I can't bear to look in her eyes; they look so lost already. "Please, darling," I plead, but her sadness turns to fury.

"No fucking way, Pink. No!" She starts to push against me, and, when I don't move, she twists and tussles with Tug. He wraps his thick arms around her and pulls her immobile and protected against his chest, if only for a minute. She looks up at him, then me.

"Please, you can't leave me in the truck." Her voice is so

broken there's no way we can stop her.

"Fuck!" Tug throws his head back and nods to me. *This is a bad idea.* He opens the door, and Finn slides out right after him. The doors to the jeep open, and I brace when I see the insignia on the lapel jackets: commander *and* captain. *Fuck.*

Tug salutes his superior officer, and I take up the slack, grabbing Finn's now free hand and coaxing her into my side. Tug makes the introductions, careful to include Finn as family.

"I think we should take this inside," the commander offers, his tone formal. We all file in, and it's just as awkward and ominous inside the house as it was outside, only we're seated and facing each other.

"I'm very sorry to inform you that Senior Chief Petty Officer Marlon Serrano has been critically injured. He underwent emergency surgery on location, has been airlifted back to base, and is scheduled for more surgery just as soon as he's stable. But I have to advise you to prepare for the worst. He was lucky to survive the crash."

"Crash?" Finn has no color left in her face, and she's gripping my hand so tight I've lost all feeling in my fingers.

"Yes, ma'am. I'm afraid I can't tell you much more than that. It's classified, but we can take you to the hospital." As if sensing my question, he looks away from Finn and directly at me. "Lieutenant Martinez is still MIA."

"How long?" Tug asks, but Finn's broken voice is the only thing I hear.

"Forty-eight hours," the captain confirms and my stomach drops.

"MIA? What's—" She breaks her own question with a sob and a cry of understanding. "No! No Pink, that can't be right? Missing? Charge is missing?" Her breathing is ragged, and the pitch of her voice is edging toward hysterical, and I really don't blame her.

"Finn." My own voice catches, but I'm trying to soothe her. I pull her into my side, but she pulls away, shaking her head with disbelief and despair. Devastation darkens her face, and her eyes fill with tears. "Please, Finn." I try to draw her back into my embrace, but she stands, wrapping her arms around her body, which is shaking, and breaking right in front of my eyes. I can't stand it—none of it. I rise as Tug does, and we enclose her in our arms to try and contain the unbearable sadness pouring from her.

"I can assure you we have every available resource searching for him, ma'am." The captain declares. I know he thinks his words might offer some comfort, but even if they do for Finn, they don't for Tug and me. It's a bigass ocean. Hell, it's a bigass world, and the first forty-eight hours are crucial. My guts twist, and my fucking chest feels like I've taken a bullet. I hate that when I catch Tug's eyes, I know his concern echoes mine. *If they haven't found him by now...*

Finn nods her understanding, but she's crumbling , piece by piece, with every tiny bit of new information, and her lips are clamped tight, so she doesn't actually speak.

"Would you like us to take you to the hospital?" the commander asks.

"No, we'll follow you. I want to pack some things, so at least one of us can stay over."

"Of course." He coughs to clear his throat, and his brows knit like he's about to give more devastating news. *What could he possibly add to this carnage?* "You and Lieutenant Gervais are next of kin, but only family will be allowed on the facility, do you understand?'"

"No, I don't fucking understand!" Finn spins round with venom and fury in her glare. The captain and commander both look shocked as hell at the outburst, but she's far from concerned about their reaction. She turns to Tug and me. "They can't. Please, they can't *not* let me see him." Her momentary outrage dissolves like spun candy in the rain, and she's a sobbing wreck in my arms once more.

"She's his fiancée, I think that counts as family, don't you?" I explain to the officers.

"It's not on his record?" the commander looks briefly at his file, but I clarify.

"It happened just before they were deployed. He was technically still on leave."

"Of course. Then that will not be an issue." They both stand. "Don't take too long following," the commander adds, and I have to scoop Finn into my arms as she buckles into a mess of uncontrollable tears. Tug shows them out and this unbearable cloak of sadness descends on us, and the only sound we hear is our girl's broken heart.

"We need to go." She sniffs back and roughly wipes the streaming wetness from her face with the back of her hand. Her eyes are raw, but she looks determined. Her shoulders stiffen, like every muscle in her body is fighting to hold her together.

"I know, baby. But why don't you go and grab a sweater and change into something comfy. Hospital waiting rooms can be cold, and the seats are like concrete, trust me. Hours sitting on them is no fun." Hoping my insight will offer some sort of distraction.

"You've done this before?" Her shocked and incredulous tone is heartbreaking, and she throws her arms around me when I nod.

"Yeah, darling, I've done this before." I pull back and sweep the slick hair, damp from her tears clear of her face. "Come on, Toxic needs us." She clenches her jaw so tight, I can hear her teeth grind, and she gives a sharp and stoic nod that breaks my fucking heart.

She returns in no time, wearing some soft-grey track pants

and a hoodie so big, I know it belongs to Charge. She looks so damn tiny in it, and her face? I have never seen something so deathly white. Even the red from all the tears adds no color or life.

"Come on, darling." I hold my arm up, and she's quick to step into my hold. One arm threads around my waist, while the other reaches out to take Tug.

I drive us to the base and straight to the military hospital only to be told he has been taken to Sharp Memorial since they had a donor match. I didn't ask what that meant, I just turned the truck around and headed into the city. The silence in the truck is oppressive, but there's nothing to say. Nothing will help. The only fragment of comfort each of us cling to is each other, our tight hands held together with hope and prayer.

We make our way to the transplant unit as instructed and are asked to wait. This is the bit I remember. I pull Finn into my lap and stroke her hair. I've been here with Tug and Toxic before, waiting on Charge. I remember everything like it was yesterday, and it's the reason I left the Navy. I didn't want this. I know it's the job, and I'd never ask the others to quit, but this nearly fucking killed us last time, though this is ten times fucking worse. Now we have Finn. Charge is missing in action, and we are damn well on the verge of losing Toxic too. I won't fucking cry, because that has never done me any good, but that doesn't mean this fucking pain in my chest isn't ripping me apart. It's tearing us all apart.

"Here, sugar." Tug offers the flimsy plastic cup filled with scalding hot tea to Finn. She stares blankly, as if she isn't registering much of anything, but she eventually shakes her head to decline the drink. He doesn't push her, just sits beside me and settles in for the long haul.

CHAPTER THIRTY-EIGHT

Finn

G OD, WITH THIS PAIN IN MY CHEST, I CAN'T FUCKING breathe; It's like a vise gripping the very life from each beat of my heart as it struggles to do its job, pumping blood and keeping me alive. It's unbearable. My life has been far from rose-tinted, but I don't ever remember pain like this. But then, I have never loved like this.

I did take the next coffee Tug offered, if just to help me stay awake. My whole body feels like it's shutting down, utterly exhausted and empty. We've been here for nine hours and there's still no news. Even with my very limited medical knowledge, I know a lengthy surgery time can't be good.

"You were here for Charge?"

"Yeah. Dumbass nearly got himself killed one time trying to be the hero."

"What happened?"

"Oh just stupid shit that involved him not listening to orders to save our asses. He went back for one last sweep and got hit."

"Is that when he got his scars?"

"I'm not telling you, Finn. This is his thing, and he will tell you. He was going to come clean about it all before he got called away, so how about we still give him the chance?" He keeps his tone so gentle, I don't feel the rejection, but I know he's right.

"Yeah, okay. I want him to tell me." I let out a sad sigh. I have to believe that day will come. I can't let anything else enter my head or I will simply curl up and die.

My sore lids close, and something catches my peripheral vision just before they seal shut—green and bloody scrubs. I scramble from Tug's lap and rush toward the tired looking surgeon, Pink and Tug by my side, quickly linking their hands in mine. The doctor rubs his neck; he's a small man, eye level with me with dark graying hair, a light tan, and sharp blue eyes.

"Marlon is stable, the surgery went well." He offers a tight smile and I start to sob, sucking the sound back in and holding it there with my clenched fist, because he isn't finished. "He's had a pancreas transplant, and there was severe damage to his liver and right lung. There was a great deal of internal bleeding that needed to be repaired, but we are cautiously optimistic. The next twenty-four hours will be critical. He's being settled into ICU right now. You can see him, but please prepare yourself. We aren't by any means, out of the woods." His tone is somber, but after that godawful list of injuries, it's understandable.

"Thank you." I grab his hand and shake it.

I know the list is horrific, but all I heard, and all I will cling to, are the words *stable* and *optimistic*. Lifesaving words for me at least.

"Yeah, thanks, Doc." Tug and Pink each shake his hand, and we are led through to the ICU.

"Oh, God." I hold back the sobs that want to burst from my heartbroken chest at the sight. Toxic's strong, fit body is covered with wires, tubes and so much bandaging there's barely a scrap of skin to be seen on his torso. I rush to his side and carefully pick up his heavy hand, holding it in both of mine. "Marlon," I whisper. His name hangs on my trembling lips, because I have no words. I don't know what to say. This is so fucking awful, my heart feels like it's been cleaved from my chest. Tug lays his hand on my shoulder, and Pink stands at my other side. I welcome his heat, their strength.

"It's gonna be okay, Finn. He's a fighter, remember that, and he loves you, so he's got something real to fight for. Just talk to him, okay?" I nod, because I know if I speak now after what he's just said, I will be a blubbering mess, and I need to think about Marlon.

Tug pushes a chair against my legs, and I sit. "Look, guys, I'm going to go back to the base, see if I can get some intel on Charge."

Another wash of pure, unadulterated agony slices through me. How the fuck am I supposed to function? This is too fucking hard. I just can't even think. *One damn fucking tragedy at a time, please.* "It's okay, sugar, stay here. I'll call when I have news, okay?" I grind my jaw and fail to swallow the lump choking me, holding back the dam of sadness.

Pink sits beside me, and we try to comfort each other in our joint desolation. I probably shouldn't compare my sorrow to his or Tug's. Toxic is a brother, Charge too, and I have only been in their lives for five minutes, but it feels like a lifetime. This certainly hurts like it's been an eternity.

"Is that a skull?" Pink's fingers twist the ring I have on my engagement finger. I let out a soft flat laugh.

"Yeah, it's the only one I have that fits the finger and I was worried someone would ask, you know, since you said we were engaged." I lean against him, my weary body utterly spent. "Thank you, by the way. I don't know what I would've done if they hadn't let me see him."

"I know, darling, and trust me, they would have stopped you. Anyway, you're here now and that's all that matters." He plants a soft kiss on my forehead. God, why does even a sweet gesture hurt so damn much. *So much pain.*

Pink is great, managed to charm the nurse in charge to let us both stay on the promise we wouldn't get in the way. He's been chatting to Toxic all night and even making me laugh on occasion, which felt wholly wrong and good at the same time. I keep checking my watch, because each second seems to take a lifetime. The doctor said the next twenty-four hours would be crucial, and we only have three more to go. Stupid, really, clinging to those words like they are Gospel, but I am. I don't want to leave even for a moment, but that coffee has finally worked its way through me, and I have to excuse myself. My legs are tingling from being in the same position for so long, and my body is numb from the agony of the last excruciating twenty-one hours. I run the corridor to the ladies. Fumbling with my sweatpants, I'm rough, urgent, and have the fastest pee in history. My pants barely cover my bum again when I burst out of the stall and run flat out back to the ICU.

All hell has broken loose in my two minute absence. How can that be? Pink is pressed back against the glass partition as a frenzy of activity, a blur of moving bodies against the soul-crushing sound of a single, unbroken heartbreaking bleep. *No. No. No.*

CHAPTER THIRTY-NINE

Finn

Four Weeks Later

I T'S BEEN ALMOST A MONTH SINCE MY HEART STOPPED beating. That sound nearly took two souls with it that night. Tug told me Toxic was a fighter, and that night, he needed to be. He flatlined for two whole agonizing motherfucking minutes, and when they brought him back, I could've killed him all over again for putting me through that. I dropped to my knees, shaking so much, my body looked like it was seizing as I sobbed, and I couldn't breathe. I've never known pain like that, high definition horror no one can touch, but I fucking felt it in every fiber, when I was a useless bystander to a real life play of life and death.

Toxic came home last week and has been taking it easy. The

sad thing is, for me it's a bittersweet reunion, because I have decided to go back to London when my Visa runs out at the end of the month. It's the hardest decision I have ever had to make, and I'm going to tell them tonight.

They called off the search for Charge and the remainder of the missing crew after the wreckage from his plane was found.

They wouldn't give much more information than that. Tug hit red tape whenever he tried to find out more, and Toxic remembers the plane being hit and not much else. His brain clearly shut down enough to focus on surviving and not much more. I don't think I have ever cried so much. I know I have never hurt like I do, and as hard as this decision is, I can't be here and not relive the nightmare time and time again. There's not a single thing in this house, or about them that doesn't remind me of him. Or remind me I had made my decision and never got the chance to tell him. Hell, I never got the chance to say goodbye. I'm never going to get over that; at least back home I can try to forgive myself, try to move on. That can't happen if I stay. *I'm a heartbroken coward.*

"Hmm… this smells so good, darling." Pink wraps his arms around me from behind. His strong body is such a comfort. He kisses my neck, and I still get a full body shiver whenever one of them touches or kisses me, though it's not the same. Nothing is the same since Charge never came home. I stir the gravy and give him a sedate smile. Everything has changed between us and I can't bear it. I know there's still a great deal of love between us, but without Charge we're not complete and the hole is just too damn big. I'm a permanent reminder of his absence and I know they won't admit it, but while I'm here they will never be able to move on. I'm here because it was what the four of them wanted. They aren't a *unit of four* anymore.

"Roast beef, Yorkshire pudding, roast potatoes, veg, followed by spotted dick and custard." I turn and watch his nose crinkle in disgust.

"I'm not eating anything made of dick." He grimaces, and I snicker.

"Don't knock it till you've tried it." I nudge him with my hip and let out a laugh when he balks and gags. "It's a steamed pudding with raisins. It's very British. You'll love it, I promise."

"I guess if anyone can make dick taste good, it's you."

"Thank you…I think," I quip, not sure where the compliment is in that remark, but his tone certainly made it sound like one. "Can you go call the others? This is just about ready."

"You want me to carve?" I falter and give a brief nod. That's what I'm talking about; everything is a reminder. Charge carved, Charge cooked, and Charge wanted me.

I wait until they all push their plates back and satisfied smiles brighten the ever-present sadness, if only for a moment.

"That was really good, Finn. It felt like an occasion meal, though. We haven't missed an anniversary, have we?" Pink gives a nervous laugh, and I shake my head.

"No, nothing like that." I can't keep the eye contact though, and my stomach is a tight knot of anxiety.

"Oh, but it's an occasion?" Tug picks up on the evasion.

"Um. Look, I'm just going to say it, because there's no easy way." The wave of dread and sickness drenches me like a tidal wave. I push through, pinch my eyes shut, and just say it. "I'm going home at the end of the month, for good." I add the last just in case there's scope for misinterpretation. I force my lids open and see what I hoped I wouldn't but really knew I would.

"Why Finn? Aren't you happy here?" Tug's voice is soft, but his jaw is twitching with tension.

"None of us are happy, Tug." I reach over, taking his hand, big and strong. My fingers thread through his, and I grip tight.

"That's not true," Pink argues, his tone clipped and hurt.

"It really is." With my free hand, I take Toxic's hand beside me and force my eyes to meet Pink's gaze opposite. "This is the hardest thing I've ever had to do, but it's the right thing, too. I'm a constant reminder of what we can no longer have. How can any one of us be happy with that?" My voice catches and tears spring to my eyes, but with my hands occupied I have to let them fall.

"We can give it time, that's what we could do. You don't have to run at the first sign of a bump in the road." Toxic's voice catches, and it's like a sucker punch.

"This isn't a bump though, is it? It's the Grand fucking Canyon in the road." I shake the tears from my eyes that keep clouding my vision.

"You can't mean this?" Pink's voice drops to a soft whisper.

"Tell me truthfully: When you look at me, you don't see us all together, you, me, Pink, Tug, and Charge. It's how this was supposed to be, and anything else just won't work." I sniff back the tears, my voice scratchy and desperately sad.

"How would you know, Finn? You've not given it time." Tug slams his fist on the table, but I know he's lashing out in frustration, and he quickly looks regretful. I squeeze his hand in understanding and face him.

"Please don't make this any harder than it is." I close my eyes, but I still see the devastation in all their faces, and it's fucking killing me. I draw in a deep breath and try to explain the unexplainable. "I can't bear the thought you will never be able to move on with me here. That I'm only here because of a plan which will never *be*. It's broken, and all we will be trying to do if I stay is fix something which is irrevocably broken."

"Do you really believe that?" Pink asks.

"This is unbearably hard for me, but yes. I'd like to think I can see a time when it won't hurt so damn much, but even if the day ever came, we'd always have something so significant missing, we'll never feel whole, and I love you all too much to let that happen. If I'm not here, you at least have the chance to have something so different, there will be no constant comparison."

"Better, you mean, because that's bullshit. Nothing is better than this—us." Toxic snaps, and I wince when he does. His sudden movement causes him obvious physical as well as emotional pain. *Shit.*

"I don't mean better. I just mean different. I'm not explaining myself very well." I shake my head and pull my hands from Toxic and Tug. I wrap my arms around my waist, trying to hold myself together.

"No, darling, you are. I get it." Pink tilts his head, and a somber edge to his striking features softens his eyes. "It's just hard to hear, after everything. It feels like a kick in the balls that we are going to lose you too, but I do understand."

"I don't fucking understand. This is bullshit!" Tug stands roughly, sending the chair flying, and I jump at his outburst, not his justified anger. He storms out the back door.

I knew that was a likely response from at least one of them. I feel unbearably guilty for having done this now, but honestly, I'm running out of time, and I wanted to give them a week at least to come to terms with it. I go to after him, but Pink calls me back.

"Let him blow off some steam, sugar. We still only want what's best for you. It's all Charge ever used to say, so if this is what you need, he'll come round."

"I think it is. It all hurts so much, I can't go on like this. I don't want to hurt anymore. I don't want you guys to hurt anymore. It breaks my fucking heart. It's so fucking unfair." My voice is raw, pitched and bordering on hysterical, and the unbearable sense of loss overwhelms me. I run for the front door needing some escape, some air, and some space. The front door swings wide, and I scream.

I jump out of my skin and scream the fucking house down at the beautiful ghost on the doorstep.

I've died. This is heaven, but the pain coursing through my very soul feels like my own personal hell.

This isn't real. Is it? Is he?

I'm still screaming when he rushes to crush my mouth and silence the noise. I'm stiff as a board and shocked through, broken and scared, elated and thankful. It's all too fucking much. My heart beats so hard, I feel bruised and battered, my head is a mess and for my sanity's sake I focus on one thing, his kiss.

His soft lips, his demanding tongue diving into my mouth like a starving man. This kiss I feel in my soul, and I don't ever want it to end. *Please don't ever let it end. Stay with me...don't ever stop.*

I clench my fists. I'm reluctant to move, because it might break the spell. It might stop this tortuous dream, even if I am so very desperate to wrap my arms around him. I don't, though. I pull my arm back and swing.

My tiny furious hand pummels his shoulder, but he just keeps kissing me. The tears are rolling in rivers, uncontrollable and soaking us both. Salty kisses on now swollen lips, and I'm yet to take a breath. I pull back on a frantic gasp of air, shocked and stunned. There's a moment in time, frozen and pure, when a heart is saved, and all the strength holding a person together is no longer needed.

I stare at the ghost of Charge and know he's real, he's here, and he's mine, and I crumple to the floor.

"Holy fucking shit!" There's a rush of thunderous footsteps behind me. Charge is on his knees, his hands on my face, strong, warm—alive.

"You could've fucking called, man!" Pink barks.

"I just wanted to get home. As soon as I got the all clear, I just wanted to come home." His hands cup my face, and his eyes bore through me.

"You're alive," I mouth, but I'm not sure there's any sound. The blood rushing in my ears drowns any noise.

"Yes, angel." His smile is a vision, and I suck in a sharp breath that makes my heart beat for the first time in what feels like forever.

"I'm sorry." I say quickly and his smile just widens.

"What are you sorry for, angel?" I'm too scared to blink in case he's not real, and I rush to say all the things that have been eroding my sanity since we parted.

"I left. I left and chose Dave, and I never got to say goodbye. You died, and I never got to say—" I break into sobs, and my words lose all intelligibility.

"Shh, shh." He threads his arm underneath me and lifts me to his chest. I hold his gaze, his lips curling in a warm and tender smile. My eyes are still the size of saucers with a mix of shock and awe. "Angel, you didn't choose Dave. You're here. You chose us." He kisses my hair, and his arms constrict a little tight. *Not tight enough.*

"You're timing is spot on, man. She's going back to London," Toxic speaks, and I can hear them follow in close behind.

"You are?" Charge quirks his perfect brow.

"Yes. I mean, I was. It's complicated. You were—Oh God, how? How are you here? God, Charge." I don't even care about the answers, I just can't believe he's here. My arms tighten, and I bury my head against his chest. I breathe him in and hold him. "I can't believe you're here," I whisper.

"I'm so sorry, angel. I know you've all been through hell." His lips press firmly into my hair, and I can feel him breathe me in, too.

"'Lil' bit, yeah." I sniff, sucking back the sobs still bubbling with the overflow of emotion I have no chance of keeping in check.

"Understatement of the year—century actually, man. Where were you?" Toxic asks. Charge looks away from me, up over to Pink, Tug, and now Toxic.

"Does it matter?" Charge rests his warm gaze back on me, and he knows the answer before I say it.

"No. No, it really doesn't." My smile splits my face, because the only thing that matters is right here.

"Classified?" Toxic asks, but it's more of a statement. Charge gives an imperceptible nod and I find I couldn't care less. He's here, he's alive, and I'm in his arms. *Perfect.*

CHAPTER FORTY

Charge

△

I HOLD HER FACE, AND I KNOW I SHOULD LET HER UP FOR AIR sometime soon, but the taste, her lips on mine, it's the sweetest fucking flavor this side of heaven. I pull back and take my time searching every millimeter of her face. Savoring the fresh image and replacing the one in my mind that has kept me alive and sane these last few weeks. I don't want to think about my nightmare when I can clearly see in her face; she has also been through hell. The hope that I would at some point be right here, kept me alive, but I can see my absence has taken its toll. No, not my absence, what they could only assume was my death. Well, I'm back, and I won't waste another second dwelling on what could've been, not when I hold my future in my palms.

"Angel." I exhale, but even to my own ears her nickname sounds like an answered prayer on my lips.

"Charge." She closes her eyes when she breathes out my name, and I wonder if she feels the same sense of divine intervention. Her lids flutter open, and her crystal blue eyes sparkle and glisten with unshed tears. She shakes herself and just holds my gaze, searching me for answers. I can't give her details about my crash, but I know those aren't the ones she really yearns for. Now the euphoria of this reunion has started to dwindle, and I can see traces of the unresolved issues creeping back into every bit of her, etching her beauty with a dark cloud of concern. Her frame begins to subtly stiffen as doubt starts to spread through her body like a disease, worry in her features and weighing heavy on her shoulders. I scoop her into my arms before her defenses kick back in, and I lock her tight against my body. The move takes her by surprise. She flashes the brightest smile and lets out a loud, unladylike belly laugh. It's the best fucking sound, and I'll take that over her shutting down.

"I'm ready to tell you everything, Finn." I hold her gaze and watch her eyes light at my words. I feel the burst of warmth in my soul. I just pray she looks at me like that afterward.

"Really?" She exhales, her tone tinged with wonder.

"Yes, angel. I promise, but not right now. Right now I need you in every filthy way possible." My voice has a rough gravelly sound to it, but the tone drops from serious to sensual, mid-sentence. She shivers in my arms, and I notice her thighs clamp tighter together.

"Really?" She bites her trembling lips flat. Her pupils are so dark, they look more black than sapphire blue, and her skin has an amazing flush of color to her cheeks. She's off-the-charts aroused by my statement, and I feel ten-feet fucking tall because of it.

"Oh, angel, you have no idea." I chuckle a throaty laugh, and start to walk us both to the stairs when Tug calls out.

"Hey, Charge, it's not your day. You're messing with the roster."

I know he's joking, but I growl back my answer just in case he isn't. "Fuck the roster and leave food and water outside the door. This week is mine." I climb the stairs two at a time, Finn's head is thrown back with full, wonderful laughter bursting from her lips, and in the distance I can just about still hear the guys' grumbles of disappointment. They are halfhearted at best, and when I turn to look back they are all grinning just as wide as I am. Well, nearly as wide as I am.

"A whole week, hmm?" She pulls her bottom lip slowly into her mouth, suppressing the stretch of her smile, but she fails to hide her delight at the idea. Her eyes sparkle, and her whole body shudders in my arms.

"Trust me, it won't be long enough." I swing my bedroom door wide and slam it shut with a hefty backward kick. I stride two steps into the room and drop her carefully, but from a height, onto my bed. She squeals and bounces, then quickly rights herself until she's perched on her knees at the edge of the bed, eager, breathless, and fucking perfect. Her gaze is intense and searching. I have never been looked at with such attention, devotion, such *love*. Unashamed and unmistakable, pure and precious, and it makes my heart feel like it's about to explode within the confines of my chest. I shuck my jacket and pull my sweater over my head. She sucks in a breath at the merest flash of skin when I raise my arms, and I panic. My stomach knots, and I feel a sudden bite of acid in the back of my throat as sickness threatens, but I fight it.

I have played this over and over in my head. Picturing the scenario a thousand times, praying I would get the chance to tell her everything she deserves to know. I know if we are to stand a chance, at the very least, I need to be honest with her so she can make up her mind whether my ugly scars are the tip of the iceberg when it comes to my confession. I lean over to the bedside table and open the top drawer. I didn't expect anything would've been moved and I'm happy that's the case. I slip the blindfold from the drawer and turn to see Finn's smile vanish and her eyes drop with instant sadness.

"It's not what you think, angel. I need this for me, just this one time, okay?" She's about to speak but snaps her mouth shut, and that's all I see, because I have the blindfold secured tight around my own eyes.

"Charge, what are you doing?" Her hand is quick to rest on my chest over the T-shirt, and I hope she can feel the fierceness of my heartbeat, because it's for her.

"Just this first time, Finn. I don't think I could take it to see your face when you look at me. I don't mean that to sound as bad as it does, but any change, however subtle, will cut me right up. I thought long and hard about this. I think this is the only way I can show you. Does that make any sense?" My hand is now over hers, pressing firmly so she can feel every beat beneath.

"It does." Her voice is soft with understanding. She pulls her hand free, and I jump when I feel her fingers at the waistband of my jeans. Feather-light touches rest against my skin, and I feel the connection like raw electricity, sparking at that tiny delicate contact. I suck in a deep breath and blow out slowly as heat rises from the pit of my stomach, and my heart continues to thump so loud, it's all I can hear. She slides the T-shirt up my chest and I squeeze my eyes tight under the blindfold when her soft lips kiss my abdomen. She follows the slow reveal of skin with tender kisses, her fingers gathering the cloth until I have to raise my arms and dip to allow her to completely remove my final layer. I haven't heard any gagging or gasps of horror, but then the scar only just reaches the front of my body around my side on the left, under my arm.

"Charge, I can't see anything." Her hands rest on my hips but I twist in her hold and clench my jaw just waiting for the horror to sink in. *Nothing*. Not a sound, no sharp intake of breath. Her hands, which have drifted over my skin as I turn and continue to move, smooth over the tortured twisted burnt skin covering most of my back. I hold my own breath as she traces the pattern of the tattoo I have, which failed to hide the burn as I'd hoped. I think it made it worse, if that was actually possible. Her lips touch between my shoulder blades, and I step away.

"You don't have to do that, Finn. I know it's—"

"You clearly know nothing," she snaps, her voice harsh and a little angry. I'm about to turn when I'm blinded by the sudden bright light. My eyelids instantly clamp tight, but quickly open to see a furious look on Finn's flawless face. "You're an idiot if you think this would make a toss of difference to how I feel about you." Her hands are tight fists on her hips, and she's radiating fury from every pore.

"It's disgusting," I retort, but hold her gaze because I'm looking for the truth in her outburst.

"It's a scar, nothing more. Honestly, I'm a little disappointed you think so little of me as to believe this would change what we have." Her throat moves in a slow swallow, and I can see the hurt in her eyes. My hand cups her cheek, and she tilts into the gentle hold. I try my best to explain something I never thought I would have to, to anyone other than my brothers.

"I didn't think that, but this is more than just twisted flesh. It's an ugliness which is part of me, so why would I want to share that, Finn? Why would you want anything to do with me once you know the truth?" I close my eyes as the pain of my memory pinches an unbearable pressure behind my eyes and in my heart.

"You will have to trust me that I will," she offers softly, her eyes crinkle and her lips curve with a tender, encouraging smile.

"I do trust you." Holding her gaze, she gives a brief nod at my earnest declaration.

"Then tell me," she whispers, though it's a demand nonetheless.

"I will, I promise. But right now, I feel all kinds of raw, exposed and desperate. I need to prove to you that I not only trust you, Finn Sanderson, but I love you too."

"You do?"

"Oh, yes, angel, heart and fucking soul. And if you still want me after I have told you everything, then I'm yours, because you already *own* me, lock, stock and barrel." She leaps into my arms, legs wrapped around my waist like a spider monkey on a tree. Her hands thread into my hair and her lips crash to mine.

Oh my fucking God, I have missed her.

Her tongue duels with mine with an urgency I return tenfold. Falling to the bed, feral passion ignites in me, and I roll my body over hers, pressing into her, dropping my full weight until she groans. Her eyes fix on mine with undiluted lust and desire. Fucking perfect, but even so, I can't stop the spiral of dark thoughts clouding in my head. Analyzing each move, each sound, trying to spot a difference now she has seen me. My heart clenches, and a warm burst of utter joy soaks my body when I realize nothing has changed—absolutely nothing. She claws at my skin like she can't get enough, her kisses devour me, and the fire in her eyes tells me she's mine. I chuckle out loud, because her actions, on the other hand, tell me she can't get me inside her quick enough.

Tugging roughly at the buckle of my belt, she groans into my mouth with pent-up lust and erotic frustration. I pull back and smile so fucking wide at the adorable whimper that escapes her throat whenever I break our connection, even if it's to breathe. In record time, I'm back in position, pitched on one arm, lying over her body, naked, hard and fucking frantic to sink into her body. Her legs hook around my hips, and she tilts her hips in invitation as I hover my impossibly hard cock just at the heat of her entrance.

"I love you." I watch her eyes light with the exact same feeling.

"Prove it."

She gasps as I sink my length inside with one carefully timed thrust. I know she wants to know everything. The cryptic statements alone must be driving her insane, and since she has seen the visual scars, which really didn't bother her, I'm just as keen to get everything else out in the open. But at this moment, I want to bury myself balls deep in the woman I love and reacquaint myself with every delectable inch of her beautiful body. I want to make her mine again.

"Oh God." She pushes her head back into the pillow, and her mouth drops open on a silent gasp that follows her words. I deftly move us so she is now on top, one of my hands captures her jaw and holds her fixed so she can't look anywhere but in my eyes. The other is grabbing a fist full of her fine ass, pulling her to meet each pounding thrust I'm driving into her. This isn't lovemaking, there's nothing sweet about the way we're clawing at each other, rolling over and over, fighting to take what we need from each other. This is feral, raw, animalistic fucking on a level I never knew existed. Our bodies slide and move as one, sweat coats our skin, and the thick smell of arousal assaults my senses and is enough to have my balls begging for release.

"You with me, angel?" I growl into her neck just before I bite down and draw her blood to the surface. I need this, so damn much, to mark her, make her *mine*.

"Yes! Oh, God, yes!" Even as her words leave her mouth on a breathless plea, her innermost muscles clamp around my cock, and my balls explode. I roar out as pleasure rips through my body, just as hers sets rigid at my fingertips, and she falls. Every contraction, every ripple of muscle feels like nirvana, and I have never come so hard, or so much.

Best laid plans and all that. It was my intention to fuck her all damn day, but that doesn't happen. Utterly spent, we both collapse and swiftly fall asleep, at least I think we both did. Whatever we did though, we fall together and are so close, wrapped around one another, and it feels like we are one entity and fucking perfect.

"Have you slept at all?" I ask, but I know the answer. Finn is pressed against my chest, her slim arm soft against my skin, draped and hugging my chest. Her face is tipped up to mine but her eyes are as wide as the smile painting her beautiful face. I doubt she closed her eyes for a second. *I'm pretty sure I actually passed out.*

"I haven't. Don't get me wrong, my body is exhausted enough to sleep for days; my mind won't let me. I have too many questions, Charge." Her lips quirk in an apologetic grin, but I understand. I'm amazed she let me sleep at all.

"I know." I lean down and kiss the tip of her nose. She's been patient, and since she took the blindfold off, I really have only one thing left to share. I draw in a steadying breath and feel her arm constrict with automatic comfort.

"There's not a thing you can say, Charge, that will change how I feel about you. I just need to know you trust me enough to share what you keep locked in here." She slides her palm flat over my heart, and I reach up to cover it with my own, entwining our fingers. I need the closeness to tell my story.

"Okay, angel." I close my eyes, and my skin tingles with tightness, I can almost feel the flames lick my skin like they did ten years ago. "After my parents died, my brother and I went to live with my guardian. "

"Your brother?" she queries, her brows shoot up in shock.

"Joshua didn't die with my parents, angel. I lied about that. You'll understand why by the time I finish."

"I'm sorry, Charge."

"It's okay, angel. You deserve to know the truth." I kiss her hair and breathe her vanilla scent in deeply; it calms and soothes, just what I need. "Donald doesn't have children and although some of the stars he deals with are brats, he'd never really encountered spoiled and troubled teenagers—well, teenager. Josh was never any trouble. I had started hanging with a gang, and I would break out of Donald's home every chance I got, despite the sphincter-tight security he had around the house and grounds. One night, I stole a bottle of his best whiskey and grabbed the keys to his Ferrari.

"After the car accident killed my parents, Donald pretty much insisted I drive an armored jeep and only that vehicle, but I knew he had the 458 in his garage, and, man, that thing was so damn fast. I had begged and begged to drive it. He flatly refused, but worse than that, he said it was too powerful for a kid. That was a dumbass thing to say to a cocky teen. Anyway, I took the liquor and keys, and climbed out my bedroom window like always, only this time Josh stopped me.

"He saw the bottle and begged me not to go. I told him he could come if he kept his noise down. He shut up but didn't want to come. I was worried he would go straight to Donald and stop my fun, so I promised him we would drop by our old home. I hated going there, but he loved it. It had been cleared of everything valuable almost right away. Some furniture and boxes had been left, but it was no longer a home. It was still on the market to be sold. Josh missed the place so much, Donald would take him back from time to time.

"I knew I had him. He ran back to his room and came back with his jacket and a flashlight. I helped him out of the window and showed him how to avoid all the spotlights and sensors that would have had the place instantly lit up like a fucking Christmas tree. Deactivating the alarm on the garage, we crawled out onto the drive, and drove out of the gates and into the night. Josh's face was stony, but he did start to relax once he recognized where I was taking him. I wasn't going to back out of a promise, even if I did have other plans for the house.

"Josh ran off to wherever, and I cracked the lock on the back door. The alarm code remained the same and again I quickly disabled that, allowing us freedom to explore. Or more accurately, giving me time to finish what I had started on my last visit. I had hidden cans of gasoline in cupboards and cut holes into the base of sofas in case those were discovered. It was unlikely anyone coming to view the place would look that close, but I wanted to make sure I could burn the place to the ground when the time was right. I had left a trail of fuel along the length of the ground floor ending in the kitchen. The empty boxes and anything else I thought might catch fire quickly I placed next to the accelerant and left a half-empty can at the other end of the house for some extra fire power.

"Josh came running into the kitchen as I struck the match and dropped it. I had almost forgotten he was there. He started yelling at me, and I got mad that he was so upset when I thought it was the best way to end my nightmares. That I didn't have to see it, think about them and our family the way it was and the way it would never be again. I wanted it gone. I grabbed him by his jacket and dragged him out. Tears were streaming down his cheeks, but his face was pale and he fell silent once he clipped his seatbelt. I drew a long pull from the whiskey and floored the car. Josh wouldn't stop shouting at me to put my damn belt on. I turned the music up so loud it drowned the annoying whining from him. The next thing I knew he was leaning over me, trying to put the damn belt on, dragging it across my chest. I struggled, and we fought, the car spun when I pulled the wheel sharply and with my foot pressed to the floor in panic, I lost control. We spun off the road and crashed through the safety barrier. The car rolled down a steep embankment, crushing my brother and knocking me unconscious.

"I had so much gasoline still on my clothes I was lucky I didn't burn alive. Some guy pulled me from the car but my cheap jacket was on fire and melting into my back. The man who pulled me out, ripped it from my body and several layers of my skin. The pain was like nothing I'd ever felt. It brought me back to consciousness and a fresh hell. The pain was unbearable but was never enough to make up for what I'd done. How fucking sorry I am. I killed my brother, and every time I look at myself, that's all I see, a murderer. These scars aren't just ugly on my outside, they are evidence of the rot inside of me, too. Ugly to the core." I blink and feel the cool trickle of tears on my cheek. Finn sweeps them dry with her fingers. She looks broken, but until she tells me, I won't know why. Long seconds pass, but she ends my agony when she speaks.

"Charge, I'm so fucking sorry, but you can't believe you're a murderer. I won't let you." Her hands fly to my face, holding me millimeters from her, nose-to-nose, eye-to-eye, and heart-to-heart. There's no escape, and I'm so thankful. "These scars are part of you, and they are beautiful. We all make mistakes, and what happened to your brother was a heartbreaking tragedy, but it was an accident. You have a kind heart and a pure soul, Charge, and I love you with every fiber of my being." She presses her full soft lips over mine, and when she pulls back, I see something shine in her eyes, something more. She swallows thickly and her wide, infectious smile makes my fucking heart sore. "You have trusted me with your heart, so it feels only right to trust you with mine. I love you, *all* of you."

"You do?" I see it in her eyes, I feel it in my soul, but I just need to make sure.

"Yeah, I really do."

She giggles and melts against my body when I pounce. *Fucking perfect.*

CHAPTER FORTY-ONE

One week later

"**I** CAN'T DO IT." I VEHEMENTLY SHAKE MY HEAD AND pout like a preschooler.

"You have to," Pink states, but four pairs of eyes are boring into me, all that's missing is the interrogation spotlight in this little intervention. "Time is up on your Visa, missy. You have to pick one of us for a husband."

"But I love you all," I huff, folding my arms across my chest. They all beam, but then sigh with frustration. I have told them this repeatedly and refused to make the decision. Not because it's at all impossible. The truth is, I could make the decision, very easily, but I do love them all, and I feel making that choice will change something, and what we have is *perfect*.

"Yes, we know that." Toxic rolls his eyes, but they are all grinning like Cheshire cats.

"Wait, I know." I jump up and scurry off into Charge's study.

I return waving four pens and some paper. "Let's do the name draw thing."

"Coward!" Charge accuses, biting back a shit-eating grin. *He knows.*

"Yep." I give a little sassy wiggle of my hips, sighing with relief when they each take a pen and scribble their names on the paper. I grab the small fruit bowl and roll the apples onto the coffee table. They each fold their pieces of paper and drop it in the bowl. I give it a little shake, and I can feel my tummy tighten. I have prayed a few times over the last month, and although I feel like I'm most definitely pushing my luck, I close my eyes and wish for one last thing. I reach my other hand into the bowl and take the piece of paper that will select my husband.

"Before I open this, I would like to say you're all so precious to me and such wonderful, kind, generous and sexy-as-all-hell men. I know for a fact I'm the luckiest girl in the world," I gush.

"Open the damn paper," Tug growls.

"Patience is a virtue, you know?" I quip. I think the power has gone to my head.

"Not one of ours. Now open." Charge demands, but I hold my hand up flat to stop him.

"Wait! I wanted to show you this first." They all groan out with frustration but I power through ignoring their dramatics. This seems like the perfect time to do this. I pull the waist of my yoga pants down to reveal the gauze dressing I said was hiding a nasty cut I got falling at the stables. I pick the tape and pull it free.

"When the hell did you get that?" Pink exclaims above the audible intake of collective breaths.

"Flick took me. I wanted to get each of your elements permanently marked on my skin, just so you know whoever is on this paper, you're all *chosen.*" I bite my lip with anticipation of their reactions.

"Angel."

"Sugar."

"Darling."

"Babe."

I beam so wide my cheeks ache. The pleasure of their expressions almost erases the pain from the tattoo, *almost*.

"Now open the—" Charge growls this time, and I quickly slip my pants back up.

"All right, all right." I un-scrunch the paper, and if it's possible my smile just got that little bit wider and my heart just swelled fit to bursting. "Charge." I say, and squeal when I'm ambushed first by Charge, then the others, all bundling me back onto the sofa and peppering me with kiss after kiss. They all look so damn happy. I can't believe... "Wait!" I had dropped the bowl when they attacked me, and I can see the papers strewn over the floor, no longer folded and all, without exception, have the name Charge written on them. *Perfect.*

EPILOGUE

Finn

Six Months Later

"**J**UST ONE MORE." CHARGE GROWLS AGAINST MY SKIN, his soft full lips pressing into my body, so I feel the vibrations from his words. His breath scorches the apex of my trembling thighs, and I suck in a breath, shaking my head at his sensual demand. I'm exhausted, utterly sated, and seconds away from falling into a sex-induced coma.

"I can't. Please." I manage to say, but it takes the very last ounce of energy left in my body to get the words out and make them even slightly audible.

"Oh, come on, angel. We both know that's not true." I tip my head up to see his piercing blue eyes sparkle with mischief. I groan and drop my head back onto the pillow. I recognize his look of determination and desire, and although I'm not the type to lie back and think of England, very occasionally, my body is so wracked, it's all it can do.

I'm not complaining, just stating a fact.

"Oh, my God!" I cry out as his devilish tongue presses flat and firm, dragging along my wetness. His fingers slide easily into my body and twist slowly, coaxing my muscles to reawaken. His sweet and sensual movements pull more pleasure from my spent body. He is relentless.

It was the same on our honeymoon, but I thought that was just because it was, well, our honeymoon, and the two weeks of utter heaven in his arms, under his body was the exception. I never expected it to be the rule.

I let out sharp little breaths, feeling the build of pressure start to ripple though me. My eyes are squeezed shut, and every muscle protests with the involuntary exertion his attention is drawing from my helpless body. His heavy hand presses on my abdomen as my hips start to roll. His other hand slides under my bottom, gripping and pulling me against his urgent, insistent mouth and its heavenly dance against my most sensitive flesh

"Come for me, angel." He exhales and the burst of air makes me jolt. His fingers push deeper, and when his lips latch around my clit, I fall from the peak he has pushed me to once more. He keeps the pressure perfect until all the ripples of pleasure have ebbed and stilled. He then languidly kisses a path from my clit up the center of my body, over my tummy, between my breasts, brushing past my lips and playfully landing on the tip of my nose. I think I smile but I can't be sure my facial muscles are cooperating with my wishes. I know the rest of my body isn't because Charge has to drag my limp form back up the bed and drape it like a comforter over his own, maneuvering me until I'm in my preferred resting position. My head on his chest, arm across his torso and our legs wrapped together like cooked spaghetti. The sun may be streaming through the shutters but I fall instantly back to sleep.

I rub the numbness in my cheek and the sleep from my eyes. I slept like the dead; it may have been five minutes but it could've been five days, I feel like I have literally been fucked unconscious. It's late morning, and I still haven't actually made it out of our bedroom. I'm sitting upright, cross-legged and sharing a steaming cup of coffee with my husband. The smile on my face, which has been a permanent fixture since Charge came back from the dead six months ago, got a little bit bigger once I became his wife. However, it's only because it's physically impossible to smile any wider without having a flip-top head. Today, however, it's tempered with some troubling thoughts that have been niggling me, and I need to address. *Number one rule, no secrets.*

"Have the others said anything to you?" I hand the cup back after taking a sip. The bitter taste makes my nose scrunch, and he chuckles. I welcome the hit of caffeine to wake me, but I prefer my morning brew with a bag, milk and lots of sugar. The need for a cup of tea is in my British DNA.

"About?" He arches a brow but his face is ever impassive.

"About me." I want to say, "*Duh*", but the skin on my bottom is still glowing from last night and judging by the look on his face, my tone holds just the right amount of sass. My bottom is safe for the moment.

"They say lots about you; you're gonna to need to be more specific, angel." He chuckles, and I purse my lips, because either he really doesn't know, or he's delighting in making this really awkward for me. Our arrangement hasn't so much changed after the wedding, but some things have certainly shifted. One of those things being, Charge is adamant he doesn't want to talk about me in a sexual way with the others. Which in itself isn't a problem. It's not like I like to compare notes or anything, but it does make this conversation a little tricky. I draw in a deep breath, because there's no subtle way to ask this.

"Have they gone off me…gone off sex with me, I mean?" I grimace, swallowing back the dry lump in my throat. He was very specific after our honeymoon that he did not want to know, talk, or even joke about me being with the others. He never did share on his days, but he just took it to a whole new level after we were married, and I'm convinced this is the source of this new development. But my core insecurity will always default to the notion that they have gone off me first. He lets out a flat laugh and quirks his lips in a wry grin.

"Not ever going to happen, but why do you ask?"

"Okay. Well, here's the thing, and I know you don't like talking about this but…" I pause, shifting in my seat. I pull my crossed legs up and wrap my arms around them, forming a tight defensive ball. I dip my eyes away from his serious glare.

"Just say it," he demands, but softly, so I know he isn't really upset by the topic, it's just, understandably, not one of his favorites.

"I haven't had sex with any of them for the last, um, I think it's over a month now." I give a tiny shrug because my arms are locked rigid around my legs.

"Really?" He uses his free hand to unpick my grip and pull me over to his side. I slide against his body, his arm holding me to his heat and I tip my head to meet his gaze and carry on the conversation.

"Yeah, really. I mean we—" Catching the twitch in his jaw, I halt mid-sentence, because he really doesn't want to hear this, like any of it. I censor the details and just give him the facts. "Haven't had sex, and I just wondered if they had said anything."

"They haven't, but have you asked?"

"I'm asking now," I state as if talking to a small and possibly dim child. He tips his head and raises a warning brow at my tone.

"I meant them. You know they are probably the best ones to answer this question," he responds flatly, and I huff out a light puff of frustrated air.

"Well, I know that now, Mr. Informative." I roll my eyes and scoot back out of his reach as he tries to grab my retreating form without spilling the coffee.

"Sass like that will get you a very sore ass."

"You know that's not really a deterrent, right?" I quip, but jump back as he lunges for me, since he no longer holds his cup. I squeal and try to run, but he's on me. His strong hands lift me high, spinning me effortlessly in the air, and plant me securely onto his shoulder. The long T-shirt I'm wearing barely covers my bottom, and he slaps his large palm sharply across the exposed skin. I scream and wriggle, but still when he swipes another hefty strike on my arse cheek.

"Oh, please continue, angel. We have all day to get your sass back where it belongs." His deep gravelly voice causes the hairs on my neck to prickle with the sensual threat, but his tone is teasing. Since we are now heading out of our room, I'm pretty confident he's not going to make good on that threat—yet. He strides along the corridor, passing Tug at the top of the stairs.

"Meeting in the kitchen in five. Tug, can you get the others?" Charge calls back and without breaking his gait, he bounces down the stairs. I have to grip his narrow hips for balance as his flimsy boxer shorts are not up to the task. He places me on one of the kitchen stools and disappears out the back toward the utility room. He returns in a flash, wearing a fresh T-shirt and has slipped on some shorts over his boxers. I pout at his new PG-rated outfit, which makes his smile beam bright and wide. It's involuntary and instant, and it makes him look so young and completely adorable.

The thunder of footsteps shakes the house as Tug bounds down the stairs. Toxic followed Charge in from out back, and I can hear Pink's truck pull up on the gravel outside. They each kiss my cheek and slide onto their preferred seats around the island. All eyes fall on Charge, who grins and points his finger directly at me.

"Our wife has a question." He isn't shy about expressing his ownership of me in private, but when we are all together he's considerate of the others' feelings and is always all inclusive when referring to me. He has, however, completely shifted the focus of the room and dropped me right in it. He winks and completely ignores my gaping jaw and narrow-eyed scowl.

"Fire away, sugar" Pink flashes a dazzling smile my way, though I feel all their eyes on me. Shifting in my seat under the sudden intensity of each of their gazes, I suck in a breath and speak in a high-pitched, rushed, and garbled mess of words.

"Oh, it's nothing really. How about some fresh coffee, or I could make some brunch, maybe, it's a little late for breakf—"

"Sit back down," Tug interrupts my word vomit, his beefy hand on my thigh, and I barely got one butt cheek off the stool before he was preventing my escape with his warning tone and his strong grip.

"What's got you all flustered, princess?" Pink's head tips with curiosity, his brow furrowed and his lips quirked.

"Come on, Finn. You can ask us anything. Surely you know this by now?" Toxic states emphatically, but each of them nod in agreement.

"I know, I just…" I let out a long, slow breath and force a tight smile. I can feel my cheeks start to heat at the thought of having this conversation.

"Oh, wow, this is going to be good," Charge teases, and the others chuckle noticing the new tint to my cheeks.

"Thank you, Mr. Helpful," I snap, and he holds his hands up, biting his lips flat to stop a knowing, shit-eating grin at my discomfort. *Arse hat.*

"I want to ask, do you not want to have sex with me anymore?" I close one eye, bracing for a slew of 'what the hells', but an unfamiliar silence blankets the men, and I can see them each pass furtive glances between one another. The odd raised brow and obvious shared understanding, just leaves me and Charge with expressions of utter confusion.

"Oh, God, you don't, do you?" I drop my embarrassed head in my hands.

"Don't be ridiculous," Toxic and Tug say together, closely followed by Pink echoing their sentiment.

"Of course we do, princess, it's just…" Pink continues, then pauses, and I search his eyes, then Tug's and Toxic's. I can see love. I have absolutely no doubt about that, and tenderness too. I can even see desire, so what the hell are they talking about?

"Okay." I state a little sharply, but I feel like my world is spiraling. *I knew it was too good to be real.* "It's just what? I don't understand. If you do still want me like that, then why aren't we fu—"

"Finn," Charge growls, and I shake my head at his sensitivity. I pinch out a placatory smile and rephrase.

"How come none of you have pursued that aspect of our relationship for weeks now?" I turn to Charge. "Was that better than saying fuck?"

"Finn!" I wave him off and focus equally on the others. They have my attention for the moment.

"Tell me what's wrong. What can I do to fix this?" I soften the rising hysteria in my voice and plead for some understanding. I reach for Tug's hand and with the other, I share a hold with Pink and Toxic.

"I don't think it can be fixed, sweetheart," Toxic says with a soft smile, and I shake my head.

"Well, not having sex is not going to work. Unless you're all intending on becoming monks?" I scoff out a humorless laugh.

"That wasn't our intention, no." Pink dismisses my flip comment with a chuckle.

"I don't understand, this is what we all wanted. What's changed?" My voice is breaking, and I look to Charge for some clarification, but he shrugs and happens to look as confused as I feel.

"You." Toxic speaks after a quick nod from his brothers.

"Me?" I almost can't get the word out, I'm in such shock.

"You two, actually," Pink continues, and judging by the way they are filling in for each other so seamlessly, it's very obvious this is something they all feel equally.

"We're the same," I protest.

"Actually, you're not." Tug reaches over and lifts me onto his lap. I welcome the contact, the heat and the comfort, because I can feel myself start to break. This isn't right. This can't be happening, can it?

"I don't think that's true." I shake my head and look at each of them with pleading eyes. Toxic picks up where Tug left off. It's like the worst tag team ever.

"It wasn't so obvious when you came back from the honeymoon, but the last few weeks it's become more noticeable, and it's definitely here to stay. Something changed. It's subtle, but it's there, and has been a game changer for all of us. Right, Charge?" Tug tags my husband.

"Charge?"

"Yeah." He drags his hand through his thick dark hair, and I'm silenced by his confession. "I understand."

"Well, I bloody don't," I snap and twist to face Tug, making sure I level my fiery glare at each of them, including Charge.

"We know you love us, Finn, that's never in question. But you can't deny there's something *more* with Charge," Pink states and, just as I'm about to protest, I'm silenced by the realization of the truth in his statement. It hits me hard in my chest, smashing my heart to smithereens.

"Are you breaking up with me?" My voice catches, and I get a sudden and completely expected burst of tears on my cheeks. There's a flurry of movement, and I'm closeted on all sides by the men who mean the world to me, each trying to assuage my breaking heart.

"Sweetheart." Tug kisses my hair.

"Sugar, that's not what we're doing. We're just trying to explain." Toxic strokes my cheek, and Pink is on my other side.

"Explain what, though?" My head is shaking away this new reality, but I can see this is very real for them. *The game has changed.*

"Look, we love you, we all love you. And as much as we had planned for us to remain a unit, things have changed, and you can't *un-change* them," Pink states softly.

"And none of us would want that anyhow. We're happy for Charge and you, couldn't be happier," Tug adds, and Toxic finishes their collective thought.

"But we can also see what we're missing, and we talked it over, and we want the same."

"Charge, did you know about this?" My chest is heaving with emotion, and I'm calmed when he shakes his head.

"First I've heard of it, angel, but I understand. It's not like this was planned. I don't believe any of us thought this would happen, but I know I definitely feel different when I know you're with one of these guys, than I did before we were married." He shrugs.

"So I'm responsible for breaking you all up. I hate this, I don't want to be Yoko." I sniff back the tears that are now trickling down my face, my nose running so much I have to swipe the back of my hand to stop from leaking onto the counter top. I'm a mess, and their comforting touches and words are just making things worse.

"Princess, you're not Yoko. We're not in any rush. We still have you, just not in a sexual way." Pink tries to soothe me.

"So you're becoming monks?" I wail dramatically, which causes a burst of laughter. It strangely helps to ease my spiraling sadness.

"No." Tug chuckles.

"Then what is the plan?" I dry my tears with my palms and suck in a steadying breath, exhaling when I feel I have gathered myself enough to hear what they have clearly been mulling. "How do you see this panning out, because this sounds a lot like 'Oh, don't worry about her, she'll just sit in the corner of the studio with a triangle while we make a few more albums.'" I snort.

"That's cute, angel, but that's not what this is," Charge states, clearly on board with this idea far quicker than me, for obvious reasons.

"It didn't work before, because we were all dating for our own ends. We just assumed the girlfriends would get on." Toxic explains, and I scoff out an unladylike laugh.

"Yeah, exactly," Pink agrees, and joins me with his own laughter. "Anyway, I think if we approach it the same way we did finding you, it will help."

"You're going to advertise for another wife?" I can't hide the shock in my voice or the hurt when it catches.

"God, no! Sorry." Pink rushes to clarify. "No, not at all. We want *you* to find us each a wife."

"What?" I gasp, and any hint of humor dies in my throat at the earnest expression on each of their handsome faces. *They can't be serious.*

"We figure the only important thing is that they get along with you. Once that's a winner, then it's just a question of our own personal chemistry," Toxic chips in, and I start to shake my head as their idea begins to sink in and not quite settle.

"This sounds all wrong," I counter, but they wave off my concern.

"It's a prototype, but the principle is sound. We just have to iron out the wrinkles." Toxic winks.

"So you *are* breaking up with me," I state, because no matter how they sugarcoat this conversation, that's the net result

"Darling, we just want what you have, and since we can't have it with you, we'd like a little help finding our *one*." Pink takes my hand and holds my gaze. I look at each of them, and my heart swells but also aches for them. Because they are right. What I have with Charge is *more,* and I love them all enough to want that for them too.

I'm sad too, but I can't blame them. It's not fair for them to never be able to experience what Charge and I have, all because of this situation we originally planned. *Plans change*

"There's no hurry. We're just putting it out there," Tug adds. "And don't forget, it took us two years to find you."

"Well, good, because this is a shock, and I need time to process." I sniff. "Besides, they would have to be pretty much the best thing since sliced bread to be good enough for any one of you. So I'm not holding out much hope, okay?" I'm only partially teasing.

"Okay, sugar, like we said. It's just an idea." Pink calls back over his shoulder because there's an almighty knock on the front door and the sound of retreating tires on the gravel drive. He opens the door and calls for me.

"Finn, think this one's for you," he hollers back into the house. I turn to the commotion on the doorstep but Pink is blocking the view. I step around him and I'm assaulted by a glass-shattering, high-pitched scream.

"Hope?" I stutter, as my mouth drops open in shock.

"Surprise!"

THE END

△▽△▽

ACKNOWLEDGEMENTS

Gah…this just gets scarier and scarier with each book. Just because I'm a worrier and I know I will miss someone, by complete accident, but I will. So i'll apologies now and know that you are supposed to be in this bit…yes you!

A huge thank you Shannon Boltin, my wonderful PA, Amanda, Nicole, Nese and Sarah who tirelessly promote and pimp me to all and sundry and I know Facebook doesn't make it easy.I am and will be forever in your debt because I literally would not be visible in the ocean of Indie authors if it wasn't for you ladies.

Joan Readsalot my go-to book-bestie. My other Beta readers, Krista Webster your chapter breakdowns were brilliant, Jane Kennedy, Amy Adkins, and Heather Callahan and Katie Fezer-Sedan thank you so much for your invaluable input into making Wanted…I think my best book…think it pipped Ethan in the end. My street team, especially, Kim , Gaynor, Jenny and Melissa(s), Lisa, Charlotte, Vickie, Charmaine, Susan, Kellee, Alison, Shannon Johnson and Lynne..But really all my street team, my new members…I love you ladies…you totally rock!

Barbara Shane Hoover my wonderful editor, and Maggie Truelove and Jane (again)…words fail me…I am so grateful for your grammar ocd…I can't even…Saya at Redquille for an extra pair of eyes this time. Stacey at Champagne formats I just hope I got this clean before it came to you…I can't count how many time my work needs …just a tweak ;) and Judi at CLP for my glorious cover…You ladies are the foundation.

Extra help this time came from John Breuggeman (Penny's son) for technical military help. Jules Godfrey Photography for my exclusive image of models Lisa Miller and David Dooner…who are expecting their first baby any day now….How cute!!

Lauren Valderrama for some extra review help and my review team…I'm not going to put your names here, because I know for a fact if I was a new author I would be hunting you all down…and I'm possessive like that YOU"RE MINE! and like Daniel Stone…I don't share ;) I am super grateful to have you, just know that is the understatement of the decade.

My Divas…most of you I've already mentioned and I know I'm taking my life in my hands giving this an extra section but, Patty, Penny, Donette, Karen, Leanne, Mandy, Kirsty and Steffy <3

Bloggers: Claire, Steph, Vicki and Vivienne at Romance Readers Retreat, Jo Booklover, Jesey at Schmexy Girl, Michelle, Yaya and Grace Afterdark Book lovers, Mel and Gayle Bloggers from Down Under, Tanya and Sharon from mom's Secret Book Blog, Rachel and Jo from Hourglass…, Neda (still keeping a watchful eye out - love you for this <3) Gitte and Jenny from Totally Booked, Ana Ives and Bri Partin andJodi Maliszewski (I know you're not bloggers but you are a champion of the book world all the same), I am super grateful to you guys. Other authors…because this is a community in every sense and I have drawn inspiration and guidance from many many talented people but here's a few and in no particular order…Alice Raine, Jodi Ellen Malpas, M Never, Stylo Fantome, JL Perry, Kitty French, Donna Alam, LP Lovell, Stevie Cole, Leslie Jones, Skye Warren, Mandi Beck, CJ Roberts, Audrey Carlan, Julieanne Lynch, Aleatha Romig, Jana Aston, and JA Huss…Don't get me wrong most of these people wouldn't know me if I sat on their face but they have affected me in a positive way and for that I am thankful.

I would also like to thank my bestie..Kymme because in all honestly there would be no books if it wasn't for her, for all the swag making for the signings…I'm gonna take you to Vegas if I ever get asked lol… I love you to the moon and back.

My family…again are quietly supportive…which is probably why I spend so much time on Facebook. Not just because of my books but there is a whole community of filthy minded lovelies happy to share this wonderful book world…you make each day a treat. I often get these utter bursts of happiness, either writing or reading and you guys are the ONLY ones that understand <3 Sorry back to my family…my husband and children (all grown up) I would like to thank you for not moaning (much)…it is your way of showing your support I know and I appreciate it… One day i'll write a story you can read…but not this day *and definitely not this story!*

But mostly, I'd like to thank you, for choosing to buy my book and taking the time to read it - a huge, I mean really huge, thank you, you will never know how incredibly grateful and honoured I am that you have and I would be even more so if you are kind enough to **leave a review** on Amazon or Goodreads. Please…please…oh and please :)

The People who make it all happen.

Dee Palmer - Author

Website - www.deepalmerwriter.com

Follow me here

www.facebook.com/Author-Dee-Palmer-
995618753806518/?ref=bookmarks

www.facebook.com/groups/902682753154708/?ref=bookmarks

www.twitter.com/deepalmerwriter

Editor-Barbara Hoover

Formatter- Champagne Formats, www.champagneformats.com

Cover Design Judi Perkins at Concierge Literary Promotions

Photography: Jules Godfrey

Models: Lisa Miller & David Dooner

OTHER BOOKS BY DEE

ABOUT THE AUTHOR

Dee Palmer lives just outside of London with her husband and (slightly embarrassed) children. Her passion is writing sexy steamy romance stories that will scorch the pages right off your kindle and are guaranteed to make your heart pound. She loves an HEA but isn't afraid to put her readers through the ringer before she delivers.

When not at her desk she can be found either fannying around on Facebook or with her nose stuck in her Kindle. Once in a while when the lights are down she might be spotted about town searching for the best French martinis and throwing some dubious shapes on the dance floor.

Stalk me On Facebook, Twitter and Instagram

Join my reader group…it's not all books ;)
Dee Palmer's Chosen One's

Printed in Great Britain
by Amazon